The End of Magic

AMBER BENSON

ACE
New York

ACE

Published by Berkley

An imprint of Penguin Random House LLC

375 Hudson Street, New York, New York 10014

Copyright © 2017 by Benson Entertainment, Inc.

Library of Congress Cataloging-in-Publication Data

Names: Benson, Amber, 1977– author.
Title: The end of magic / Amber Benson.
Description: First Edition. | New York : Ace, 2017. |
Series: An Echo Park Coven novel ; 3
Identifiers: LCCN 2017002519 (print) | LCCN 2017006709 (ebook) |
ISBN 9780425268698 (paperback) | ISBN 9781101630563 (ebook)
Subjects: LCSH: Witches—Fiction. | Magic—Fiction. | BISAC: FICTION /
Fantasy / Contemporary. | FICTION / Urban Life. | FICTION /
Contemporary Women. | GSAFD: Occult fiction. | Fantasy fiction.
Classification: LCC PS3602.E685 E53 2017 (print) |
LCC PS3602.E685 (ebook) | DDC 813/.6—dc23
LC record available at https://lccn.loc.gov/2017002519

First Edition: May 2017

Printed in the United States of America
1 3 5 7 9 10 8 6 4 2

Cover illustration by Larry Rostant
Cover design by Diana Kolsky
Book design by Kelly Lipovich

And many of them that sleep in the dust of the earth shall awake, some to everlasting life, and some to shame and *everlasting contempt.*

—Daniel 12:2

The End of Magic

The Book of The Flood

In the beginning there was magic. It laced the world together, binding its many pieces into their proper place and maintaining balance. It filled the universe with a sense of the extraordinary, turning journeys into quests, learning into power, life into destiny.

But change is as inevitable as it is necessary. So the days of magic's dominance waned, and the world shifted, swapping the variables from one side of the equation to the other. The disparate pieces of the old world lost their shape and were torn asunder. Humanity shucked its innocence and magic was discarded. The sense of wonder that once suffused the world was slowly extinguished, leaving a darker void in its wake. A sense of complacency rose up to cradle us and we gave in, settled for eschewing the old ways in favor of the new.

To our horror, the world became a place of soulless evil and corruption. One in which we chose to bow down before an altar dedicated wholly to ourselves . . .

—Dawn 1:3
The Book of The Flood

Lyse

One powerful dream that went out across the world and reawakened the slumbering power of magic. *One* coven of blood sisters—or witches, as they'd been called before the word took on such negative connotations—standing against a Machiavellian syndicate called The Flood. *One* woman who didn't know what the hell she was doing but who'd been thrust into the middle of a battle between good and evil.

This was Lyse MacAllister: a woman who had straddled the line of living up to her responsibility and shirking it . . . choosing the former. She was the uninitiated woman. The unwitting master of a coven that stood between the world remaining as it was and being destroyed under The Flood's new world order. She was woefully unprepared for the job, but, in the end, it kind of hadn't mattered.

Lyse had seen what The Flood was capable of, had experienced their evil firsthand. They had captured and tortured many of her blood sisters, using up the women's powers to further their own nefarious ends. Lyse and her coven mates had freed the poor wretches they'd found in The Flood's secret underground lair, but the damage had been done and many of the women were now only shells of their former selves. A human body could only endure so much—and to be caged like an animal, experimented on, and have your powers drained from you like tree sap . . . ? Well, it was merely a matter of time before you ceased to function. Before everything that made you a person was sucked out and you were left an empty husk. No longer the glorious and unique human being you once were. And these atrocities were carried out against young girls, too—children, really, who had just begun to move toward womanhood.

Lyse likened what she and her coven mates—Arrabelle, Evan, and Niamh—discovered in The Flood's subterranean warehouse laboratory to the World War II horrors of Josef Mengele's "experimentations" at Auschwitz. The inhumanity they'd found there had chilled Lyse and the others to their very cores.

Evan and Arrabelle were trained herbalists, but their magical gifts could do little to help. They'd done what they could, helping Lyse and Niamh free the women and children—and soothing those who seemed somewhat cognizant of what was happening—but most of the victims were so far gone that "fixing" them was not on the table.

Evan had been the first one to realize that they needed help to get the victims to safety, and so he'd encouraged Lyse to reach out to the few blood sisters that he trusted, those who'd stayed on the fringes of blood sister society and hadn't been co-opted by the corruption inside the Greater Council, the governing body that presided over the world's witch covens. After Lyse and her coven mates had discovered a mole inside the Greater Council's ranks, anyone associated with the Council had become subject to suspicion. And Lyse doubted that Desmond Delay—the man she'd only recently learned was her grandfather—was the only bad apple.

She didn't want to think about him, didn't want to give

him the satisfaction of taking up space in her mind. He'd blown her world wide open when he'd informed her of her parentage and now she felt sullied, tainted by having his blood running in her veins. He'd made her question who she was and where she'd come from. Made her question the tenuous relationship she'd forged with the woman who'd raised her, her grandmother Eleanora. For now she was ignoring all the bad feelings that bubbled up inside her, but she knew that one day soon she would be forced to unpack them, possibly forfeiting the leadership of a coven she'd only recently accepted her place in.

"You're lost in your head," her coven mate Niamh—a diviner of great talent—said, sweeping her long dark hair into a bun at the nape of her neck.

Lyse could only agree with Niamh. She knew she'd disconnected from the present moment. Knew she'd been cast adrift in her own thoughts as she'd tried to process all the pain and suffering and fear she'd experienced in The Flood's underground laboratory.

"Sorry," Lyse said. "You're right. It's all a bit overwhelming."

The others had followed her lead, shepherding the victims into a safe area, then heading topside with her by way of a bank of industrial-sized elevators that served as the only entrance and exit into the bowels of the mountain—leaving The Flood's underground labyrinthine research facility behind them physically if not emotionally. Now they were in the Nevada desert, looking to Lyse's continued leadership to get them the hell out of there.

"It's a lot," Arrabelle said, resting a hand on Lyse's shoulder, but Lyse could feel her friend's body shudder as she turned to look back at the bank of elevators that led to the lab. "We all feel it. This place has bad juju—evil things happened here . . . even before The Flood took it over. It's full of nasty vibes."

Lyse knew Arrabelle was convinced the place had once housed a secret U.S. military compound, and Lyse had to agree that there *was* something cold and clinical, and vaguely government-issue, about the facility.

"You know we're not far from where Area 51 is purported to be," Evan said, joining Lyse, Niamh, and Arrabelle's conversation. "Who knows what the government had in there before The Flood got their hands on it?"

The old mine shaft that housed the facility was in the mountains bordering Groom Lake, Nevada—maybe Arrabelle and Evan weren't too far off the mark.

"I'm gonna reach out to the Eagles if you guys are still all right with it."

Lyse nodded and watched as Evan took out his cell phone. There was little small talk. He quickly got to the heart of the matter, asking his friends to send reinforcements who would be prepped and ready to help care for the women and children Lyse's coven had rescued.

"I'm going to take a walk," Lyse told Arrabelle.

She needed some space to think.

"We're on it," Arrabelle said, and nodded.

Lyse turned to go, but then she felt Niamh's long fingers encircling her upper arm.

"I wanted to tell you that we did the right thing," Niamh said, a haunted look in her eyes. "Now no one else will die like my sister."

They'd arrived too late to save Niamh's identical twin, Laragh—who'd been kidnapped, tortured, and murdered by The Flood. Lyse knew that Niamh had been damaged in some visceral way by her sister's death and that the loss of the psychic connection between them—the same connection that had helped guide Niamh and the others to the location of the secret facility—was ripping Niamh apart.

"I wish we'd gotten here sooner," Lyse said, filled with guilt by the loss of the blood sisters they hadn't been able to save.

"Me, too."

Niamh let her go, but not before giving Lyse's arm a firm

squeeze. It was as if she were saying . . . *It's not your fault*. But Lyse didn't believe her . . . or anyone else.

She gave Niamh a quick nod, then stepped out onto the uneven desert floor. She felt Niamh's gaze pinned to her back as she stumbled along the rocky terrain, but she didn't look back. Embarrassed by the tears that blinded her vision.

She was feeling unsure of herself, and she needed some space in order to think, to figure out what their next move would be and what the future might bring them.

She moved farther away from the others, taking one of the paths that led away from the mouth of the mine shaft toward the dusty brown horizon. She was so happy to be aboveground again she didn't even mind the heat as she walked, watching the blue sky shift into late-afternoon streaks of burnt orange and dark indigo. She was dirty, sweaty, and she could smell herself. She realized she had no idea how long she had been held captive by The Flood before she escaped and hooked up with the others, but the last time she'd showered was at least twenty-four hours in the past.

The rubber soles of her shoes offered little protection from the jagged stones she was trying to maneuver over, so she stopped and hauled herself up onto an outcropping of beige rock. She felt exhausted, both mentally and physically, her tired feet aching from too much time spent standing upright. Hopping over a crevice in the outcropping of stone, she saw flecks of greenery growing in the shaded dirt beneath the rocks.

Even when things look darkest, life goes on, she thought, then tore her gaze away from the growing things to gently make her way over to the edge. She plopped down on the warm stone, the heat radiating up through the seat of her black jeans, and closed her eyes.

She lifted her face, catching some of the dwindling sunlight. She tried to relax the kinks out of her shoulders and back, but it was no use. She felt tight as a knot, her whole body aching from the last few hours. She let her mind drift, remembering all the awful things she'd endured: She'd watched a man die—a man she'd been in love with. She'd let down her coven mates, especially empath Daniela and Dream Keeper Lizbeth. She'd allowed Desmond Delay—the man she was now forced to acknowledge as her grandfather (the thought made her skin prickle)—to escape without taking any responsibility for his heinous crimes.

She was a shitty coven master, and even though she hadn't asked for the gig, she still felt the weight of the position pressing down on her. Yet she was only one person. There was only so much she could do. For someone else, those words might have absolved them from guilt, but for Lyse, they did nothing. As far as she was concerned, they were a cop-out, and they did zero to assuage the anger she directed at herself for failing to be a better leader.

She opened her mouth and screamed, the sound raw and terrifying as it ripped itself from her throat. It left her gasping when it was done, but she ignored the burning in her throat and repeated the action one more time. She felt like there was some kind of murderous poison bubbling up from deep inside her and the only way to get it out was to scream. So she did— again and again until the scream became a sob and then she was forced to let the tears flow. She didn't think crying made her weak. More the opposite. With tears came acceptance and the will to go on in the face of utter impossibility.

Because Lyse finally understood—sitting on that outcropping of rocks in "the middle of nowhere" Nevada—that the battle she and her blood sisters were entrenched in would probably be the end of them and of everyone they knew and loved.

She and her coven mates were on what amounted to a suicide mission.

As this realization blossomed inside her, it took up the

space where fear and anger had been hiding, filling her soul with a sense of righteous purpose.

So she died doing what was right? Well, then . . . that was just gonna be the way it went down. And if she could protect her blood sisters from the same fate, she would—but she was comfortable with the knowledge that death loomed large in her future.

Today, she decided, was as good a day as any to die for what she believed in and knew to be right.

She came back to find the others crowded around Evan. Well, to be more precise: Evan's phone.

"What's going on?" she asked.

Arrabelle, with her aquiline face and smoldering brown eyes, was the only one to look up. She'd stripped down to a tank top, and even in the fading afternoon light, her toned brown arms stood out in stark contrast to the cream fabric. Her look spoke volumes to Lyse.

"Shit," Lyse murmured.

"Yeah, shit's the word," Arrabelle said, her words coming out in a whisper—as if by keeping her voice quiet, she could stop whatever she was about to tell Lyse from being true. "You think the Inquisition was bad news? What happened today makes the Roman Catholic Church look like a bunch of witch lovers."

As Lyse got closer, she could see that Niamh's face was wet with tears, her shoulders heaving as she cried. Even Evan, who was the most stoic of the three, looked shaken.

"Tell me," Lyse said, a deep sense of *wrong* eating a hole in the pit of her stomach.

"They burned down a school in West Africa," Arrabelle said. "Some of the children began exhibiting powers and the villagers just burned the whole thing to the ground. Ninety-four kids dead. And there's more."

"More?" Lyse said.

Arrabelle raised an eyebrow, arms crossed over her chest. Lyse could feel her friend trying to distance herself from the words coming out of her mouth.

"Someone posted a list online of every coven in the United States. With names. It has to be The Flood's work. It's the only thing that makes sense."

"And . . . ?" Lyse prodded.

"They're picking up everyone who is named on the list. 'Quarantining' them," Evan said.

"Who is 'they'?"

"The police," Arrabelle answered before Evan could. "Rounding us all up. Like we're criminals."

Lyse was having trouble processing what Evan and Arrabelle were saying.

"I don't understand."

"They're picking up every blood sister they can lay their hands on," Evan replied. "And not just here. It's starting to happen across the world."

Lyse was speechless. It was like they'd survived a nightmare only to step into an apocalypse.

"My God," she said, finally.

So the hunt for witches had begun. Lyse saw why the blood sisters had gone underground all those centuries ago after the witch trials of the Dark Ages had nearly wiped them out. Why they had let magic seep out of the human world and had practiced their trade secretly and silently to avoid detection by the mass of humanity.

Fear.

Death.

Obliteration.

This was what awaited Lyse and her fellow coven mates now. Because humans had a nasty reputation of killing what they didn't understand . . . and only asking questions later.

"So Lizbeth's dream . . . it's doomed us," Lyse said.

Arrabelle nodded.

"Looks like it. Lizbeth fulfilled her destiny. Her dream brought magic back to the Earth, but, at the same time, it beamed the truth about our existence into every human mind in the world. It heralded our return—but it damned us, too. Witches are real now. We can't hide in the shadows anymore."

"No," Niamh said, speaking up now. "Without Lizbeth's dream, our magic was weak, almost nonexistent. With our new power, we are so much stronger. It was a necessary step forward. I believe we have to go to an extreme before we can ever hope to return to a balance."

"So we open the door to The Flood? Show them our vulnerabilities so they can expose us to humanity . . . ? They're rounding us up like criminals," Arrabelle murmured.

Niamh sighed.

"Yes, all of it. Even the bad stuff. Because there can't be any more secrets. If we'd stayed hidden, we would've been doomed. We're real again and now we can fight back."

What Niamh said made a queer sort of sense, Lyse thought. It seemed counterintuitive, but maybe that was just the way the world worked.

"But what about what we've done here?" Lyse asked, indicating the entrance to the mine shaft and all the unsettling things that lay inside it. "Since we've destroyed their research labs, doesn't that put The Flood at a disadvantage? They've outed us, but we've cut them off at the knees."

"We don't really know what they accomplished here," Evan said, his hand unconsciously going to the wound on his side— or the scar that was there now that the wound had been miraculously healed by the power of magic. "They might not have gotten what they wanted from these women. I think, more than anything, they created the opposite of what they were expecting. They forced a psychic connection between all of those blood sisters they tortured. They built a monster down in that hellhole."

Lyse knew Evan was right. There was something terribly powerful loose in the research facility. It was like a psychic monster created by all the suffering and pain. The Flood's test subjects had unwittingly created the psychic beast and it had come to their aid when they'd needed it—but it would not be controlled. It did what it wanted and could not be relied upon to help anyone unless it felt moved to do so. Its unpredictability had made Lyse and the others decide to leave it to its own devices. Trying to corral it or force it to come with them didn't seem like a viable option.

"You'll have to let your friends know what's down there," Lyse said. "That it probably won't hurt them, but they should be aware that it's very powerful and intense."

"Of course," Evan agreed. "And they should be here soon. Jessika and her blood sisters were coming from Las Vegas. I doubt they know about the website posting, but maybe I'm underestimating them. I hope they're careful getting to us."

Lyse hoped so, too.

"So we wait for them and then what?" Arrabelle asked.

This was what Lyse had taken her walk to figure out. She'd had her epiphany about what the future held—danger and death—but the smaller details were still murky.

"Well, we need to get ahold of Daniela and Lizbeth. Touch base with Dev. Make sure she's been holding down the fort in Echo Park without too much trouble," Lyse said. "Let her know about the website. That maybe she and Freddy should take the girls and make themselves scarce for a little while just to be on the safe side."

"Agreed," Arrabelle said, nodding. "I'll call her now."

Now, Lyse thought, *if I can only get ahold of Daniela and Lizbeth that easily.*

But she needn't have worried about finding them. As soon as Arrabelle powered up her phone, it began to beep with voice mails and texts.

"Damn, I'm blowing up," she said, scrolling through the texts.

Then her finger froze and her mouth dropped open. "There're like ten from Freddy. Jesus . . ."

She clicked on the screen, eyes flicking horizontally as she read.

"We have to get back to Echo Park. Dev's whole family . . . the girls . . . the house . . . it's all gone."

Lyse thought she'd misheard.

"That can't be right—"

"It *is* right, Lyse. There are dozens of messages here. He says Dev's destroyed, almost catatonic with grief. He says we need to come back now. The last text is dated two days ago . . . radio silence after that."

How long have we been down there? Lyse wondered. *It couldn't have been that long, could it?*

But if Arrabelle's phone was correct, then they'd lost at least forty-eight hours. Lyse, who'd been down there longer, had probably lost more time than that even. She suspected that time ran differently down in the underground lab. This seemed to prove it.

She wished she had her own phone, but The Flood had taken it—and everything else she owned—leaving her with only the clothes she had on her back when they'd captured her in Italy.

Italy . . . where Weir had died.

She didn't want to think about it, but the image of his cold body, stiff with rigor mortis, filled her mind and would not be banished. She felt her heart break again—like it would every time she relived that horrible moment in the Italian catacombs when she'd first realized he was gone.

Gone, she thought. *No, gone was too easy a word. It didn't begin to encompass what had happened to Weir when they'd run into The Flood's operatives.*

Murdered . . . destroyed . . . obliterated . . . *these words were more appropriate.*

"You're a million miles away," Arrabelle said, running her

hands over her newly shorn head. She'd shaved it down before they'd performed the Releasing Ritual for Eleanora, the last master of the Echo Park coven. It was upon Eleanora's death that the leadership of the coven had passed to Lyse, her grand-daughter. Only Lyse hadn't known the true nature of their relationship at the time, having been led to believe that El-eanora was just her great-aunt. It was hard to believe that Eleanora's death was still so recent. So much had happened since then that it felt like decades, not days or weeks.

"I'm here," Lyse said, dragging herself back to reality. She would tell the others about Weir's death soon. She just couldn't face it, and everything else they'd just learned, right at that moment. "Anything from Lizbeth or Daniela?"

Arrabelle shook her head.

"No . . . wait, hold on." She tapped the screen, bringing up a voice mail on speaker. "It's an Italian number."

The message played out in short bursts of heavily accented English. It was a woman's voice, an administrator from a private Italian hospital, letting them know Daniela was their patient. The message rambled on, but the gist was that Daniela wasn't doing well, had been in a coma since she'd been admitted, and Arrabelle's was the name they'd been given from the emergency room as a contact. Please would she be in touch?

Arrabelle replayed the message again for clarity, but the intent was the same: Someone needed to go to Rome and take care of whatever the hell was happening with Daniela.

"And there's no mention of Lizbeth," Lyse said, thought-fully, "but she has to be the one who gave them your number, Arrabelle."

"Seems like a reasonable assumption," Arrabelle agreed. "Something bad happened to Daniela, forcing Lizbeth to leave her behind."

"She had a dream to get out to the world," Niamh said in a quiet voice. "She did what she had to do to make that happen."

It was clear from this voice mail that fate had splintered

the Echo Park coven to the four corners of the Earth. Yet, Lyse felt, should she and Arrabelle ever come together with Daniela, Dev, and Lizbeth again, their reunited coven's power would be more than impressive. It would be unbelievable.

"We can get to Los Angeles in a few hours, and then we'll go to Italy from there," Arrabelle said, looking to Lyse and Evan for approval.

"I think it's the only plan that makes sense," Evan said, reaching out and taking Arrabelle's hand in his own. "We should stay together. There's power in that."

"Yes." Niamh nodded. "Together is best. They'll have a harder time getting us if we stick close to one another."

"When they came for Niamh's and my coven," Evan said, his voice tight, "they played 'divide and conquer.' I've wondered since then . . . if we hadn't let them separate us, maybe the outcome would've been different."

"I don't think it would've mattered," Niamh said—she and Evan had been members of a coven on an island in the Pacific Northwest. When their coven had been attacked, they'd lost their coven master, Yesinia, and two of their other members, including the coven's empath, Laragh.

Niamh had watched The Flood burn her blood sisters at the stake and then steal away with Laragh. Niamh's connection to her twin had led Arrabelle and Evan to the mine shaft near Groom Lake—but Laragh was already too far gone when they'd arrived. Lyse and the others had watched as Niamh held her emaciated twin in her arms, the sisters together one last time before Laragh died. It had been heartbreaking, and had made Lyse hate Desmond Delay and the rest of The Flood even more.

"No?" Evan asked. "You really think we were screwed, no matter what we did?"

Niamh nodded.

"We weren't prepared, and they were. We could never have beaten them."

The low-pitched hum of an approaching helicopter interrupted them.

"Shit," Arrabelle said, squeezing Evan's hand. "They know we're here. We need to get clear of the entrance and hide . . ."

She turned on her heel and headed back to the mine's entrance, dragging Evan with her. Lyse and Niamh followed behind them as the sound of the helicopter's blades cut through the purpling dusk. Lyse pulled her flannel from her waist and slipped it back on, the cool air from the mine shaft making her shiver. Arrabelle found a crevice in the shaft big enough for them all to fit, and they crammed inside, waiting.

"Are you sure—" Niamh started to ask, but Arrabelle shushed her.

The helicopter was close, kicking up the dust outside the mine's entrance as it set down on the scorched brown earth. The four of them waited with bated breath as the giant machine shut down and a long, uninterrupted silence filled the air. This was eventually followed by the crack of a metal door opening.

"Evan?! You in residence here, ya crazy bastard, or was that a bogus call you made?"

The tension went out of Evan's shoulders as he recognized the voice.

"It's Jessika," he said, bringing Arrabelle's hand to his lips and giving it a quick kiss. "The lady nabbed herself a bird to get here."

"Jess! Right behind you," he called out before striding toward the mouth of the mine shaft.

"Shall we?" Arrabelle asked, quirking an eyebrow as she watched Evan's retreating back.

"Wouldn't miss it for the world," Lyse said, and grinned.

She loved seeing the usually taciturn Arrabelle acting as smitten as a schoolgirl over Evan, her former flame. It was the one bright spot in what was proving to be an otherwise miserable existence.

"After you," Arrabelle said. "You *are* the master of the Echo Park coven."

She poked Lyse in the upper arm to let her know she was just teasing. Even though Arrabelle had wanted the job—would have probably made a better coven master than Lyse—she had been a gracious loser. But she still enjoyed harassing Lyse about it.

"Okie-doke," Lyse said, and led the way, Arrabelle and Niamh hot on her heels.

They left the cool dark of the mine entrance, returning to the last dregs of afternoon heat, but Lyse was too busy staring at the helicopter to notice.

"Holy crap, that thing is giant," she said. "It looks just like one of those Black Hawk ones from the movie."

The three women who'd arrived in the helicopter had enveloped Evan, ribbing him between hugs, but at Lyse's comment, they broke rank and came over to surround her. They were all wearing camouflage T-shirts, dungarees, and combat boots—which would've made them seem imposing even if they hadn't been well over six feet, each possessing a seriously muscled body and a fierce expression on her tan face.

"Uh," Lyse said, taking a step back—and hoping she hadn't offended them.

"You think we'd roll in on a civilian chopper? Like we were the local news?" the tallest of them said and snorted with derision. Her short blond hair was pulled back into a tight ponytail at the nape of her neck, and her mirrored aviator shades made it impossible to tell what she was thinking. "We only travel in style, little lady. And we have reinforcements on the way. About five Humvees' worth so we can get your refugees all tucked up safe inside."

"Arrabelle, Lyse, Niamh . . . this is Jessika," Evan said, grinning at his friends' shocked expressions. "When I say I'm calling in the cavalry, *I mean I'm calling in the cavalry*. They're blood sisters . . . but also members of an elite group of covens who act as mercenaries for some big guns . . ."

"Not the Greater Council?" Lyse asked, almost choking on the words. This was a huge mistake. The Council was compromised, and she'd warned Evan and the others that this was the case . . .

"Stop looking like a wolf ate your supper," Jessika said, whipping off her aviators to reveal intense violet eyes. "We may do jobs for those guys, but we operate on our own. And we don't do any kind of shit that we don't want to do. Right, sisters?"

The other two women, both blond and as tan as Jessika, nodded.

"Besides," Jessika continued, "I dreamed about you, Lyse MacAllister. You and the rest of your coven are famous—and any blood sister worth her salt knows that if we don't help you, well, we're all pretty much fucked."

With a rakish grin, Jessika offered her hand to Lyse,

"We're famous?" Lyse asked, incredulous.

"You're more than famous," Jessika said, grabbing Lyse's hand and giving it a firm shake. "You're the only thing standing between this world . . . and the end. So, me and my sisters, we're here to help you, protect you, and keep you and *your* sisters safe."

And with that, she pulled Lyse into a bear hug, almost crushing the smaller woman in her heavily muscled arms.

"Good to meet you, too," Lyse murmured, dazed, as Jessika finally released her.

"Now where are the prisoners?" Jessika bellowed, beckoning for her sisters to follow her inside the entrance of the mine shaft. "Let's grab 'em and then let's get the hell out of here before the government calls and says they want Area 51 back."

Lizbeth

They were in the dreamlands. All the power she'd been imbued with when she'd been hurtling toward her destiny— being the last Dream Keeper, the one who would dream the return of magic—was gone. She no longer felt the souls of the trapped Dream Keepers. They had been released from one prison into another (the second just happened to be Lizbeth's body) until she finally set them free—but she did find herself missing them just a little and the way they filled her brain and blood with their song. Now there was only Lizbeth—no one else was rattling around in there with her—and she thought that was probably for the best.

She took a deep breath.

She thought she would be okay.

And then she began to cry.

She felt Tem wrap his long arms around her. He pulled her to him as she gulped down air, her sobs so powerful they shook her whole body. All the fear and tension drained out of her as she cried, like her heart had been lanced with a sharpened needle. It was a visceral thing, something she had no control over. So she let the hysteria consume her. Let her brain float away for a little while. Even though the crying made her head feel large and unwieldy, made her temples throb, there was nothing for it.

Temistocles held her as she broke down. He didn't say a word, only stroked her russet hair and let her cry. He seemed to understand she needed this. That without the tears, there would be no healing of the wound.

She nestled her cheek against the warm hollow of his neck, the soft skin at his throat as inviting as a pillow. She wished she could go to sleep right there in his arms—and if she could've managed it, she would've. She didn't care that she was standing up.

"Daniela . . . the others . . . will they be . . . okay? I . . . can't . . . stop . . . crying," she whispered. She was having trouble getting the words out because she was gritting her teeth in between the sobs, trying to stop them from chattering.

"I don't know. And you do what you need to do," he said, then kissed the top of her head.

"I've . . . ruined your shirt." The thin linen at his throat was wet with her snot and tears.

He laughed, the sound coming from deep in his belly and rolling over her like a wave of joy.

"What?" she demanded, smiling despite herself.

"*That's* what's got you worried?" he said, snorting with more laughter. "After all that . . . after thwarting the bad guys and personally—with your own damn body as the vessel— dragging magic back into your world . . . getting boogers on my shirt's what gives you pause?"

He squeezed her tight.

"You are a precious jewel. I'd die a hundred more times to get to spend my death with you."

She pulled away from him, for the first time realizing that though he was warm to the touch, she could hear no heart beating in his chest. She stared up at his face—the long nose, the sad gray eyes that turned down at the corners, the soft pink lips—and her own heart thudded.

"I don't want you to be dead," she said, the words coming out in a rasp. Her mouth was dry from crying. "I want you to be alive so we can be together."

He grinned down at her—as tall as she was, he was even taller.

"I'm stuck in the dreamlands, love. It's a life, of sorts. I can see you and touch you while you're here . . ." He trailed off, as if realizing just how lame this sounded.

Thunder cracked across the sky, the sound rolling in percussive bursts toward them. For the first time since she'd left behind the human world, Lizbeth looked at her surroundings. The dreamlands were another dimension from the one she'd been born into. It was where you went in your dreams, and since Lizbeth was a Dream Walker, she'd spent a lot of time there. But the dreamlands were so changeable, so fickle and unpredictable, that even with her experience spending time there, she was often surprised by the new things she discovered.

This trip was no exception. She'd been standing on a monolith of rock in Georgia—the country, not the state—before Tem had spirited her away, and part of her expected to see a similar terrain here in the dreamlands. That happened more often than not when she visited. It would resemble where she'd been in her real life, and then, after a while, it would start to morph and change into something new. The dreamlands were skilled at mirroring whatever was in the dreamer's mind, whatever the dreamer happened to be thinking about or obsessing over in their waking life. She was pretty sure the dreamlands were crafted from pure thought, making them impermanent and easy to manipulate, if only you knew how to do it.

And she did . . . but this trip was different.

"Where are we?" Lizbeth asked, eyes adjusting to the darkness.

She saw a velvety black sky with a shining globe—the orb as pale as fresh butter—stitched into the fabric above them, and then farther away a sea of angry gray thunderheads fast approaching. They were standing on a surface made entirely of water. It stretched out around them in an unbroken line of liquid for as far as the eye could see. She lifted her foot and felt wetness slosh against her ankles, saw that not only were her feet bare, but so were her legs. She lifted her arms, examining the rest of herself, and discovered that she'd magically shed her cold-weather clothing for a thick white muslin nightshift. She knew she should have been cold standing in four inches of cool water, but the muslin made her feel warm and toasty.

"These are the true dreamlands. Their 'resting' shape, if you will, when they're not molding to whatever they think a dreamer wants to see," Tem said—he was still in the same long green leather coat he'd worn when she first met him, his black hair in the same tall mohawk. Unlike Lizbeth, he remained unchanged in the dreamlands.

"Why do you look the same, then?" she asked, her eyes not on him but still marveling at the beauty that surrounded them. This place was *everything* and *nothing* at the same time. The vastness of what she saw made her feel small, imbued her with the sting of what it meant to be truly alone—except she wasn't. *He* was here with her.

"Because I'm dead and you're alive. I'm trapped here, an echo of what I once was, still moving and thinking and doing, but only because of the power I draw from the dreamlands," he replied—after a long silence where, he, too, seemed to be contemplating the vastness of the space. "It gives me a little play in your human world, but not for long or with much power. All of your Dream Walkers are like me. Those witches who choose not to move on to the next plane, but to stay behind, as I have, because they still feel the call of life and the needs of the living, the ones whom they left behind in death and sorely miss."

"Like Eleanora," Lizbeth said, and Tem nodded his agreement.

"And there are many others," he said, then added sadly: "And more will be coming."

"What do you mean?"

"More of your blood sisters will die, Lizbeth," he replied. "The balance has to shift before it can come back to the middle."

Lizbeth felt like a tear had opened in her heart.

"I don't want anyone else to die," she said—and she heard an edge of hysteria in her voice. "I just want things to be as they were. I want to go back to before all of this happened. Before my coven was split apart. Before I went up on that rock and used my dreaming powers to call magic back into the world . . ."

Tem let her speak, understanding that she needed to exorcise the fear and guilt she was feeling.

"I want to go back to Echo Park. I want Eleanora to be alive again. I want Lyse to never have come home. I want Daniela to be well. I want Weir. I want my mom to be alive . . ." The last word—*alive*—poured out of her in a piti-ful moan, and on its heels came more tears. But this time they sprang from the deepest part of her, from the small child that lay buried in the dark corners of her brain—damaged and inconsolable and full of the basest of emotions: Need.

"But doesn't this place give you reassurance? That death isn't the end?" he asked, but she shook her head.

"It's not that . . ."

"Then what?"

She shook her head, unable to give voice to the feeling. More than anything, it was being in this place. It intensified things. Made her *feel* with a sharpness that was disconcerting.

No more tears, she thought. *They get me nowhere.*

She swallowed back the sadness that had invaded her without warning. Fought the lump in her throat, demanding it melt away. After a few moments, she was more composed.

"I just want it all to be like it was," she said, finally managing to corral her emotions.

Tem smiled down at her, lifting his fingers to her cheek and brushing away the wetness there.

"But, my little dreamer, change is the greatest gift of all. To be alive is to change and grow and accept loss and death. It's all of it . . . and without those sad and wonderful things that happened to you recently, we wouldn't be standing here, together, right now."

"I still don't like it," she said.

"Of course not," he replied. "Because you're young now. But wait a while and see how you feel then. I guarantee that one day you'll be so tired of life that you'll beg death to come. Eventually we all move on, Lizbeth. It's an inevitability that cannot be changed."

She grimaced, not liking what he was saying at all.

A flash of bright blue light filled the sky, followed by a rolling crack of thunder. Tem craned his neck, frowning as he looked up at the storm clouds gathering above them. He shook his head as if to clear it, then returned his gaze to Lizbeth.

"I believe that's our cue to get moving."

"Where are we going? There's only . . . *this* . . ." She pointed at the liquid landscape just as another flash of blue lightning lit up the water, making it shimmer like cut glass.

"The waters of the dreamlands," Tem said. "They're whatever or wherever we want them to be."

As he spoke, a small boat appeared on the water in front of them. It was little more than a dinghy made of weathered slats of pale gray birch wood, but it sat primly on the surface of the water, waiting for them.

"Your chariot awaits," he said, gesturing to the boat.

"But who sent for a boat?" she asked.

"Neither of us, at least not consciously," he replied, "but the dreamlands sensed our need and acted accordingly. Now we really do need to shake a leg. A storm is coming."

He offered her his hand, and she took it, letting him help her into the boat. The dinghy took her weight easily, barely swaying as Tem climbed in beside her. They sat side by side on the little wooden bench seat, their arms and legs touching. It was all very intimate and Lizbeth felt herself blushing as the boat began to glide silently across the top of the water, propelled by absolutely nothing.

"Are you comfortable?" he asked.

She nodded and the dinghy picked up speed, the wind ruffling her long hair. A drop of rain fell on her nose and she wiped it away.

"So what now?" she asked.

"We stay in the dreamlands for as long as we can. It's safer for you . . . and there are things you can only learn here."

"Like what?" she asked, the rain beginning in earnest.

It fell in sheets so thick it was hard to believe they were made up of individual raindrops. She shivered, finally feeling cold for the first time since they'd arrived.

"Here," Tem said, pulling an umbrella from the ether. He opened it, the slick black fabric canopy large enough to cover them both. "And that's what I meant by learning."

"Making an umbrella appear out of nowhere?" she asked.

"Exactly."

As more and more rainwater fell, the water around them began to rise. Lizbeth only knew this because when she looked down past the mini-ripples made by the raindrops, she could see that a vast ocean lay beneath them. There were massive reefs made of red and purple coral and filled with swaying green kelp and multicolored fish. She gasped when she saw the silhouette of a mermaid streak past them.

"It's so beautiful," she murmured—then shrieked as a giant bright pink tentacle broke the surface of the water and slammed across their path, narrowly missing the front end of the dinghy.

"And dangerous," Tem said, taking her hand and giving it a squeeze. "Even for us magicians."

"You said that before, when we first met."

"I did," he agreed.

"What did you mean?"

"My brother, Thomas, and I come from a universe similar to yours, but different in many ways. The darkness that has seeped into your world overtook ours. There were some who fought back, but, in the end, it wasn't enough."

He sighed and scratched at his nose with a long, delicate finger.

"Unlike you, we had magic. It hadn't been hidden away and forgotten, stripped from the very fabric of our existence," he continued. "Not like in your world. Where I come from, we know that many different universes coexist, vibrating so closely together that they seem to rest on top of one another. For those of us who are born lucky—like Thomas and me— we can travel between the different alternate realities using the dreamlands as a conduit . . . because they connect everything and everyone together."

"So why is my world different?" Lizbeth asked.

Tem shrugged, then shook his head. He lowered the umbrella, the rain having finally stopped.

"It's all in the details. Major events occur that cause a divergence—like maybe there was a war and in my world one side was victorious, but in yours the other side won. Whatever happened that made magic disappear from your world? Well, it just didn't happen in my universe."

The boat was beginning to slow down now that they'd outrun the storm, and they drifted on the endless sea, no land in sight. There was only a blanket of fog ahead of them, a fine white mist that they seemed to be heading straight toward.

"And what I did? It brought that magic back into my world?"

"It was never wholly gone," Tem said. "But you've unbound it again. You dreamed its return and you can't put that genie back in a bottle."

"And now what? That's the end of The Flood?"

Tem snorted.

"Hardly. The Flood is only a manifestation of the darkness that's been sweeping across all of the worlds. But for some reason, your universe has become a pivotal holdout. If you fall, I don't know what will become of everything else."

"I feel like all I'm doing is asking questions," Lizbeth murmured, then sighed; she was tired and emotionally wrung out. She wished she could just close her eyes and sleep for a thousand years.

"That's how you get answers," Tem said, smiling, as the dinghy bumped into something under the water and came to a stop.

Lizbeth leaned forward, but because of the fog she couldn't see what they'd hit.

"Well, now, it appears that we have arrived."

She stared at him.

"Arrived *where*?"

"The Red Chapel," he said, his eyes trained on something just over her shoulder.

She turned, following his gaze, and a long sloping beach made of bloodred stones seemed to magically appear out of the fog. The beach led to a rectangular patch of green grass upon which sat a tiny redwood cabin. As more of the fog lifted, it became clear to Lizbeth that this was the extent of the island: one little building on one little piece of land set adrift in the middle of an endless sea.

"We'll be safe here. For a little while, at least," Tem said as he hopped out of the boat. He offered her his hand, and she felt a small shock of electricity pass between them as their fingers touched. He blinked but seemed unsurprised by the intensity of the connection.

"Oh . . . okay then . . ." she murmured, blushing for what felt like the thousandth time in his presence. It was hard not to have a crush on him. He was so handsome and kind, charming and funny. He was anything and everything she would've wanted in a man . . . except for one niggling little detail.

He was dead.

"Don't look so maudlin, half-caste," he said, his voice a purr as he grabbed her other hand and swung her out of the boat.

He made her feel like a delicate flower (even though she knew she was really a gangling beanpole) by lifting her into the air and setting her down on the red stone beach as if she weighed absolutely nothing at all. The pebbles felt warm underneath her toes, smooth and round.

"Thank you," she said, lowering her eyes, not able to meet his gaze. She may have been safely on dry land, but she felt anything but safe when Tem was nearby.

"My pleasure." He gave her a low bow and she laughed at the courtliness of the gesture.

He was such a mix of things. Chivalrous and strong, on one hand, but also silly and awkward, too. Handsome, but all gawky elbows and knees. She liked that he was such a hodgepodge of disparate things, liked that the first time she'd met him he'd appeared to her in the guise of a dragon, all fierce and wise.

He really was a magician, really could manipulate the fabric of the dreamlands—like calling up the boat or the umbrella— and she found herself wishing that she could do the same.

"You can and you will," he said, reading her mind.

This was something they'd been able to do from the moment they'd met. A damaged childhood spent in an institution had rendered Lizbeth mute, and so he'd communicated with her telepathically. It had been unsettling at first, but after a while she'd grown used to it—though she'd been unable to stop herself from thinking inappropriate things about him. Like how cute she thought he was.

Now it was his turn to blush.

"Sorry about that," she said.

"You're just stating a truth, half-caste. I *am* very cute," he replied, taking her hand and leading her up the slope of the beach.

He called her "half-caste" because he said all Dream Keepers were part human and part his universe. That was why they could travel to the dreamlands and talk to Dream Walkers. It was what set them apart from the rest of their coven blood sisters and made them rare. So rare Lizbeth was the first to be born in almost fifty years—an important secret that had been closely guarded by her fellow witches in the Echo Park coven. They'd done well in protecting her from The Flood, who wanted nothing more than to capture her for her power, harnessing it to further their own ends—which included wiping the witches off the face of the Earth. But Lizbeth knew there was even more to it than that. Once they'd used her powers up, they'd destroy her. There would be no stay of execution.

It all sounded ridiculous when she thought about it, so melodramatic, but it was the truth. And it was why she was here, in the dreamlands, with Tem, safe for now—but who knew how long that would last.

"Mind your step."

He trod upon the beach, his long legs gracefully finding them a path through the stony shore. The fog was mostly gone now and the night began to recede with it. Still, Lizbeth wasn't sure if the sun had risen because a hazy sheen of clouds covered the sky, blocking her view of the sun and hiding the landscape in deep shadow. She turned back, expecting to see the dinghy at the edge of the beach, calmly waiting for their return, but it was gone. For some reason unknown to her, they were to stay here on this strange island in the middle of nowhere. At least until Tem magicked up a helicopter or something else ridiculous to help them leave.

"LB!"

Lizbeth's head whipped around at the sound of the young girl's voice, her russet hair flying in her face. She dropped Tem's hand, pushing the hair out of her eyes.

"Ginny . . . ?" She couldn't keep the shock from her voice as she caught sight of her friend Dev's younger daughter, arms and legs all akimbo, as she ran toward them—and her heart lurched as she wondered if the girl was dead.

"No need to worry," Tem said, once again reading her mind. "A living human can be brought here by creatures like you and myself. Our magic is strong enough."

"Thank God," she said as Ginny flung herself at Lizbeth.

She caught the small body up in her arms and hugged her tight. Ginny squirmed in the embrace.

"Too tight," the little girl whispered—and Lizbeth released her, a sheepish smile on her face.

"What are you doing here, Ginny?" she asked, trying to seem calm and more adultlike than she felt.

"Not just me, LB. Marji, too." Ginny's long dark hair was loose around her shoulders, the wind catching bits of it as she spoke. The little girl unconsciously reached up and grabbed for a hank, sticking it in her mouth to suck on.

This was something Lizbeth hadn't seen Ginny do in a long time. At seven, she was far too old for such childish things. Lizbeth realized Ginny was nervous, maybe even scared. Not something she was used to seeing in Ginny. Marji, Dev's older child, was the more delicate one, always letting her little sister take on the role of fearless leader.

"Where?" Lizbeth asked, taking Ginny's hand. She threw Tem a worried look.

Had he known Devandra's daughters were here in the dreamlands?

"I knew Thomas was here," he said. "But not the girls."

He seemed apologetic and Lizbeth wondered why.

"C'mon, LB. It's creepy in the house! And it's really big

inside, too," Ginny said, getting back some of her usual vim and vigor as she dragged Lizbeth behind her. Maybe now that Lizbeth was here, she felt safer.

But before they could reach the threshold of the entrance, Marji was rushing out the door of the cabin, tears streaking her face.

"They're all dead," she sobbed, and threw herself at Lizbeth.

Lizbeth caught the older girl and held her tight, feeling Marji's skinny shoulders shake with grief.

"Marji, what are you talking about? Who's dead?" But Lizbeth couldn't get a word out of the girl.

Instead, Ginny answered the question, looking up at Lizbeth with her solemn brown eyes.

"Oh, Marji means Mama and Gramma and the aunties."

And then Lizbeth understood.

Arrabelle

Arrabelle was impressed by the Shrieking Eagles—the banner under which Jessika and her blood sisters operated. Made up of women with military, law enforcement, and governmental agency backgrounds, the Eagles encompassed members of seven disparate covens that had banded together to offer their services to other blood sisters.

"We're mercenaries whose agenda is *all* blood sister, *all* the bloody time," Jessika had said as they'd stepped into the elevator that led down into the guts of the former research facility.

Arrabelle appreciated the specificity of their agenda. They were smart and fierce and worked with a military precision that was unreal. Until the moment they'd arrived, Arrabelle had been unaware of their existence, but it made sense. The blood sisters were a secret organization with many enemies. Of course the Greater Council would find itself employing a mercenary group like the Shrieking Eagles to protect its interests every now and then.

Upon first seeing the laboratory—the polished chrome-and-steel surfaces, the strange concrete block rooms with shatterproof observation windows cut into their exteriors at human eye level, the tech equipment, operating tables, surgical implements that resembled torture devices—Jessika had whistled through her teeth.

"Damn, this place looks like it came right out of one of those torture porn movies."

She pointed at the cages lining the walls of the lab, empty now, save for the few that held corpses—blood sisters who were already beyond help when Arrabelle and the others had found them. These cages Arrabelle and Evan had left alone, but they'd managed to free everyone else from captivity and lead them to an empty airplane hangar. Which was crazy, to have an airplane hangar underground? But Evan had found it after roaming the empty corridors, looking for a safe place to put the women until help arrived.

The fluorescent lighting above them was oppressive.

Like a headache in the making, she thought—and part of her wanted to demur, to go back topside and get as far away from this horrible place as she could. But Arrabelle was never one to run from her fears. In fact, she was quite the opposite, always running at full speed toward the things that scared her the most.

Like this place . . . and the creature The Flood had created with their horrific experiments. The one who haunted the facility in poltergeist form.

She was pretty sure *it* was the reason the paramilitary members of The Flood had evacuated their underground lair. It was obvious from their behavior that they were scared of the creature—and even though it had come to the blood sisters' aid when they needed it, it had unsettled Arrabelle as much as it had The Flood's soldiers.

"They're so small," one of the Eagles said, an edge to her voice. Her name was Belinda and she was one of the two women who'd arrived in the helicopter with Jessika. "These tiny cages were for people?"

She sounded incredulous, as if she couldn't imagine anyone doing something so inhumane. Arrabelle was pretty certain that if she'd been a mercenary, one who'd supposedly seen it all, she would be way more jaded. She barely had any faith in humanity left as it was. Right then it was really hard to have anything but rage for The Flood and its members. Not after what she'd seen . . . cages housing young girls who were barely near puberty and who wore the haunted expression of the brutalized.

"They did this to children," Arrabelle said, as the group of women gingerly made their way through the abandoned lab toward an industrial-sized metal roll-up door that opened onto one of the many twisting underground corridors.

"There's no rhyme or reason for why these bastards do what they do," Jessika said to Belinda.

"Oh, they have a very good reason . . . they're true believers," Lyse said, as she stabbed a large red button on the wall with her palm and the door began to roll upward. "The Flood thinks if they erase us from the Earth, then they wipe out magic forever. And then the world is cleansed of our evil influence and everything is set for their new world order to begin."

"It's kind of biblical," Evan said as he led them down the darkened corridor.

Lyse agreed.

"It's no different than the crazies who believe that starting World War Three will bring about the end of days."

"You mean, they think God will take all the good guys up to heaven and damn the rest of us sinners to an eternity spent on some apocalyptic version of Earth?" Even asked.

"As far as The Flood is concerned," Lyse replied, "I'd say you're dead on. It's a very similar idea."

Arrabelle stepped up in line with Evan and took his hand. She found it hard not to be touching him—especially since she'd been thoroughly convinced he was going to die only hours earlier. But via their sheer force of will, the caged blood sisters had healed him so he could fight off the remaining members of The Flood for them. He was better now, almost an entirely different person from the ill man she'd spent the last few days with—and he was using this newfound energy and good health to do what was necessary to help those who'd saved him.

The click of heels on the polished cement floor was so loud that Arrabelle hoped they didn't run into anyone else down here. The element of surprise would be woefully lost in the clatter of the Eagles' heavy tread. Belinda and Evan had taken out their cell phones and were using the bright lights from their screens to illuminate the way in the murky darkness. Arrabelle felt Evan squeeze her hand and her heart fluttered.

Though he'd been on the periphery of her life for the last decade or so—his choice, not hers—there'd never been another person for Arrabelle. Evan was her big love, had been since she was eighteen, and, now that he was back in her life and safe, she wasn't going to ever let him get away again.

"How do you know all of this stuff?" Jessika asked Lyse.

"Lyse got an earful from Desmond Delay—" Evan said, and Jessika stopped in her tracks, turning to stare at him. This made everyone else stop, too.

"He's involved in this?" Jessika asked, and for the first time she didn't look like the calm, assertive woman they'd met topside.

"He is," Lyse said. "He's up to his neck in it. And just so all the cards are on the table—he's my grandfather. So if that's a problem . . ."

She put her hands on her hips, holding her ground. Firm and tough.

So unlike the will-o'-the-wisp she'd been when she'd first come back to Echo Park, Arrabelle thought. She hadn't expected much from Lyse back then, but now, after a trial by fire, Arrabelle was proud to call Lyse her coven master.

Jessika put up her hands in mock surrender.

"Not a problem. At least, not for me or my gals," Jessika said. "He's tried to get us to do some sketchy stuff over the years, and I've always said no. He made it sound like it was at the Greater Council's behest, but he never fooled me. Him and that son of his . . . a real nasty piece of work."

Arrabelle watched Lyse's face pinch with anger.

"You've met my uncle?" Lyse asked, and Arrabelle remembered the unsettling conversation she and the other members of the Echo Park coven had had with the man . . . before Lyse dosed him with a heavy helping of medicinal marijuana, the drug seriously messing him up. Once he wasn't a threat anymore, Arrabelle and her other coven mates had sent him packing. Needless to say, he was a nasty piece of work.

"Yup," Jessika said, nodding. "He was a creep."

"I knew it from the beginning," Lyse said. "I wanted to be wrong, wanted him to be a decent human being, but unfortunately I was right." She sighed. "I wanted to have a family again, but living in denial isn't the way to get it."

"You have a family . . . of sisters," Niamh said. "Blood sisters stand by each other no matter what."

Arrabelle appreciated Niamh's quiet strength. Though she wasn't very verbal, when she did have something to say it was usually pretty important. The girl trafficked in cold hard truths. As if she knew she was being assessed, she shot Arrabelle a small smile, then nervously tucked her long brown hair behind her ears.

"Thanks, Niamh," Lyse said. "I know you're right."

"Well, if the Delay thing is all settled . . ." Jessika said, indicating that they should continue moving. "Let's walk and talk. I get the impression we need to lock and load before we wear out our welcome here."

"Agreed," Evan said. "It's this way."

He turned the corner and they entered another dark warren of tunnels.

"The women are mostly in shock, but they'll do what you ask. Arrabelle and I started passing out some lemon balm tincture I brought with us. It seemed to have a calming effect."

Arrabelle felt a hand on her wrist, and she turned to see Niamh walking beside her. The other woman's gait was slow, her stride not nearly as long as Arrabelle's own. Arrabelle released Evan's hand and slowed to match the younger woman's step. The rest of the group pulled ahead of them.

"Can we talk for a minute? Alone?"

Arrabelle knew where Evan was headed, so she nodded. Niamh's request was more than reasonable.

"Of course."

Niamh slowed even more before finally coming to a complete stop—and in the half light, her face looked white and drawn. She leaned back against the wall, her bony shoulders pressing into the cold concrete.

"I wanted to let you know that I'm not alone."

Arrabelle raised an eyebrow and Niamh smiled.

"That's one of your go-to expressions," Niamh continued. "The raised eyebrow. You look like you don't believe a word anyone says, period."

Arrabelle didn't like learning that she was so predictable. She lowered the eyebrow and tried to compose her face.

"It's not a bad thing. I like that I sometimes know what you're gonna do before you do it," Niamh continued. "It makes me feel safer. Well, a bit safer. I don't feel good about much these days."

Arrabelle understood. She'd been a closet cynic for most of her life, but the experiences she'd had the last few weeks had hardened her in a way that even the trauma of losing her beloved father hadn't been able to.

"What's that mean?" Arrabelle asked. "That you're not alone."

Niamh shrugged. Arrabelle watched as the young woman scratched her chin with nails that had been bitten to the quick.

"It sounds odd, but when Laragh died . . ."

She stopped there, silent for a moment. Arrabelle knew it was hard for Niamh to talk about her dead sister. Their unspoken twin connection, a psychic link that transcended space and time, had led them here to this underground facility. The sisters' bond was so strong that Arrabelle wondered if even death could truly separate them.

"She's in my head. Has been for a little while, only at first, I didn't realize. That's all I wanted to say."

"Can you be more specific . . . ?" Arrabelle asked—she thought she knew what Niamh was saying, but it was so outlandish that she wanted it confirmed first.

"The thing that was born down here from all the tests and death—Laragh says you call it a poltergeist—it's in here with us, too. Laragh can handle it. It listens to her. So you don't have to be afraid. It won't hurt anyone. Laragh has it under control. See?"

She reached out and touched Arrabelle's arm—and Arrabelle felt a jolt of electricity cut through her.

WE ARE ONE AND WE ARE ALL HERE. OUR BODIES ARE ONLY VESSELS.

The voice—if that was even what it was . . . in some ways the words were more like an image flashing across her brain—continued inside her head:

SAVE OUR BODIES, BUT WE WILL NOT LIVE AGAIN UNTIL THE FLOOD IS DESTROYED.

"You . . . *she* . . . can read my mind?" Arrabelle asked, stepping away from Niamh's touch as her body thrummed with an electric charge.

Niamh frowned, began to nod, then stopped herself, thinking out loud.

"No, not really. I mean, it's not mind reading. It's more like she . . . *we* . . . get flashes of stuff. Maybe they're thoughts sometimes, but it's more like impressions, mostly. Like starbursts in the sky, bright but fleeting."

"Okay," Arrabelle said, digesting the information as she noticed that the light from the cell phones was gradually disappearing down the corridor. Soon she and Niamh—and whoever the hell was sharing Niamh's body—would be alone in darkness.

"You're not scared?"

Arrabelle shook her head.

"What's there to be frightened of? It's just another bizarre thing that I can't really explain."

"I don't know," Niamh said, nervously running a finger through her long brown hair. "I get really freaked out about the stuff I don't understand. I wish I could be as strong as you . . ."

Arrabelle rested her hand on the younger woman's shoulder.

"You're plenty strong. And don't be freaked out, okay? 'Cause no one is gonna let anything bad happen to you. Not on my watch."

Niamh gave Arrabelle a half smile, but it disappeared quickly. It was strange to hear her speak about her sister as though she were standing right there in the hall with them.

"Oh, it's not for me I worry," Niamh said. "It's for everyone else and what's going to happen to them. I don't know what's coming, but it's terrifying. I can feel it in my gut—and Laragh agrees. Something bad is going to happen . . . and it won't spare you, Arrabelle. You or Lyse."

Niamh's words bore the hallmarks of a surreal prophecy, and they sent a shiver down Arrabelle's spine.

"The Flood is coming, Arrabelle," Niamh continued. "But where it will take any of us, I just don't know."

Arrabelle swallowed hard, the hairs on the back of her arms standing on end.

"We should get back to the others."

"Yeah, that's probably a good idea," Niamh agreed, and then her whole body trembled. "Is it cold for you, too?"

Arrabelle shook her head. She was sweating like a pig and

had been ever since she and Niamh had stopped to talk in the corridor.

"No, you're burning up, aren't you," Niamh said, her tone matter-of-fact. Then she took a deep breath and pushed off the wall.

She was correct—Arrabelle *was* burning up, and Niamh knew it even though she hadn't laid a hand on Arrabelle's skin.

"It's just a reminder that you're still among the living," Niamh continued, replying to Arrabelle's unspoken question. "That's all."

They brought out the survivors in small groups, filling the elevator time and again, until there was not a single living soul left down below. By then, the rest of the Eagles had arrived and they worked tirelessly to get the victims settled into five Humvees they'd brought with them from Las Vegas. It was such a stark contrast, two disparate groups—the able-bodied Eagles and the emaciated blood sisters from the lab—stepping out of the darkness of the mine shaft into the purple-hued Nevada desert night.

Arrabelle wanted to reach out to the young girls, the ones who'd lived such short lives and experienced more evil than good in that brief time, but she couldn't find a way to connect. It was impossible to break through the walls their damaged minds had built to protect them. Even the adults were inaccessible, locked away behind blank eyes.

They were all so gaunt, so starved, you could see the bones pushing against their skin, trying to break through the thin flesh. There were women—blood sisters—of every age, shape, and ethnicity. The Flood had gone through and chosen them not for their physical looks, but for something more ephemeral . . .

"They're like Lyse," Niamh said.

She stood with Evan and Arrabelle at the entrance, the

three of them watching as the last woman was loaded into the remaining Humvee. "They're different than the rest of us. They must have shown abilities that transcend that of a normal blood sister. My sister, Laragh, was the same. It's why they took her and left or killed the rest of our coven."

"They wanted the special ones," Evan said. "The ones who had evolved into something greater than the rest of us."

Lyse, who'd been talking to Jessika by the helicopter, came to join them.

"They're gonna take off now," she said. "Head out of here and hopefully find a way to get these women some medical and psychiatric attention."

"They know about the website?" Arrabelle asked. "They know the police might be waiting in Vegas to collect them?"

Evan snorted.

"I wouldn't want to put money on that encounter going in the police's favor."

Arrabelle agreed with him, but she knew what guns could do against unarmed civilians and it was not a pleasant thought. It made her worry about the Eagles and about the women they'd rescued.

"They know," Lyse said. "And I don't think they're worried. But I encouraged them to stay under the radar. Jessika said she has a friend in naval intelligence who owes her a favor. She didn't say so, but I think she might be commandeering a ship so they can stay out at sea, bring in people to help the women offshore . . . where it's safe. All of this not in Las Vegas, obviously."

"If they *can* be helped," Arrabelle said, looking at Niamh. The poltergeist creature had said the women's bodies were just vessels and would stay that way until The Flood was defeated. She wasn't sure what any medical doctor, herbalist, or psychiatrist could do to make a difference in the face of something like that.

"See you guys on the other side," Jessika called over to them, giving a wave.

They watched as she hopped into the helicopter's cabin and climbed into the pilot's seat, the door closing behind her.

"That woman is incredible. I wish my brain worked the way hers does," Arrabelle murmured.

They watched Jessika put on a headset, then flip a few switches on the control panel. There was a loud hiss and then the helicopter's rotor blades began to engage. Jessika gave them a quick wave through the glass of the cockpit, and the metal machine slowly lifted into the air.

"She's not someone I'd ever want to screw with," Evan said, shaking his head. "I met her at a sweat lodge in North Dakota. We were both there studying with a Cree shaman—she's an herbalist like us, Arrabelle. She was finishing her time with him and I was about to start mine. We hit it off right away, but, honestly, she's always kind of intimidated me. She's a real badass."

Arrabelle wondered if she should feel jealous about Evan's friendship with the other woman. But she was just so in awe of Jessika, she wouldn't have faulted Evan if he was a little in love with her. Heck, she might be a little in love with Jessika and the rest of the Shrieking Eagles herself.

As the helicopter lifted into the sky, the Humvee engines roared to life and began the arduous journey of returning to civilization. Their giant wheels kicked up dust as the convoy headed out into the desert, the sound of their progress echoing back at Arrabelle and the others for a long time after they'd gone. But soon even that last trace of the Shrieking Eagles and their charges died away, the night swallowing them whole . . . and leaving the four of them—Arrabelle, Evan, Lyse, and Niamh—alone by the entrance to the now-empty mine.

"Now we walk," Arrabelle said, answering the unspoken question in all their minds. "The car's parked about two miles away. From there, we head back to Los Angeles."

There was no acknowledgment that they were exhausted,

that they'd already battled the forces of evil once that day and deserved some well-earned rest. Instead, there was merely silence as they embarked on what would prove to be the beginning of a very long journey.

"No word from Freddy or Dev?" Lyse asked, leaning her chin on the back of Arrabelle's seat. "No word back from Italy?"

Arrabelle knew she'd received nothing since the last time she'd looked at her phone—five minutes previously—but she rechecked it again anyway. As the screen lit up in the darkness, she held the cell phone up so Lyse could see it.

Nothing.

"Maybe we can try texting again in a few minutes?" Lyse asked, and Arrabelle nodded, letting the screen go dark again as she set the phone back in her lap.

"Of course. But Freddy hasn't replied to anything I've sent, and when I call it goes straight to voice mail."

"It *was* two days ago," Evan said from the driver's seat. "Maybe something else happened. Two days is a long time to be incommunicado."

"I hope nothing else has happened to them," Lyse murmured, sitting back in her seat. "It's bad enough already."

She and Niamh were in the rear of Arrabelle's rental car, the same one she'd put on her credit card at the Sea-Tac airport Hertz Rent-A-Car days earlier. It was crazy how long ago that felt . . . like she'd lived a whole lifetime since then. She knew she was going to get killed on the overages—she hadn't even called to let them know she was taking the little red car out of Washington State—but, at this point in time, she didn't really give a shit what they charged her. She was obviously not going to be returning the car anytime soon, and they had her card. Let them have fun running it up to its limit.

"Not that we even really know *what* happened to your

friend, Dev," Evan said, trying to roll the stiffness out of his shoulders. He'd been driving for six hours nonstop and they were getting close to Los Angeles.

Arrabelle had been working hard not to let her mind go down that path. If anything terrible had befallen Dev and the girls . . . no, Arrabelle couldn't let herself go there.

"Well, we'll be in L.A. soon," Arrabelle said, catching Lyse's eye in the rearview mirror. "And then we won't have to speculate anymore—"

The words were no sooner out of her mouth than the car hit something—a pothole, maybe—in the road and began to fishtail. Evan took his foot off the brake and turned the wheel, trying to keep the car under control.

"Hold on!" he shouted, gripping the steering wheel hard. Arrabelle could see his tense expression reflected back at her in the rearview mirror, lit green by the dashboard light.

A moment later the car righted itself. Evan sighed and began to pull off to the side of the road.

"No!" Niamh screamed, grasping the sides of her head in her hands as if she were in terrible pain. "They're right behind us."

"Keep going!" Lyse screamed, leaning forward and grabbing the back of Evan's seat. "Listen to Niamh and put your foot back on the goddamned gas!"

Evan did as he was told and slammed his foot down on the accelerator—but not before a pickup truck slammed into the back of them. It sent the red rental car sailing forward, the spinning wheels losing traction as Evan tried to accelerate.

"Go!" Niamh cried, her voice hoarse with fear. "They've got guns and they're going to kill us!"

A bullet slammed into the back window, cracking the glass, and Niamh screamed.

"Go, Evan! Go!" Lyse yelled, but Evan didn't seem to register what she was saying. He stared blankly ahead, head lolling—and that was when Arrabelle realized the bullet had found its mark.

Without thinking, she crawled halfway into the driver's seat and pressed her foot on the gas. The car shot forward, swerving wildly. The movement roused Evan and he grabbed the steering wheel, straightening out their path so they shot forward down the dark and empty highway.

"Are you okay?" Arrabelle cried, terror racing inside her as she tried to discover where he'd been hit.

"Okay," he said, gritting his teeth. "Just the top of my shoulder. I'm in shock, I think. You can take your foot off the gas now, Bell."

He turned his head and gave her a rakish grin. In that moment, with his chiseled cheekbones and shining eyes, she thought he was the most handsome man she'd ever seen.

"Evan," she cried, overwhelmed by the sense of relief that flooded through her.

"You can still drive?" Lyse asked.

Evan nodded.

"Then we have to get off this road," Lyse said. She had her seat belt off and was turned in her seat so she could stare out into the darkness through the busted window.

The bullet hole was tiny, but the glass had fractured like a giant spiderweb, making it hard to see through.

"Where?" Evan asked.

Lyse had a ready answer.

"There." She pointed ahead of them through the windshield at the bright lights of an all-night diner.

"No way," Arrabelle said. "We can't endanger anyone else's life—"

"Trust me," Lyse said. "I've got this. Just exit up there."

Arrabelle wanted to argue, but Evan placed a hand on her thigh.

"Let's do what Lyse says, Bell."

He gave Arrabelle a grin, and she swallowed hard, then nodded. Lyse was the master of their splintered coven, and Arrabelle still needed to learn to trust the other woman's instincts.

"Okay, here we go," Evan said as he indicated with his blinker and made the turn, exiting off the road and toward the diner.

"Go into the parking lot," Lyse said, "and then follow the asphalt around to the back."

"But it's a dead end," Arrabelle said, looking through the windshield. "There's nothing back there but a Dumpster."

"Yup," Lyse agreed, but she did not elaborate.

Arrabelle bit her lip as Evan reduced his speed and cruised through the brightly lit parking lot. A big, square sign flashed the name of the place—*Tessa's Roadsider*—in glaring fuchsia and hot pink, the acid colors washing across the black asphalt in psychedelic swirls of neon. There were about half a dozen cars parked in the lot and maybe double that number of people in the diner. No one gave the rental car a glance, their faces turned away from the plate-glass front windows of the retro diner.

Evan headed toward the back of the diner, and Arrabelle could see nothing but a Dumpster waiting for them.

"Stop now. I'm getting out," Lyse said.

Arrabelle shook her head, glaring at Lyse in the rearview.

"No way," Arrabelle said, her hand reaching for the door handle.

With her disheveled hair and fiery blue eyes, Lyse looked all of sixteen. There was no way Arrabelle was gonna let her get out of the car alone.

"You can't come with me, Arrabelle." And the tenor of Lyse's voice stopped her cold. "Because you have no hands to open the door with."

Arrabelle looked down at her lap and, to her shock, saw that Lyse was correct. She didn't have any hands—just cauterized stubs where her hands had been severed at the wrist.

"What the hell—" Arrabelle shrieked, but Lyse was already climbing out of the car. She slammed the door behind her and began walking back toward the main parking lot.

As soon as Lyse was gone, Arrabelle looked down at her hands and was not surprised to find that they had been made whole again. She was sure Lyse had used some kind of hypnotic suggestion to pull that trick—and it pissed Arrabelle off that she'd fallen for it.

"She can't go on her own," Arrabelle said, and reached for the door handle again.

"I don't think she needs us," Evan said, mouth agape as he stared into the rearview mirror.

"What are you talking about?" Arrabelle said—and then she followed his gaze to the rearview mirror and saw Lyse performing a feat that nothing in Arrabelle's wildest dreams could have prepared her for seeing.

"Holy shit," Evan said, unfastening his seat belt and opening the driver's door.

Arrabelle climbed out behind him, unfolding herself from the cramped car interior, and shivered as the cold wind buffeted her skin. Niamh had already exited the car and was leaning against the back bumper, eyes on their coven master. Arrabelle and Evan joined her there, staring at Lyse, who stood twenty feet ahead of them, arms outstretched. A glowing blue light arced from her palms, creating a shimmering orb of energy.

As Arrabelle watched, Lyse opened her mouth and began to sing. It was a wordless tune, full of sorrow and grief, and as it grew in volume and pitch, the orb grew with it—until, finally, the rental car and all of its passengers were enveloped inside it. The driver of the white pickup truck either didn't see the massive ball of energy or didn't care.

"No!" Arrabelle screamed as the driver put his foot on the accelerator and the truck barreled toward them.

The pickup truck hit the edge of the orb and, in a flash of

neon blue light, disappeared. The orb fizzed and hummed as a streak of lightning shot across the night sky and slammed into it, popping it like a soap bubble.

"Holy crap," Evan said, his voice filled with wonder.

Niamh said nothing, just stared at Lyse with hero worship in her eyes.

"What the hell kind of magic was *that?*" Arrabelle demanded as Lyse turned to face them. Arrabelle had no idea what in the hell they'd just witnessed, but she knew it existed outside a normal blood sister's abilities.

"I have no idea," Lyse said, and she shot Arrabelle an exhausted grin. "But welcome to the dreamlands."

And that was when Arrabelle realized the white pickup truck hadn't disappeared . . . *they* had.

Devandra

The burnt-out Victorian that had once played host to Devandra Montrose, and generations of Montrose women before her, was now just another dark spot on the elegant street in Echo Park. Dev loved the houses in her neighborhood because they had a sense of history about them. With their Easter-candy-colored clapboard siding and peaked roofs, the early Craftsmans and Victorians reminded her of sugary confections. Of course, these elderly beauties—as in most Los Angeles neighborhoods—were sandwiched in between derelict apartment buildings and tiny cottages with cracked glass windowpanes, unkempt yards, and owners who refused to pay for the upkeep on their rentals.

Some people in her neighborhood complained about these lesser buildings, saying they were blots on the grandeur of their showier neighbors, but Dev didn't agree. She thought all the homes and apartment buildings were unique in their own way, had always argued that each of them added a layer to the eccentric character of the street.

But the horror of the last two days had drained her and

now she didn't have the energy to argue about anything—let alone the worthiness of the run-down houses in her neighborhood. Her world had been upended and now it took every bit of energy inside her, energy that had been stored up over her thirty-plus years of living, to get out of bed in the morning.

Her partner, Freddy, was beside himself with worry. He was grieving, too, but he'd put his own feelings aside—as much as one could compartmentalize something so awful—to help Dev battle the morass of depression that was threatening to overwhelm her. No, it was more than depression, it was an unwillingness to keep living.

Her mother and sisters were dead, her daughters gone (in all probability dead, too), and her blood sisters unreachable . . . it all felt pointless. A life not worth living. She knew she should want to live for Freddy. That her partner was still there and alive should have given her will enough to live, but her grief had been so absolute that it was like living in a fog. One that would never lift and that Freddy couldn't penetrate—even though, bless him, he really had tried.

The truth was that Dev felt like all the color had been drained from the world—and she had no interest in living if it meant she had to do it in monochrome.

It had been two days since Dev's bedeviled mother—and her mother's former lover—had brought about the end of the Montrose line. Dev didn't understand how time could continue after a tragedy like that—how life could go on after an emotional earthquake so powerful, it had changed her very brain chemistry. Her whole life, she'd been the mellow one, the laid-back sister, the passive daughter, the indulgent mother . . . but that woman was dead. It felt like she'd been poisoned and burned alive, flayed and dismembered, stabbed and strangled . . . her heart weeping as she'd died a slow and gruesome death, forced to watch everything she'd ever loved taken away from her.

"Dev?"

She was lying in a fetal position on Eleanora's bed, the

covers bunched up around her waist, one of the soft down pillows pressed against her cheek, still wet from the last round of tears she'd shed. She felt a hand on the back of her neck, and she flinched at the touch. Freddy instantly pulled his fingers back as if she'd burned him—and maybe the impotent rage she felt *had* turned her skin into fire.

"Sorry," she murmured, slowly turning her head to look at him. There was a sickly yellow undertone to his dark skin, and his handsome face was pinched with worry. Stress lines spiraled out around his eyes and mouth, creating deep indentations in the flesh.

"It's okay," he said, smiling down at her from his perch on the edge of the bed. "I just wanted to let you know that Arrabelle got in touch. She and Lyse are on their way home now. Should be here in a few hours."

Dev's neck began to ache from holding the awkward position, so she rolled over until she was facing Freddy. Normally, she would've reached out and taken his hand, but she found it almost impossible to touch or be touched by anyone. Even the gentle press of his fingers on her neck made her feel claustrophobic.

"Do they know we're at Eleanora's?" she asked, and he shook his head.

"I'll tell them," he said, reaching for his cell phone.

She nodded, but her gaze was already drifting away from his face, her thoughts taking her far away from the pain of her shattered reality.

They sat at the round oak table, the yellow damask tablecloth pinned beneath their elbows. Three women, one gray and two in the prime of their lives. Three faces she knew almost as well as her own. The room was filled with a hazy smoke that made it hard to see. Dev stepped farther into the room, out of the shadows where she'd been standing, and, abruptly, the smoke cleared and the room came into sharp focus.

"Devandra?" Her mother's voice. From cradle to grave, Melisande

Montrose's dulcet tone would be the first and last thing Dev would ever hear. How she knew this, she was unsure, but it was the truth. Her mother had cooed her name when she was born, and when she died, it would be her mother who came to greet her on the other side.

"But you're on the other side already, Devandra," Melisande continued, cocking her head. She had a bowl of soup in front of her—soup Dev had made for them all—but the bowl was different than any Dev had in her kitchen.

You have no kitchen, *a little voice said in Dev's head.* You have nothing anymore.

She ignored the voice, concentrating on the soup bowl. After a few seconds of intense concentration, she remembered where she'd seen it before. It was an orange ceramic thing that had lived on a shelf in Eleanora's kitchen. She'd never seen the former master of her coven use it for food, but once, a long time ago, she'd heard Eleanora refer to it as "Hessika's scrying bowl."

"Why are you eating out of that bowl?" Dev asked.

She noticed that the pot of soup on the stove was starting to burn. Without thinking, she reached over and turned down the burner of her old O'Keefe and Merritt stove. Inside the pot, the soup—which was not the soup she'd made, but a concoction that resembled bright red borscht—still roiled and bubbled. It seemed not to care that Dev had cut the gas in half, lowering the flame to the point where it was barely a pale blue ring of fire.

"We're not eating," her sister Darrah said. "We're watching the future."

Darrah and Dev had only been eighteen months apart, so close in age they'd experienced their adolescence as a shared one. What happened to Dev also happened to Darrah and vice versa.

Until now, *the tight little voice said.* Now she's going where you can't.

Anyone who saw the Montrose girls knew they were siblings: golden strawberry blond hair that verged on red, peaches-and-cream complexion with rosy cheeks, piercing eyes. The older three were round and soft; only the youngest, Delilah—probably because she never stopped moving—had managed to keep the curves at bay.

"*The future is here,*" *Delilah said, her eyes sad. Dev wanted nothing more than to rush across the room and run her hands over the bristly stubble of Delilah's shaved head. Once again, Delilah was the nonconformist, unwilling to act or look like the rest of her sisters.*

"*The future sucks,*" *Dev said.*

Her mother and sisters did not respond to her bitter words.

"*Come look, Dev,*" *Melisande said, her bobbed gray hair neatly combed so it curled around her ears. She gestured to the orange bowl as a head of steam began to rise from inside it.*

"*I don't think I want to,*" *Dev said, shaking her head, her feet planted on the thick-slatted wood floor.*

"*But don't you want to know what happens?*" *Darrah asked, pursing her lips into a frown.*

The kitchen felt smaller here than it had in reality. The wooden cabinets were so tall that they seemed to reach up into the sky—and when Dev looked up, she saw there was no ceiling to the room, merely a layer of smoke. Dev felt something hot singe her hip, and she realized she was leaning against the heated stove.

"*What're you cooking in the oven?*" *Dev asked. "It's so hot I've burned myself.*"

"*No one gets away without a scar,*" *Melisande said, fingers plucking at the metal spectacles she kept on a chain around her neck. Dev watched as she slipped them onto her nose and then peered into the orange bowl.*

"*We just want you to know something important,*" *Delilah said. "It's only a little of the future. Come look. Please?*"

Dev felt herself being drawn toward the table, a place she did not want to go. So she did the only thing she could think to do in order to stop herself: She plunged her hand into the pot of soup. The liquid heat was intense, a burning sensation shooting up her arm as she cried out in pain and bit her lip.

"*Don't do that, Devandra,*" *Melisande said, scolding her naughty child. She waved her hand at the pot, and the pain in Dev's arm instantly disappeared.*

Surprised, Dev looked down into the pot. She found the cast-iron pot empty, its innards scrubbed clean.

"Come on," Melisande added. "Don't dillydally."

"But you killed everyone and you let him take my girls," Dev wailed, wanting nothing more than to pick up the heavy soup pot and slam it into her Judas-of-a-mother's temple.

Melisande shook her head, shooting Dev a dismissive frown.

"Are you kidding me? You really believe I would do something like that?" Melisande asked, her annoyance at Dev's stupidity plain in her words.

"I saw you—" Dev began, but Melisande interrupted her.

"You saw nothing," Melisande replied, ignoring Dev's frustration. "And you really think that soup was what did this to us? You ate some, too, Devandra Montrose. So how come you're still alive?"

Dev had just assumed that she hadn't eaten enough of it to kill her.

"But Thomas made you bind the ghosts to the house, bind us to the house—"

"To protect us, Dev," Darrah said with a sigh. "But it was already too late. The seed had already been planted."

"What do you mean?" Dev asked, her voice rising in pitch as a wave of hysteria shot through her. "A seed? Who planted a seed here?"

Melisande pointed at the orange bowl.

"Come and see."

"No," Dev said as she closed her eyes, not wanting to see.

She found herself physically repulsed by the scrying bowl and whatever was inside it. Just the thought of peering into its depths made Dev's stomach lurch. She felt the blood rushing in her head, her temples throbbing with each heartbeat.

"Come."

Her mother beckoned her forward and, against her will, Dev opened her eyes and went to the woman who had borne her. Melisande took Dev's hand and guided her to the fourth chair at the table. Dev sat down and Melisande pushed the bowl in front of her.

"Take my hand," her mother said, and Dev did what she was told, taking Melisande's right hand and Delilah's left one, so that the Montrose women were linked together in an unbroken circle.

"Now looooooooooooooook."

The word seemed to drag on into eternity; a whole universe was born and died in the space of time it took for the final consonant to sound. Dev stared down into the bowl of crystal-clear water . . . and she saw.

It was one of those old, rambling bungalows whose wooden shingles had turned a silvery gray with age and exposure to the elements, its windows caked with grit from the salty sea air. It sat perched on the edge of a cliff, a snaking staircase made of driftwood leading to the sandy beach. There were four bedrooms, a tiny kitchen, and a living room whose back wall was made from three large plate-glass windows—so at sunrise and sunset you could stare out at an unadulterated view of the sea.

They went on a Friday night and stayed until Sunday, a weekend trip, a benevolent gift from Freddy's boss, whose family owned the house in Laguna Beach. On their way out of town, they stopped at the store and loaded up on groceries. They filled the cart with yummy delicacies—ones they eschewed at home because of the expense—and suntan lotion that smelled like a Hawaiian coconut. Freddy even bought two bottles of expensive cabernet for the two of them to drink on the porch when the girls had gone to sleep.

It was a weekend slice of heaven and they'd sorely needed it. The girls spent sunup to sundown outside, building sand castles and chasing waves, their giddy shrieks of joy echoing on the empty beach. They'd only fought once during the whole trip—though Dev had quickly intervened, ending the dispute before there were any tears.

What was it they'd been fighting over? She tried to remember. It was something small and unimportant . . . ah, yes . . . *a piece of sea glass.*

Dev had been making lunch, homemade egg salad sandwiches with bread-and-butter pickles and store-bought Tater Tots—a rarity at their house, but the girls loved them and so they'd splurged at the store. Though she could see the beach from the kitchen window, she wasn't worried about keeping an eye on the girls. Freddy was with them, set up in an old beach chair in the sand, rereading *The Stand*. He was wearing a ratty old sombrero he'd found in one of the bedrooms, the wide straw brim so long it covered his black caterpillar eyebrows, making his dark eyes look permanently surprised.

She'd giggled like a little kid when he'd first put it on—*Mama, you snorted!* Ginny had said—and that only seemed to egg him on more. He'd taken to wearing the hat like a new head of hair and Dev knew he was doing it just to amuse her.

"Lunch!" she'd called as she'd stepped out onto the porch with the plates of food. The porch held a weathered teak table and four mismatched chairs, and they'd taken to having most of their meals out there.

The girls had come up the stairs arguing, Freddy behind them, sombrero in one hand and *The Stand* in the other. He was shaking his head, obviously frustrated by the bickering.

"Let your mama see," he said as he put his stuff down in one of the patio chairs and placed a hand on each of Ginny's nut-brown shoulders.

"It's *miiiiiine*," Ginny whined, dragging out the *i* in *mine*. Freddy rolled his eyes at Dev as if to say: *I've been dealing with it all day and now it's your turn.*

"What's yours, peach pie?" Dev asked Ginny, but Marji answered for her.

"He gave it to me. It's *mine*."

A definitive *mine* from Marji meant that this was probably not going to end well.

"What is it?" Dev asked again.

With Freddy's prodding, Ginny lifted her right hand and opened her fist. Sitting on the fleshy mound of her palm was a small, perfectly round pebble made of what Dev assumed was red sea glass.

"It's mine," Marji reiterated. "The man gave it to me."

Marji reached for the stone and Ginny's hand snapped shut like a clam.

"No!" she howled, and ran into the house, still clutching her prize. Marji started to go after her, but Freddy lightly grasped his older daughter's arm.

"Marj . . . be the older sister."

Marji stared up at her dad, wearing a look of utter betrayal on her face.

"But, Dad, it's not fair!" she cried, eyebrows scrunching together the way they always did right before the tears started.

"Marjoram, please, no tears," Dev said, letting out a long sigh. "Why don't you and your dad sit down and eat? I'll go get Ginny and we'll talk about this reasonably, all right?"

Marji didn't look satisfied with this solution, her frown deepening.

"I'm not going to give the pebble to anyone else without us all talking about it, okay?" Dev added, and this seemed to appease Marji. She nodded, a lone tear snaking down her cheek.

Dev went back inside and called Ginny's name.

"In the baby's room, Mama!" her younger daughter replied from down the hallway.

The rest of the house was decorated in a seafaring motif: wooden fish sculptures and seashells on every available surface, nautical-themed minutiae and woven fishing nets hanging on the walls . . . only the back bedroom was unique. It was the smallest of the four bedrooms, and, as soon as they'd arrived, Ginny had immediately claimed it for her own. It had none of the nautical trappings of the other rooms, but instead was kitted out like a baby's nursery. There was a carved wooden cradle, a rainbow-hued parade of dancing bears stenciled on the walls, and soft, baby-blue pile carpeting. At some point, someone had shoved a tiny twin bed in the corner under the window, and this was where Dev found Ginny, the little girl sprawled out on the bed, staring at the red pebble cupped in her hand.

"See the light, Mama?" Ginny said, holding the pebble up to the window, so that, like a prism, rectangles of red light reflected around the room. "It's so pretty."

Dev sat down on the edge of the bed, pulling her long skirt up around her knees.

"It *is* really pretty," she said, reaching out and stroking Ginny's long brown hair. Both of the girls took after their father, who was Filipino, inheriting none of the ginger coloring that plagued Dev's side of the family. "And if it belongs to your sister, then I think you need to give it back to her."

Ginny continued to stare at the pebble, not looking up at her mother.

"But I like it. It sings."

"I'm sure she'll let you look at it sometimes . . ."

"No, she won't," Ginny said, matter-of-factly.

Dev sighed, wishing that both girls were a little older, so they'd be easier to reason with.

"Let's go eat lunch and we can have a family powwow about it, okay?"

Eyes still on the stone, Ginny frowned.

"Mama, I don't wanna."

"Well, I'm your mama and I say you gotta eat those Tater Tots before they get cold!"

She grabbed Ginny around the waist, hoisting her up into the air and swinging her around until she pealed with laughter.

"Tater Tot monster!" Dev cried as she set Ginny down on her feet and gave her a big bear hug.

"You're so silly, Mama," Ginny said, hugging Dev back.

"I know I am," Dev said, and took her younger daughter's hand, guiding them back down the hall toward the porch, where Freddy and Marji were waiting.

Freddy was eating his sandwich, but Marji was glaring down at her lunch, her finger rolling a Tater Tot back and forth on the paper plate. She looked up when Dev and Ginny came outside, but she didn't say anything, only scowled at her baby sister.

"Let me see the stone, Ginny," Dev said.

"But I wanna hold it—"

"Ginny," Freddy said, voice firm as he set down his sandwich.

Ginny sat in one of the teak chairs and looked from her father to her mother. Then with a pout, she unwillingly relinquished the stone to Dev.

"Thank you," Freddy said, picking up his sandwich and taking another bite. "Good stuff, babe."

He gave Dev a wink.

"It's mine," Marji said, jaw clenched in anger. "Not that anyone cares."

"Marjoram," Dev said, hefting the stone's weight in her palm. "Now as pretty as this pebble is, I don't think it belongs to either of you. I think it lives here at the beach and we can play with it while we're here, but it's not going home with us."

"Mama, no!" Marji said, smushing the Tater Tot under her thumb. "Not fair!"

"It's gonna stay here on the patio and when we leave, I'm gonna let you girls give it back to the sea."

Ginny frowned.

"But it's not from the sea. It's from the man."

Dev looked at Freddy, who shrugged.

"They said an old man came up and gave it to Marji, but I didn't see a soul down there."

"There was an old man," Ginny shouted. "There was an old man. With a funny cane!"

"Ginny!" Marji said. "You're not supposed to tell."

"Tell what?" Dev asked, not liking what she was hearing. She exchanged a nervous look with Freddy.

"It's a secret," Marji said, lowering her voice until Dev could barely understand her.

"He had a lion, Mama," Ginny said, not shouting this time. "On his cane and he said it was a secret and the pebble was a secret, too. But then he gave it to Marji and I yelled at him, so I don't care."

Leave it to sibling jealousy to foil a would-be pedophile's plan.

"Marjoram, you know you're not supposed to talk to strangers."

"He talked to me," Marji said, getting churlish.

"Same difference," Freddy said.

"You were asleep, Daddy," Ginny said. "He came over to talk to us when you were snoring."

Freddy looked sheepish.

"I might have fallen asleep for a minute, but . . ." He trailed off and sighed. "But that's more than enough time."

Dev wasn't mad at him. The girls could wear you out—had worn her out on many occasions—so she knew it was an honest mistake. Now she found herself wishing she'd kept more of an eye on them through the kitchen window when she was making lunch.

"He wasn't doing anything bad," Marji said, defending the old man. "He said he found the pebble and thought we would like it."

"But he gave it to Marji," Ginny said, shifting in her seat so she was closer to the table . . . and the Tater Tots. Two of which she stuffed into her mouth.

"He said it was magic and it was a secret only for us—then he said he had to go."

Dev wanted to ask if he'd done or said anything inappropriate, but she was afraid to scare the girls.

"Well, there are no secrets at our house and you both know this," Dev said, instead. "And you both know that people you don't know can steal you away from your daddy and me. As nice as they seem. As friendly as they are. As many gifts as they try to give you—they are still strangers."

Marji rolled her eyes.

"I wouldn't have gone anywhere with him."

"That's not the point," Dev said, reaching for her own sandwich. "You're supposed to set a good example for Ginny—"

"You seth a bath one," Ginny said, her mouth full of Tater Tots.

"Ginny." Freddy's tone was a warning. Then he turned to his elder daughter: "Marji, you know why your mom and I are upset . . ."

He waited for her answer. Finally, she nodded, still sullen.

"Yeah, I know. Stranger danger."

"If anything happened to either of you, it would be the end of our world," Dev said. "We just want you safe."

She put a hand on Marji's shoulder and felt the tension there.

"Just think about how sad we would be if anything happened to you. Can you do that for me?"

Marji nodded.

"Now let's eat our lunch before the bread turns into a soggy mess," Dev continued, and squeezed Marji's shoulder.

"Okay, Mama."

Later, Dev had put the red pebble on the stone mantelpiece and promptly forgotten about it. Neither of the girls had ever mentioned it again and she was pretty sure that had been the end of it. But now as she stared into the orange scrying bowl, she saw Marji pick up the stone and put it in her pocket as they closed up the house and left for home.

She watched as they returned to their home in Echo Park and Marji placed the pebble, and some other shells they'd collected at the beach, onto the windowsill above the kitchen sink. With a sinking feeling in the pit of her stomach, Dev realized the stone had been there all the time. It had been right in front of her nose and she'd never noticed it.

She looked up from the image in the bowl.

"Wait," she started to say, but then stopped, at a loss for words.

"It was magic and once it was in this house, there was no stopping

it," her mother said. "Thomas and I worked the binding spell and the stone stole the spell's power, using that power, which was supposed to protect us, against us."

"No," Dev said, her voice so high that she didn't recognize it as her own.

"Yes," Darrah said. "Marjoram had no idea what she was doing. The Flood used her like they use everyone. You couldn't have known what was going to happen."

Dev realized her sister was right, but she still felt awful. Like she'd failed her mother and sisters, her daughters, Freddy . . .

"I wish I were dead, too," she moaned, and wrapped her arms around herself.

"Don't ever wish that," Delilah said. "We need you."

"I'm such a failure."

Melisande took her eldest daughter in her arms.

"Stay alive, Devandra. You and the girls. Get them from the dreamlands and stop The Flood. Don't let our deaths be in vain."

Dev nodded, relief flooding her heart as she recognized the truth in her mother's words . . . and also understood that her daughters were still among the living.

"I won't, Mama," she said, closing her eyes as tears overflowed them.

She was back in Eleanora's room. Back in the bungalow on Curran Street where she'd spent so many happy hours with her beloved blood sisters. Freddy was staring down at her and she saw fear in his eyes. He was terrified he was going to lose her like he'd lost the girls. She reached out and took his hand, the first real touch between them since the tragedy . . . since their house had burned to the ground with her mother and sisters inside it—and the girls had disappeared with Thomas, an almost-stranger.

"I'm still here," she whispered as she brought his hand to her lips and kissed his knuckles. *"And I'm not going anywhere."*

Desmond

The old man held vigil over Daniela's bed, sitting in a hard-backed wooden chair his son had found for him. The armchair the hospital provided for visitors was much too soft and hurt his already aching back. As he waited, whiling away the minutes and hours, he often reached out a hand as if to touch her. But he would always bring it back to his lap, never once actually making contact. He knew that to touch Daniela would only send her farther away from him, from their world. So he sat and did nothing. Just watched the gentle rise and fall of his daughter's chest and prayed she would survive.

Desmond Delay—this was the name he'd chosen for himself and it suited him well, he thought—was old and dying. It didn't matter *what* was killing him, only that it was. He wished to live long enough to see the new beginning The Flood would create, but he didn't hold out too much hope. His days were numbered and he knew it—plus, he wasn't so sure The Flood would be delivering on what they'd promised him and its other followers.

Not that he would ever voice those thoughts out loud—and definitely not to his son, David, who came and went from the cold hospital room with the regularity of an automaton. He was worried about his father, afraid this "trial by bedside" would be the end of the old man. He didn't say as much, but Desmond could almost read his son's mind these days. He knew the younger man was worried that Desmond would die and then he would have to enact The Flood's plans on his own, the responsibility of which scared the hell out of him. The strange thing was that Desmond was also worried about this—though for a very different reason.

Though his son was loyal to a fault, there was something wicked about the child he'd created. Not quite a sociopath, but not terribly far from it, either. He took too much pleasure in carrying out his duties, in expunging the Earth of the witches that, even now, held humanity back from its destiny. That the situation was thus—well, it was more Desmond's fault than anyone realized. He had always been too lenient with the witches (the self-named blood sisters) and had even fallen in love with two of them. Though both women had borne him children—three in all—Desmond had been responsible for each of the witches' deaths . . . something he was not proud of. He had known as he'd bedded them and loved them that one day he would have to destroy their world.

But the children he had wanted and had tried to protect— in his own way.

He had failed with one child, a daughter, who had been killed in a car crash that he had no hand in . . . though he suspected other members of his order were not so guiltless. She'd left him a grandchild, but the girl, Lyse, had been lost to him before he'd even found her. She was one of the evolved blood sisters, whose powers came from all the disciplines of magic. Once the other members of The Flood had realized this, he'd been forced to let his plans for her go.

Now only his son and Daniela remained. His son was his

right-hand man. Did as he was told and worked tirelessly for The Flood. Daniela was another story. She'd been raised by her mother, Marie-Faith Altonelli, a member of the witches' Greater Council and an extremely powerful witch in her own right. Daniela was her only child and a formidable magic wielder, as well. A talented empath, she could not only feel the emotions of those she touched, but she could manipulate them into thinking and doing what she wanted of them . . . not that she willingly abused her powers in this way. Desmond had used her talent to manipulate things to his liking— though she had no idea at the time that he was doing it.

Marie-Faith had never told the girl of her parentage, had never let Desmond reveal the truth to his daughter, either . . . but he'd stayed close to them throughout Daniela's childhood, behaving as much like a real father to her as Marie-Faith would allow.

He thought he'd done a good job with Daniela, had made her feel loved and understood, and because of this loving connection, he felt sure that if she woke up from her coma, he would be able to turn her to his ways. He was certain he could convince her to become part of The Flood, using her incredible talent to do the good work . . . and now that unadulterated magic had returned to the world her incredible talent would become even more magnificent.

Magic had been returned full force to the Earth, magnifying every blood sister's power—and The Flood had plans, so many plans, for that power. They'd been unsuccessful in creating the last and final weapon because the witches they'd captured, the evolved ones, hadn't been "awake" enough yet. This was what their scientists had learned after performing all sorts of psychological and neurological tests on the women. The failure of these noninvasive tests had, finally, led to the witches' bodies being cracked open like sardine tins and their brains harvested for further study.

Their own damn fault, he thought, but it was more out of

habit. He didn't actually believe the words he was thinking. Hadn't for a long time now.

In truth, Desmond was disillusioned with the dogma he'd once wholeheartedly embraced. He was so entrenched in the movement, though, that, at this point, it seemed ridiculous to do anything but continue forward with the Bataan Death March he'd set himself on all those years ago. He hadn't known back then that The Flood would make a monster out of him. Only . . . he should've seen it even then, should've understood what he was sacrificing. He'd just been so angry and hurt by Eleanora's rejection of him: He'd loved her and she'd taken their unborn twins away from him, without even telling him he was a father. Then, to add insult to injury, she'd given the children away—he would've taken them both had he known—and subjected them to the horrors of adoption. Their daughter had come out all right in the end, but their son, well, Desmond only found David later in life and, by then, his personality (with all its imperfect traits) was already set.

So he'd brought him into the fold, made him a foot soldier in the war for a new world order. Only with time he'd become disillusioned and now he wasn't so sure that the future The Flood sought to bring about would actually make the world a better place. Human beings were flawed and imperfect. Magic, or the utter destruction of it, was not going to change that.

Now he wanted Daniela to wake up, to see her once more before he no longer counted among the living. This was the one hope he held on to, the only thing that kept him going.

"Father?"

Desmond was pulled from his thoughts by his son's rumbling voice. David stood in the doorway of the hospital room, and Desmond realized he'd probably been standing there for a while. Had probably already called to his father once, maybe twice, and Desmond hadn't heard it. He really *was* getting old.

Both of his witch lovers, Marie-Faith and Eleanora, dead

and gone before him, and, here he was, still tenaciously holding on to life. It was surreal.

"Father?"

Desmond realized he'd disappeared into his head again.

"Yes," he replied, giving David an indulgent smile.

The man was physically handsome with a charming countenance, even if his brain was rotten. Tall, with perfect posture and silver hair cropped close to his skull, all holdovers from his years in the military, David looked very much like Desmond when he was younger.

"We should go. You're wanted."

Desmond nodded. He knew he couldn't sit by Daniela's bed forever—he would have to leave her for now. At least he knew she would get the best possible care here. He'd had her transferred to a clinic where many expatriates living in Italy went for treatment, the doctors and medical staff known for their top-drawer medical care. Besides, he'd be back—and, maybe, by then she'd be awake.

Desmond climbed to his feet, using his trusted cane for support. Every time he wrapped his fingers around the polished metal lion's head handle, he was reminded of Daniela. It had been her gift to him many years ago, and he cherished it.

"I'll come by and check on her while you're gone," David said. "Just in case she wakes up."

"Good," Desmond said, and then he took his son's arm and followed him out of the hospital room.

Daniela

Daniela floated, barely aware of her father's, or anyone else's, visits. She didn't know where she was, or even *why* she was there—just that she was alive and in pain. It was a strange surreal feeling. Like she was sleeping and not sleeping at the same time, her awareness of reality so tenuous that it hardly existed at all. Except for the pain . . . that was the one thing that kept her tethered to what was left of herself. The damage to her anterior insular cortex had been severe—had anyone done an MRI of her brain, they'd have seen a lesion the size of a quarter there.

Daniela could not quite remember what had happened to her, and she was only aware of the continued damage she was being unwittingly subjected to by the clinic staff because it hurt—and the pain brought her closer to reality. The men and women treating her didn't know that every time they touched her, they were only making her worse. That she was an empath, a very powerful one, and now that magic had returned to the world, instead of just her hands, her whole *body* had become a conduit for her empathic talents.

Touch her arm to take blood—damage done.

Lift her up to change the sheets of her bed—damage done.

Check her pulse—damage done.

The list went on and on—and all the damage done would be a constant reminder that the gloves she'd worn for most of her life would not be able to protect her anymore.

That she was, for all intents and purposes . . . untouchable.

Lizbeth

"Hello, there."

Lizbeth looked up to find Tem's brother, Thomas, standing in the doorway of the Red Chapel. He was wearing a ripped T-shirt and tight black jeans, his thin frame well-muscled. Though they were both tall and lanky with pale skin and dark hair, their features were so different you would have to know they were related in order to see the resemblance. There was a sadness to Tem that didn't exist in his brother. The gangling awkwardness that made her Tem so charming was reversed in his brother. Thomas had a fierceness to his gaze, his bright blue eyes scalpel sharp.

This only hinted at their different personalities. Lizbeth could sense one was a giver and the other a taker. One put others before himself and the other . . . he was ambitious and out to succeed. She just hoped that didn't mean Thomas would throw them all under the bus to further his own ends.

"You don't look happy to see us," Thomas continued, leaning against the doorjamb. His voice purred and Lizbeth remembered that he, too, could be very charming, but in a brasher, more confident way than his brother.

"LB?" Ginny said, a tremor in her voice.

Lizbeth swallowed hard, shaking herself from her thoughts. She tried to focus on the little girl standing in front of her, tried to compartmentalize her own feelings so she could be there for Dev's daughters. Marji was shaking, her body so ridiculously thin and small in her bright red cotton dress that Lizbeth wanted to hold her even tighter. Hug the grief out of her. Instead, she began to unconsciously stroke Marji's long dark hair, a gesture she'd seen Dev perform a thousand times.

"It's okay. It'll all be okay," Lizbeth said to the girls, though her eyes searched out Tem. He looked grim, his jaw set, gray eyes flashing with concern.

—I'll find out what happened.

He spoke the words in Lizbeth's mind and she was glad they had this link, could discuss things without frightening the girls. She nodded, letting him know she would keep an eye on the girls so he could go speak privately with his brother.

"Shall we go inside, Thomas?" Tem asked. Thomas quirked an eyebrow but didn't argue.

"Of course. Let's leave the ladies to their reunion."

He turned and went back inside, disappearing into the darkness.

—I'll be right inside if you need me.

She nodded and watched him follow his brother into the cabin. When they were gone, Lizbeth turned her attention to Marji and Ginny.

"You have a pretty voice," Marji whispered, tilting her chin up to look at Lizbeth. But her gaze was empty, her eyes hollow and without luster. It was as if she was looking through Lizbeth. Or, rather, her gaze was directed inward, but she was going through the motions of interacting with the outside world.

Despite the shock of what they'd been through and the

awfulness of the situation, leave it to the girls to be unfazed by Lizbeth's newfound ability to speak.

At least Marji isn't shaking now, Lizbeth thought, but then she realized this zombielike stare was somehow worse.

"Can we go to the playground?" Ginny chirped.

"The playground?" Lizbeth asked, not sure where someone would hide a playground here on this miniature island.

"It's behind the chapel," Marji said, in a listless voice.

"Can we?" Ginny repeated, grabbing at the hem of Lizbeth's plaid shirt.

Wait a minute, Lizbeth thought. *I'm not wearing a plaid shirt.* Yet when she looked down at herself, she was, indeed, wearing a purple plaid shirt and a pair of cuffed indigo jeans with black moccasins. This was an outfit from her past . . . *before* all of the craziness had started. When Eleanora was alive, when Lyse was still living in Athens, Georgia, and when The Flood wasn't even on Lizbeth's radar. It made her realize something important: The dreamlands had tried to cater to what they thought she wanted.

It was odd to realize she'd totally misunderstood the place. She'd always thought the dreamlands changed of their own volition, creating the places they wanted you to visit. Now she wasn't so sure about this. It was actually more like the dreamlands sensed a need in you and then changed themselves accordingly. Trying, in a not very straightforward way, to fulfill that need. A few people, like Tem, had found a way to bend this aspect of the dreamlands to their will, but everyone else was at the dreamlands' mercy . . . trapped in a land that was trying desperately to please them. It had been frightening here in the dreamlands when she was a child and had visited them without meaning to. She'd been lucky enough—or maybe luck wasn't the right word—*blessed* enough that the Tall Lady had found her and had made sure of her safety during her childish wanderings. Now she would do the same for Dev's girls, protecting them and making sure they were never at the mercy of the dreamlands' whims.

"Why don't you show me this playground," Lizbeth said, indicating the far side of the Red Chapel.

"Yay!" Ginny squealed. Lizbeth noticed the change in the girl and realized that Ginny had decided everything would be all right now that Lizbeth was here. She held tight to Lizbeth's shirt, leading the three of them past the front of the cabin but giving the entrance a wide berth.

"It's a real place," Marji said, taking Lizbeth's hand. The girl's fingers were cold and clammy, the palm slicked with sweat. "But Thomas says it looks different back home."

"It's called the Red Chapel 'cause it's made out of red trees," Ginny piped up, pleased to be able to share what she'd learned.

"Yeah?" Lizbeth asked, encouraging the girls to keep talking.

"Yeah," Ginny continued. "Thomas says that they cut down big redwood trees to make it—"

"Like the one you can drive through in Northern California," Marji added, still not her normal self but some instinctive part of her not wanting her little sister to hog the conversation.

"It's magic." This came from Ginny, who wore a wide grin, exposing tiny bone-white baby teeth. "See!"

They'd rounded the side of the cabin, and the sight that greeted them took Lizbeth's breath away. This wasn't a traditional playground. It was a *fairy garden*. Earlier in the summer, she and Dev had helped the girls build a smaller version of this same fairy land in the Montrose backyard—but theirs had been nowhere near as elaborate as this one.

The dreamlands had outdone themselves: There were tall glass spires in a rainbow of colors with brightly colored pinwheels in shimmering gold fabric resting atop them; strings of twinkling lights wrapped themselves around human-sized sunflowers whose faces were like soft brown fur wreathed in a halo of mustard-colored petals. A rose quartz fountain cut into the shape of a dolphin sat in the middle of the garden, a purple waterfall of soap bubbles burbling pleasantly from the creature's nose. A border of blooming hydrangea bushes in shades of baby blue, mauve, and opalescent cream lined the circumference of the garden, walling it in completely—except for a child-sized entrance cut into the shrubbery.

Ginny fit easily, but it took some creative maneuvering—aka crawling—for Lizbeth to get her adult body through the doorway. Marji brought up the rear, only ducking her head slightly to clear the top of the entrance. As soon as they were inside, both girls grabbed for Lizbeth's hand.

"It's just like ours," Ginny said, pulling down the bottom of her T-shirt, the front of which was emblazoned with shiny pink butterflies.

"But it's all real," Marji added.

"Real in a different kind of way," Lizbeth said, letting the girls give her the tour of the garden. "This place is called the dreamlands—"

"We know."

"Oh," Lizbeth said.

"Thomas told us," Marji continued. "He said his brother lives here and that it's like a magical playland. That you can make it change if you use your mind."

"I don't like Thomas, LB," Ginny said with a seven-year-old's bluntness.

"He's not so bad." Marji spoke quickly, blushing bright pink and avoiding Lizbeth's eyes.

Someone thinks Thomas is cute, Lizbeth thought—which made total sense. Marjoram was almost twelve and puberty was about to hit the Montrose family like a hurricane.

And Lizbeth knew exactly why Thomas appealed to the preteen: He greatly resembled the poster of Benedict Cumberbatch hidden on the inside of Marji's closet door—a place she *thought* was private but obviously was not. At least not with an overcurious kid sister hanging around. Dev had heard all about it—"Sherlock Holmes lives in Marji's closet!"—from motormouth Ginny and, finding the whole thing just "adorable," she'd relayed the story to the rest of the coven. Only Lizbeth, who at eighteen was still in the process of leaving her own teenage years behind, realized how humiliated Marji would be to know her mother's friends had giggled over her crush on the dapper British movie star.

Thomas may have gotten a pass with Marji because of his resemblance to her crush, but Lizbeth had to agree with Ginny. There was definitely something about Thomas that rubbed her the wrong way. He wasn't bad, per se, just full of himself and hard to read.

So unlike Tem.

"So what else did Thomas tell you," Lizbeth asked, as they stopped at the fountain and the girls sat down on the stone bench that curved alongside it.

"That you can drink it 'cause it's grape soda," Ginny said, pointing at the frothing water pouring from the dolphin.

"Whose idea was that? I don't remember anything about grape soda—or even this fountain—being in the fairy garden in your backyard."

Marji shrugged, but Ginny was full of information.

"Thomas asked us what we wanted and Marji said, 'Fairy garden'—"

Marji's brow furrowed.

"I did not."

"Did, too," Ginny crowed.

"I said," Marji corrected, "that I didn't think he could make a fairy garden like the one at our house, and then he did."

"That's what I said."

Marji rolled her eyes at Ginny—and it was such a specific gesture, the look of utter disdain for a sibling, that it made Lizbeth miss her older brother. She didn't know what Weir would think about all this. Or what he would have to say when she was able to go home again. He would be mad, of course, angry she'd gone away and left him in a catacomb in Rome. She'd have a lot of explaining to do: why she'd taken off, how she'd been compelled by magic—and the power of the trapped souls of the dead Dream Keepers she and Daniela had found in the catacombs—to go to that awful monolith of rock in the Ural Mountains and use the power of the Blood Moon to telegraph her dream of magic to an unwitting human world.

It was all unbelievable to her—and she was the witch. She knew about strange and unbelievable things . . . had seen stuff that was both terrifying and awe-inspiring. She was the last blood sister of her kind, a Dream Keeper (when almost no others remained) who until recently had been mute and maimed, damaged beyond all reason by the death of her mother and her forced incarceration in a mental institution by the cruel selfishness of her father.

God, her life sounded like a soap opera . . . and maybe it was.

"—he said Mama was gone . . ." Lizbeth had gotten lost in her thoughts and had missed some of what Ginny was saying.

"Did he say how?"

The little girl shook her head, her usually tan complexion ashen.

"He just said she was gone," Marji added, picking at her thumbnail.

"So maybe he just meant that, literally, your mom had gone somewhere."

Marji frowned and then her lower lip curled as she tried not to cry.

"No, he said our grandma and our aunties were dead. That Mama was gone, too."

A tear plopped onto Marji's cheek, and Ginny reached out and took her sister's hand.

"It's okay, Marji."

Marji shook her head.

"No, it's not," she sobbed. "It's not okay and it will never be okay again."

She dropped her chin to her chest and cried in earnest, her shoulders shaking as she took in deep, wheezing breaths. This upset Ginny, who until that point had been relatively calm. She looked up at Lizbeth, her own lip trembling and pronounced: "LB will fix it."

Lizbeth was surprised. If what the girls said was true, she didn't think *anyone* could fix this mess. Ginny's words were like a balm on her sister's nerves, and slowly Marji began to calm down. Her face was still pale and her eyes red-rimmed, but she'd stopped hyperventilating.

"You will?" she asked Lizbeth, eyebrows shooting up in a hopeful smile.

Lizbeth didn't know what to do. She hated lying to the girls, but she couldn't bear to see them so distraught. The words she settled on were vague enough that she didn't feel too terrible saying them.

"I will do everything in my power to fix what I can."

Ginny caught her older sister's eye. Marji took a deep breath and nodded.

"Okay," she said, her voice shaky as she held Ginny's hand. "We believe you."

And that was all it took.

It was different being in the dreamlands this time. She wasn't just visiting them in her sleep (like she'd always done before). She was now physically here—she and the girls—brought by the two odd brothers from another universe who seemed to know just how exactly to manipulate the dreamlands to do their bidding. It was exhilarating. She felt more alive, the colors around her were more vivid, the heat from the sun warmer . . . it was like being in a video-game version of normal reality.

They'd stayed in the fairy garden for a long time, Ginny half in Lizbeth's lap and Marji leaning against Lizbeth's shoulder. It had gotten toastier as they'd rested beside the fountain, the fog lifting as the sky burst into a cloudless neon blue—and the girls had fallen asleep.

One minute Ginny was quietly prattling on about how fairies only ate honey and flower nectar, and then there was silence. Lizbeth let her own eyes close, the sun's heat spreading across her scalp and face, down her shoulders and torso, until she was floating in a sea of golden warmth. She sat in the silence for a while, her mind adrift in a hazy fog of exhaustion, until a long shadow cut across her face, blocking the sun. She lazily opened her eyes, expecting to see Tem standing above her. To her surprise, it was not him.

"Shh, we don't want to wake them."

Lizbeth's brown eyes widened at the sight of the two older women, one a giantess with a halo of wispy, strawberry-blond hair and the other small and gray-haired, her no-nonsense attitude apparent in the rigid set of her posture and her granite countenance. The Tall Lady, as Lizbeth had referred to Hessika when she was a child, had cast the shadow. Her companion, Eleanora, knelt down so that she and Lizbeth were at eye level, and Lizbeth noticed that the long brown shift she wore was too big for her small frame. That, and the contrast of the towering giant of a woman beside her, made Eleanora look elfin.

"You're here . . . ?" Lizbeth said, her voice full of confusion as she shifted in place, trying to stand up.

"Take care," Eleanora said, smiling down at the sleeping girls. "They need their rest."

Lizbeth nodded, careful not to disturb the two sleeping beauties as she climbed to her knees. The next moment she was in Eleanora's arms, clinging to the smaller woman the way Ginny and Marji had clung to *her* earlier that day.

"I was so scared," she whispered.

"I know," Eleanora said, stroking Lizbeth's long hair. "But you did what needed doing. As hard as it was."

They must've made a sight: two sleeping girls, two giant women—Hessika and Lizbeth were both tall as trees—and Eleanora, the no-nonsense, birdlike creature who bound them all together.

"Sorry," Lizbeth murmured, and pulled out of Eleanora's embrace, embarrassed by her outburst. She wasn't a child anymore, yet she'd gone to Eleanora like one, wanting the older woman to make everything better.

As if she could read Lizbeth's mind—and maybe she could—Hessika said: "There's no weakness in needing folks, *ma chère*. We are born alone, but we mustn't stay that way." Her voice was soft and lilting, with strong brushstrokes of the Lower Alabama accent that had made her seem so exotic to Lizbeth as a child.

The leader of the Echo Park coven before Eleanora, Hessika had been long dead by the time Lizbeth was born. But she'd chosen to stay on this plane of existence as a Dream Walker, her ghostly presence a part of Lizbeth's life since she was small. Like Lizbeth, Hessika had been a Dream Keeper, her dream prophecies kept in journals that Eleanora had hidden away until Lizbeth needed them most—because Hessika, alone, had dreamed of The Flood and knew that their ultimate goal was to destroy the covens. These Dream Journals had led Lizbeth to Italy, where she'd separated from her coven mates Lyse and Daniela and her brother, Weir—compelled to do so by magic. This had set into motion a series of events that, she hoped, would stop The Flood.

"So you found us then, did you?"

Thomas stood near the entrance of the fairy garden, lounging against one of the glass spires. His pose may have been casual, but there was a rigid set to his jaw and his eyes flashed with warning.

"What have you done?" Eleanora said, lips pursed in anger. "Bringing them here—"

She gestured at the sleeping girls.

"They're safer," Thomas argued, as he stood up straight. "I had no choice after what happened."

Eleanora got to her feet, shaking her head as Lizbeth tried to follow.

"Stay, this is between him and me," Eleanora said to her, the words coming out in a low growl. She strode across the lawn, the hiss of grass crunching under her bare feet.

Thomas met her halfway, moving with a feline grace that belied his anxiety. He was trying to intimidate Eleanora, but she was having none of it. She marched right up to him and jammed her finger into his chest.

"How could you do it? You sold them out and now they're all gone."

Thomas held his ground, but his shoulders slumped.

"I didn't do it. I know it looks bad for me, but you have to believe I would never harm a hair on the head of a Montrose woman."

Eleanora was like a pit bull with its teeth locked on its prey.

"How dare you plead innocent," she said, her voice tight with rage. "You bound all of them to the house and then you burned it to the ground. You would have done the same to Hessika and me, but unlike the others, we didn't belong to the house. We exist in the dreamlands like your brother."

"Speak of the Devil," Thomas said, turning around and indicating that Tem should join them. "Come in, brother. No one here will bite you."

Tem ducked his head so he could fit through the entrance cut into the hydrangeas.

"I don't expect to be bitten, brother."

He moved toward Thomas and Eleanora, but then he by-passed them and made a beeline for Lizbeth, kneeling down beside her.

"Everything okay here, half-caste?" He took her hand in his and brought it to his lips. The back of her hand tingled where he kissed it.

—Thomas may be a self-righteous prick, but he can be trusted. I promise.

He spoke only to her, using their telepathic bond.

"I'm fine. Everything is okay," she replied, giving him a

quick smile. She didn't know if Thomas could be trusted or not, but she believed in Tem. She was just going to have to trust him when it came to his brother's intentions.

"I was just telling the ladies that I didn't hurt their friends."

Tem raised an eyebrow, turning his attention to Eleanora.

"He helped to destroy the Montrose line—" Eleanora began, but Thomas interrupted her.

"I saved the girls. If I had meant to wipe them all out, why would I have done that?"

Eleanora shook her head.

"I can't begin to imagine what's going on in that horrid mind of yours."

Thomas snorted.

"A powerful witch wants in my mind. Not the kind of place for your sort, dearie," he spat back. "Don't think you can handle what's in there."

"So much anger, *ma chère*," Hessika said, stepping between them, her height dwarfing them both as she looked at Thomas. "We must put it all aside in these dark times. Fight among ourselves, and we will surely lose this war."

"But he murdered them," Eleanora said as her gaze lingered on the sleeping girls, sadness filling her eyes.

"We don't know who perpetrated this atrocity," Hessika replied, a light breeze rippling the hem of her diaphanous cream-colored robe. "Appearances can be deceiving."

Hessika's pronouncement seemed to relax Thomas, his shoulders sagging and the tension lines dissolving from his face.

"I appreciate your judicious words," Thomas said. "I understand I was not myself before and that my behavior was, well, unforgivable. For that I am truly sorry. I was under the spell of the darkness . . . The Flood, as you call it in your universe. It was not my choice to attack Devandra Montrose or her children that day."

Tem stood beside his brother, placing a hand on his arm.

"Where we come from, we are you," Tem said, directing

his words to Hessika. "Unlike in your universe, magic was never forgotten in ours; it's flourished and grown, helping us to create a more egalitarian society. We, the magicians, are its stewards and we do its bidding. Some of your kind, like Lizbeth and yourself, Hessika"—he lifted his chin toward the Tall Lady—"are half-castes. Somewhere in your family line is a link to our universe. It's why you are Dream Keepers, why you can visit the dreamlands of your own volition. How you can control what you see here. In this place where time is fluid. Where the past, present, and future meet, and if you're lucky, you can get a taste of your destiny."

Hessika nodded.

"I've always wondered . . ."

"Why you were so special?" Thomas asked.

"How we came to be," Hessika said. "Why we could do so much more than just dream."

"It's because you are us," Tem said. "There's so much more you can learn, so much more available to you. You have no idea the power you wield—"

He broke off, realizing he'd gotten carried away with himself.

"What my overly passionate brother is trying to say is: We are Magicians," Thomas said, turning to Lizbeth, his blue eyes flashing with power.

"Which means that we have so much to teach *you*, last of the human Dream Keepers."

Hessika and Eleanora had disappeared with Thomas, leaving Lizbeth and Tem alone with the girls, who were sleeping the drugged sleep of the dreamlands.

"It isn't like it is in the real world."

Tem slipped his hands underneath Marji's slumbering form and lifted her into the air. She was almost too big to carry, but he cradled her dead weight to his chest with such care and gentleness—as if she were a tiny flower needing delicate handling—that Lizbeth's heart beat a little faster watching him.

"Sleep, I mean. We have to be careful and wake them soon, or they'll sleep forever," he continued. "And that's not an exaggeration. I really mean *forever.*"

The words sent a chill down Lizbeth's spine.

"Are you serious?" she asked, kneeling down to scoop Ginny up in her arms.

The girl was skinny as a rail, all gangling arms and legs; easy for Lizbeth to manage.

"*Dead* serious," he said in mock seriousness, like he was doing an old-school Clint Eastwood impression. "But in true 'all seriousness,' just think about it. We come here to the dreamlands when we sleep, so where do we go when we sleep while we're here?"

What he was saying made a certain kind of sense. She'd never thought about what would happen if she fell asleep while she was visiting the dreamlands—a trip she'd been making almost nightly since she was a child.

"I don't know," she said, truly curious about the answer.

He grinned back at her, inclining his head in the direction of the Red Chapel—and she was reminded again of how handsome he was, especially when he smiled.

"Let's take them inside and I'll tell you."

"All right," she said, and grinned back at him as she followed him away from the fairyland.

They walked in silence, and like a mood ring, the dreamlands began to change with her emotional state. The scent of the small child in her arms had made her nostalgic for her mother, and while she watched, the landscape followed this bittersweet train of thought, morphing into a field of flowers she'd played in once when she was a child . . . a sea of yellow buttercups that she'd run through with her mother, their squeals of delight trapped in the amber of her mind. Lizbeth was impressed by the depth of detail the dreamlands took away when it plumbed her memories. She bit back tears as she and Tem moved through the plain of bright flowers, their honey-yellow pollen staining her feet and legs.

"You're doing this, you know," Tem said, as the wind gusted across the field, the song of a hundred thousand petals dancing on the breeze filling the air.

"Not on purpose," she said.

"No, not on purpose," he agreed.

They finally reached the edge of the buttercups and stepped across a moat of neon-green grass encircling the Red Chapel. Only now the chapel was just a giant square box assembled from long beams of hammered redwood timber with an oddly slanted bloodred door cut into its side. The door was a gnarly-looking thing that reminded Lizbeth of a bloody gash. It was unsettling and she found herself shrinking away from it.

"Bad things have happened in this place," Lizbeth said.

"They have," Tem said as he stood before the horrible door, one hand on the doorknob. "Blood sisters died at the Red Chapel."

Lizbeth shivered.

"But death, as you know, is not the end."

She nodded.

"I know."

"Step inside and put your burden down," Tem said, turning the knob and pushing the door open. All Lizbeth could see inside was darkness. "This way."

He crossed the threshold, Marji still sleeping in his arms, and disappeared inside.

All Lizbeth could do was follow.

Lyse

There were just some things you didn't know you could do until, all of a sudden, you were just doing them. That was how Lyse learned she could physically go to the dreamlands . . . *and bring other people along with her.*

"Holy hell," Arrabelle said, staring at Lyse like she'd just watched her eat a newborn baby. "How the hell did you do that?"

Lyse wished she had a better answer than "I don't really know," but she didn't. As soon as the blue orb had popped, she'd known exactly where she'd taken them, but not *how*. It had all come from instinct . . . a little voice inside her head that told her to pull off at the diner and head for the back of the parking lot. Part of her, the same part that encouraged her to follow this instinct, wondered if she'd been drawn to the specific place because there was a flow line running through it. That her personal magic was even more powerful when she drew from the bands of magical energy encircling the Earth. It seemed like a reasonable assumption, but she had so little training in magic that it was only a guess.

As much as she loved Eleanora, Lyse would always be a

little angry with her grandmother for shielding her from the truth: that they were both witches. If only Eleanora had trusted her enough to bring Lyse into the fold sooner, maybe then she wouldn't be so in the dark about her abilities. She knew that Eleanora had wanted her to have a normal life—had "protected" Lyse from the supernatural world of the covens because she loved Lyse—but dammit, sometimes she just wanted to punch her grandmother in the arm and yell at her for being so stupid.

Once again, she found herself frustrated by this train of thought and decided that it was a dead end for her. Best to put it away and focus on the problems at hand.

"Well, I don't know for sure," Lyse said, wishing she had more info and wasn't just making an educated guess. "But I think my abilities were augmented by a flow line."

Lyse shrugged. She knew this wasn't the answer Arrabelle was looking for, but it was all she had.

"So these are the dreamlands," Niamh said, green eyes wide as she took in the landscape around them.

It wasn't too terribly different from the earthly plane they'd just left behind them. They were still in a parking lot. It was still night. There were still the same glowing neon letters spelling out *Tessa's Roadsider* in hot pink and fuchsia . . . only as Lyse and the others watched, the neon letters in the giant sign began to melt like cotton candy stuffed into a microwave and set to high.

"Are you seeing this?" Arrabelle asked, but it was rhetorical. No question that they were *all* seeing it.

"Watch out, Bell," Evan said, taking a protective stance in front of Arrabelle. "The Dumpster's going the same way as the neon sign."

Lyse followed Evan's example and moved out of the way just as a load of sludge (which, until only moments before, had been a heavy-gauge-steel trash bin) headed for her feet. The sludge had a mind of its own, and that mind did not

follow the rules of traditional Earth-based physics. It immediately changed its direction, veering to the left as it chased
after Lyse and the others.

"Head for the car," Evan said, but Arrabelle shook her head.

"*What* car?"

Arrabelle's little red rental was gone, replaced by a grinning red plastic skull the size of a car.

"What the hell is that?" Evan asked.

"Skull," Niamh replied, which got a withering look from
Arrabelle.

"No, I got that," Evan said, grinning. "But why?"

"That's the million-dollar question," Lyse said, as she began
to circle around the edge of the diner toward the front of the
building. "Maybe there's an answer in there."

She pointed to the entrance of Tessa's Roadsider diner.

"C'mon," she said, jogging toward the chrome-and-glass
double doors.

"Are you sure this is a good idea?" Arrabelle asked, but
she and Evan were already following Lyse toward the entrance.
Niamh was the only holdout, still staring at the neon sign as
it slowly began to melt into a pile of sludge the color and tex-
ture of Pepto-Bismol.

"I think the sludge is coming with us," Niamh said, pointing to the pink goo that was getting dangerously close to her
sneakers.

"Start walking," Lyse said as she reached the entrance and
pushed open the door marked *In*, getting a blast of chilled air
to the face. "We don't know what it'll do if it touches you."

"I've seen *The Blob*," Niamh said, joining the others at the
entrance. "I know what goo can do."

"It smells amazing in here," Lyse said, holding the door
open for Evan and Arrabelle as the greasy perfume of French
fries bubbling in a deep fryer and burger patties sizzling on
the grill assailed their nostrils.

From the sparkly, ruby-red vinyl booths, the polished

chrome-and-Formica dine-in counter—with requisite ruby-red vinyl-covered swivel seats—and the pristine white-tiled floors, this place was old-school/retro diner heaven.

"It's like America on steroids," Arrabelle said, wrinkling her nose as she passed Lyse. "Not a huge fan of all that fried crap."

Niamh, the last one of them inside, disagreed.

"Oh, yeah, I like it in here," she said, a wistful smile on her face. "Our parents took Laragh and me to a place like this near Seattle once. We could order anything we wanted . . . it was the first time I ever had a milkshake . . . it was strawberry."

"Do you smell that?" Arrabelle asked—and Lyse nodded: *She sure did.*

Fresh strawberries, vanilla, and heavy whipping cream. This new aroma displaced the diner smells, though no matter where Lyse looked she could find no one doing any cooking.

"Uh, I think we're being followed," Arrabelle said, looking pointedly at the white-tiled floor.

Lyse followed Arrabelle's gaze to the entrance. The Pepto-Bismol-colored sludge had pushed open one of the glass doors and was now making its way inside the diner. The closer the sludge got to them, the stronger the strawberry milkshake aroma became until it was almost overpowering.

"I think we've found the origin of the milkshake smell," Evan said, pulling Arrabelle along with him as he moved away from the sludge and farther into the diner.

"No kidding," Lyse said. As a finger of sludge snaked toward her sneaker, she hopped up onto the seat of one of the booths, the soles of her shoes squeaking on the red vinyl. "Niamh! Get on a booth or one of the counter stools."

"No, I think it's okay," Niamh said—and Lyse watched in horror as the younger woman knelt down beside the goop to examine it.

"Niamh—" Evan said, a warning in his tone.

"It's okay, Evan," she said, and tentatively stuck a finger into the thick goo.

Lyse closed her eyes, not wanting to see Niamh's finger dissolved down to the bone.

"Mmm . . . that's yummy."

"It didn't eat you?" Lyse asked, still not wanting to look.

"Nope," Niamh said—and Lyse opened her eyes in time to catch Niamh licking her finger. "I ate *it*."

"C'mon, Niamh," Evan said, shaking his head. "Really? You had to eat it?"

Niamh, still squatting by the doorway, turned to face the others, a big grin on her face.

"It's strawberry milkshake."

The sludge had surrounded Niamh, leaving a tiny island of white tile where she knelt. Now that it had what it wanted—Niamh under its guard—it remained where it was, unmoving. Whatever the sludge was, it was clearly interested in Niamh and wanted to be as close to her as possible.

"Niamh," Lyse said, "I want you to think about turning the strawberry milkshake into a chocolate one."

Niamh looked up at her, frowning.

"I know it sounds super weird, but can you do that?" Lyse continued.

Niamh nodded, but she looked skeptical.

"I'll try," she said.

She scrunched up her face and closed her eyes, doing as Lyse asked. At first, nothing happened, but then the sludge began to bubble—hesitantly and then with more energy. Lyse watched as the gooey sludge began to get darker and darker until it was no longer a pale Pepto-pink, but a rich chocolatey brown.

"Smells like chocolate," Arrabelle said. Lyse could smell it, too, the warm sugary goodness of chocolate filling the air.

Niamh dipped her finger into the brown goop.

"You don't have to eat it," Evan began, but too late—Niamh had already popped the goop-covered finger into her mouth.

"Yep, that's chocolate, all right," Niamh said, and grinned.

Lyse realized that Niamh's ability to manipulate the physical form of things here in the dreamlands made a weird kind of sense. She'd never been able to control what happened in her dreams, but Lyse had read about other people who possessed the talent—and she had the distinct feeling Niamh was one of them. Which meant that they were much safer traveling in the dreamlands with Niamh to navigate their way.

"I think it's okay to come down now," Niamh said, standing up and wiping the goo from her hands onto the front of her jeans. "It's just a milkshake."

She offered her hand to Lyse, and Lyse took it, letting Niamh help her climb down from her perch on the red vinyl seat. As she alighted from the booth, the sludge moved out of her way, leaving a clean spot for her to stand in. Evan and Arrabelle did the same, and the sludge obliged by clearing a path for them to join Niamh and Lyse.

"You're controlling the sludge," Lyse said.

Niamh nodded.

"I see that. It was kind of obvious when the sludge went all chocolatey."

Evan seemed to catch on to the implication of what Lyse was saying.

"Niamh, you were manipulating the diner and you didn't even realize it," he said. "I've heard you tell Yesinia—she was the master of *our* coven," he explained to Lyse and Arrabelle, "about making stuff happen in your dreams. Controlling your nightmares . . ."

Niamh shrugged, shoving her hands into her pants pockets.

"But that's different."

Lyse disagreed—it was *exactly* the same thing.

"If you can control stuff in your dreams, then you can do it here. These are the *dreamlands*. This is where you come when you dream."

Lyse knelt down and dragged her finger through the sludge. She held it up to the light for the others to see.

"This place is made of dreams, Niamh," she said. "You ate a dream."

Niamh laughed.

"Yeah, I guess I did."

"I think it's time we got out of here," Arrabelle said. "Let's see what's here and then let's figure out how to get home."

"Agreed," Lyse said.

The four of them headed toward the double doors.

"The world is a new place, Niamh," Arrabelle said. "What was impossible before? Well, who's to say it's impossible now . . ."

Arrabelle let her words trail off as she placed her hands against the glass and pushed the *Out* door open. It swung forward and she stepped into the night, pressing her back against the door and holding it wide so the others could pass. Niamh looked uncertain, her eyes switching from Evan to Lyse, then to Arrabelle and back again.

"Maybe. It's a little scary to realize that whatever I think can become reality here. Makes me not want to think . . ."

"You're looking at it the wrong way," Evan said. "You have a gift. Use it wisely and you don't have to worry about it."

"I had no idea I could take us all to the dreamlands," Lyse said, smiling at Niamh. "It freaked me out, too. But it saved us from the bad guys, and that's something."

"I just *imagined* and a neon sign turned into a puddle of strawberry milkshake."

"You never know when that 'imagining' gift of yours could be the thing that saves the entire world," Lyse said, putting her hand on Niamh's arm and gently guiding them both out into the night.

Niamh snorted—but she didn't argue.

They'd been walking in the desert for what felt like forever.

After they'd left the diner, they'd headed out onto the highway, following the road signs that pointed them toward

Los Angeles. It was an empty stretch of road. No cars, no bikes, no buses, no airplanes . . . no other travelers. The dreamlands must be such a vast place that you could walk forever and never run into another person.

It was also an incredibly changeable landscape. You blinked and things were different—which was how they'd found themselves not on a highway at night anymore, but on a flat plain of bloodred desert in the middle of the afternoon, their shoes sinking into the sand. Lyse missed the firm asphalt of the road under her feet, and she hated missing something as important as watching night being instantly swapped for day.

We could spend forever wandering the dreamlands, Lyse thought, *and never reach a real destination.*

She knew they needed to get back to the real world—and soon. Things were already a mess in their reality, and the four of them being gone so long was a bad idea. The only problem was that since she had no experience with venturing in and out of the dreamlands, she wasn't really sure where they'd end up if she did manage to get them out. Would they be right back where they started—with the white pickup truck barreling toward them? Did where you were in the dreamlands correspond with where you were in reality, or was it all arbitrary?

Lyse didn't want to do something that might endanger them all.

Her uncertainty made her unwilling to act. She recognized that logic was unhelpful because it didn't really work that way in the dreamlands . . . a place where Niamh could turn cars into skulls and neon signs into milkshakes. And the only time she'd ever seen someone moving in and out of the dreamlands was watching Lizbeth do it in Elysian Park. Her physical form had remained behind while her spirit traveled here—but their situation was totally different. Lyse and the others hadn't left their bodies behind. They'd been awake when they'd entered the dreamlands.

I wonder if this was what Weir experienced when he died? This untethering from the world? Lyse thought—and then his face appeared in her mind, the charming smile and mercurial eyes. She wished with all her heart that he were with them here in the dreamlands. He'd help her make the right decisions, make sure they all got back to the real world in one piece.

"What's wrong? Why are you crying?" Arrabelle asked, her voice soft.

They were walking side by side, and Lyse hadn't even realized there were tears on her face until she reached up and felt the wetness on her cheeks.

Evan and Niamh were ahead of them, lost in their own conversation.

"Weir," she said, her voice cracking—and she knew she could no longer keep the poisonous knowledge to herself. It was eating her alive, dogging her every step and making it hard for her to think straight. She needed all of her faculties about her if they were going to get back home, and maybe telling someone else about Weir's death would help.

"Lyse?" Arrabelle asked, deep concern in her voice.

She encircled both of Lyse's wrists with her hands, stopping them both where they stood.

"What is going on?"

Lyse just shook her head, unable to speak.

"Did something happen? Did you get in a fight?"

Lyse continued to shake her head, fighting back the tears she knew were coming. Her throat burned from the effort, a lump lodged there so hard it was like a stone.

"Lyse, please," Arrabelle said, and pulled Lyse into her chest, hugging her tight. "Tell me what's going on?"

Lyse pressed her face against Arrabelle's collarbone, her bangs in her eyes. *I'm not going to cry. I'm not going to cry. I'm not going to cry . . .* But that was exactly what she was doing, the tears coursing down her face. Arrabelle's long fingers stroked Lyse's hair as she made calming noises low in her throat.

"Hush, hush . . . it's okay, baby . . ."

Lyse could hear Evan asking what was wrong—and Arrabelle shooing him and Niamh away, giving her and Lyse some privacy. She remembered that Arrabelle had taken care of her once before, when Eleanora had died. She'd collected Lyse from the police station and made sure she'd gotten home in one piece. Something Lyse had not had the presence of mind to do for herself.

Lyse was glad that of all the people in the world, it was Arrabelle who would hear her confession.

"He's . . . I . . . it's my fault."

"What's your fault?"

Lyse shook her head.

"He died because of me."

Arrabelle pushed Lyse back so she could see her face.

"Did you just say that Weir's dead?" She wasn't being accusatory or judging Lyse—she was just shocked. Lyse knew this intellectually, but she still felt the guilt well up inside her like a fountain.

"It was in Italy. After Lizbeth took off—"

Arrabelle's face fell, as much for Lyse's pain as for the news itself.

"Oh, God . . . does Lizbeth know?"

Lyse shook her head.

"How could she? It was just the two of us—I sent Daniela off after her—and now Daniela's in the hospital"—something else she also felt tremendous guilt about—"it was just a chaotic mess and then The Flood's people attacked us. I lost it and when I came to, Weir was just lying there . . . on the floor of the catacombs . . ."

Arrabelle swallowed back her own tears.

"Oh, Lyse, I'm so sorry. For you both." She shook her head, trying to clear it. "Poor Lizbeth."

"She'll blame me," Lyse said, "and she'll have every right to. It was my job to protect all of you and I failed."

She hated herself in that moment. She wished nothing more than that she'd never been born. She should've protected Daniela and Weir . . . and Lizbeth, wherever she was. She'd let her just run away like a spoiled little child instead of keeping her in hand.

I'm not even thirty and I feel the weight of being a caretaker to too many souls, she thought, miserably.

"You are one person, Lyse MacAllister," Arrabelle said, a firmness in her voice. "Not God. You did what you could do and it didn't work. Someone died, someone got hurt. That's the price of doing business in this messed-up world. Everyone knows that this isn't going to end well, that some of us aren't going to make it. But we do it because it's the right thing. *You* do it because it's the right thing."

Lyse swallowed, the lump in her throat beginning to dissolve.

"You didn't ask to be a part of this," Arrabelle continued. "It was forced on you. But you're still here. And I'll follow you into the pit of hell if that's where you think we need to go. You didn't kill Weir, but you will avenge him. I promise you that."

She pulled Lyse back in, squeezing her tight.

"Now stop crying," Arrabelle said, finally letting Lyse go. "I might not have been premature when I said that bit about hell. I think we're there now."

Lyse looked around them, the red desert stretching out in all directions.

"I think I can jump us out of here again—"

"Yeah?" Arrabelle asked.

"Yeah, but I want to see if I can't get us somewhere interesting . . ."

Arrabelle caught the glint in Lyse's eye.

"Like go-big-or-go-home interesting?"

Lyse smiled.

"Exactly."

Lyse asked them to form a circle and join hands. Four witches—each one powerful and unique in their own way: two herbalists, a diviner, and whatever the hell Lyse was . . . an *evolved one*, she supposed she should call herself—standing in the middle of a bloodred desert about to perform some crazy-ass magic. Until she'd come back to Echo Park and learned that blood sisters and magic were real, she would've peed her pants laughing at the absurdity of what they were doing now. It felt like that silly slumber party game kids played—*Stiff as a board, light as a feather*—only with four grown-ups as the participants instead of a bunch of giggly preteen girls.

"Niamh," Lyse said. "I want you to imagine us in Daniela's hospital room. Sounds crazy. Sounds impossible, but, dammit, you have the gift of controlling dreams, so if anyone can make it happen, it's you."

"I'll do it," Niamh said. "I mean, I'll try. If you can make the jump, then I will do exactly what you tell me to."

"Good," Lyse said. "Evan, Arrabelle, I think you should just concentrate on this insanity working and us getting back to Earth in one piece."

Nods from them both.

"Can do," Evan said, and gave Lyse a wink.

She was happy to have the three of them on her side. It gave her the feeling that she could do anything . . . and maybe she could. She closed her eyes and tried to remember what exactly had happened the first time she'd attempted this.

You didn't think about it, she told herself. *You just did it.*

"Light as a feather, stiff as a board. Light as a feather, stiff as a board."

She knew the others were looking at her.

"I don't have a spell or anything to say," she muttered, eyes still closed. "So I'm borrowing this one. I'll just say it in my head."

She heard Niamh giggle.

It was hotter than heck in this bloodred desert, and Lyse felt sweat pooling on her upper lip and in the crook of her lower back. She wanted a one-way ticket out of the dreamlands and straight into their own reality—so that was what she concentrated on as she thought . . . *Light as a feather, stiff as a board* . . . in her head. She repeated the mantra over and over again until she felt the top of her head burn with the heat of the dreamlands desert sun. She opened her eyes, expecting to see a glowing blue orb encircling them, but there was nothing. Only the same blazing dreamlands sun beating down on them. Like small red mirrors, the surface of the sand was reflecting the sun back at them, and Lyse felt the skin on her cheeks starting to burn.

"It's not working," she said, looking at the others. "I'm just sweating and repeating that stupid phrase in my head for nothing."

"Uh, I think maybe you need to repeat it again, faster."

Lyse frowned at Niamh, but the other girl wasn't looking at her. She was staring at something over Lyse's shoulder, eyes wide.

"What?" Lyse asked, turning to follow Niamh's gaze.

Her mouth dropped when she saw a pink dust storm—why it was that color, Lyse had no idea—heading directly for them.

"Can you make it change direction?" Evan asked Niamh.

"No, I just tried. It's not part of the dreamlands . . . it's something else . . . something older and much, much scarier."

Lyse tore her eyes away from the approaching darkness and began to mumble under her breath.

"What're you saying?" Arrabelle asked.

"I'm begging the Goddess or whatever is up there to get us the hell out of here—"

There was a *cracking* sound as a brilliant blue bolt of lightning shot down from the sky and struck the sand in front of Lyse's feet.

"What the—" Arrabelle shouted, but then she began to smile. "Look."

A pale blue orb had appeared in the middle of their circle, floating a few feet away from Lyse's face. It was small and almost translucent, but it was a start.

Get bigger, Lyse thought. *WAY bigger.*

She turned her head and heard the incessant hissing of the wind as it reached out from the edges of the storm, eager to draw the four of them into the heart of its darkness.

"Get us the hell out of here!" Lyse screamed at the orb as she dragged her gaze away from the monstrous cloud of evil moving swiftly toward them. "Please, little guy!"

The orb began to swirl in place, growing larger as it spun. Within seconds, it was so big that it had enveloped the four of them, each of their faces bathed in the orb's neon-blue light.

"Think Rome. Think Daniela. Think hospital room!" Lyse screamed at the others, though her words were mostly directed at Niamh.

There was a loud *crunch* as the dust storm hit them with all its force and they spun forward—but then the orb popped.

The Book of The Flood

. . . so the responsibility to act is thrust upon the chosen ones. For they are the light and the power of The Flood. Through them will come the final cleansing of mankind's sins, and their pains will bring about the beginning of a new epoch for humanity. And the witches that have toiled in their evil for so long will find themselves without succor and will be brought low to their knees and destroyed. So is the power of The Flood on this Earth and beyond . . .

—Pariah 2:12
The Book of The Flood

Niamh

She wasn't alone, and that made the thing Lyse asked of her much easier. Though she couldn't really tap into the power in any conscious way—other than to ask for their help—because Niamh was only the vessel. Inside her she carried the energy that had once comprised her twin sister, Laragh—and with her twin came the creature that The Flood had created.

Though she didn't understand the logistics of how any of it was possible, Niamh's hunch was that it had something to do with electricity. She'd been holding Laragh when her sister died, and in that breadth of time between life and death, Niamh had felt the electrical energy that *was* her sister being transferred into her own body. A wave of fire shot through her skin in an electrical burst that felt like she was sticking her finger in a light socket—but the pain had immediately subsided and she'd been left as she was before . . . only with the impression that she was somehow "fuller." Not physically, but spiritually. Like she was made up of more psychic mass than her frail human body was supposed to contain.

Whether or not her body was capable of supporting two or maybe three or more persons—who knew how many women's lives had gone into creating The Flood's creature—she was glad for the extra battery power. She focused her thoughts on taking the four of them away from the dreamlands and toward a woman (whom she did not know) and a hospital room half a world and a dimension away.

She heard a second *pop* as Lyse's blue orb physically pulled them out of the dreamlands, and her sense of "up" and "down" shifted as she began to somersault in the air, so fast she could hardly think straight—but then she realized that part of her consciousness recognized that she was still standing firmly on hard-packed earth, holding hands with two of her blood sisters . . . that the disorientation was only in her head.

Daniela. Take me to Daniela.

She thought these words but did not speak them out loud. She wished she knew what Daniela looked like, thought maybe it would make this whole thing way easier. But that was an impossibility, so she decided, instead, to craft a stand-in version of Daniela in her mind. She imagined a woman with icy blond hair and pale blue eyes—but just as the picture began to come into focus, it began to change, the hair morphing from blond to dark brown and finally to purple and pink, the wide face narrowing at the temples and chin.

That's not me, she thought. *I'm not doing that . . .*

WE ARE. AND WE WANT YOU TO FIND HER.

There was another voice in her head, a loud one that had nothing to do with her own unconscious. It belonged to The Flood's creation . . . the monster crafted from the stolen energy of all the broken women inside The Flood's underground lab. Their energy—which was really the essence of their magic— had come together, morphing into one powerful psychic creature. The Flood had been successful in making a monster, but that had not been their intention. This was obvious because The Flood's soldiers had been terrified of it, had even *fled* the lab because of it. The creature was merely a by-product of their efforts to build something else . . . but *what?*

Niamh had no idea.

The creature's voice echoed in her head again and the sound was cacophonous—almost as if there were a chorale of women speaking to Niamh.

WE WANT YOU TO SUCCEED.

Next, her sister's voice spoke to her from inside her head, Laragh's spirit riding the pulse of electricity that made up Niamh's life force.

—We *want you to succeed. We'll help you go to Daniela.*

Her head began to throb as she felt the creature tapping into her neural pathways, searching through her memories to find different images it could cobble together like it was building a jigsaw puzzle of a human face. It took Jenny Franklin's chin—Jenny owned the Seafaring Merchant, a junk store two streets over from the house Niamh and Laragh had grown up in. Next, the creature stole her Aunt Estelle's delicate upper lip. It borrowed Lyse's dark eyebrows and cadged the ears right off an unnamed trapeze artist Niamh had seen perform when she was eight, the woman sailing gracefully across the orange-and-red-striped fabric of the circus big top.

When the creature was done mixing and matching, Niamh realized that—though she'd never met the woman before—she now possessed a reasonable facsimile of Daniela Altonelli's face to help guide her to their destination.

Daniela Altonelli, we are coming for you, she thought as the swirling patchwork of images that made up Daniela's pixie face filled her mind's eye like a kaleidoscope.

And then Niamh felt someone squeeze her hand.

"We're here," Lyse whispered in her ear.

Niamh opened her eyes. She was standing in a pool of sunlight by a window, a hospital bed in front of her that held an achingly frail body tucked inside it like a chrysalis. Daniela was a wraith, so pale you could see the outline of her veins beneath the delicate flesh of her face. She looked almost nothing like the woman in Niamh's mind.

Maybe if she weren't so sick, Niamh thought.

But Daniela was sick. *Really* sick . . . her translucent skin was tinged a shade of purpley-blue, and she had shadowed hollows under her eyes and beneath her cheekbones that were so dark they looked like bruises. Her breathing came in shallow, ragged bursts. A quiet hiss in her throat.

It was apparent to anyone who looked at her that Daniela was not long for this world.

"Oh, God," Lyse said, her hands on the bed railing as she peered down at Daniela's lifeless body. "How did this happen?"

She hadn't even seen Lyse move. One moment she was standing beside Niamh, the next she was leaning over the hospital bed.

Arrabelle slipped past Niamh and joined Lyse at Daniela's side. She put her hand on Lyse's shoulder, but her face was ashen, too. She looked like she needed as much comforting as Lyse did.

Niamh took a few steps back, moving away from the two women in order to give them some space. She didn't know Lyse and Arrabelle well, but she understood the deep, familial connection that existed between coven mates.

"She's going to die," Niamh whispered to Evan, who nodded in agreement.

"Is that what I looked like?" he asked. "When I was sick."

Evan had been at death's door, the same as Daniela, and he hadn't looked much better.

"Not too far off the mark," Niamh replied, and heard Evan's sharp intake of breath.

Back at Daniela's bedside, Lyse lifted a hand to touch Daniela's face but then thought better of it. "Daniela?" she murmured.

There was no response.

"Dammit, I hate that I can't touch her!" Her voice was

hard and even Niamh, who was not an empath, could feel the bristling of Lyse's anger. Lyse turned away from the bed and began to pace, her frustration an electrical current in the room.

"Isn't there anything you guys can do?" Lyse asked, turning back to face Arrabelle. Lyse was trying not to cry. Niamh could hear the pleading note in the other woman's voice. "You and Evan. You know magic potions. Can't you fix her?"

Arrabelle swallowed hard, tears in her dark eyes. She looked back at Evan, too emotional to speak herself, and he answered for her.

"There are things we can do to prolong life, but she's been so damaged . . . parts of her brain are probably broken beyond repair and it all happened so quickly . . . I don't think it's possible," he said and sighed. "This happens to empaths. Their circuitry just gets blown and there's nothing you can do to fix it. Nothing herbal, at least. Especially once they're this far gone. It's one of the side effects of their kind of magic—and it gets every one of them."

"Come on," Lyse said, her voice a growl. "What the hell is magic good for if it can't save someone you love?"

Niamh had pondered this question more than once in the last twenty-four hours. Her sister had died and magic hadn't been able to save her. In fact, it was precisely because of Laragh's magic that her sister had been tortured and killed.

GO TO HER.

It was the creature—it's voices humming in Niamh's head.

I can't, Niamh thought, her words for the creature in her head. *She's an empath. If I touch her, I'll kill her.*

GO TO HER.

The creature was insistent.

No, Niamh thought. *I'm not a killer.*

—*Who said you were?* This was Laragh getting in on the action. Niamh wished the others could hear the crazy conversation that was going on inside her head: a psychic creature and her dead twin, both arguing with Niamh about killing a woman whom none of them had ever met.

Well, I will be if I listen to you, Niamh said.

—*Nonsense.*

Laragh had always been the more dominant twin—she was born first and she'd been given all the gifts: She could bend people to her will, was always getting what she wanted in any situation, and was a clever arguer (as was evidenced in the argument they were having now). She was just the better person overall, and she was the one who should've been there in that hospital room helping to fix things. Boy, had the universe made a stupid mistake when it allowed Niamh to live and Laragh to die.

You should be here, Niamh thought. *This should be your fight, not mine.*

—*You were the one who realized what was happening. I didn't believe you.*

Laragh's voice was earnest, and what she said was true. Niamh had seen the future in her cards, in a tarot spread that predicted a horrific future. She'd gone to their coven master, Yesinia, and Yesinia had believed, but the others—Laragh, Evan, and Honey—didn't want to live in a world where witches could be killed without recourse for the crime of being what they were.

I didn't want to be right, Niamh thought. *I wish I had been wrong.*

—*But you weren't. And now we have to step up and do something about it.*

Niamh must've nodded because Evan shot her a questioning glance.

"Niamh?" he asked.

"I need to do something," she said, steeling herself for the argument that was about to ensue when she told them what she, Laragh, and the creature had planned.

"What are you talking about?" Evan asked, his voice quiet, trying to keep the conversation between them.

It didn't work.

"Niamh?" Lyse asked—and Niamh saw that her hands were clenched into fists. She'd stopped pacing, was standing by the bed again, her shoulders curved inward, her posture protective.

Arrabelle was looking at her, too.

"What do you need to do, Niamh?" Arrabelle asked, happy to focus on anything but Lyse's anger and what was happening to Daniela in that hospital bed.

TELL THEM.

Niamh swallowed hard, nervous. She'd let the creature and Laragh push her into this, and now she was going to have to own it.

"I need to touch her."

Arrabelle immediately stepped between Niamh and the bed.

"No way. You'll kill her—"

"Arrabelle—" Evan was trying to calm her down, but Arrabelle was fierce and immovable, her expression that of a mama bear protecting her cubs.

"If you come anywhere near this bed—" Arrabelle continued, her voice rising.

"Stop!"

The word rang in the air with the clarity of a silver bell, the sound cutting through the chaos and bringing silence in its wake. Everyone turned to look at Lyse, who had shut them all up with one word. She, in turn, looked at each of them, establishing her leadership with a fierce glare.

She saved Niamh for last.

"You want to touch her," Lyse said, "because you think you can save her?"

YES.

The creature spoke in Niamh's mind, but from the funny expression on Lyse's face, Niamh was pretty sure Lyse had heard it, too.

WE CAN SAVE HER. LET US TRY. THIS IS WHY WE ARE HERE.

Niamh saw Lyse blink, the passion in the creature's words washing over them both. Lyse swallowed hard, fixing her attention on Niamh. Though she was physically speaking to Niamh, Niamh knew that Lyse's words were meant for the creature.

"Go ahead," she said. "I trust you. All of you. Do it."

Niamh nodded—this was all the go-ahead she was going to get—and started to move closer to the bed, but Arrabelle blocked her path.

"If you kill her, or hurt her any more than she already is," Arrabelle said, her voice as low and dangerous as a leopard's growl. "I'll kill you."

The look Arrabelle gave Niamh was deadly. Niamh believed Arrabelle would do exactly as she said.

"Bell," Evan said, drawing Arrabelle's gaze away from Niamh. "Come stand by me."

With a final look at Niamh, Arrabelle stepped out of her way.

"You better fix her, dammit," Arrabelle murmured as she passed Niamh, the emotion in her voice palpable. She might have just threatened her life, but Niamh knew Arrabelle wanted this to work, too.

As she neared Daniela's hospital bed, she felt like one of those old-time faith healers that practiced the laying on of hands. She wasn't sure where she was supposed to touch Daniela—the head, the shoulders, the arm—so she decided to just go for it and let the voices in her head direct her if she guessed wrong.

The head, she thought. *That's where the damage is and that's where I should go.*

She raised her hands, her fingers trembling, and kept walking until she hit the metal guardrail with her hip. Daniela's eyelashes fluttered as Niamh's body connected with the bed, but they didn't open.

"Daniela, my name is Niamh," Niamh said, feeling silly talking to someone who appeared comatose. "I'm gonna work on making you better. So try not to worry too much and we'll get you all fixed up, if we can."

She didn't know why she was saying all this, trying to reassure a person who couldn't hear her. Maybe all the babbling was just her nervousness coming out. It was a trial by fire—and she hoped she didn't fail.

"Okay, I'm gonna touch your head now. Don't be scared."

She placed her hands on Daniela's temples, and, at first, she felt nothing.

It's not working, she thought.

WE ARE HERE.

Niamh realized this was the creature's way of reassuring her. She wondered if—

And then she lost control of her thoughts as it began . . .

. . . a rectangular prism of polished crystal dipped into Niamh's field of view, dangling as if it were hanging on a piece of invisible filament. It began to spin, moving slowly . . . slowly . . . slowly . . . making lazy circles that caught the light from an open window—she didn't know where this window was, or if she was only imagining that the window existed and the light was actually coming from some artificial place. Heck, she didn't know where she was, or even if she was . . . she felt weightless, bodiless, cut loose from the bindings of corporeal reality—maybe she was even a freewheeling spirit now.

But then the prism drew her attention again, filling every corner of her vision with halos of concentrated rainbow-hued light. She was fascinated by the richness of the colors: the drenched-in-blood-reds, the newborn-springtime-violets, the salty-ocean-blues, the sunburst-

summer-yellows. It was a kaleidoscope of beauty so powerful and full of life that Niamh ached with want as she experienced it. Every molecule that existed—and didn't exist—thrummed with the need to create. It was being as close to God as Niamh could imagine . . .

Arrabelle's dulcet tones were the first thing she heard.

"She's coming around."

Niamh opened her eyes and found industrial-grade ceiling tile staring back at her. Lots of big, square acoustical tiles with a smattering of little brown holes in them . . . holes to fixate on and count and see imaginary animals in when you looked at them. She felt woozy, felt the room spinning around her, but she just stayed focused on those holes and they kept her anchored to reality.

"I'm okay," she heard herself saying, though she couldn't feel her lips moving. "I'm all right."

"Don't let her sit up yet," she heard Evan say. "She still looks green around the gills."

Niamh had never understood what people meant when they said they felt close to God. She'd just assumed they were being melodramatic. Now she knew that wasn't true. She'd felt it, knew it, wanted it again.

Was that being dead? she thought, and waited for an answer from the creature or Laragh.

She got no response.

Hello?

Still no answer, not even from her sister. She started to panic. Where was Laragh? She'd lost her once before and she couldn't . . . wouldn't . . . lose her again.

Laragh? Are you there?

But there was nothing—and for the first time in her life, Niamh felt alone. The panic grew inside her; the fear that she was now and forever on her own was becoming a reality. She was terrified that she'd never talk to her twin again.

"Laragh . . . ? Laragh, don't go . . . Laragh . . ." Her sister's name died on her lips and she covered her face with her hands.

"What happened, Niamh?"

She lowered her hands from her eyes and found Lyse kneeling on the ground beside her, a worried expression on her face.

"She's gone. I thought she would stay, but she left me . . ."

All the panic and fear streamed out of her in a flood of words, and with the wound lanced, she began to weep. Lyse helped her sit up, then wrapped an arm around her shoulder, pulling her close. She could smell Lyse's spicy perfume, the warmth of the other woman's body, and it made her cry harder, the missing of her twin even more urgent when she was so close to another living person.

"They're not inside you anymore, are they?" Lyse asked, her voice a respectful whisper.

Niamh shook her head.

"They were the ones who wanted you to help Daniela."

It was a statement, not a question. Once again, Niamh nodded.

"Do you want to see what you did?"

From the tone of Lyse's voice, Niamh couldn't tell what she was going to see when she looked in that hospital bed, but she knew she couldn't sit on the cold white floor forever. She reached for Lyse's hand and Lyse, immediately understanding what she wanted, helped Niamh to her feet.

"Look," Lyse said, guiding her over to the bed and placing Niamh's hands on the metal so she could lean her weight against it.

Niamh didn't think Lyse would force her to look at something terrible. She didn't think Lyse was capable of something so cruel. If the laying on of her hands had not healed Daniela, had, in fact, done the opposite, someone would have told her. This knowledge gave her the courage to do as Lyse commanded: to look.

She let her eyes trail up the heavy cotton blanket, past the light cream sheets—where Daniela's hands were balled into fists at her sides—to the deep hollow at Daniela's throat just above the V-neck of her thin hospital gown, and, finally, to her sunken cheeks and eyes . . . only to Niamh's surprise this was no longer the case. Daniela's face had plumped since she'd last seen her; the dark shadows were lighter and the color had returned to her skin. Daniela was breathing easier; the shallow hissing sound that had preceded every inhalation had gone.

Niamh's body began to shake and she felt her knees buckle, but Evan and Lyse were there to hold her up.

"She's better," Niamh murmured.

"Whatever you did," Arrabelle said. "Whatever your sister and that poor trapped creature did . . . all of you saved Daniela."

Niamh nodded, thinking of the sacrifice her sister had made. Then another thought danced through her mind, and suddenly Niamh didn't feel so heartbroken. *If she was inside my brain,* Niamh thought, *then she could be there with Daniela, too.*

The thought was enough to give Niamh hope. Maybe she wouldn't be alone, after all. She had something to look forward to now. She would wait and when Daniela woke up—as Niamh knew she would—then they would see. They would *see* just how much of the creature and of Laragh had fused itself with Daniela's brain in order to save the empath.

"What are you thinking?" Lyse asked, confused by the abrupt change in Niamh's demeanor—and the secret smile that played across her lips. "It's like a light just went on inside your brain."

"It's nothing," Niamh said. "Just something I realized. It's not important."

But that was a lie.

To Niamh, it was the most important thing in the entire world, and, for now, it was her secret—and her secret alone—to pin her hopes on.

Arrabelle

Arrabelle had to sit down. She'd been staring at the television screen too long, her eyes not wanting to believe what they were seeing. Watching the BBC World News, it was easy to decipher what was happening in the world . . . and why.

"So that's it," Arrabelle said finally—though there was no one in the well-appointed waiting room to hear her. "Decision made, no questions, no thought . . . just action."

She sat back against the plush leather couch, covered her mouth with her palm, and shook her head in disbelief. She would've expected better from humanity. She *had* expected better. She'd believed that someone in charge would want to discover what the blood sisters were all about. Wouldn't just round the witches up and put them in internment camps—jerry-rigged from abandoned prisons and schools . . . basically any building they could throw camp beds in and then police with the military.

The United States was spearheading the international campaign to collect and imprison blood sisters. The European Union, China, and Russia were following suit, as well as many of the former Eastern bloc countries and most of Asia and Africa. New Zealand, Australia, some of Central and South America, Cuba, Canada, and Iceland were the holdouts.

"You're still watching." It wasn't a question.

Evan stood in the doorway, leaning against the doorjamb. He looked wiped out but healthier than he'd been only a day earlier. The women they'd rescued from the underground warehouse had saved him—pouring their own psychic energy into his body to heal him. Arrabelle understood their reasoning: Maybe he and the others . . . Lyse, Niamh, Arrabelle . . . could actually fight The Flood. Stop them, even.

Though this was an outcome Arrabelle was becoming less and less sure about reaching.

"Train wreck," she said, thinking about more than just what was happening up on the television screen. "This shit, what's happened before this . . . it's getting really bad and we're not doing anything to stop it."

"It's the twenty-four-hour news cycle. Makes it look worse than it is," Evan replied. "But I feel you. I don't like sitting around, either. I want to be doing something."

"It's so frustrating. And I don't think the news is blowing it out of proportion. I believe it's bad out there. Really bad."

Evan didn't argue with her.

Probably because he knows I'm right, Arrabelle thought.

She returned her gaze to the flat-screen television on the wall, watching as three older women were forcibly removed by police officers from a house in Glastonbury. The women were all brown-skinned with white fluffy clouds of hair puffing out around lined faces and frightened eyes. Only the oldest woman, so frail she used a walker to maneuver down the stairs of the semidetached house, looked disdainful of the proceedings. When one of the policemen tried to take her arm to hurry her along, she shooed him away with a feral growl.

A news anchor was talking over the picture, but as Arrabelle watched, the sound abruptly went out.

"Evan, did you mute the TV?" she asked, but Evan raised his hands in the air to show that his hands were empty.

"Not me," he said as Arrabelle found the remote control on a small side table by the couch and pressed the volume button until it was all the way up.

Still no sound.

Piercing green eyes looked out at them from the screen. The old woman was staring directly into the lens of the news camera. The semidetached house, the policemen . . . they were still there, but out of focus. Like the background had been frozen in time so this elderly blood sister could reach out across time and space to connect with them.

"What the—" Arrabelle began, but the old woman let out a hacking cough and the sound stopped Arrabelle short.

"Bell, they've come for us—" the old woman said, then covered her mouth with a shaking hand as she fought back another cough.

Arrabelle climbed off her perch on the couch, moving closer to the television screen.

"Bell, they've come for us—" the old woman began again.

"Evan? Are you seeing this? She just said my name—"

Evan nodded and left his place by the doorway to join her in front of the television. He stood close enough to take her hand in his own.

"—and we will wait for the sign," the old woman continued, and Arrabelle could see the wrinkles on her worn face as she spoke. "But don't make us wait too long."

She winked at them and then the picture and sound returned to normal. Of course, they'd forgotten the volume was now on its highest setting and it made them both jump. Arrabelle raised the remote and quickly turned the volume down.

The picture changed again and a coiffed, male news presenter sat in a studio, chattering about the newly discovered existence of magic. Evan took the remote from Arrabelle and pressed the power button. The screen went dark, cutting off the man midsentence.

"Enough."

Even under the best of circumstances, Arrabelle was a total news junkie. Now she was obsessed.

"I think we need to know—" Arrabelle said, grabbing for the remote as she protested.

"We know all we need to know, Bell. We're screwed."

Arrabelle shut her mouth. Evan was right. There was no amount of knowledge that was going to save them from the hatred being directed toward them and their sisters.

"What do you think she meant when she said they would wait for 'the sign'?" Evan added when he was sure Arrabelle wasn't going to argue further.

"Your guess is as good as mine," she said, shrugging. It was cold in the waiting room, and Arrabelle shivered.

A young nurse passed by the doorway and nodded at them. Arrabelle inclined her head in return, grateful that the nurse didn't stop to chat. She was also grateful they were the only people there in the waiting room, so that she didn't have to make small talk with other restless families as they waited for their loved ones to get better.

"You haven't slept in days," Evan said as he guided Arrabelle back to the couch where they sat down together, their bodies so close Arrabelle could feel the heat of Evan's skin against her own.

"You haven't slept, either," Arrabelle said.

"Let me just take care of you for a minute, dammit," he said, as he took her by the shoulders and turned her around in her seat, so that her back faced him. She sighed as he began to rub her shoulders.

"God, that feels good," she said, closing her eyes.

"You're so tense. Just relax." She could hear the command in his voice and she tried to let the tension in her body flow out of her. "You've always run hot, Bell. Your skin is like a furnace."

Though Arrabelle had been in love with Evan since she

was a teenager, this new evolution in their relationship—him actually reciprocating her interest—made her nervous. Which only made her more tense—and she could feel her shoulders hunching again.

She heard Evan laugh, and she turned her head to glare at him. "What?" she demanded.

"You're the only woman I know who gets *more* tense when you give her a massage."

Arrabelle snorted.

"I'm not more tense," she protested.

"I'm touching you. I think I can feel when you tense up— like right now—"

Arrabelle pushed him away but kept her outrage playful.

"How dare you?! I can't believe—"

Evan silenced her with a kiss. She felt herself relax, the tension in her body replaced by longing. She tried to extend the kiss, her teeth nipping at his lips, but he pulled away.

"When this is all over," he said, grinning at her. "I promise."

She wished it were "all over" now. She felt impatience growing inside her.

"One more kiss?" she begged.

At first, Evan shook his head, but then he relented. He turned her back so she was facing him again and wrapped his arms around her, pulling her in close. She waited, anticipation building as she let him run the show.

"You're very beautiful," he said, staring deep into her eyes, and she felt like she was falling, tumbling head over heels toward him.

"Thank you," she murmured, her eyes dropping to his mouth.

"You're welcome," he said, softly.

She watched his lips form the words, felt the sound travel to her ears, slip into her brain. She loved the cadence of his voice, the low tremble of his words. She closed her eyes, letting the nearness of their bodies overwhelm her senses.

"Where'd you go?" he asked after a few moments of silence. She opened her eyes and smiled.

"Somewhere far away from here. Where it's okay to be what we are."

Evan's eyes dropped to his hands, where they rested in his lap.

"Yeah, I'd like to go to that world."

Arrabelle's grin faded. They'd moved away from a romantic moment to something . . . well, the subject didn't bring pleasant thoughts with it. The mood broken, Evan sighed and got to his feet. Arrabelle was annoyed with herself for wrecking the only nice thing that had happened in hours.

"I don't know why I brought that up," she said, her throat constricting. "I do want it to be okay. But I'm just so scared things will never be right again."

Evan pivoted on his heel, turning back to look at her.

"Things change, Bell," he said. "And there's nothing we can do to stop that. We can only hope that, eventually, these changes will bring about something good . . . an empathy and compassion in humanity that until now, I think, has been buried so deep inside that we forget we have it."

Arrabelle didn't have a ready answer for this.

"But we're in the transition phase," he continued. "We have to bear the suffering so others who come later . . . they don't. It's a beautiful gift we give . . . and as awful as all this is"— he indicated that he meant their situation by stretching out his arms—"we do it because it's the right thing. We do it selflessly, and for others, because we can."

She loved Evan so much in that moment she could hardly bear it. A wave of pure, unadulterated, unconditional love so powerful it left her empty after it had surged through her.

"I love you." She murmured the words quietly, letting their weight speak for them.

Evan seemed embarrassed by this show of affection, but he swallowed and nodded.

"I know you do . . . I love you, too."

But there was a sense of futility beneath his words, and Arrabelle wondered what he'd been thinking about when he'd said them.

Arrabelle found Lyse in the bathroom. She felt intrusive cornering her coven master there, but she wanted to speak to Lyse in private.

"Can we talk?"

Lyse was leaning against the counter, her back to the door, but her reflection caught Arrabelle's eye and beckoned her inside the room.

"Come on into my office," Lyse said, raising an eyebrow at her surroundings.

"I'm just trying to understand what we're doing," Arrabelle said, moving farther into the space. "What the game plan is."

"We need Daniela. We wait for her to wake up," Lyse said, still facing the mirror—and Arrabelle felt like she was having a conversation with Lyse's reflection instead of the woman herself.

"And then?" Arrabelle asked, joining Lyse in front of the row of sinks.

"And then we go to Devandra," Lyse replied.

"I'm with you so far . . ."

"But *what* after that? That's what you want to know," Lyse said, her shoulders slumping as she deflected Arrabelle's question.

"Yes, that's the crux of it," Arrabelle agreed, her eyes wandering across the face of the mirror, seeing the row of closed toilet stall doors. Her mind decided there were monsters hidden behind the beige metal doors, all of them just waiting for her to leave so they could gobble Lyse up.

It was an eerie feeling.

"To be honest," Lyse said as she pushed off the counter and turned to face Arrabelle, "I'm waiting for a sign."

It was the exact same phrase the old woman on the television screen had uttered. Lyse seemed to sense Arrabelle's confusion—or maybe it showed on her face. Arrabelle had never been great at hiding her feelings.

"That's crazy."

"What's crazy?" Lyse asked.

"Evan and I were watching the news and then something weird happened . . . this old woman—a blood sister from the U.K. the police were 'collecting'—started speaking to me," Arrabelle began. "She looked right at us, like we were on Skype, and then she said my name."

"She was using magic?" Lyse asked.

Arrabelle nodded.

"Yeah, pretty sure she was. But the weird part was after that. When she said, 'We will wait for the sign.'"

Lyse frowned, then lowered her gaze, thinking.

"What the hell does it mean," Arrabelle asked, "that you just said the exact same thing?"

Lyse shook her head. She had no more insight into things than Arrabelle did.

"I don't know why we both said the same thing. I can only tell you that every time I've been confused or uncertain, I take a leap of faith and some sign appears, directing my course," Lyse said, and then she shrugged, looking embarrassed. "It's a lame answer. I know."

Arrabelle laughed.

"At least, like you just said, you're honest about your lameness."

"Well, I've got *that* going for me," Lyse said, and rolled her eyes. "God, I'm not good at all this, Arrabelle—"

"You're doing it, though," Arrabelle said.

"That I am. It scares the shit outta me, but I just keep moving forward. It's all I know how to do right now. Run toward the thing that scares me?"

The last idea came out as a question, and Arrabelle wondered if there was a part of Lyse that was asking her for reassurance. That she felt alone in all this and wanted Arrabelle's support.

"I don't think it's a terrible plan," Arrabelle said, finally. "We should be more proactive. We should go to The Flood ourselves, cut the head off—and by that I mean take care of Desmond Delay—and then we'll see if they can function with him gone."

"I like it, in theory," Lyse said, "if we only knew where to start . . ."

Arrabelle had been thinking the same thing. It was an idea that she'd been kicking around in her head for a while: how to find The Flood and dispatch them on their own turf?

"They're elusive," Lyse continued. "They cleared out of their underground lair and left nothing for us to use to find them."

"I think . . . if you're amenable," Arrabelle said, choosing her words carefully, "that I might have a way to find them. But we'd need the whole coven to do it."

"Go on," Lyse said, as she retrieved a rubber band from her jeans pocket and caught her dark hair into a ponytail.

"We can do what they're terrified of us doing: We can use our magic and cast a spell."

"Do you think we have the kind of power to do that?" Lyse asked—and Arrabelle kicked herself for forgetting how new Lyse was to the whole "witch" thing.

"Um, you transported four people to another dimension," Arrabelle said. "I think we can manage a location spell."

"Why didn't I think of that?" Lyse said, shaking her head. "You should be the coven master, not me."

"Well, I'm not and you are," Arrabelle said. "So suck it up and stop beating yourself up. We're a coven and we'll figure this out together. We're not monsters, we're not evil, we use our powers for good. That's all you need to know."

Lyse leaned against the countertop and gave Arrabelle a sheepish grin.

"Can I admit something else to you?"

"Of course."

"I don't even believe magic is real," Lyse said. "I watched you guys perform your 'rites' and I wanted to laugh. It all looked so silly and didn't seem to accomplish much of anything."

She paused, gauging Arrabelle's response—but Arrabelle kept her expression neutral, waiting to hear Lyse out.

"And then all this stuff happened . . . we went into the dreamlands, we saw what The Flood did to all those women and girls," Lyse continued. "And I'm not forgetting about the ghosts—sorry, *Dream Walkers*, you call them . . . it all scares the shit out of me."

"It's a lot," Arrabelle agreed. "And I'm sorry that it's hard for you to believe—"

"No, that's not what I'm saying," Lyse said, interrupting Arrabelle. "I'm saying that it's taken me a while, but I believe in it. All of it. I accept that what I know can't rationally be true . . . *is* true."

"Eleanora was trying to protect you," Arrabelle said, pulling herself up onto the countertop to sit. "But she did you a disservice."

"I know she did," Lyse agreed.

"It wasn't because she was trying to screw you over," Arrabelle said. "It was because she loved you and wanted you to be 'normal' for as long as possible. She knew what was coming and knew it would be bad, so she gave you the gift of time. Time to live a real, nonmagical life."

Lyse nodded.

"Yeah, I know. I know she loved me, too."

"Hessika dreamed it all," Arrabelle added. "Eleanora knew you would be involved somehow."

"Yeah, she did," Lyse said. "Why did no one believe them?"

"That's the million-dollar question," Arrabelle replied. "I think because we like the status quo . . . no one wants to believe anything bad can happen—and then the bad things happen and we're blindsided."

"We're all so stupid," Lyse said.

"There's definitely a balance in life. Between good and evil, stupidity and intelligence, awareness and denial . . ."

Arrabelle leaned back against the sink counter and sighed.

"I feel like I've had a healthy dose of the stupidity and the denial," Lyse said.

Arrabelle saw that Lyse was being self-deprecating.

"You're learning not to see things in terms of being black and white. To be cognizant of the gradations," Arrabelle said. "Just remember that we are working to make things better, to tip the scales in the other direction a little, so that the scales stay balanced. That's it. That's our job."

"The Flood wants to tip it all the way over," Lyse said, her voice rising in anger. "I hate them and everything they stand for."

"They think they're right," Arrabelle said. "They think they're on the side of good. They want humanity to change, and they think the only way to do it is to wipe the slate clean—"

"Which is messed up," Lyse said.

Arrabelle shrugged.

"Without change, the world is stagnant—"

"Without *good* change, you mean," Lyse said.

"No. Change is neither bad nor good. It sides with no one. It just *is*."

Lyse began to pace, pinching the bridge of her nose between her fingers.

"This conversation is giving me a headache."

Arrabelle didn't disagree.

"The blood sisters have always tried to maintain the balance," Arrabelle said, hating that she sounded like a teacher lecturing to a class. She hoped Lyse appreciated the effort. "When we perform our magical rites, it's more about the power of connection. We connect to our sisters and, through each other, we connect to the flow lines. We draw our power from the Earth—and that power goes out into the world through us and through our good acts. Does that make sense?"

"Yes," Lyse said. "I think so."

"In other terms, the blood sisters bring connection to the world—"

"And The Flood brings bad?"

Arrabelle shook her head.

"They bring imbalance and *that's* bad," Lyse said, amending her answer.

"The good guys shouldn't control the world any more than the bad guys should," Arrabelle said. "The good guys telling everyone what to do would be just as bad—in its own way—as what The Flood is doing."

Lyse seemed to accept this answer. She stopped pacing and stuffed her hands deep into her jeans pockets.

"Okay, so we don't work for the good guys *or* the bad guys . . . we work for the *balance*."

Arrabelle smiled. Lyse was learning fast.

"Let's do that spell you were talking about," Lyse said. "The locating one."

"Perfect," Arrabelle replied. "We'll try when we have Daniela and Devandra back with us."

Lyse gave her a tight smile.

"Sold. Now let's get the hell out of this stupid bathroom."

Arrabelle laughed.

"But I liked your office," she said, grinning as she hopped off the countertop and headed for the door, Lyse's footsteps echoing behind her.

Lost in her thoughts, Arrabelle stepped out into the corridor and headed down the hallway toward Daniela's room. Her mind raced as she tried to fashion a plan for when they found The Flood . . . because she knew that stopping them would be the only thing that tipped the balance back into place—and returned the world to normal again.

Of that, Arrabelle was *almost* certain.

Lizbeth

"This can't be," Lizbeth said, her jaw dropping as she looked through the doorway. She was still holding Ginny in her arms, but for a few moments she felt bodiless, untethered from reality—*all* realities—as she tried to process what she was seeing inside the interior of the Red Chapel.

It was an exact replica of her first home—the downtown Los Angeles loft that she'd come home to as a newborn . . . before her parents ended their marriage and she'd gone to live with her mother and Weir had stayed with their father. It had been so long ago, and her memories so fractured by the trauma she'd experienced after her mother's death, that she was surprised she remembered it at all.

"Oh my God," she murmured. "I can't . . . it's not . . ."

There were no words, no way to take in everything she was seeing and feeling. It was just too overwhelming.

While Lizbeth stood in the doorway and tried to control her breathing, Tem laid his charge down on the white leather sectional couch that took up one side of the front room before coming over to Lizbeth and relieving her of her own burden.

He placed Ginny on the other side of the couch so she was head to toe with her sister, and then he took Lizbeth by the crook of the arm and led her toward the kitchen. Once there, he sat her down at the white granite kitchen island—Lizbeth had forgotten how *white* the loft had been. Starkness met the eye at every turn. It was the kind of colorless apartment that eschewed comfort for glamour. It was a glacier-white showplace for her father to flaunt his money. Not one bit of it had ever been home to Lizbeth.

She waited while Tem brought out two tall water glasses from a kitchen cabinet and set them on the island in front of her. Then he turned to the massive built-in refrigerator and began digging around inside it.

"Why?" she asked, shaking her head in disbelief. "This place is awful."

But looking around, she realized this wasn't an entirely true statement. It was cold—that was a fact—yet revisiting the loft now, through the lens of adulthood, Lizbeth saw the touches her mother had wrought from her father's sparseness: the heavy plate-glass windows that let in copious amounts of light and afforded views of the downtown Los Angeles skyline—but hanging from the ceiling in front of them were stained-glass art pieces that belonged to her mother, their colored panes catching the cold winter light and turning it into glorious diamonds of color that danced across the walls; the floor that had been fashioned from whitewashed planks of oak, distressed by age and use—but there was the pink-and-blue handwoven Navajo rug her mother had bought for a song at an estate sale in Los Feliz and somehow its cheerful color brightened the whole room; the skylights built into the plaster ceilings that funneled even more light into the large, open-plan space—and illuminated by this light were the faint pencil marks on the back kitchen wall that Lizbeth's mother had used to document Weir's height, and then Lizbeth's own, as they each grew older.

Any feeling of life that Lizbeth saw in the loft came from her mother.

"Your brain crafted it," Tem said, his back to her as he continued to rummage in the fridge. Finally, he found what he was looking for, and triumphant, he pulled out a carton of pulp-heavy orange juice.

"I was thinking about my mom," she said, honestly. "I guess that's why. But *this* place? It's so much more my dad's taste, but then . . ."

". . . your mom is here, too," he finished for her.

She nodded.

"Yeah, I feel her in the space, and that's not something I would've expected."

Tem handed her a glass of juice, then extended his own toward her.

"Cheers," he said as they clinked glasses.

It felt odd to do that here, in this place. To be anything other than the small helpless kid who'd felt so alone after her mother had died. A child who'd needed love, but who, instead, had been ignored. Her father's hope . . . ? That she'd just disappear.

"I miss her," Lizbeth said, barely tasting the sugary juice. "I needed her. I *really* needed her and she was gone. I was alone."

The weight of Tem's hand settled over her own and she felt the cool of the granite beneath her palm.

"You were never alone. The Dream Walker Hessika was always with you," he said. "And your brother never stopped missing you."

God, she'd forgotten all about Weir! Guilt, and the orange juice, soured her stomach. She'd left him back in the Italian catacombs with no explanation as to why she was behaving so oddly. She wished he were here now, wished she could tell him her brain hadn't been her own, that she'd been at the mercy of something greater than herself.

"Before . . . you asked me where you go when you dream in the dreamlands," Tem said, drawing her attention back to him.

She looked up, surprised, her curiosity piqued.

"Yeah, it was a strange thing . . . the idea that . . ."

". . . you're already where you dream?" he finished for her. He was always doing that to Lizbeth—finishing her thoughts, knowing what she was going to say before she said it. He gestured to the sectional couch where Dev's girls lay sleeping.

"Yeah," she said.

She watched the girls, their faces smooth and dewy—with none of the tension she'd seen on them earlier.

"Here, when you sleep, you walk the line between life and death," he said. "Death can't have you yet because it's not your time, but it likes the taste of life, so it tries to keep you there as long as it can."

Lizbeth frowned.

"I think we should wake the girls up now," she said, climbing to her feet.

He laughed, and held up his hands for her to relax.

"Don't freak out, half-caste. They're also sleeping a healing sleep. And those girls need it. They've been through a lot."

She settled back into her seat but decided to keep an eye on the young dreamers just to calm her mind.

"Dream Walkers—like me and Hessika and Eleanora—stay here," he continued. "I know it seems like we're trapped, but we're not. We chose this and we have enough magic left inside us to make it so."

"But you can go to death?" she asked. "If you want to?"

"If I sleep here, then, yes, I can will death to take me. If I want."

She yawned, the exhaustion she'd been keeping at bay for so long finally settling over her.

"You should sleep, too, love," Tem said. "You look so tired and sad."

She shook her head.

"No, I don't want to—"

"Afraid you'll never wake up?" he asked, raising an eyebrow as he voiced her fears for her. "Don't you trust me?"

"Yes, but . . ." She stopped, not actually sure if she was being truthful or not. "Wait. I just . . . I don't know."

"Do as the man says, ma chère."

Lizbeth turned in her seat to find the Tall Lady standing behind her. *Hessika*—she had to remember the woman had a real name.

"I'm not tired—" she started to say, but was foiled by another yawn she couldn't control.

Hessika wore an amused expression on her face. Lizbeth was almost certain that the woman hadn't been there before. *Where had she come from?* Hit by another jaw-cracking yawn, Lizbeth fought to keep her eyes open. She was so tired that her bones ached.

"Of course, you are," Tem said. "You're wiped out, dead on your feet. A walking zombie of sleep deprivation."

She had to admit it was true. The thought of closing her eyes for a few minutes sounded so appealing . . .

Hessika's voice sounded in her head: "The little ones cannot stay long, ma chère. Tell your sisters that we are watching, but they must come to the Red Chapel and soon."

Lizbeth opened her eyes to find herself alone in a now-darkened kitchen, her arms folded on the granite countertop like a pillow, her head tucked inside them. She sat up and stretched, her whole body stiff. She looked around, but Tem and Hessika were long gone. She yawned and noticed something wet on her chin, but her fingertips came away clear and she realized she must've drooled a little while she'd slept.

Wait, I didn't sleep, *she thought.* I was just awake. I was talking to Tem and Hessika and then . . . this makes no sense.

She turned, searching for Dev's girls, but they weren't on the couch where she'd left them. No one was here. She was on her own. Just Lizbeth, alone, in a loft she'd hated since she was a child.

"I hate you," she said out loud. "I hate what you represent. What you are."

The loft didn't seem offended by Lizbeth's outburst. Instead, it began turning on lights, muting the darkness outside and bathing Lizbeth in pale yellow lamplight.

"I'm sorry," she said to the loft. "I'm just overwhelmed. There's so much emotion here."

I feel stupid talking to an inanimate building, *she thought.* I need to get my act together.

She pushed the bar stool back, expecting a loud screech as the metal legs scraped against the floor, but there was nothing. She squatted down but saw no wheels or padding to protect the wood. She stood up and rapped her hand against the countertop. Nothing, no hollow knock or resounding echo, only an absence of sound.

It was unsettling.

She began to wonder if she was asleep . . . in the dreamlands . . . in death.

The front door opened silently—and she would never have known had she not been staring at it when it happened. A moment later, her mother and Weir—a much younger version of him, at least— came into the loft.

Bit-na was carrying a grocery bag in one arm and a large purple purse under the other. She was above average height with a slender frame that made her look like a model. Her black hair was cut pixie short and she wore bright red lipstick but no other makeup. Dressed well—black linen pants, strappy leather sandals, and an asymmetrical, sleeveless cotton blouse—she was talking animatedly to Weir, who stared up at his stepmom adoringly.

Lizbeth could not hear what they were saying. The strange silence extended even to them.

I wish I could tell you both that I love you, *she thought,* staring at the baby version of Weir, her eyes filling with tears.

In this weird past/limbo/memory/dream state, her Caucasian half brother was probably no more than twelve, but he already came to Bit-na's shoulder. He had a shock of bleached blond bangs that fell *into his eyes, the rest of his head shaved. He also had a brown paper grocery bag just like the one Bit-na carried.*

If Weir is twelve here in this dream, I'm not even born yet, *Lizbeth thought.* This is *pre*-me.

This was before her parents had divorced and Bit-na had taken Lizbeth away. Before her mother had died, leaving Lizbeth at the mercy of a father who thought she was "retarded" (she had a visceral memory of her father spitting the slur out at her mother, a crying baby Lizbeth in Bit-na's arms). What she was watching now? These were the good days . . . before Lizbeth had ripped the family apart by being "different."

Lizbeth stared at the tableau, unable to move. She wanted to run to her mother and brother and touch them, hold them close one more time, but a part of her brain knew that this was impossible. What a shock that would've been, to have a gangling giant of a girl appear out of nowhere and pull you into a bear hug.

"That's not true, you know."

"What?" Lizbeth asked. She was so used to hearing her brother's voice that she answered him automatically.

"That you ruined our family."

She turned and saw the adult version of her brother standing beside her, leaning against the kitchen island. He was dressed in a pair of khaki cutoffs and a black T-shirt, his hair wet, as if he'd just come from a shower. He grinned at her.

"Weir?" she said, her voice cracking.

"I missed you, pipsqueak."

"I missed you, too," she said, letting him pull her into a hug.

He smelled like burnt leaves and metal. She was so happy to see him that she almost cried.

"I didn't mean to leave you guys in the catacombs. I didn't have any control over myself. I didn't know what I was doing. I'm so sorry—"

"Shhh . . ." he said, squeezing her tight. "None of it matters."

She nodded, letting his touch melt away her guilt.

"I get to be here with you now. That's the important thing."

"It's true," she agreed.

After a few more moments of holding her close, he let her go—and she looked up into his face. The eyes she found staring back at her bore such intense sadness that she felt like crying all over again . . . but then the sadness disappeared and he was just good old Weir.

"I meant what I said, LB," he continued. "It wasn't you. And it wasn't me, either. Though, at the time, I thought it was. We were only kids back then and we had zero to do with our family falling apart. The truth is always sadder and more complicated than we can imagine."

He pointed back to where Bit-na and the younger incarnation of himself had been standing, but now they were gone. In their place, Lizbeth and Weir's father stood, an angry expression on his face. He began pacing back and forth by the front door, brown hair sticking up in unkempt tufts, eyes red-rimmed and wild. Lizbeth turned to Weir, opening her mouth to ask him what was happening, but he just shook his head.

"Watch," he said. "We can only see the past. We can't hear it."

She returned her attention back to their father in time to see the front door open and Bit-na come into the room. She was wearing a raincoat, her dark hair drenched.

"She's pregnant with you," Weir continued, "but the bastard doesn't care. This happened while I was in Iceland with the Nordic Ice Queen."

Weir's mother was a blond former model who pretended she didn't have a child. He'd lived with her for one summer when he was a teenager and she'd spent the entire time ignoring him. Because she'd been so cold and uninterested in her own son, Weir and Lizbeth had labeled her the "Nordic Ice Queen."

Lizbeth watched as Bit-na reached out a hand, her long fingers searching for her husband's cheek. He turned away, his face bright with anger. She looked confused, not sure why he was upset with her. Though Lizbeth couldn't hear what they were saying, she watched Bit-na implore her husband to tell her what was wrong. Instead of answering her, he just started screaming.

"Don't look away."

Lizbeth couldn't have torn her eyes away from the scene had she tried. Bit-na, her belly as swollen as a watermelon, tried one final time to reach out to her husband—but it was a mistake.

Lizbeth watched in horror as her father punched her mother in the stomach.

Bit-na's face went pale, her mouth open in a silent O of pain. She fell backward, her hands clutching her distended belly protectively as she hit the floor. It was a hard fall and the side of her head connected with the wooden leg of the sectional couch. Blood blossomed from her scalp, staining the white leather of the couch a dark brown.

"No." Lizbeth clutched Weir's arm. Then, unable to keep looking, she buried her face in his chest, biting back the urge to scream.

"She was protecting you," he said, no emotion in his voice. "You almost died . . . and the idiot doctors told Bit-na that your cognitive problems stemmed from what happened to you in utero. This is what drove our parents apart and why our father was always so awful to you. He couldn't deal with his guilt."

When she'd collected herself enough to look again, the scene was gone, but her mother's blood still stained the white fabric of the couch. I hope that stain never went away, *Lizbeth thought.*

"He's just a man. Fallible and stupid. He fucked up and he lost everything. I know I should feel sorry for him," Weir added, "but it's hard, LB. Even here where it doesn't matter anymore."

Something about the words Weir chose bothered Lizbeth. When she really stopped to think about it, something about this whole ex-perience was *sitting wrong inside her.*

"What do you mean?" Lizbeth said, her brain beginning to spin. "When you say that it doesn't matter anymore? What do you mean?"

She heard the plaintive whine in her voice.

"LB," Weir said, his voice laced with sadness.

Lizbeth tried to tamp down the nausea that was burning her throat, her thoughts all tangled together like a skein of yarn . . . and then she found the thread.

"No," she murmured. "No, I don't want to pull the thread."

She turned to face her older brother, understanding dawning in her eyes.

"Please, no," she continued, grabbing him by the arm and shaking him. "No, no, no . . ."

He didn't have to answer. His silence said it all. Her fingers caught the loose thread—the thread that would lead to the answer she already knew, but did not want—and she began to pull.

"You're here. In this place . . . the place between the dreamer and death. So that means . . ."

She couldn't bring herself to say the word.

"I'm dead," he said for her.

"Why . . . ?" she moaned. "Why are you dead . . . ?"

She felt disbelief and the realization that she didn't have the power to change any of it.

"I can't . . ." she said, her voice catching in her throat. "You can't. I need you."

He put a hand under her chin and lifted her face up so that he could look into her eyes.

"LB, I am always with you." He placed a finger against her forehead. "Inside here . . . I live on in your heart and your memories."

It was all too much to process. She began to cry, the tears leaking from the corners of her eyes.

"I have to go now," he said, pulling her to his chest and squeezing her tight. "But I wanted you to know the truth about our family. Let it set you free, my sweet sister."

He released her and took a step back—and she saw that he was crying, too.

"I love you, Weir," she said, the hot tears running down the sides of her face.

"I love you, too, LB."

And then her brother faded away to nothing.

She stayed in the loft for a long time, but no one else came to visit her. No images of the past, no ghosts of the present . . . and the future didn't belong here. She felt numb, the cold hardwood biting into the back of her thighs where she sat cross-legged on the floor. The white shift dress she wore left her arms and legs unprotected from the chill.

She loosed her hair, letting the long strands envelop her face, hiding her away. She wanted to close her eyes and go to sleep, but every time she lay down and closed her eyes, an image of Weir's face flashed through her mind. She had to immediately open her eyes again or else give in to the panic that wanted to eat her up.

In order to keep her mind off her grief, she hummed snatches of Korean lullabies that Bit-na had sung to her when she was small and songs she'd heard on the radio . . . anything to make sure her mind stayed blank.

She wove her hair into a long braid, singing as she worked. After a while, she heard the soft rustle of fabric, and she lifted her gaze, not surprised to find that she was no longer alone.

Daniela

Lizbeth's dream was the world's dream. Even as she slipped in and out of this reality, Daniela was not unaware of the changes happening around her. She felt the power of magic as it reentered their world and took hold once more. Things had shifted; a drastic transformation had been wrought with this one act. Where the blood sisters had once been unknown to the world . . . now—for better or for worse—their legacy had been foisted on an unsuspecting humanity.

And then she was alone again. Lost in a sea of sensation and tranquillity. A place from which she did not want to return.

Until the voices came, and then she was forced to listen.

. . . like swimming in a vat of molasses, everything sticky sweet and sludgy . . . can't open my eyes . . . can't open my mouth . . . can't breathe . . . like a heavy stone pressing on my chest . . . so dark, but not empty . . . lights playing . . . pink, purple, cerulean blue, Day-Glo green . . . like fireworks . . .

WAKE UP.

The voice broke through to her brain—the only thing that had reached her since her coma had begun—and Daniela surfaced. She couldn't feel her body, but she knew she was back in reality, if only for the most fleeting of moments. There were voices, speaking a language she didn't understand, or maybe her brain was garbling their words. She didn't know.

. . . back under . . . floating on the sludge, my body part of it . . . I'm made of the sludge . . . I hear them singing . . . like mermaids singing each to each . . . like a line of poetry I can't remember . . . the colors dancing . . . pink, purple, cerulean blue, Day-Glo green . . . like fireworks . . .

WAKE UP.

The voice was jarring, ripping her back into reality. She was cognizant again. She'd come up from the abyss before, but only for brief bits and pieces of disjointed time. Now it was different. The stone that had been holding her down in the dark place was gone and she felt a lightness in her chest.

But then a slicing pain cut through her body and she cried out in agony. She tried to swallow, the raw skin of her throat dry and cracked, and nausea hit her like a car accident, unexpected and violent. She began to retch, her body doing work she had no control over. But she couldn't move, couldn't turn her head to evacuate the bile that rose up into her mouth.

She began to cough, aspirating liquid and phlegm into her lungs. She heard an alarm go off, the sound piercing. It beat a rhythm of pain into her brain, each note a nail being hammered directly into her central cortex.

. . . floating again . . . the pain gone . . . lost to that old reality I am no longer in . . . floating, floating, floating . . .

WAKE UP. DO IT NOW.

The voice was insistent, jolting her awake . . . and then another voice, this one familiar to her, reached out from beyond.

"Daniela?"

A siren's call from outer space. Totally improbable . . . but

Lyse was here. Lyse had come for her. Her sister . . . no, Lyse wasn't her sister . . . was more like her cousin . . . the terminology was unimportant. She was related to Lyse by blood and that's all that mattered.

Lyse is here for me, Daniela thought. *How is that possible?*

She'd been so alone for so long . . . and now that loneliness was replaced by the joyful knowledge that she was joined to Lyse forever. They were *family.*

"I know you can hear me," Lyse said, her voice scratchy. She sounded like she'd been crying.

Daniela wanted to open her eyes, wanted to see if the voice truly belonged to Lyse, but it was just too difficult to make her body do what she wanted. Near impossible, even.

"I explained about the gloves. They've put them on you. They didn't understand, at first, didn't realize they were making you worse . . ."

Lyse's voice trailed off.

. . . no, I trailed off . . . back to floating in the sludge . . . I want to stay here . . . so warm and safe . . . only the floating . . .

WAKE UP, DANIELA.

The voice demanded action from her and so she followed it back to life:

"She's coming around."

Another voice she recognized, low and mellifluous . . . it could only be Arrabelle. She really wanted to open her eyes and see if she was right, but her eyelids only seemed willing to flutter.

"I think she's trying to open her eyes."

This voice she didn't know. It was softer than the others, younger and broken-sounding. It was as if upon hearing it for the first time, a well of sadness opened up underneath Daniela and she fell headlong into it. Fell far and fell fast.

. . . I am falling . . . but not the same . . . black . . . black . . . blackness . . . no lights . . . no warmth . . . tentacles slithering around me . . . searching me out . . . wanting to pull me down further . . .

wanting to wrap around me and squeeze me into oblivion . . . not death . . . but a death of some sort . . . an end I won't be able to escape from if I stay . . .

WAKE UP. THIS WILL BE THE LAST TIME. WE PROMISE.

She believed the voice and she fought to return to the old reality, aggressively wanting to come back now. She didn't want to go down to the sludgy place ever again. Something had changed and it wasn't the same as when she'd left it. Not safe and warm, not womblike.

". . . she's here. I feel her for the first time. She's coming back."

Open your eyes, Daniela thought. *Open, dammit!*

It was working. Her eyelids were fluttering . . . but disappointment flooded her brain when she realized they still wouldn't budge.

"Daniela?"

Lyse was close to her. She could smell the other woman's scent like a talisman, drawing her out of the abyss. Back to true consciousness.

"I can't touch you—even though I want to," she heard Lyse say, a catch in her voice. "But I'm here and I need you back. Do you understand? I won't lose you, too."

Daniela felt something hot and wet fall onto her cheek. A tear. Lyse's tear.

". . . yse . . ." she moaned, her lips barely moving. ". . . yse . . ."

"I'm here," she felt Lyse murmur close to her ear. "I'm not going anywhere."

This time when the fingers of unconsciousness grabbed her, they did not try to steal her soul . . . they merely took her to the oblivion of sleep.

She dreamed—and her dreams were crazy. A collage of images that made no sense.

At one point she was inside a strange metal box made from

sheets of aluminum soldered together to form a perfect square. She was alone, lying there, staring up at the cold metal ceiling, but then she turned her head and realized that she was actually lying on a hospital gurney—and the box was not a box . . . but something much more sinister . . . a giant metal *oven*.

She lifted her head, her chin pressing into her throat, and ahead of her she could see an observation window cut into the metal. There were men in camouflage fatigues standing on the other side of the window, staring at her, the assault rifles in their hands trained on her through the glass. She tried to sit up further, but her ankles and wrists were bound to the hospital gurney by stiff metal cuffs that cut into her skin, drawing a circle of blood in the flesh.

She blinked and her world shifted . . .

Now she stood on a slender wooden dock that was shrouded in a thick, gray fog that blotted out the landscape around her. Glowing orbs of light stood like sentinels on either side of the deck, providing the only illumination visible in the fog. She reached out with both hands and discovered that the orbs were actually candles, their flames flickering in the wind. She looked up, but there was no moon to light the sky. Only a velvety black cover that seemed to spread out above her for eternity. She felt cold, goose bumps breaking out on her arms and legs—and when she looked down, she was surprised to find herself naked and not wearing her own skin. The body she was clothed in was utterly alien to her, its curves of rounded flesh unrecognizable. She didn't try to understand what had happened to her. She just stared down at the curling mound of soft pubic hair, the wide hips and flat stomach, the whiskey-colored skin that gleamed with glittery flecks of gold as she stood in the soft glow of the candlelight.

She reached down and touched her new belly, pressing her long fingers into the softness of the flesh. It was a sensual feeling. Like she was touching herself . . . but *not* touching herself—and it felt both thrilling and taboo.

She felt soft fingertips drop onto her bare shoulder, this new flesh molding onto hers, and she turned her head. She had no idea what her borrowed face looked like, but she imagined it as beautiful and feminine with soft full lips and expressive brown eyes. A tall, bare-chested man stood behind her, the length of his body sliding up against her, her ass pressing into the length of his manhood. She tried to find his face, but here things got bizarre. The man's body was human from the neck down, but he wore a ghastly, skeletal stag's-head mask over his head.

She tried to move away from him, disgusted by the animal musk that exuded from the man/death stag's body, but he held her fast. He caught her up in his arms and lifted her into the air, carrying her with him as he strode down the deck. She wanted to fight him, didn't like the aggressive way he held her, but when she opened her mouth to protest, he silenced her with a kiss, his long black stag's tongue laced with a poison that burned her mouth.

Daniela realized that this was some kind of bastardized version of the Horned God ritual. Usually, this magical rite—an induction ceremony, really—occurred when a blood sister first joined her coven and spiritually gave herself to the Horned God as a way of binding herself to the sisterhood. It was a beautiful moment in every blood sister's initiation, and Daniela hated that it was being twisted in this nasty way.

She beat her fists against his chest, the foul scent of animal filling her nostrils, and he bent his antlered head toward her face, slipping the same thick animal tongue back into her mouth again. She gagged, unable to stop him as he bit at her lips, fur and something that was not teeth, but maybe a hard palate, grinding against her mouth.

He finally pulled away from her and when she opened her eyes again, she was lying on a silken bed, soft down pillows fluffed around her nude body. The death stag was poised above her, naked now, his giant throbbing cock angled toward her

nether regions. She dragged herself away, not wanting anything to do with the creature or his giant penis. He reached
for her middle, and she knew he was going to try to flip her
over so he could have his way with her from behind. She did
the only thing she could think of to save herself. She grabbed
the death stag's skeletal white antlers and yanked on them,
pulling his head toward her chest. The antlers—no, the whole
death stag's head—came away in her hands, the sharpened
tips embedding themselves into her chest.

She gasped as pain flooded her body, rivulets of warm
blood spilling down her naked breasts. She reached up and
pulled the antlers from her chest, letting them drop onto the
bed beside her. She stared down at the gory twin wounds cut
into her skin, and then she pressed her palms against them,
trying to stanch the flow of her lifeblood out onto the sheets.

When she finally tore her gaze away from all the blood
and looked up, she found a grinning human skull staring
down at her. She tried to speak, to ask the beast why he'd
done this to her, but its empty eye sockets beckoned her to
follow it into death. She shook her head, not wanting to go
but also not able to fully resist. She couldn't think straight.
Had lost too much blood. The whole bed was sticky with the
stuff.

She reached up a hand, fingers digging into the skull's
mouth, trying to yank away its lower jaw—but it bit her and
she began to cry. After a few moments, it released the fleshy
digits and she let the hand fall back to her chest, slipping on
the slickness there, unable to keep her hands pressed against
the wound any longer.

The skull lowered itself toward her face, grinning as it
came close and closer . . .

She woke up after the first real sleep she'd had since they'd
left Echo Park for Italy. In her mind, it all seemed like years,

decades, centuries ago . . . she felt old and wizened, no longer a young woman. A husk of her former self.

She felt all this and she hadn't even opened her eyes yet.

The weight of the past and the future were already pushing down on her, dragging her back toward things she wished she could forget.

Not wanting to be awake but knowing she had to rejoin the world, she asked her eyes to open, and this time they obeyed her. Light flooded in, blinding her—and the morning sunlight was so bright that tears began to course down her cheeks, not attached to any emotion. She blinked back the wetness, reaching up to discover that one hand was tethered to an IV drip, so she used the other to brush away the salty tears. At first, she thought she was alone, but she quickly realized this was not the case. A woman with uncombed brown hair sat in a plush chair directly across from Daniela's hospital bed. Her eyes were closed, left elbow crooked on the arm of the chair so her chin rested on the back of her hand. She was creamy skinned with a spray of freckles dotting her nose. Her dark lashes splayed fetchingly across the top of her cheeks as she slumbered.

With clumsy fingers, Daniela grabbed the top of the sheet that covered her, raising it toward her face to blot away the last of her tears. She hated the way they felt, hated how their warmth disappeared almost as soon as they hit the air, leaving her skin chilled.

"You're awake."

She looked up to find the woman staring at her, forest-green eyes appraising Daniela's face, their warmth almost hidden under a fringe of long lashes. She was thin, collarbones protruding from the V-neck of her white T-shirt, and she had long arms, which she now looped around jeans-clad knees as she lifted her feet up onto the seat of the chair. While Daniela watched, the woman made herself smaller, folding up her arms and legs like human origami until she was a neatly wrapped package of exposed feet, head, and torso.

"Neat," Daniela rasped, her throat hoarse and sore from whatever tubes had been stuck down there to keep her alive and breathing.

The woman smiled, but it was slight and fleeting.

"I was asleep," the other woman said, her voice pitched higher than before. "I wasn't supposed to do that. Fall asleep, that is."

Nervous, Daniela thought. *I make her nervous.*

"S'okay," Daniela said, her own voice cracking. *"Won't tell."*

"I'm Niamh."

The woman began to rock back and forth in the chair, like a child, eyes downcast.

"Dan . . . iela," Daniela croaked.

"I know."

"Lyse . . ."

"She and Arrabelle and Evan . . . Well, I'm on watch until they get back."

There was a tentative quality to Niamh's voice, a sadness that Daniela remembered from before. This was the voice she hadn't recognized. This was the creature who had opened the well of sadness and almost dropped Daniela into the abyss.

A dark gray shadow coalesced around Niamh, a living aura unlike anything Daniela had ever seen before. It raged around the woman like a maelstrom, sparks of black fire shooting out like tentacles, searching for a hold on Daniela's soul. Fear coursed through Daniela's body, adrenaline snaking like fire in her veins. She tried to sit up, but she was too weak.

"No . . ." she moaned, shaking her head.

Niamh began to unwrap herself, worry creasing her brow. "You okay?"

"Stay away," Daniela said, flinching as Niamh and her hungry aura climbed out of the chair and moved to the other side of the hospital bed.

"What? Why?" Niamh asked, confused.

Daniela tried to cower away from her, to put as much space between them as she could, but there was only so much real estate.

"Are you all right?" Niamh asked, reaching out a hand.

Daniela squeezed her eyes tight, bracing for the worst, but when nothing happened, she opened them again. She saw that Niamh had retracted her hand, staring down at her fingers as if they were diseased.

"I—I'm sorry." She stumbled over her words . . . and the gray aura began to fade.

Daniela forced herself to un-grit her jaw and relax. Niamh seemed to intuitively understand that she needed to stay as far away from Daniela as possible. Whatever atrocity had befallen the woman had opened up her psyche like a cracked nut, the shell split in two and all the raw meat glistening on display. She was an open wound, a veritable trap for any empath. Touch someone like Niamh, who'd been damaged that badly, and you'd get sucked down into the abyss.

"*I . . .*" Daniela began, wanting to explain, but at that moment a slender man with horn-rimmed spectacles pushed open the door.

"You're up," he said, setting a coffee cup on the ledge of the nearest window and moving to Daniela's bedside. "And you don't look like death warmed over anymore."

She was used to Arrabelle's blunt honesty, but she didn't appreciate it from someone she didn't know.

"*Who are you?*" Daniela rasped, her voice shot.

"I'm Arrabelle's friend Evan, and Niamh is my coven mate."

The pieces began to fall into place. Her mind flashed back to Devandra's house, to the Mucho Man Cave and to the last time their coven had all been together . . . *might be the last time that they were all together.* She remembered that Arrabelle's friend Evan had reached out to warn Arrabelle about the danger from The Flood. That Arrabelle had left her coven mates behind to go and rescue him.

Well, it seemed that Arrabelle had accomplished what she'd set out to do.

The young woman, Niamh, stopped just shy of Daniela, not wanting to get too close.

"Since you've been comatose, a lot of things have changed," she began, turning to look at Evan.

"And not for the better," Evan interrupted, resting his hands on the bed's metal guardrail.

"Where's Lizbeth?" Daniela rasped, almost crying with gratitude when Evan plucked a plastic cup of water from the side table and handed it to her. She sipped the cool liquid, her raw throat feeling a bit better. *"I saw her . . . in my dreams . . ."*

"She's gone. Somewhere in the dreamlands," Niamh said—and Daniela felt a deep worry in her heart.

"What aren't you telling me?" She wanted them to give her all the bad news at once. Otherwise, it would just draw out the pain.

"The world has changed . . ." Niamh paused. "Your coven mate Lizbeth brought magic back into the world through her dreams."

"But humanity's not taking it very well," Evan added.

Daniela's heart sank. She couldn't help but feel responsible. She was the idiot who'd trusted Desmond Delay—that traitor—and unwittingly sold out her blood sisters to him. In her defense, she really had been in the dark. But ignorance was not an excuse. She, of all people—a fucking empath—should've known better. Maybe if she'd been smarter, she'd have controlled Lizbeth better and worked out a way to share the dream gradually . . . to manipulate the flow of information and allow humanity time to process it properly. Everyone was highly aware that human beings were bad at dealing with the unknown. Humans loved to shoot first and ask questions later.

Weeks before the insanity had begun—before Lyse had even left Athens, Georgia, and come home to look after a dying Eleanora—Devandra had drawn a tarot spread that intimated there was a Judas among the Echo Park coven.

The spread had been a simple one:

The World
The Magician
The Hierophant
The Devil
The Fool

No one knew who The Fool belonged to, but it turned out to be Daniela's card. *She* was the Judas—

As if something hot and blazing had been conjured into life by her thoughts, Daniela saw orangey-red flames flare up in her peripheral vision. When she turned her head, she saw that Niamh's body had been engulfed in flame.

"You're on fire," Daniela said, as she stared at Niamh— though it had only taken her a moment to realize that Niamh wasn't on fire. Her aura was burning so bright.

"What're you talking about?" Niamh said, her eyes wide and scared.

"Your aura, it's burning up."

And I'm terrified of what all that anger would do to me if I ever touched you, Daniela thought.

Niamh closed her eyes and took a deep breath. The orange-red glow instantly began to fade away.

"Better?" Niamh asked, opening her eyes.

Daniela nodded.

"I've never . . . I couldn't see auras before," Daniela said.

"It's the magic returning to our world," Evan replied. "It's making everyone's powers manifest in new ways." He turned to Daniela. "You're an empath, so why *shouldn't* you start seeing auras, or at least some kind of visual manifestation of the emotions you feel when you touch someone."

She felt herself nodding. What Evan said made sense—the gray and orangey-red changes in Niamh's aura had to be manifestations of Niamh's sadness and anger. If the negative emotions she felt from Niamh could hurt her, she wondered, would the positive ones—like love or joy—act in the opposite way? She wanted to try her theory out, but there was so much else to discuss, so many things that she needed to know. And she was already worn out from this minor interaction with Niamh and Evan. In fact, her eyes were already starting to close.

"Daniela?" she heard Evan say, but she didn't answer. She was already drifting to sleep . . . and out of their reality.

"Hi, Daniela," Lizbeth said. "You're in the dreamlands. Sort of."

Her friend sat in front of her, cross-legged on the floor, her long russet hair tied back in a loose braid. She was wearing a white shift dress that exposed her thin arms and delicate shoulders, but Daniela was not deceived by the delicate image Lizbeth presented. The Dream Keeper was anything but fragile. She was imbued with so much power that Daniela could see it sparking off the teenager's body in streaks of shining gold.

"You brought me here," Daniela said, realizing—after the fact—that the pain in her throat was gone. She looked down and saw that she was in a matching shift dress to Lizbeth's, her own short hair a frazzled purple-and-pink rat's nest.

They were sitting in a room that was the color of bone. It wasn't a place Daniela had ever been before, and the coldness that emanated from the space, the crisp emptiness that filled the room, made her shiver.

"I did bring you here," Lizbeth said. "I wanted you to know that Dev's girls are here with me and Eleanora and Hessika. They're safe for now, but they can't stay forever."

"Dev's girls are with you, okay," Daniela replied, nodding. "Even though I have no idea why Dev would let them out of her sight . . ."

Lizbeth's face fell.

"Not enough time. Just tell them that I have to stay here to learn to use my powers—but the girls can't stay. We will all be with the magicians at the Red Chapel—"

"*The magicians? At the Red Chapel?*" *Daniela interrupted, her confusion growing.*

Lizbeth nodded.

"*I know it doesn't make sense right now, but just remember what I say. Go to the Red Chapel. It's a real place in our world* and *in the dreamlands. We will be there with the girls. But go soon. As soon as you can. It won't be safe for them here for long.*"

"*Who are the magicians?*" *Daniela asked as she tried to commit Lizbeth's words to memory.*

"*The brothers. Tem and Thomas,*" *she said, a secret smile pulling on the corners of her lips.* "*They're magicians. They're going to teach me how to use the powers I have—*"

"*And Eleanora and Hessika are okay with all this?*" *Daniela asked.*

Lizbeth frowned.

"*They don't like it. But they understand why it's necessary. They're taking care of the girls. When you find Marji and Ginny, you'll find Eleanora and Hessika, too. If I don't see you again, I love you and the others. Tell them I said that!*"

"*I will, but why wouldn't we see you again—*" *Daniela started to ask, but Lizbeth only shook her head.*

"*You're about to wake up. Remember . . . the Red Chapel—*"

Daniela opened her eyes.

"Lizbeth, tell me . . ."

But Lizbeth was gone.

Daniela sat up in her hospital bed.

"What's wrong?" Niamh asked—she and Evan were still standing by the side of the bed. For them, time had barely inched forward; for Daniela . . . it was like she'd been asleep for centuries.

"We have to go," Daniela said—sending a silent thank-you to Lizbeth for somehow making the fix on her throat cross over into the real world. "The Red Chapel. Dev's girls are there waiting for us."

She didn't stop to call a nurse to remove her IV. She simply yanked the needle from her hand—blood flying—and threw the tubes onto the bedclothes. She dragged herself off the mattress, her feet hitting the cold tile floor and sending shivers up her spine.

"The Red Chapel? We know it . . . of course, we do . . . but it burned down—" Niamh began, but Daniela cut her off.

"Don't ask questions," she said, hunting for her old clothes. She found her pants and a clean T-shirt in the chest of drawers. "Just go get the others."

As Niamh shot out the door, Daniela slipped her pants over her bare legs, her body shivering with the cold.

"What did you see?" Evan asked—and Daniela could tell that he wished he could help her get ready. But she was an empath. No one could touch her.

"I saw Lizbeth. She's in the dreamlands with Dev's girls. She said we need to go to the Red Chapel. That the girls would be there waiting for us . . . and she said they wouldn't be safe there for long."

"Jesus . . ." Evan said.

"Exactly . . ." Daniela replied. "I just hope we're not too late already."

Devandra

The dreamlands. The girls were in the dreamlands.

Dev's mother had said it and so Dev believed it. The question then became: *How could she and Freddy get to the Dreamlands to rescue them?*

These were the thoughts flowing through her head as she stood at the kitchen sink, washing the dishes from their late-afternoon lunch of store-bought chicken soup.

"There's someone at the door."

They'd been expecting Lyse and Arrabelle, but as soon as she turned her head, her hands wet from the soapy water, she realized something was wrong. The panicked look on Freddy's face gave it all away.

Freddy had seemed to instinctively understand something was different about the woman he'd loved for so many years, and he'd been acting accordingly. Giving her the space she needed in order to figure out who this new person she'd become . . . *was*. But whoever was at the door had upset him so much he wasn't walking on eggshells. He was just reacting.

"What's wrong?" she asked.

"Police. At the door. I could see them through the peephole."

Peephole. Freddy's nervous chirp of a voice, coupled with the absurdity of the word itself, made Dev giggle.

Freddy's mouth fell open and he stared at her.

"You're laughing."

She shook her head.

"No . . . I'm not . . . laughing," she said, in between giggles.

"It's not funny," he replied, frowning at her, his caterpillar-thick eyebrows turning down in the middle so they formed a V.

This made Dev laugh even harder. Which did not please Freddy.

"This isn't the time to be laughing, Devandra."

He only used her full name when he was mad at her. Otherwise, it was *Dev* or *darling* or *honey pie* or *sweet-ums*—her man very much liked his terms of endearment.

"Don't be mad," she said, drawing a deep breath and hoping it would stifle any further giggles.

"You saw the news," he said—and gone was the smooth charming voice he usually employed. It was replaced by a tight, strained cadence that spoke to his fear and unease. "They're here to take you away."

"They're not taking anyone away, love," she said, patting his arm as she crossed the kitchen and headed for the front of the house.

Freddy was hot on her heels, and she could smell the terror oozing out of his pores like a foul musk.

"Devandra," he said in a harsh whisper. "Stop!"

She did as he asked, but only long enough to set him straight.

"Love," she said, placing her hands on his upper arms. "I have this. You don't need to worry."

She looked deeply into his eyes, channeling a wave of calm that she hoped would relax him. The police would know she was a liar in two seconds if they caught sight of him. He needed to chill out, or else she'd send him to the back bedroom where he wouldn't be a liability.

"Go to the back of the house, Freddy," she said, letting the confidence in her voice cajole him into doing her bidding.

"I can't lose you," he said, his voice cracking. "I just . . . I can't."

She nodded. She wanted him to know that she understood—and she really did. He'd lost everything, too, and she had no intention of adding to his grief.

"You don't have to worry," she said, reaching up and stroking his cheek with her index finger. "Trust me. I won't let anything happen to me . . . or to you . . . or to the girls."

He swallowed back a sob, and nodded.

"Okay."

"Thank you," she said, leaning forward and giving him a quick kiss on the lips. "Thank you for trusting me. Now go to the back of the house."

He stood there for a moment, locked in uncertainty, then did as she asked and padded down the hallway toward the bedrooms. With Freddy out of the way, she could do exactly what she pleased. Whoever was on the other side of the door would be no match for her.

Dev had not been born assertive. In her family, she was always the peacemaker. The one to settle arguments, not start them. But with the life-changing experience of losing most of her family in one fell swoop, something switched on inside her—or maybe it was more truthful to say that something switched *off* inside her. She'd stopped giving a shit, stopped caring about what anyone else thought. Not in a bad way. But in the sense that she didn't feel the need to please other people anymore. Especially the people she didn't love and care about—like whoever the hell was at that front door.

As if the person on the other side of the door knew she'd been thinking about them, they gave another knock. This was followed by a muffled: "Ms. Eleanora Eames? This is the police. Please open the door."

Dev felt like laughing again. *They're so stupid that they don't even know she's dead. So much easier for me, then.*

She gathered her wits about her and opened the door.

Two men in ill-fitting suits stood on the threshold waiting for her. She smiled warmly at them.

"Sadly, Ms. Eames passed away not too long ago. I'm Ellen Mendoza. My husband and I are house-sitting while Ms. Eames's niece, who lives here now, is away."

A little kernel of truth always gave a lie more credence—and the real beauty was that there was very little lying being done. Her middle name was Ellen, and if she and Freddy ever made it official, she'd take Mendoza as her last name.

One of the men—he wore old-fashioned round spectacles and his greasy hair was probably longer than regulation allowed—took out a notepad and began flipping through it.

"This niece," he said, looking up from his notepad. "Would that be Lyse MacAllister?"

Dev nodded.

"Why, yes, it would be. I don't really know her, though. I was acquainted with Eleanora through neighborhood meetings and such."

The other man nodded. He was older and gruffer, with a nervous tic that made the muscle above his right cheek twitch. It was hard not to look at it when she talked to him, but she managed.

She was not interested in offending him or giving him a reason to stay longer than necessary.

"Do you know when she'll be back?" the man with the spectacles said, giving her a strange grin. It split his lips but did not touch his eyes.

A sociopath's smile, Dev thought, and put on her kid gloves. As far as she was concerned, they were both dangerous predators that she wanted off her scent as soon as possible.

"Next week. She was visiting abroad. Italy, I think."

She continued to stick close to the truth. They could easily check and see that a Lyse MacAllister had booked a flight to Italy.

The older man pulled a card from his suit jacket pocket and offered it to her.

"If you hear from Ms. MacAllister, please give us a call."

Dev nodded, giving them what she hoped was a helpful look. "I will."

They seemed satisfied with their mini-interrogation and turned to go—but then the one with the spectacles pivoted back to face her.

"We have the house under surveillance, Ms. Mendoza. We're tapping the phones, all perfectly legal and obtained under special court order. So should you try to warn your little witch friend not to come back home, we'll know it."

He gave her that strange cold smile again—*The smile of a snake,* Dev thought—and then he rejoined his partner, who was waiting for him farther down the deck. Dev watched them go, keeping the smile pasted on her face until she was sure they'd crossed the koi pond and were heading back out onto the street.

"You sons of bitches," she murmured.

She stepped back inside and closed the door, leaned against the smooth wooden surface. Her body was taut as piano wire. She hadn't realized how much the two policemen had affected her until they were gone.

"Freddy?" she called.

He was out of the back rooms in a flash, looking sheepish.

"I shouldn't have let you handle that all by yourself," he said, running a hand through his thick, dark hair.

"No, you did the right thing," she said. "They were here looking for Eleanora and Lyse, but I put them off. I used your last name. They won't have that on their list. I'm Devandra Montrose to them. There's no Ellen Mendoza to go chasing after."

The words came out in a rush, disjointed and frenetic. She was more upset than she'd realized.

Freddy came to her and wrapped his arms around her

shoulders, pulling her in close. The stench of fear had dissipated and he smelled like himself again.

"I can't lose you, Dev," he whispered in her ear.

"I know," she whispered back.

They stood clinging to one another for a long while. Until the shadows of the afternoon leaked in through the windows and cast them into darkness.

Dev wasn't surprised that the first test of this new, improved version of herself had followed so closely on the heels of saying good-bye to her mother and sisters. *What doesn't kill you, makes you stronger,* she thought—and she believed this mantra because it had proved true in her case.

As she and Freddy lay in Eleanora's bed, snuggled up together like two bugs in a rug, Devandra knew she had to reach out to the others. No one had called her, but Freddy had received a text from Arrabelle, letting them know they were in Italy (which was craziness), that Daniela was ill, and they would come as soon as they could manage.

You can't come back here, ladies, Dev thought, while Freddy's soft snores tickled the back of her neck. *It's just not safe anymore.*

It was heartrending to think the place she'd called home was now an alien thing. No longer would she feel protected. Her house was gone. Her family was gone. The warmth and safety she'd known walking the streets of her beloved neighborhood were gone. There was nothing left for her in Echo Park.

Taking care not to wake Freddy, she wiggled out of his arms and crawled out of the bed. She wore her long strawberry-blond hair loose at night, and it grew so fast these days that it trailed almost to her waist. Her feet protested at the coldness of the floor, but she ignored them and went to Eleanora's dressing table. Here she found Freddy's phone and carried it with her out of the bedroom.

The house was silent as a tomb, the air chilly enough to

make goose bumps appear on Dev's exposed arms and throat. She scuttled down the darkened hallway on tiptoe, careful not to turn on any lights as she went. When she reached the living room, she made her way to the couch and settled in, pulling an afghan from its back and bundling up.

"Better," she said, still shivering. But she could already feel the crocheted afghan doing its job. Warmth was returning again.

She took out the phone and the screen flared to life, the phone vibrating in her hand. She searched through the contacts and selected Arrabelle's name from the list. She sent her friend a text message:

Don't come back. We will meet you in another place. Xoxo D

She deleted the text from Freddy's phone—it was instinctual, there was no logical reason for the move—and then she depressed the power button, putting the phone back to sleep.

She was back in bed five minutes later, Freddy's phone exactly where he'd left it when he'd gone to bed that night.

Dev dreamed of the girls. They were in a garden with Lizbeth and everything was okay. She wasn't close enough to speak to them. All her observations came from far away—almost as if she were watching them through the eye of a telescope, so that, at first, they looked close, but then it became clear they were actually light-years away. Like watching a star being born only to realize that it was already long dead. That what she was seeing had happened billions of years ago.

This was how far the image traveled to reach her. She wept, thinking of the girls. It was all so devastating, the wanting to be there to watch them grow up, to help them when they needed her most . . . and not being allowed to.

She must've cried out in her sleep because she found herself being shaken awake, Freddy's worried face staring down at her as she opened her eyes.

"You okay?" he asked. She wasn't fully awake yet and the dream still held on tightly to her. "Dev?"

She rolled over and sat up, wiping the sleep from her eyes. She looked around the room—Eleanora's room with its delicate vanity and warped mirror, the light cream curtains under heavy drapes, the thick-slatted wooden floor—and she began to relax, the familiar smells and sights calming her panic.

"Bad dream," she said finally, pressing her body back into the mound of pillows and closing her eyes. "The girls were far away and I couldn't reach them . . . it was awful."

Freddy took her hand, pulling her knuckles to his lips.

"We'll get them back. I don't know how, but we will," he said, and kissed her hand.

"I wonder . . ." she murmured under her breath. "Freddy, hold on a second."

She sat up and swung her legs off the bed, gathering her nightdress around her.

"The Dream Journals," she said, and quickly padded across the uneven hardwood floor to the smallest closet in the room. This was where she and Lyse had stored Eleanora's things. "Well, the one Lizbeth left behind, at least."

She opened the door and knelt down, beginning to pull stuff from the bottom.

"We made her leave one book behind, just in case," Dev continued, digging out shoes and boxes in order to get to the false floor. "Of what? I don't know."

"Can I help?" Freddy asked.

"Take these," she said, handing him two small boxes followed by two more. "And these. I need to make some room."

Once Freddy had joined her in her efforts, the work went quickly, and they were able to get the floor cleared in no time.

"It's under here," Dev said, feeling around the empty floor with her fingers. "It's like a little latch—"

There was a small *click*, and with a triumphant smile, she lifted part of the wooden floor.

"Yes," she murmured, slipping her hands inside the depression until she found what she was looking for. "Here we go."

She pulled out an oilskin-wrapped square and sat back, the package resting on her lap. With nimble fingers, she began unwrapping it, creating a cloud of dust that made her nose twitch. She pulled the journal from the oilskin and lifted it up in the air. It wasn't a large book, but there was a weight to it that belied the flimsy cardboard covering. Inside, there would only be blank sheets of paper, but Dev knew the translucent lined pages bore the stamp of magic.

"Dream Journal acquired," she said, and smiled at Freddy. "Now I need Eleanora's cards."

They sat at the round oak table, the morning sun streaming through the windows and setting the kitchen aglow with pale light. Dev was still in her nightdress, but she'd tied up her long hair in a loose bun, tendrils of it curling around her face. Freddy sat across from her, a look of intense concentration on his usually relaxed features.

This magic stuff was all new to him. Dev was sure that in the past, he'd wondered about what she did—was the magic for real or was she just pretending to read the tarot cards? He knew she saw clients out in the redone garage—the Mucho Man Cave, as they'd lovingly christened it—but she doubted he really believed she was doing anything magical out there among the mismatched tables and chairs. In light of everything that had happened to them, he was forced to accept that his partner was special. That Dev could do impressive feats of real magic—feats like the one she was about to attempt right there in Eleanora's kitchen.

"You really think it will work?" Freddy asked.

Dev didn't know for sure, but she had a feeling that it might. Because things were different in the world now. Like a spigot turned to full blast—when before there'd barely been a trickle—magic was everywhere.

"All we can do is give it a shot," she replied, setting the Dream Journal down on the table between them.

It was a faded thing, tattered and worn out like it had spent too long in the sun. Someone had drawn an ouroboros on the cover in pen and ink: smooth strokes from a sure hand. Dev had never given the symbol much thought, but as she stared down at it, she could feel the magic it represented almost leaping off the paper.

"What is it?" Freddy asked.

"The ouroboros?" Dev answered, making sure the image of a snake eating its own tail was what Freddy was referring to.

He nodded.

"It's creepy."

"You feel that?" Dev asked, surprised. The symbol made her skin crawl, but she hadn't expected Freddy to pick up on it, too.

"It's repellent," he said, biting his lip. "Like I'm not supposed to look at it."

Dev knew what he meant.

"It represents the Eternal . . . that which has no beginning, no middle, and no end. Something we humans can't and shouldn't try too hard to understand."

"I'm fine with that," Freddy said, giving her a tight smile. "It doesn't want me to look at it and I'd rather not look at it, either."

Since they'd lost the girls, Freddy's marvelous sense of humor had been tamped down by grief, but, finally, it was starting to rear its head again. She gave him a wink, pleased to see it reemerging.

"Don't think you can charm me *that* easily," he continued, enjoying the flirtation between them. "You'll have to work harder than a wink to get me."

Dev laid her hands down on the tabletop. She needed to

take a moment here, tell Freddy how important he was to her. She'd let that slide in her exhaustion and terror. She'd put her feelings above his when she should have given them parity with her own. Marji and Ginny were half his, and he'd loved her family as much as she had. He was dealing with the same complex emotions, only she hadn't been there to protect him the way he'd protected her.

"I'm sorry," she said, her throat tight as she tried to hold back her emotions. "I went away and I wasn't there for you."

He looked up at the ceiling, then down at his nail-bitten hands, anything not to meet her gaze.

"I miss you."

He nodded, taking it in. Then he looked up at her, his eyes wet with tears.

"Don't apologize to me like that, Dev," he said. "It was my honor to look after you when you needed me. You are my other half, the better part of me—you know that—and I never don't feel connected to you. Even through all of this, through losing the girls and your mother and sisters . . . the house . . . everything . . . I still feel . . . felt connected to you. So just . . . don't apologize for needing a moment to collect yourself. It's my job to look out for you. And, honestly, I can't bear you thinking you needed to apologize. It's a given, Dev. I love you. That doesn't change."

"But you needed me, too," she said, wiping at the tears that streamed down her face.

"And I *have* you. I'm getting what I need, Dev."

He magically produced a handkerchief from his pocket, and she saw his initials embroidered on the white fabric in light blue stitches. It had been his gift from her on their fifth anniversary. She took the proffered handkerchief and blew her nose.

"You don't hate me?" she asked

"For snotting up my handkerchief?" he said, grinning. "Hell, no."

Sobs and laughter burbled out of her, mixing together

until Dev didn't know if she was crying or laughing. *Probably both,* she thought.

"We're so stupid," she said, climbing out of her chair to hug the man she loved. "If we just lean on each other, we can get through anything."

She kissed the side of his face, pokey bits of dark stubble scratching at her cheek.

"We can do that," Freddy agreed. "We can definitely do that."

He kissed her back, this time on the lips, and for the first time in days, Dev began to feel safe again. As they broke apart, Freddy stared up into Dev's eyes.

"I want to marry you," he said.

She was taken aback, shocked even. The idea seemed to come out of nowhere.

"What?"

"When this is all over, I want you to be my wife. Officially."

Dev swallowed, her mouth suddenly dry.

"I didn't mean—" She started to protest, but he shushed her with another kiss.

"Just say yes," he murmured against her mouth once they'd parted again.

She opened her eyes, his love encircling her like a cocoon.

"Yes," she whispered.

"Now go do this magic spell, or whatever it is," he said, grinning like a little boy who'd just gotten the birthday present he wanted.

She left him, her fingers brushing his arm as she circled past him and returned to her chair. She was giddy, her body thrumming with excitement—but she reined her happiness in and took her seat. She reached across the table, picking up the blue velvet drawstring bag that contained Eleanora's deck of tarot cards.

"I am a cartomancer."

She intoned the words to the cards as she removed them from their bag and set them out in front of her.

"I have the gift of divination and with your blessing, I will ply my trade."

She set her hand palm down on the topmost card, letting the cards get a sense of her. She knew she would be able to wield the deck if, and only if, the deck gave her its permission.

"Dev—"

She knew what Freddy was going to say—*Why are you asking permission? They're just cards*—but she silenced him with a wave of her hand. She needed silence and goodwill in the room. There could be no doubting. Freddy seemed to get what she was asking of him and he nodded, sitting back in his chair and waiting for her to continue.

"If I have your goodwill, show me a sign—"

Dev cried out, the palm of her hand on fire. The pain was so terrible that she almost drew her hand back, but something inside her told her this would be a fatal mistake. Instead, she gritted her teeth and let the fiery sensation burn her hand. Just as she almost couldn't take anymore, the pain eased and a cooling balm spread across the flesh of her palm. There was a heady scent of ambergris and myrrh, as if someone had turned the two scents to ash inside an incense burner.

"You once belonged to Eleanora Eames and before her to Svetlana Aoki and before her to Mary Westover and before her to your original maker Lady Frieda Harris . . ."

The cards seemed to warm at the mention of that last name, as if they missed their first mistress, the woman who had painted all the imagery for Aleister Crowley's *Book of Thoth* tarot cards—for this had been one of Lady Harris's own decks. The warmth grew until the cards were toasty, but they never got as hot as they were during that first interaction.

"Thank you for offering us your services," Dev said to the cards—and then she lifted them in her hand and began to cut them, setting four separate piles down on the tabletop.

"We do not seek your help in divination but in reaching out to the spirit world . . . to the dreamlands."

She took the top card from each pile and placed them at the cardinal directions around the Dream Journal: North was The Star to guide them, West was The Moon to light their way, East was The Sun behind them, and South was The Chariot upon which they would attempt this journey.

She'd loved these cards from the first moment she'd seen them. Eleanora had shown them to her not long after she'd been initiated into the coven, and since that day she'd been obsessed with owning them for herself. The *Book of Thoth* tarot's Major and Minor Arcana were an art deco masterpiece, gloriously rendered in brassy gold, moss green, and lavender geometric patterns . . . and their provenance made them even more special.

Dev just hadn't imagined them coming into her possession so soon or in such a tragic way. With Eleanora's untimely death.

The ring of a telephone cracked through the air, jarring them both out of the calm Dev had created with her intonations to the cards.

"Is that the landline?" Freddy asked.

He didn't wait for an answer, just got up and reached for the corded phone hanging on the kitchen wall near the refrigerator. He held the receiver to his ear and frowned.

"Just dial tone."

Dev wasn't surprised, certain the ringing had come from the back. Where Freddy's cell phone lay on the side table in Eleanora's bedroom.

"It's yours."

The ring came again, louder and more insistent. Wailing like a baby to be picked up.

"Go get it?" Dev asked—and Freddy took off like a shot.

She looked down at the cards and was shocked to find that two of the cards had rearranged themselves: The Moon had swapped places with The Sun.

Guided by the sun, the moon at our backs, Dev thought.

"This is crazy. I heard ringing, but I pick up the phone and it's *not* ringing," Freddy said, as he jogged back into the room, his phone held out in front of him like it was possessed—and maybe it was. "Here."

He handed Dev the cold, dark hunk of plastic and metal—but as soon as the phone touched her skin, it roared to life, vibrating in her hand.

"Damn," she said, almost dropping it.

"Should we answer?" Freddy asked, and Dev nodded, staring at the screen, which read *Unknown Caller.*

"Yeah, I think so," she said—and pressed the accept button.

She put the cell phone to her ear.

"Hello?"

She listened for a moment, disbelief dawning across her face.

"Who is it?" Freddy asked, rocking back and forth on the balls of his feet.

Dev removed the phone from her ear and set it on top of the Dream Journal, engaging the speakerphone.

"*. . . and Auntie E is here, too, and the Tall Lady . . . and we can make things happen that are like magic . . . you're talking too much, Ginny . . . No, you're talking too much, Marji . . .*"

A tear rolled down Dev's cheek as, together, she and Freddy huddled around Eleanora's round oak table, listening to their daughters reaching out to them from across many universes.

Lyse

Lyse had heard the commotion in the hallway—saw Arrabelle taking off after an excited Niamh, both women heading for Daniela's room—and knew something had happened. Logic told her that Daniela had woken up . . . there was no way she could've taken a turn for the worse. But that didn't make her feel any better as she ran down the long white hall, the squeak of her sneakers echoing through the corridor. She could feel her heart rate increasing, hear the hiss of her own labored breathing in her ears.

She was not paying attention to her surroundings, her worry for Daniela ruling her senses. She didn't see the well-built man with the silver cropped hair until he'd stepped out in front of her. Her instincts kicked in and she screeched to a stop on the linoleum-tiled floor, hands out in front of her as if to ward off an attack. The silver-haired man wore a snarl of disdain. It was obvious he hated her, and he didn't make any bones about it.

She began to back away from him, a surge of fear-based adrenaline shooting through her. Every encounter she'd had with her long-lost uncle David had ended badly . . . and she was pretty sure this one was destined for the same outcome.

"Leave me alone, you son of a bitch." She spat the words at him, anger taking over.

"That's not a nice thing to say about Eleanora. Though I concur. My mother—*your* grandmother—was a real bitch."

She was shaking, her impotent rage blossoming into tears. As she fought them back, praying they wouldn't fall, she realized how weak it made her feel when her anger crested over the peak into emotion. Every time she needed to appear strong, the emotional side kicked in, undercutting her strength.

"You don't even get to say her name. Murderer."

He cocked his head and narrowed his eyes, really looking at her.

"I did her a favor," he said, finally, and shrugged.

"A favor?" Lyse was incredulous. *What the hell was wrong with this guy?* "You killed her. You took the most sacred thing in the world—someone else's life—and you crushed it."

He took a step toward her, and she unconsciously moved back, reaching out with a hand to brace herself against the corridor wall. She did not intend to let him push her back any more than he already had . . . because every step she took put the power dynamic more firmly in his favor.

"Are you frightened of me?" he asked, and she could sense his excitement radiating outward, gunning for her.

Everything inside of her ached to put more distance between them, but she held her ground. She would not let her fear of him bully her into submission.

"That's not fear. It's disgust," she said, putting as much passion as she could into her words. "Because I find you repulsive."

He laughed, a low and malevolent thing that made the hairs on the back of her neck rise to attention. Gooseflesh broke out along her arms and she was, once again, tempted to give over and step away . . . but she steeled herself and did not move.

"Laugh all you want," she said. "You're not winning this thing."

He shook his head, eyebrow raised.

"What *thing*?" he asked.

"You and The Flood. You're not getting this world. Not if it's the last thing I do."

"Well, that's a given," he said. "That it's the last thing you're going to do. And you're going to fail at it. Just like you do with everything else in your life."

His words were like bullets, each one primed to hit her in one of her weak spots. They were strategically played to worm their way inside her and ferret out her insecurities, splitting her confidence apart from the inside out. He knew he'd hit the mark, saw the emotional impact on her face, and was gleeful, pleased at his ability to wound her.

"Really?" Lyse asked after she'd caught her breath. "Did you think I'd go down so easily?"

"You've let everyone down. Your coven is in ruins and Daniela is dying," he said.

Lyse wanted him to shut up, but he just kept talking.

"When she's dead, my father—and your grandfather—will be broken. He's old and sick, and her death will push him over the edge," he continued, "and then I can step into his place. *I* can be the one to lead The Flood to its zenith. *My* name will be the one the world remembers."

"You're crazy," Lyse murmured—she knew anyone associated with The Flood was insane.

"No, I'm smart," he said. This was followed by a guttural growl, low in his throat. "You really don't know anything about me, do you?"

It was true. She knew zero about her uncle, her dead mother's twin. Hell, she didn't know much about her own mother and father, either—other than the tangle of childhood memories she'd shoved into the recesses of her mind because thinking about them was just too painful.

"You were my mother's twin," Lyse said. "You grew in the same womb. How could you do all of these horrible things to me?"

He laughed again, and Lyse wanted to cover her ears—because something inside her sensed he only laughed when he was about to something terrible. Something inhumane.

"She was nothing to me," he said, grinning. "And she was less than nothing to me when I killed her and your father."

"No," she said, raising her hands to cover her ears. She did *not* want to hear this.

"So easy to run them off the road. My only mistake was that you should've died with them."

She took a step toward him, all the fear and insecurity and guilt and anger filling her like a balloon until she was ready to pop. She felt disconnected from her body but still in control of it—and so, fully conscious of what she was about to do, she took another step and then another . . . reaching out with her hands, the power inside her rising to a fever pitch. How dare he try to push the blame for Eleanora's death onto her shoulders? How dare he call her a failure as a human being and as a blood sister . . . *and as a friend*? How dare he murder her parents in cold blood and let her live with their absence for the rest of her life?

"This ends now," she said, when she was close enough to touch the man she hated so much.

She grabbed his wrists in her hands and held tight. Her magic called up a neon-blue orb that coalesced around them, growing larger until they were both consumed by it.

"What are you doing?" he cried, fighting to pull out of her grip, but she would not let go.

"I want to go somewhere dark and hidden," she screamed into the ether as the orb swirled around her, the hiss of air and energy so loud it pummeled her eardrums. "I want to throw this man away—hurl him into an abyss from which he can never return!"

She saw uncertainty dawn in his eyes. Felt his body stiffen as he started to understand that this was real magic—her magic—and that he'd pushed her past the fail-safe point. There was no coming back from the fervor of rage in her eyes. She was powerful and strong . . . and she would show him exactly where he belonged. In fact, she would leave him there to think long and hard, possibly for an eternity, about what kind of a human being he was.

He fought her in earnest now, struggling to escape the pull of her magic. He squirmed under her touch, writhing and yanking, working desperately to unbind himself from her.

But it was too late.

They were already gone.

Only this time the orb did not pop. It stayed intact and went with them on their journey.

It took Lyse a moment to understand where the orb had brought them, but once she did, the perfection of it made her smile.

"Where are we?!" her uncle screamed, fear ratcheting up his voice an octave. He was the one clutching at her now, his fingers pressing into her skin as he fought to keep his balance. The orb hadn't liked the taste of her uncle David, and so it had expelled him. Now his hands—the one place where his flesh touched her own—were the only part of him still inside the orb.

"You're where you belong!" Lyse screamed back at him.

Had she been asked to describe the singularity that would be her uncle's eternal punishment and final resting place, Lyse would've said it was visually unimpressive. No more than a small black dot.

She knew her brain couldn't understand what it was experiencing. That this small black dot she saw wasn't really the singularity's true shape, just a construct for her simple human mind to hold on to. But the power it exerted over everything around it was very real. It made her want to throw herself at the singularity and become one with it forever.

Luckily, she was fully inside the orb's swirling magic and was only psychologically affected by the pull of the celestial body. Unlike her uncle, who was no longer protected by magic.

"Help me!" David screamed, and Lyse knew it would be only a matter of seconds before he succumbed to the singularity's pull.

Her magic had brought them here, and she gladly accepted the role of judge, jury, and executioner as they stood on the precipice of time and space.

Inside the orb there was chaos, magic swirling around her like a maelstrom . . . outside there was a soundless vacuum, the infinite silence pierced only by her uncle's cries. And then the singularity exerted its final pull and David was sucked backward. One minute he was there and the next, he had ceased to exist.

Lyse knew she couldn't stay here any longer. That her magic could only protect her for so long before the singularity broke through and stole her away, too.

"Take me home," she murmured.

And the orb popped.

"Holy shit!" Freddy yelped—as Lyse's body magically appeared on top of the round oak table in front of him.

Lyse grinned back at him, enjoying the shocked expression on his face. He was wearing a white embroidered Mexican wedding shirt with a coffee stain down its front. He was also holding a coffee-stained mug in his hand. She felt bad. Her surprise appearance must've freaked him out so much he'd spilled his coffee down his shirt front.

"Nice to see you, too," she said. "Sorry about the coffee."

She groaned as she tried to sit up, every muscle in her body aching.

"Wait . . . Uh, what, uh . . . *How?*" he whispered, sitting back in his chair and pointing at her with the coffee mug.

"I said I wanted to come home, and this is where my magic brought me."

He nodded, as if this made all the sense in the world.

"Sure, yeah . . . *yeah* . . ." he said, and took a sip from his mostly empty coffee mug.

Lyse ignored the pain in her limbs and climbed off the table-top, only feeling human when she had both feet on the floor again. She pushed away the bad feelings—though she knew she'd have to deal with the knowledge of her parents' murder eventually—and tried to clear her mind. For now she just needed a break from all the emotional shit.

"Where's Dev?" she asked.

"Uh, she's in the bedroom . . . would you like some coffee?" Freddy asked.

Lyse thought about it for a second, then nodded.

"Why the hell not?" she said, feeling giddy and full of crazy energy after what she'd just done.

She knew she should feel racked with guilt—she'd just hurled a human being into a singularity—but since it existed within the landscape of the dreamlands, a place where anything was possible, it didn't one hundred percent mean that she'd killed him. She had a strange feeling her uncle was more alive than dead, though she doubted he'd be coming back to their world any time soon. And, if she was lucky, maybe he'd *never* come back again.

Wishful thinking, Lyse thought.

Dev came into the kitchen and found Lyse sitting there having a cup of coffee with Freddy. Somehow she'd missed all the commotion, and her shocked *Oh!* of surprise made Lyse laugh.

"You're here," Dev said, switching gears in a heartbeat. "Do you have the girls? Where are the others? We've been so worried. The house is gone, everything inside it, too. We've missed you!"

Too many questions and feelings all at once. The only thing Lyse could think to do in response was to pull Dev in for a hug.

"I'm so sorry," she whispered in her friend's ear. "I can't even imagine . . ."

Dev pulled away from the embrace and looked Lyse right in the eye.

"Yes, you can," she said. "*You* of all people can understand."

Dev was right. Lyse had lost so much. So many of the people she'd loved were gone. She felt like she was a bad omen. Being friends with her was like having a deathwatch beetle quietly ticking away inside the walls of your house. She wondered if her love should come with a warning label.

"Lyse . . . ?"

She realized Dev had been talking to her and she'd missed every word.

"I'm sorry," she apologized. "What were you saying?"

"The girls, we spoke to them. They're with Lizbeth and Eleanora in the dreamlands. A place called the Red Chapel . . . ?"

"I can take you there," Lyse said, excited that she could do something to erase the sadness etched into Dev's features. "To the dreamlands . . . it's something we discovered . . . now that magic is loose in the world again, *real* magic, all of our powers, everything we can do . . . it's heightened."

Dev nodded. She had come to the same conclusion herself.

"That was why I could use the cards to reach out to the girls," she said to Freddy. Then she turned to Lyse: "It was the strangest thing. I just knew it was possible and then I made it happen. And Freddy saw it all."

Freddy shook his head in agreement—and Lyse wouldn't

have blamed him at all if he'd told the ladies he needed to go take a lie-down. He seemed genuinely overwhelmed by everything he'd seen and heard. Poor Freddy. Lyse was a blood sister who could wield magic and travel to other dimensions . . . and *she* felt like she was in way over her head. Freddy was a layman and he'd been exposed to some truly awful stuff. She didn't know how he was coping so well.

"Well, I left the others with Daniela at the hospital. I got sidetracked by a run-in with my uncle."

"Oh, God," Dev said, the color draining from her face.

"You don't have to worry about him," Lyse said. "He's not going to bother us anymore."

She finished the last dregs of her coffee and set the mug in the sink. Even though she'd just downed a ton of caffeine, she yawned, her lack of sleep finally catching up with her. Too bad for that. There was no time to think about taking a nap. They needed to reconnect with the others and then go get Marji and Ginny.

"What do you mean?" Dev asked.

"I dropped him off in a place that he's going to have a hard time finding his way back from."

"Okay," Dev said, but she refrained from asking for further details. "So how do we do this? Do you work a spell or . . . ?"

"No, it's even simpler than that—" Lyse started to say, but she was interrupted by a pounding on the back kitchen door.

The three of them turned to see the wood of the door frame splinter as someone shot three bullets into the lock.

"We have to go!" Lyse cried—as a furious kick from outside sent the kitchen door flying.

Lyse grabbed Dev's wrist and began the mental work of forming the blue orb that would take them to the dreamlands.

"Freddy!" Dev screamed, reaching out to her partner with her free hand. But he was already running toward the door, trying to block the intruders from entering.

"Go, Dev! They won't hurt me!" he called back to her, as

the first black-clad man burst into the kitchen, holding an assault weapon in his hands. "I love you!"

The blue orb encircled Lyse and Dev just in time to stop a hail of bullets that came from the men in the doorway. Lyse felt sick. She knew if her magic hadn't been protecting them, they'd have been dead.

One of the men—it was hard to tell them apart because of the camouflage blacking on their faces—slammed the butt of his Kalashnikov into the back of Freddy's head. Freddy fell to his knees, then pitched forward onto the floor, either dazed or unconscious, Lyse wasn't sure which.

"Freddy!" Dev screamed as more men in black camo poured into the room and encircled his body. *"No!"*

She tried to break free from Lyse's grip so she could run to Freddy, but Lyse wouldn't release her.

"The girls need you, Dev!" Lyse cried, wanting Dev to understand what she'd be sacrificing by leaving the safety of the magical orb. She wasn't going to be able to help Freddy. There were just too many men with guns out there and more were still arriving.

She felt Dev stop trying to pull away, saw her deflate as they watched two of the men pick Freddy up by the armpits and drag him outside.

"Desist working magic and stand down," one of the men screamed at Lyse. He seemed like the one who was calling the shots for this mission.

"No way!" Lyse yelled back at him. "You have no authority here!"

He raised his hand and another volley of bullets slammed into the neon-blue orb, but none of them penetrated Lyse's magic.

"We have to go," Dev murmured, tears of impotent rage rolling down her cheeks. "If we stay any longer, I'm not gonna be able to take it."

Lyse picked up what Dev was putting down. Her friend

could only stand there so long, letting those bastards man-handle Freddy, before she broke free of Lyse's grasp and did something stupid . . . like try to stop them herself.

"Okay, we're out of here," Lyse said, before Dev could change her mind.

Lyse didn't think about where they were going, just wished them out of the kitchen. She was just sorry she couldn't see the look of confusion on the soldiers' faces as the orb winked out of existence . . . she and Dev with it.

The magical orb took them to the clinic in Rome, to the long white corridor that led to Daniela's hospital room. Lyse shook her head, trying to figure out what had happened: *Why weren't they in the dreamlands?*

"Get back," Dev whispered, pushing Lyse into an empty room just as Arrabelle came striding down the corridor, moving at a brisk pace. Behind her, less than ten feet away from where Dev and Lyse were hiding . . . was *Lyse*.

"Holy shit, that's me . . ." Lyse started to say, but Dev put a finger to her lips to shush her.

They watched as a man—Lyse's uncle David—stepped out of the elevator just in time to block the Lyse doppelgänger's path.

The doppelgänger came to a stop in front of him—and Lyse could see the doppelgänger shake with fear. It was insane, but now she knew exactly what she looked like when she was scared.

"Leave me alone, you son of a bitch," the doppelgänger yelled at David.

"That's not a nice thing to say about Eleanora," he replied, looking amused.

Lyse watched as the scene played out in front of her.

"I can't . . ." she whispered to Dev, and slipped back into the empty room.

She found one of the windows open a crack, and so she stood in front of it, gulping down the fresh air, trying not to think about what David was telling her doppelgänger out there in the hallway. After a moment, Dev came to stand beside her.

"That can't be true," she said, putting her hand on Lyse's arm. "About your parents . . ."

But there was no conviction in Dev's words.

"It's true," Lyse said, her voice flat. "As true as those idiots taking Freddy. We don't want to believe what's happening, but our world has gone to hell . . . and I'm not sure we can stop it."

Dev didn't try to argue. Instead, she went back to the doorway to watch. A moment later she called back to Lyse: "They're . . . *you're* gone now."

"Good," she said. "Let's go find Arrabelle and the others."

As much as she didn't want to, she might have to tell them that traveling to the dreamlands wasn't her only magical ability . . . *She could travel through time, too.*

Evan

Evan wasn't sure *what* he was supposed to be feeling any-more. There was a gnawing emptiness in the pit of his stomach that wouldn't go away, and he knew it was directly tied to the woman standing next to him. But until that moment he hadn't wanted to acknowledge he had a problem . . . a problem that came directly from him still being alive.

He'd been pretty sure he was going to die, so he'd thought a lot about death. And while standing on the precipice of the great beyond, he'd looked back at the life he'd led and found it to be a decent one. Nothing super exciting, more of an emotionally walled-off existence than he'd have wished for himself, but that was all.

He felt like he'd made his peace with death—and then, abruptly, and against all reason, he'd been released from the Grim Reaper's clutches. To his surprise, he'd found himself almost—but not quite—disappointed by the reprieve. Not that he'd *wanted* to die. The opposite, in fact. It was just that when you'd given up the lease, sold all the stock, and closed up shop, it was kind of hard to start all over again.

Which made him think, once again, of Arrabelle.

They'd reconnected at a time when he thought everything was lost. He felt guilty about the messed-up state of their friendship, and so he'd let her believe that if things were different—aka, he wasn't dying—he'd be willing to start a relationship with her. Of course, now that death wasn't on the table anymore, he was realizing just how selfish that choice had been.

Well, it was partly selfishness. He really *did* want to make her happy. But he should never have given her hope. Not when he knew he could never love her the way she needed to be loved.

He knew trying to explain was useless. His inability to act on feelings he may or may not have was not personal to her. He didn't think he was capable of being with *anybody*. If he could've chosen for himself, Arrabelle would be the first and only person on the list. But there was just too much . . . *past*. Too many things had happened to him as a kid and he'd been so damaged that the part of him that was supposed to want to be in a relationship . . . well . . . it had died.

It wasn't that he was asexual. He just couldn't be in a relationship. Vulnerability was not something available to him—and so he'd chosen to remain utterly alone to save someone else the heartbreak of falling in love with a man who couldn't love them back. He was broken, and keeping his distance was the kindest thing he could do in the situation.

But then he'd let Arrabelle get too close. They'd been best friends in college, and he'd thought maybe he could learn to be different with her. But when she'd tried to kiss him, just as always, the wall had gone up. He'd shut down, locked her out, and totally hurt her feelings. Their friendship had recovered, but it had never really been the same after that. They'd drifted apart and he hadn't encouraged her to visit once he'd gone up to the Pacific Northwest.

He'd missed her a lot over the years, but he knew the separation was for her sake. He'd already hurt her more than he'd hurt any other person, and he didn't want to reopen the old wounds.

Dying had changed all that. The walls had crumbled as soon as he'd realized the wound in his side was going to slowly kill him. He'd thought about her more and more—and then he'd gotten Niamh to mail her the letter and the journal documenting their coven's destruction. He didn't know what he'd expected to happen. He just knew that he wanted her holding his hand when he died. Wanted her beautiful face to be the last thing he saw before he closed his eyes for the final time. In hindsight, it was ridiculous. They hadn't been close in years, she had no impetus to come find him . . . for all he knew, she would read the letter and ignore it.

No, that was a lie. He knew Arrabelle, knew the force of her personality, and knew she would find him—or his dead body—if it was the last thing she did. He knew how she operated, and he'd known she'd be a part of his limited future come hell or high water. He hadn't been wrong. She'd done exactly as he'd (unconsciously) expected and now here she was . . . a woman who deserved much better than his sorry ass could provide.

He was going to have to be honest with her sooner rather than later. No lies, no subterfuge, no half-truths. Arrabelle deserved the truth from him.

Now as they stood next to each other listening to Lyse, he sensed Arrabelle's eyes on him, as if he could feel her love radiating out at him like a heater. He looked over at her, and she caught his eye, smiling so hard that the skin around the corners of her eyes crinkled in happiness. It only made him feel worse.

"Are we ready?" Lyse asked—and Evan turned his attention away from Arrabelle and back to their de facto leader.

His own coven master, Yesinia, was dead. Burned at the stake in front of the Red Chapel—the very place he was letting Lyse and the others lead him back to against his will. As difficult as it had been, he'd let his loyalty to Yesinia be put on hold in favor of the Echo Park coven's master. Even though Lyse was inexperienced, he'd taken her as his new coven master because he could sense the power and strength at her core. She would be a formidable ally, so long as she stopped doubting herself and just let her instincts guide her way.

"Niamh, you said you know the Red Chapel," Lyse continued—and Niamh nodded, her face pale. Evan could see that she was clenching her jaw so hard the muscles were twitching. "If you keep your mind's eye on it, we won't get lost out there when I call up the orb."

Evan thought Lyse had gotten pretty good at navigating herself in and out of the dreamlands, but now she seemed uncertain again. And the look she shot Dev, the Echo Park coven's diviner, upped the suspicion Evan was feeling. She'd gone off to get Dev—without telling any of the others and at a super random time when everyone was so concerned about Daniela—and now she was acting funny. Only Dev knew what had happened to make Lyse so squirrely . . . and she was keeping her mouth shut about it.

They stood in a circle in Daniela's hospital room, a coven of witches that included two diviners (Dev and Niamh), two herbalists (Evan and Arrabelle), one empath, and Lyse, who, by some trick of genetics, possessed the power of all five of the disciplines of magic. They were a ragtag bunch—and as Evan looked at each weary face, he could see how bone tired they all were.

"Do you think it will work, Lyse?" Daniela asked, arms folded over her chest protectively. "Do you think that you can get all of us to the Red Chapel?"

It was amazing to see her standing there, alive and rosy cheeked. Because by all rights, she should be dead.

"I think so," Lyse said.

"I think Daniela should stand in the middle of the circle," Arrabelle said. She turned to Daniela. "You can't touch any of us—gloves or no gloves, it isn't safe. Niamh brought you back from the brink once and I'm not risking you again."

Daniela nodded.

"I'm not a delicate baby, Arrabelle. But I think you're right in this situation."

Lyse turned to Niamh and Evan. Her blue eyes looked troubled. "I know the Red Chapel is not where either of you would choose to go, but it's where Dev's girls are and we have to go get them."

"I understand," Evan said. He patted Niamh's arm. "You're okay with it?"

"No," Niamh said, "not really, but I know we have to."

"The dreamland version will be different," Arrabelle said, trying to be helpful.

"I appreciate you worrying about me," Niamh said. "But you don't have to. I can handle it."

Evan knew from experience how strong Niamh was, but his coven mate had been dealt a serious blow. The loss of her twin, Laragh, had changed her irrevocably. He knew she was putting on a brave face, but he trusted that she would say something if she didn't think she could handle it. He wished they didn't have to go back to the place where he'd been mortally wounded and Niamh had watched The Flood burn Yesinia and Honey to death. But there was nothing for it—they couldn't leave Dev's little girls to fend for themselves in an alternate universe.

"Let's do it, then," Lyse said, and nodded to let them know they should clasp hands. Everyone—except Daniela, who stood in the middle of the circle—did as she asked.

Evan found himself holding Lyse's right hand and Arrabelle's left hand. With a sigh, Lyse closed her eyes and pressed her lips together. Then she murmured: "Red Chapel."

As Lyse uttered those two small words, Evan felt his body begin to thrum with energy. He looked over at Arrabelle, whose eyes were wide as saucers, and he knew she was feeling the exact same thing.

"You're glowing," Arrabelle whispered, her eyes flicking to Evan's left hand. He followed her gaze and was surprised to discover that where his fingers entwined with Lyse's, they were glowing neon blue.

"Yours, too," he said, indicating that Arrabelle should look at her own hand.

"Wow," she said, and grinned.

They both watched as the light snaked down the line of witches, turning everyone's hands blue.

"It's working," Dev said, her face full of wonder. "Even though there are so many of us."

"Quiet," Lyse murmured, her attention fixed on some internal point. "Red Chapel, Niamh. Only there. Only *now*."

Evan was confused by this last statement. *Only now?* What did that mean? But he didn't have time to ponder the thought further because the blue orb grew out of their interconnected hands, slowly enveloping the six of them inside its magic.

"Do you feel anything, Daniela?" Arrabelle asked.

"Oh, hell, yeah," Daniela said, in awe of what was happening around her. "I'm going with you guys, no problem."

"Red Chapel," Lyse cried. *"Take us to the Red Chapel!"*

There was a loud *screech* and then the hospital bed flew up into the air, slamming against the ceiling. Dev screamed as the bed bounced off the acoustic tile and hit the side of the orb. Luckily, the orb was impenetrable and the bed did nothing to damage the swirling blue magic.

"Red Chapel!" Lyse screamed. *"Red Chapel!"*

There was another *screech*, as more furniture in the room began to take off, lifting into the air and eddying around them like the orb was the eye of a hurricane.

"Stand down, witch!" a loud voice called from the doorway.

Evan turned his head to see who was using this aggressive

command. A tall, masculine woman with short, curly blond hair stood in the doorway, the sneer on her face pulling her bland features into a hideous gargoyle-like grimace. She was holding up her arms, the sleeves of her boxy khaki pantsuit pulled back to reveal raw, red, misshapen wrists. The stink of camphor bit into Evan's nostrils and he wanted to drop Arrabelle's hand so he could pinch his nose closed against the smell.

There was something *wrong* about the woman—something seriously deranged—and he wasn't thinking this just because she'd commanded all the furniture in the room to attack them.

"Stand down, witch, before I end you!" the woman shrieked, her gray eyes wide enough that you could see the rounded whites of her eyeballs.

"The Red Chapel . . . the Red Chapel . . ." Lyse continued to chant, her voice getting louder in pitch as the ECG monitor, a heavy beige behemoth, rose in the air and pitched itself at them. A crackle of electricity shot through the sphere as it connected with the monitor.

The orb began to pulse with more energy—too much energy—because the ECG monitor was still plugged into the wall. The surge of electricity was short-circuiting Lyse's magic. The woman in the doorway began to smile as she realized what was happening, and her hands began to move with the frenzy of a conductor guiding an orchestra through Grieg's *In the Hall of the Mountain King*.

"She's going to break the circle!" Dev shouted. "Lyse, do something!"

Lyse nodded, still chanting. Evan didn't know what Dev thought Lyse was going to do other than what she was doing now. The woman in the doorway was doing something to stop them from leaving, using her powers to block their way—but maybe if all of them threw their energy behind Lyse, it would be enough to break free of the other woman's magical hold.

"The Red Chapel!" Evan began to yell, looking around at the others, using his eyes to encourage them to do the same.

Arrabelle was the first to understand what he was doing. She gave him a curt nod and began chanting. Dev and Daniela joined in next. Niamh was the last to add her voice to Lyse's spell—but the effect was instantaneous. The blue orb popped and they were free.

"Who was that?" Arrabelle asked as soon as they arrived.

They were in a part of the dreamlands that Evan and the others hadn't seen on their last trip, a flat expanse of land covered by a foot of water as far as the eye could see.

"I don't know. But whoever she was, I wanted to punch her," Daniela said, eyes blazing with anger.

Niamh raised her hand, the shy kid at the back of the classroom, waiting patiently to be called on.

"I think she knows," Evan said, pointing over at Niamh.

The others turned, silent now as they waited for Niamh to elaborate. Lyse stood with her hands on her hips, a modern-day Boadicea. Arrabelle, with her shorn head and athletic body, was Lyse's second-in-command. Daniela, small and scrappy, looked better than she had when they'd first gotten to the hospital, but her cheekbones still protruded from her elfin face and, in contrast to her brightly dyed hair, there were brown roots at the base of her scalp. With her physical softness, Dev looked maternal and easygoing, but Evan sensed a steely strength resonating inside her, undercutting that softness.

And then there was Niamh.

Evan had known Niamh and her twin, Laragh, since they were teenagers. He'd treated them both like they were his kid sisters. He knew how tough and strong Niamh was, knew she'd been battered down by this experience but that she was a survivor.

They were a ragtag bunch—but Evan was proud to be going into battle with each and every one of them.

"They came to Yesinia's house. Just knocked on the door," Niamh said.

"She was our coven master," Evan elaborated, for those, like Dev, who might not have known.

Niamh continued: "I'd gone there, to Yesinia's house, to talk to her about this tarot spread I drew that just kept repeating and repeating." She turned to Dev, who was also a diviner. "Did the cards do the same for you?"

"Yes, I got the spread, too," Dev replied. "The tarot was adamant. The spread wouldn't stop, just kept repeating. It's something blood sisters in my family had experienced for centuries . . . they tried to let me know, but I . . . didn't understand."

Evan noticed that Daniela was being particularly silent, her head down, eyes on her gloved hands. Hands that she was squeezing into double fists. Lyse had noticed Daniela's silence, too, but she wasn't being subtle about it like Evan.

"What's wrong?" Lyse asked. Daniela looked up, eyes darting back and forth as though she'd been caught doing something wrong.

"Nothing," Daniela hedged.

"I don't believe you," Lyse said. "You have this strange look on your face . . ."

Daniela sighed, and Evan was pretty sure she was trying not to get emotional. There was a telling tic in the cheek muscle just below her right eye.

"I . . ." she began, then stopped, frowning so deeply that the worry lines in her forehead came together like a triangle made of wrinkles.

"No one here blames you for anything," Arrabelle said, but Daniela just shook her head.

"After I'm done talking, that might not be true anymore," Daniela said, and swallowed hard. Once again Evan could see the emotions warring inside her.

"All you can do is tell us," Evan said. "It can't be that bad."

Daniela took a deep breath, letting it out slowly.

"I'm The Fool. The Judas. The one who sold us out."

Lyse stepped toward her but remembered the "no touching" rule before she'd gotten too close. She quickly pulled her hand back.

"What're you talking about?"

"Don't you know already?" she asked Lyse, her frustration building so that she began to pace, trying to expel some of her nervous energy. "Desmond. My father, your grandfather . . . I didn't know and I told him everything. I told him Lizbeth was the last Dream Keeper. I thought he was on our side, but he was the mole. He had my mother and Eleanora killed. He destroyed our coven and split us apart. He goaded us into doing all of this. Getting Lizbeth to bring magic back into our world . . . it's all part of The Flood's plan!"

She stopped moving, the *plosh* of displaced water stopping, too, as she stared at them.

"I screwed us all. It's my fault," she continued, punching at her hip with a balled fist, trying to punish herself with physical pain. "Lizbeth was under their spell, she was being used . . . once Pandora's box was opened, The Flood could use our powers against us. Turn humanity into a Dark Ages mob of witch-hunters—which Arrabelle says has already happened—and the battle between us and the humans would bring about World War Three—the end of days, the beginning of the apocalypse. They want to wipe us *and* humanity off the face of the Earth and start all over again. It's why they call themselves *The Flood.*"

"Jesus, how do you know all this?" Evan asked.

Daniela had a ready answer.

"When Niamh over there saved me . . . she put *them* inside me—"

Evan realized Daniela was talking about the creature from the underground bunker. *So it's moved bodies,* Evan thought. *Looking for a better host. Can't blame them. Daniela's perfect. A*

*talented empath who can not only feel emotions but influence them,
as well.*

Daniela was still talking:

"*They* were there for all of it. While they were being tortured in some underground lab, The Flood has been using
the witches' powers to jump-start their version of the end of
days. That's why they stole the evolved ones like Lyse"—she
turned to Niamh—"and your sister, Laragh. They had the
most magic inside them . . . and when they died, their energy
began to come together . . . to form the creature you put inside me."

"What would all this accomplish for The Flood?"

"They were trying to find the last Dream Keeper, the *mes-
siah*, for lack of a better word. They used the power they'd
collected from the evolved ones to make the spell . . . the one
that pushed Lizbeth to dream the final dream. The one that
would bring magic back into the world and start a war."

She pointed to Lyse.

"At first, they thought *you* were the last Dream Keeper,
but *I told them the truth. I* gave *them Lizbeth.*"

She stood frozen in the middle of the endless sea, hands
clenched at her sides, her cheeks red with humiliation. She
looked so miserable in that moment that Evan, who was about
as un-touchy-feely as they came, felt the urge to hug her. Not
that this was even an option.

No one said anything. Daniela just stood there and gritted
her teeth, her anger bubbling just under the surface—though
it was directed only at herself. She was rigid, her posture that
of a small child on the brink of having a temper tantrum.
Evan opened his mouth to say something—*anything*—that
might break the uncomfortable silence, but Lyse beat him
to it.

"You think you're the only fool here, Daniela?"

Daniela lifted her eyes, red-rimmed and shiny with unshed
tears. She stared defiantly back at Lyse.

"No. You don't get to do that—" Daniela said, fighting back her anger and grief with every syllable.

"—do what? Forgive you for being human?" Lyse asked. "For screwing shit up? For not being perfect or knowing the future? It's impossible to be anything other than what you are, Daniela. An imperfect person who makes mistakes but has a good heart and learns from their experiences. That's it. That's the best any of us can hope for."

"Stop. Please . . . just stop," Daniela said, tears in her eyes. "I can't bear it."

"*You* are being so cruel to *you*," Lyse continued, ignoring Daniela's pleas. "You would never treat any of us as poorly as you treat yourself. You would never be so cruel to me if I were the one confessing a mistake to you."

"But it's not you," Daniela cried. "It's *me*."

"And I love *you*," Lyse said. "Regardless of the fact that your trust was abused. That you were taken advantage of and used—"

"But I should've *known*," Daniela moaned as she crouched down in the water and wrapped her arms protectively around herself. *"I should've known who he was . . ."*

"You should've known that Desmond Delay was my grand-father, your father . . . and an all-around bastard?" Lyse asked. "What're you? Psychic? How could you have known any of it? Your mother and Eleanora kept the information from us."

"He never loved me . . . or my mom," Daniela sobbed. *"Never."*

Lyse got on her knees and crawled over to Daniela. When there were only a few inches between them, she smiled and said: "But I love you. Isn't that enough?"

Daniela looked up at Lyse, the tears flowing down her face like twin tributaries.

"You do?"

Lyse nodded.

"Of course, I love you. You're Daniela . . . my blood sister, my blood sibling of a sort . . . *my friend*. And if I could hug you right now, I would."

"God, we're pathetic," Daniela said, wiping at her face with the back of her arm. "Getting our asses wet in whatever the hell this place is, having an emotional moment out in public and I can't even hug you."

Evan, who was not an emotional person, found himself very moved by what he'd just seen.

"It's pretty sucky," Lyse said, grinning back at Daniela. "Now can you get up and get your wet ass in gear? We need to go find Marji and Ginny."

As Daniela and Lyse climbed out of the water, Evan and Arrabelle shared a look. But before either of them could say anything, an icy breeze cut across the water and a disembodied voice flowed around them:

"And we've come to be your guides."

The Book of The Flood

. . . and so comes the end of days. We fear this change and the upending of human society as we know it. It seems as though we have sacrificed greatly to reach this paradigm of existence, but trust in The Flood, sisters and brothers, for only The Flood will bring about the creator's true plan. Only with suffering and sacrifice will we attain true perfection. Only with the blossoming and harnessing of magic and the destruction of those who stand in our way will we reach our goal.

Though we toil humbly at the feet of the one, the true, the perfection . . . it is only through our own debasement that we will find the path. Only then, when our feet tread the way, will The Flood follow behind in our wake and a new world order will be born.

—Horatio 7:4
The Book of The Flood

Arrabelle

Arrabelle had never been happier to see a dead person in her life. When she turned her head and caught sight of Eleanora Eames, the former head of the Echo Park coven and Lyse's grandmother, she was overwhelmed by a feeling of joy so great that she wanted to cry. Arrabelle, who did not like to show emotion, welcomed the tightness in her throat. It was all a jumble inside her: tears, joy, relief. The sense of being alone in a dark wood with no source of light had lifted and she felt better. For the first time in a long time, Arrabelle knew they would make a plan. That Eleanora would take charge and make sure things ended well.

It was a naïve thought. That Eleanora could fix everything. But Arrabelle decided not to question it. Maybe the little voice in her head was right: Eleanora couldn't solve all their problems. But just having her there to help guide them made Arrabelle relax.

She recognized the giantess standing beside Eleanora from the picture on Eleanora's bookshelf. This was Hessika, the Echo Park coven's Dream Keeper before Lizbeth. Her appearance was jarring at first—you just wanted to stand there and stare at her. She was tall and imposing but with a true sweetness and joy to her face. Obviously, she'd chosen to stay behind after her death and become a Dream Walker, so she was on their side. And if Eleanora trusted her . . . then Arrabelle trusted her, too.

"Thank the Goddess," Arrabelle said, unable to stop herself from grinning with pleasure. "You're a sight for sore eyes."

Here in the dreamlands, Eleanora and Hessika looked as if they were made of flesh and blood—they couldn't manifest so strongly back in the real world—but Arrabelle still didn't want to try to touch either of them in case it wrecked the illusion.

"Hessika and I have been preparing for your arrival," Eleanora said, smiling back at Arrabelle. "But we should get moving. The girls are at the Red Chapel and as much as they are safe there with Lizbeth for now . . . soon she will not be there to protect them."

Eleanora turned to Dev.

"They've been waiting for you."

"And I've been waiting for them," Dev said, eyes shining with tears.

"So you're our maker, *ma belle?*" Hessika asked, her gaze fixed on Niamh. "You can build here, make us something to travel with?"

Niamh nodded, and until the giantess turned her attention to the young woman, Arrabelle hadn't realized how unsettled Niamh was. She was deathly pale, her thin body shaking with nerves. Arrabelle had read Niamh's journal, knew that back in their reality she and Evan had lost their whole coven at the Red Chapel. She could only imagine how terrifying it would be to go back there—even if it was only the dreamlands' version of the actual place.

"Why did you call her a maker?" Lyse asked.

Hessika gave Lyse a lazy smile.

"'Cause it's their particular energy that vibrates here in the dreamlands, dear heart," Hessika replied. "Their very existence powers this place. Shall we say—just as an analogy—that they are the dreamers who dream the dreamlands into existence? Does that make sense? It's how come they can manipulate matter here. Dream Keepers have a bit of a talent for weaving in the dreamlands, but it's impermanent. Only builders can make things that stand the test of time."

"What do you want me to make?" Niamh asked, her face still pale.

Hessika waved a long, thin arm in the air.

"I've always been partial to pontoon boats . . . but that's just because my papaw had himself a little catamaran I used to love as a child."

Arrabelle had a feeling that even on a "little catamaran" Hessika would still look regal.

"The sooner we get there the better," Dev said, looking expectantly at Niamh.

"So you want her to put a motor on it," Arrabelle asked dryly.

"Whatever gets us there sooner," Dev said, grinning back at Arrabelle.

"Let Hessika and me take care of that," Eleanora replied as Niamh took a deep breath, raised her hands in the air, palms up, and closed her eyes.

The others stood in a semicircle watching her work.

"I'm not sure I really know what a pontoon boat looks like," Niamh murmured from behind closed lids. "So I'm just gonna give you what I think it is."

There was no shock wave of magic, no loud noise to connote the arrival of something that a maker had built. It was so much simpler than that. One moment there was nothing, the next, a big, flat-bottomed behemoth floated on the water in front of them.

To Arrabelle, it was more raft than boat, its thick round

timbers lashed together with heavy twine—but there was more than enough room for all of them. It seemed buoyant even with their combined weight as they climbed aboard—although Arrabelle was pretty sure that neither Eleanora nor Hessika contributed to the weight load. There was just something about the way the two Dream Walkers moved that clued Arrabelle in. The difference was so slight, almost as if they were floating, and Arrabelle would never have noticed it if she hadn't been paying attention.

"Will it work?" Niamh asked once they'd all embarked.

"Yes," Eleanora said from her perch at the bow of the boat—she and Hessika had taken up places at the front while the others had filled in toward the stern. "Now let us handle the power."

She waved a hand and a swirl of wind encircled the makeshift boat, pushing them forward. The wind picked up speed and soon they were skimming along the surface of the water toward their final destination. Hessika and Eleanora remained standing, no matter what speed the boat was going. The rest of them had to sit down and hold on to the twine that kept the timbers in place, afraid they'd be knocked overboard by the wind buffeting the boat.

Arrabelle stayed close to Evan. She didn't need to touch him to feel the tension he held in his shoulders. The more time they spent together, the better able she was to read him. It was like she'd developed a sixth sense attuned only to him and his needs. She'd never felt this way about another person before, never cared as much about someone as she did about Evan. And as much as she wanted him, she was afraid of the vulnerable way he made her feel.

It was like balancing on a seesaw, fear and need vying for precedence in her mind.

Unable to help herself, she reached over and placed her hand on Evan's shoulder. She felt the muscles of his back go rigid under her fingers. She removed her hand, and when he didn't turn and acknowledge her in any way, the rejection she experienced was heart-wrenching.

She hadn't felt as close to him since he'd been miraculously healed by the blood sisters in the underground lab—and though she knew Evan was still guarded about his feelings, part of her worried that he'd only been open to her love because he was dying. She felt bad about judging him so harshly. He wasn't fickle and she knew he wouldn't play with her heart like that.

But still, round and round she went, her brain unable to stop trying to fit the pieces of the puzzle together. She hated being in a holding pattern. Was the worst when it came to patience. She would rather push things to a resolution, even a negative one, so long as it ended the uncertainty. She was trying really hard to not do that in this situation. She cared too much about Evan to screw things up with her impatience . . . and, besides, they were in the middle of a crisis and her attention needed to be directed elsewhere. Her brain should be focused on problem solving, not on whether Evan wanted her.

But it was hard not to reflect on that kind of stuff when you were trapped on a raft cruising down an endless sea, the sound of the wind filling your ears and making it impossible to talk. All she had were her own thoughts to occupy her. Thoughts that did nothing to ease her worry.

"It's coming," Eleanora called out over the hiss of the wind. "We need to go faster."

At first, Arrabelle didn't know what Eleanora was talking about, but a few moments later she saw it: A cloud of darkness had formed behind them, eating up the water they'd left in their wake.

"What the hell is that?" Arrabelle cried, pointing at the swirl of storm clouds that were quickly gaining on them.

"It's what animates The Flood—here the darkness is in its true form," Eleanora yelled back at her.

They'd picked up more speed, the front of the boat slamming into the cresting waves as it went faster and faster, trying to escape the oncoming storm. Now Arrabelle could see that the darkness was sucking up funnels of water into the clouds.

Too late, they realized the darkness had a plan.

"Hold on tight!" Lyse screamed as the boat went airborne. A moment later, it crashed back into the surface of the water. Only the water had become so shallow that the stern of the boat slammed into the solid ground underneath it and the raft split apart, sending everyone flying. Arrabelle felt fingers grasping at her ankle, trying to hold her back, but then her own velocity ripped her out of its grasp and she sailed away. With a *thwack*, Arrabelle's hip connected with the ground and she cried out in pain, holding on to her side.

The water was freezing, soaking into her pants and shirt, and she began to shiver uncontrollably. Her hip throbbed— she'd probably taken a layer of skin off as she hit the ground— but she gritted her teeth against the pain, rolled over, and crawled to her knees. She'd been thrown on the other side of the darkness, but instead of a maelstrom of cloud and water and wind, she found herself inside the calm.

She was in the eye of a storm.

There was no wind here and the sky had been blotted out by the black clouds swirling above her. Inside the eye, the air was heavy with water, and her lungs fought to pull oxygen from it.

"Evan!" she cried. "Lyse?!"

There was no reply. She felt her ears pop as the pressure changed, and she knew that she had passed out of the eye of the storm. All around her, there was nothing but sand. She realized that the dreamlands had changed again on her. The water was gone and a powdery red sand had taken its place.

"*Hello?!*" she screamed, the heaviness of the air blunting her cries. "*Help me!*"

After a while, she gave up calling for help and began to

wander, looking for a way out of the darkness. But it was like being trapped in smoke. The gray smog made it hard to see very far in any direction. And the more she walked, the less confident she was that she wasn't going in the wrong direction.

She must've walked for hours, anger giving way to frustration and then frustration giving way to fear. She was in a strange place and she had no idea how to get back to her own reality. She gave up on finding the rest of her coven and began to try to call up one of those orbs Lyse used to transport them in and out of the dreamlands. She went around and around, working on figuring out a way to use magic to get herself out of the darkness.

As an herbalist, she knew how to manipulate plants to make tinctures and poultices and powders . . . what she *didn't* know how to do was take those skills and use them to save herself.

It didn't take long for her to give up and start walking again. The red sand began to change, replaced, instead, by bright white rocks in various shapes and sizes. It only took stepping on one of the "rocks" to discover that it was made of a soft and fluffy material—and not a rock, at all. She knelt down and picked up one of the smaller "rocks" and held it up in the palm of her hand.

"What are you?" she asked it, lifting it to her nose and sniffing. It smelled like steamed sweet rice, a heady sugary scent that made her stomach growl.

She raised an eyebrow, not really believing that the dreamlands were trying to feed her. She pinched off a section of the "rock" and put it in her mouth. It tasted heavenly. Starving, she stuffed the rest of the "rock" in her mouth and barely chewed, the fluffy rice ball melting as she swallowed.

She knew it was a mistake the moment it hit her belly, the ache she felt there spiraling out to the rest of her body. She clutched her stomach and groaned, but she was in such pain that she was hardly conscious of doing it. All she could see was the darkness. All she could feel was the evil in her stomach slowly dissolving her from the inside out. Black dots appeared in her peripheral vision, and a deep ache of pain filled her every cell. It took over her senses and leached all the life from her veins. She fell forward, her body sprawled across the ground, smooshing the "rocks" beneath her.

If she'd been aware, she would've quickly understood her mistake. She would've realized the "rocks" were actually mushrooms, and, as an herbalist, she would've kicked herself for touching the poisonous things to begin with, let alone eating them. It was the stupidest of mistakes.

The mushrooms began to expand and grow, surrounding and covering Arrabelle until she disappeared underneath them. Unconsciousness settled over her and, for all intents and purposes, she appeared to be dead and buried . . . even though she was not.

She was merely sleeping the sleep of the dreamlands.

Lizbeth

L izbeth stood by the edge of a lake filled with grape Nehi (the only soft drink she liked), watching as three glowing suns, the size and color of a trio of blood oranges, began to set on the eastern horizon. Three suns and a grape soda lake . . . ? Just another indicator of how bizarre things were in the dreamlands. It was like stepping into a world where the only limitations were your imagination.

The wind was picking up, blowing bits of her russet hair into her face. She sighed as she pushed an errant strand from her eyes. She wished she had a pair of scissors so she could just cut the whole mess of it off. She felt like she needed a change, and lopping her long hair would be an easy way to accomplish it. Finally, she just reached up and grasped the long strands of hair, tying them in a knot at the back of her neck.

"I'm going to be trite, but a penny for your thoughts?"

Lizbeth turned to find Thomas standing behind her, gazing out at the effervescent purple water. He was wearing a long woven caftan that came to his ankles, the fabric thick and homespun, so that he resembled a wandering mendicant monk. He didn't look at her as he spoke, just kept his face to the water, eyes fixed on something in the far distance.

"If not a penny, then a silver dollar."

He snapped his fingers and a small silver coin appeared in his palm—which he then held out for her to see.

"Magic tricks don't impress me," she said, her voice even.

She didn't like Thomas, had real trouble reconciling his familial relationship to Tem—they were like night and day, as far as Lizbeth was concerned—and yet she sensed there was something important he needed to say to her, so she tried to keep her dislike in check.

"There are magic tricks anyone can learn," he said, his gaze still focused far out in the distance. "And then there is the magic that a creature like you is born with, and *this* must be cultivated for a higher purpose."

"What? So I can be like you?" She stared at him, willing him to turn and look her way—to tell her this bit about a "higher purpose" directly to her face.

Reading her mind, he pivoted so his eyes locked on her own. Then he smiled, baring his canines, and immediately she wished she could travel back in time and make a different choice. Not to goad him, but to walk away from the conversation before he looked her way. Because now she was trapped, the full power of his gaze pinning her to the spot where she stood as it burrowed into her, tunneling through skin and muscle, aiming for her heart.

"Yes, so you can be like me . . . and Temistocles. You may only be a half-caste, but that still means part of you is like us. And because of that, you will be called up to defend the innocent against the darkness."

With a concerted effort, Lizbeth was able to ratchet her eyes away from the granite planes of his face. She dropped her gaze to her feet, digging into the sandy shoreline and teasing out a clump of dirty brown mud with her toes. The purple lake and the three suns hadn't been there when she and Tem had carried the girls into the Red Chapel. They had only appeared when she'd come outside to think.

"I'm already doing what you say," she murmured, her chin dipped toward the ground. "Isn't that what combating The Flood is? Fighting the darkness?"

"You're afraid to look at me," Thomas said, and she shrugged.

"It's like looking into the sun."

He laughed. The first uncalculated sound she'd heard out of his mouth. She looked up and found his countenance much changed. Now there was a welcoming air about him, as if he'd flipped a switch and changed his entire attitude.

"You and your blood sisters think you know me, but I know none of you have ever understood a whit about me. Not really. I loved Devandra's mother, Melisande. And I would have made her mine if I hadn't been called back to take my place, to fight the darkness in my own world."

"Not The Flood?" Lizbeth asked, curious now.

He shrugged.

"You have The Flood. For us it was called *the darkness*. But though it goes by many names, it is always the same . . . a sickness that slowly overtakes a world and destroys it."

"Why?" Lizbeth asked.

"If I knew the answer to that, well, I don't think we'd be staring at your soda lake and having this conversation."

Lizbeth stared back at him.

"Wait? Are you saying this lake is really and truly filled with my favorite soda?"

She was shocked. She'd just assumed the lake had been created to *look* like grape Nehi. She'd never in a million years have dreamed that it *actually* was made of the stuff.

"Why not?" Thomas asked.

Lizbeth didn't have an answer for him, instead, she murmured under her breath: "This place is so weird."

Amber Benson

"This is the crossroads of *everywhere*, the hub upon which all universes spin. Of course it's going to be 'weird.'"

He has a point, Lizbeth thought, not *wanting* to like Thomas, but starting to . . . at least a little bit.

"You said you're a magician and you want to train me. But so I can do what?"

"Stop The Flood in your world. Do that and it affects all the rest of the universes, as well."

"Why are we so important?" Lyse asked.

"Because your Earth expelled magic. No other universe was ever able to do so. If you can excommunicate magic . . . you can do the same to the darkness."

Lyse shook her head.

"No, that's not right. There was still magic there."

"It was only the residual of what once was," Thomas said, and sighed. "It's why The Flood had to use you to bring magic back fully. What none of you modern witches realize is that the blood sisters were the ones who exiled magic from your world. And then they used the residual magic that was left to keep magic out."

"I don't believe you," Lizbeth said.

"The rituals you did . . . they weren't to keep the balance," he said. "They were to keep magic at bay. Magic is what almost destroyed them. Magic is why they were hunted and burned. Magic was the great divider between the blood sisters and normal human beings."

Lizbeth didn't know what to say . . . or what to believe.

"Yes," he said. "I can see the questions on your face. You don't believe me. Though part of you knows that I'm right. By the way, I'm not reading your mind—though I could if I wanted to."

"Well, don't," she said, glaring at him.

He raised his arms, palms out in supplication.

"Only with your permission. Though I don't think Temistocles asked for your permission, did he?"

She glared at him.

"That was different. I couldn't speak. It was how we were able to communicate."

Thomas raised an eyebrow.

"He could easily have given you a voice. That is within his power."

She hated how he was trying to sow seeds of discord between her and his brother . . . and she hated how it was working. She could hear the doubt in her own head. The cynical voice questioning Tem's motives, pulling on this single thread until, if she didn't get a handle on it, the whole sweater would come undone.

"No, I'm not gonna let you do this!" she said, pushing back with her mind and shoving the thoughts away.

He smiled, pleased—and it dawned on Lizbeth he was provoking her for a reason.

"First lesson. Don't let anyone in your head. Not me, not even Temistocles. Not *anyone*."

She nodded, realizing with a start that her training had already begun.

"What if I don't want this?" she asked.

"Destiny is destiny."

His tone was light, but the meaning was clear: *You don't get a say in this, Dream Keeper.*

The slam of a door undercut the moment. Lizbeth turned to see Ginny and Marji running toward her. She'd left them dreaming in the Red Chapel, but Tem must've woken them up. They were bright-eyed and full of energy, speeding down the path that led to the lake.

"Girls?" Lizbeth called.

"We talked to Mama and Daddy," Ginny cried as she flung herself at Lizbeth's waist. "On the phone! There's a lake behind you. Why is there a lake?"

The little girl's mouth was moving a mile a minute.

"Slow down and tell me all that again," Lizbeth said, stroking Ginny's hair. The girl was clinging to her like a little mollusk, her stick-thin arms stronger than Lizbeth could've imagined.

"There's a phone in the Red Chapel," Marji said, breathless from running. "And it started ringing and Ginny answered it. It was Mama and Daddy."

The girls were ecstatic from the effects of one phone call. Lizbeth could imagine the sheer joy they'd experience once they'd been reunited with their parents.

"LB," Marji continued as she sat down in the sand and looked up at Lizbeth. "Are we going home soon?"

Lizbeth wasn't sure what kind of home the girls would be going back to, but she supposed that wherever Freddy and Dev were, it would be home enough.

"I think so, lovey," Thomas said, before Lizbeth could answer.

The girls looked back at him and he smiled. Neither of them seemed afraid of the man, and that made Lizbeth feel better about him.

"I miss home," Ginny said, turning back to Lizbeth.

"Soon, Ginny," Lizbeth said, letting the girl tuck in under her arm. "Did your mom and dad ask you to tell me anything?"

Marji nodded her head with vigor.

"They said to take care of us and keep us safe."

Nothing could've crushed Lizbeth's heart more—

"That I can do," Lizbeth said, pulling them both to her and hugging them tight. She felt responsible for Dev's daughters, and she vowed right then and there to do everything in her power to keep them as safe and sound as possible.

"We need to get the girls away from here—"

Lizbeth was surprised to hear fear in Tem's voice as he ran up the path toward them. His eyes were on Thomas as he spoke, but he came right to Lizbeth and the girls, his hand grasping Lizbeth's shoulder.

"What's happening?" Lizbeth asked, trying to keep her voice neutral so she wouldn't scare Marji and Ginny.

"*It's* coming," Marji said, matter-of-factly.

"What're you talking about?" Lizbeth asked her.

Marji shivered.

"The bad thing. It wants you, LB. And it wants me and Ginny, too," she said. "If it can get us, it will."

Tem gripped Lizbeth's shoulder harder and began leading her away.

"We won't let it get you," Tem said, still looking at Thomas.

Thomas nodded.

"No, that's not going to happen. But I don't think going back to the Red Chapel will protect us."

"All right," Tem said.

"At least, not the Red Chapel here in the dreamlands," Thomas added.

"You think it's safer in the real world?" Lizbeth asked.

Thomas frowned, surveying the landscape ahead of them.

"Dealing with The Flood, in some ways, is easier than with the darkness here."

"Then let's go," Tem said.

"But Mama's coming," Marji said. "We can't go. Mama's here. I can feel her."

Tem and Thomas exchanged a look.

"You can feel her?" Thomas asked Marji—but it was Ginny who spoke up.

"Marji feels stuff sometimes, and if she says Mama's here she means it."

Thomas patted the small girl's hair.

"You're a good sister, Ginny," he said, then turned to Marji. "And you're lucky to have her and she, you. Stay together always. No matter what happens. Stay close to each other."

Ginny nodded and reached out to take Marji's hand.

Thomas returned his attention to Tem and Lizbeth.

"I wanted to keep the girls here because I felt like it was safer, but I was wrong. Tem, you feel it coming and so does Marji. I trust the two of you and your instincts," he said. "Do you feel Devandra here in the dreamlands?"

Tem closed his eyes. To Lizbeth, it looked like he was dreaming, his eyeballs flicking back and forth underneath his eyelids—but then he opened them and shook his head.

"I feel something, but it's being blocked by the darkness. It doesn't want me to know," he said. "So I assume that means *someone* is here to collect the girls."

"Then we stay and wait as long as we can," Thomas said. "And when we can't stay any longer, we go.

The girls stared at Thomas with round, wide eyes. They seemed to understand that he was giving Dev, and anyone else with her, a chance to find them.

"Eleanora and Hessika will know what's happening," Lizbeth said to Tem. "Can you reach them?"

Tem shook his head.

"It's as if I'm reaching out through murky psychic waters, pet," he said, giving her a sad smile. "The darkness is close and it's insistent about keeping us out of the loop."

"Why has it taken so long for it to find us?" Lizbeth asked, uncertain about the wisdom of staying put.

Tem looked at Thomas.

"There was witch blood spilled here at the Red Chapel in the recent past, and the energy released by the slaying can be drawn upon to cast a protection spell—"

"Which is what Thomas did as soon as he arrived with Marji and Ginny," Tem finished for his brother.

"But we knew it would only last for so long," Thomas said. "And now the time has come to move on."

"Thomas really did make a spell, LB," Ginny said. "It was magic!"

Thomas grinned down at Ginny.

"The girls helped me," he said. "They said a magic spell while I worked."

"Moon shadow fall on me, protect all the important things you see," Ginny said, emphasizing the rhyming quality of the spell. "We had to say it a lot, LB."

"I bet you did," Lizbeth said, then mouthed a *Thank you* to Thomas. Obviously, he'd given the girls a task to take their minds off all of the awful things that had happened to them.

"It was an important part of the spell," Thomas said, as if to dispel the thought he'd given the girls a mindless job to do. "Less about the words and more about the intent, correct, Marjoram?"

"Yes, sir," she replied, smiling shyly back at him.

"Shall we play a game while we wait?" Tem asked, guiding Lizbeth and the girls away from the lake. "I bet if we wish very hard, we might be able to find a lovely yellow bag of Bananagrams somewhere inside the Red Chapel."

Lizbeth let him lead them away, but not before she caught the look of intense worry on Thomas's face. That look sealed her trust . . . and terrified her to the bone.

Lizbeth enjoyed watching Tem with Marji and Ginny as he occupied them with Bananagrams. He didn't *let* the girls win, per se, but it was obvious after the first round, when he was losing by a wide margin, that his concentration wasn't fully on the game at hand. He looked up at Lizbeth a few times from his perch at the kitchen island and gave her a wink, letting her know that he knew she was watching.

It was hard for her not to stare at him. They had this strange, intimate connection—had had it from the very moment they'd met—and even though Lizbeth knew that he was not truly available to her, she couldn't help wishing that he were alive again. It wasn't that she wanted to be his girlfriend, or anything so normal . . . she just wanted him to be a part of her life. And if he was trapped here in the dreamlands, she wasn't sure how their continued friendship would be possible. She guessed she could visit him here whenever she wanted, but it just wasn't the same. Just didn't feel right.

"Let Temistocles entertain them and we finish our conversation," Thomas said as he came to sit on the couch beside Lizbeth.

"Okay," she said—the first time she'd had a reasonably pleasant interaction with him.

He noticed and his whole demeanor changed. He seemed to relax, his shoulders lowering and his eyes brightening. Lizbeth realized he'd been waiting a long time for her to give him permission to be himself.

"Yes, it's been difficult," he said, then held up his hand, "and, no, I wasn't reading your mind. It's clear what you were thinking."

"What happened to you?" she asked, beginning to see that there were more similarities between Thomas and Tem than she'd been willing to acknowledge.

"We were cocky, Tem and me. We thought we could control the darkness, but we were naïve. The darkness cannot be controlled . . . only kept at bay," he said, a catch in his voice as he spoke. "We were caught and Tem was spelled out of existence, but I was given to your world, to The Flood, so my powers might be used against the woman I loved . . . and her family."

Lizbeth's heart broke for him. She couldn't imagine what that would be like—to be used as a tool to destroy the person you loved. It was a terrifying proposition.

"Time runs differently in our universe than in yours," he continued. "When I left Devandra's mother, she was a young woman . . . and I truly did think I'd find a way to get back to her. But sadly, time does not run backward anymore and the window passed. So shocking to see the one you loved grow old without you. And you only having left her days before. It's chilling."

"Will that happen to us here?" Lizbeth asked, and Thomas shook his head.

"The difference in time between your world and the dreamlands is very slight. That cannot be said for our world—"

His eyes flicked over to Tem, who was trying to convince the girls that *stegalump* was a word. To his pretend consternation, Marji and Ginny were having none of it.

"—but that's neither here nor there. Suffice it to say, I was used against my will to do damage and it was only the combined effort of your coven that broke the spell I was under. Of course, I don't expect any of you to believe me."

He said the last part with a yawning sadness that made Lizbeth feel awful for treating him badly.

"You brought the girls here. You saved them."

He shrugged.

"It was all I could do. I didn't know the house had been compromised until it was too late."

"By what?" Lizbeth wasn't sure she understood what he was talking about.

"The girls were given a magical object. A stone. They didn't know what it was or what it would do, but its presence made all the work we'd done less than worthless—it made our spells *dangerous*. It borrowed the energy we'd expended and turned it back on us," he finished.

Sitting at the kitchen island, the girls were giving Tem a hard time, but he was taking it like a champ. He was good with them, treating them not like children, but like human beings that had opinions and thoughts and needs of their own.

"You say we can't stop it, but we can keep it at bay?" Lizbeth asked. "How do we do that?"

"We train you so that you can take Tem's place."

Lizbeth shook her head and sat up straighter on the clean, white couch.

"His place?" She felt ridiculous asking so many questions, but she really didn't know.

"We are—were—the guardians between the dreamlands and your world. Our job was to make sure the darkness didn't slip past us and leak fully into your world like it did into ours and countless others . . ."

"But what about when the blood sisters banished the magic. Didn't that protect us?"

Thomas weighed the question.

"When magic disappeared from your world . . . it *did* keep the darkness away. For a while."

"But not forever. It found a way in," Lizbeth offered.

Thomas agreed. "Yes, it found a way in . . . through us . . . our negligence. We should've been on guard, but we were on Earth, enjoying the fruits of your world and not minding what we should've been minding. And just as bad, we should've found you and looked after you."

"Because I'm the last Dream Keeper?" Lizbeth asked, and Thomas nodded. "Hessika knew The Flood was coming and that I was part of it. She made sure the Echo Park coven took me in and protected me. So that worked out okay."

"Yes, they did well by you," Thomas said. "But now it is my and Tem's turn to look after you. You belong with us."

"And what will happen to The Flood?" she asked.

"The Flood is just the earthly manifestation of the darkness. The mask it wears, if you will. When we banish the darkness, The Flood will cease to have power."

Lizbeth thought she was beginning to piece it all together.

"And how do you banish the darkness? Can you keep it just here in the dreamlands . . . ?"

"That would be nice," Thomas said. "Though I'm not sure it's even possible now."

Lizbeth disagreed. This was exactly what Hessika and the other Dream Keepers had foreseen. That The Flood would come and only a handful of blood sisters would be able to stem the tide. She and *her* witches from the Echo Park coven. If anyone had a chance of fixing things, it would be them. Lizbeth didn't argue with him. She would let Thomas and Tem train her . . . but only *after* she and her coven mates had tried their hand at stopping The Flood.

"What happens if we fail and The Flood wins?"

"The darkness will own your world and it will become like ours."

Lizbeth hadn't heard Tem speak much of his world, but she sensed Thomas wanted to talk about it even less.

"What does that mean?"

Thomas looked at his hands, his fingers clasped so tight they were white and bloodless.

"Our world is a wasteland, Lizbeth, and we are part of only a handful of our kind left. It's why we need you. You have enough of our blood to help us."

She didn't push him to illuminate.

"I'll make a deal with you," she said, finding herself speaking before she'd really thought the idea through. "So long as you help us kick The Flood's ass, I'll give you my word that I'll do whatever you ask of me after."

"Just like that? No further negotiation?"

She shook her head.

"That's it. No further negotiation."

"Well, we'd already planned to help in any and all ways that we can—"

Lizbeth laughed.

"Then it's a deal."

They shook hands.

"This may all be for naught," Thomas said, suddenly serious.

Lizbeth smiled at him.

"Then we go out trying."

Daniela

At first, Daniela thought they were all doomed. The boat had crashed nose first into the shallow water, timbers breaking apart, twine unlashing, but somehow Niamh had managed to hold it all together, and those still left clinging to the wooden pieces had been saved.

Daniela had seen Arrabelle go flying. She'd tried to grab hold of her coven mate, but she'd slipped out of Daniela's grasp and disappeared into the darkness—though not before Daniela's touch had brought her directly into Arrabelle's mind. There she'd been exposed to the kind of personal information that no one needs or wants to know about their closest friends. It was a different experience than she'd ever had before. Within two seconds of touching her friend's skin, the essence of Arrabelle had been downloaded into Daniela's mind.

She felt like a magnet, collecting psychic energy, and she knew it had everything to do with the creature Niamh had put inside her. It was what had wrought this change in her power, and the strangest part was she seemed to suffer no ill effects from the experience. It was bizarre to think that before her deathbed revival, if she'd touched Arrabelle, she would've been destroyed for days. All her life, her brain had been jacked up royally every time she'd used her powers . . . but now she felt free, no more fear that her power would kill her because the worst had already happened: It kind of *had*.

"We need to go back!" Daniela screamed—eyes hungrily scanning the landscape for any sign of Arrabelle.

The others were fine. Dev sat hunched in the corner with Lyse, eyes wild with terror. Evan was turned around so he could face the back of the boat and look out for Arrabelle, too. Niamh just sat in the middle of the boat looking shell-shocked.

"Do you see her?" Lyse called back to Arrabelle and Evan.

Daniela wished the answer were different: "No!"

The darkness was beginning to fade behind them, and with it went any hope of finding Arrabelle. No matter how hard Daniela looked, there was zero sign of her friend.

"We have to stop and go back," Evan yelled to Niamh, though she wasn't in charge of their progress—Eleanora and Hessika were the ones who needed to make the wind turn them around.

"She's gone," Eleanora said, but their progress did slow, the boat not shaking so badly now that it was buffeted by less wind. "There's no going back."

"We can't leave her," Evan said, hands waving in emphasis. "She would never leave any of us!"

Eleanora listened to his outburst, but then she firmly held her ground.

"It took her. Don't you see that?" she said, voice full of anger. "She's not here to be found. I should've known it would come to this . . . picking us off one by one, the bastards."

Daniela knew in her heart that Eleanora was right. The darkness was gone. No sign left to show it had ever been there, at all. Only miles and miles of placid, water-covered land stretching out behind them.

Daniela felt heartsick, but at least knowing that a part of Arrabelle had become one with the creature inside her was a kind of consolation. Crazy to think she had access to layer upon layer of Arrabelle's thoughts and memories. She pushed it all away, not quite feeling right about invading her friend's privacy. She decided she would keep that door locked for now.

"I'm not leaving her back there," Evan said, ignoring Eleanora. "Stop this thing."

Hessika waved her hand and the wind dropped away.

"It's a waste of time," Eleanora said, but Evan shook his head.

"You do what you have to do, but I'm going back to find her."

The boat had slowed enough for Evan to get off easily. He clambered over the side, his feet sinking into the silt beneath the waterline.

"Niamh?" he asked, but she didn't move.

"I'm sorry. I feel like I need to go with them," she said.

He looked disappointed, but he didn't get angry with her.

"I guess you have to do what you have to do," he said, and then, without ceremony, he began heading back the way they'd come.

They watched him trudge through the murky, ankle-high water, his form getting smaller and smaller the farther away from them he got. No one said anything, just watched him slowly disappear as he headed off into the unknown.

"Will he be okay?" Dev asked.

There was no answer.

The irony was they only traveled for another half hour before they reached the Red Chapel. To have lost both Arrabelle and Evan when they'd been so close was ridiculous. And Daniela still wasn't sure it was the right decision to let Evan go. Not that she had any idea what they could've done to make him stay. He'd been determined to go back and look for Arrabelle, and Daniela couldn't fault him for it. She knew it was a futile gesture. Whatever the darkness was, it had swallowed Arrabelle whole and spirited her far away. If she'd thought there was any hope of finding Arrabelle, she'd have joined Evan—but her gut instinct told her his search would bear no fruit.

The loss of Arrabelle had affected them all. Lyse had remained stoically quiet, but Niamh had curled up into a ball in the middle of the boat and refused to talk to Dev when she'd made overtures of conversation. Daniela knew part of it was feeling guilty she hadn't gone with Evan. He was the last remaining tie to her old life, and he'd been her coven mate for much longer than she'd known any of the Echo Park blood sisters. And yet she'd thrown her lot in with them without question.

Eleanora was harder to read. Death, and the process of becoming a Dream Walker, had changed her friend. The flinty granite of Eleanora's personality had fully asserted itself, killing any softness left inside her. She wasn't cold or mean in any way; there was just nothing left for Daniela to catch hold of . . . any empathic ability to connect to her old friend had been severed.

While Daniela watched, the landscape changed, the water drying up and becoming solid ground again. This didn't seem to deter the boat; it just kept floating along as if it were still on a liquid surface.

"Should we walk?" Daniela asked, but Eleanora shook her head.

She decided that this was Eleanora's ship and she, Daniela, was merely one of its passengers. After that, she'd kept her mouth shut. She would just have to wait and see how it all developed. She knew she was ready to leave the dreamlands behind and return to their world. There were a whole bunch of idiots back there who needed their asses kicked . . . and she was the one who was going to do it.

"That can't be it," Lyse said, and Daniela followed her gaze out toward the horizon.

She had to agree with Lyse . . . there was no way that squat wooden building ahead of them could be the Red Chapel.

"Remember, the dreamlands can be misleading," Eleanora said. "Things aren't always as they seem."

The Red Chapel truly was nothing to look at it. Merely a small wooden square on a patch of green grass, a sprawling purple lake stretching out behind it. Daniela didn't know what she'd expected, but it was not this. Maybe something grandiose to match the larger-than-life name? Instead, she found herself underwhelmed.

Niamh, on the other hand, had relaxed visibly when she'd caught sight of the place. Whatever she'd been expecting to see, it was obviously not this small wooden box.

Hessika slowed their speed as they got closer. Daniela felt Dev's nervousness grow as they neared the building, her sense of excitement building, too.

"They're inside," she said to Daniela, her voice shaking. "I can't believe I'm going to see them again."

Daniela patted Dev's shoulder, the leather fabric of her gloves separating her touch from Dev's skin—but even this small gesture alarmed Dev.

"Are you sure you should be doing that?" Dev asked, a spike of fear punctuating her words.

"Can I tell you a secret?" Daniela whispered, putting her lips as close to Dev's ear as she dared. "I think it's done. I think I don't have to use the gloves anymore."

Dev looked startled.

"Wait. You're kidding! How is that even possible?"

"It's the creature inside me . . . I think it protects me. I think it consumes the energy I take in when I touch someone. I think it's using me," Daniela continued, keeping her voice low for Dev's ears only. "But I'm using it, too."

Dev shook her head, her focus wholly on Daniela.

"Are you going to tell the others?" she asked.

"Soon," Daniela said. "Let's get the girls first and I'll do a little testing. See if I'm right about this."

"Just be careful," Dev said, seemingly satisfied by Daniela's answer. "We've already lost Arrabelle and Evan. We can't lose you, too."

Daniela didn't have the heart to tell Dev that she didn't care what happened to herself anymore. If she died, it didn't really matter. She just wanted to destroy Desmond Delay and The Flood, and then she could cease to exist forever and that would be fine by her.

Thankfully, their talk was cut short when the boat finally came to a stop. They touched down on the edge of the grass and as soon as they'd all disembarked, the boat began to fall apart, leaving a mess of timber and twine behind.

Dev, followed by Eleanora, went straight to the front door and pushed her way in. She was eager to see the girls.

"That was well done, *ma belle*," Hessika said to Niamh.

"I'm so tired," Niamh said. "I feel like I could sleep for ages—"

She didn't finish her thought because her eyes rolled up into her head and she crumpled forward. Daniela was closest to her and, without thinking, she reached out and caught Niamh around the waist before she could hit the ground.

"Daniela! No!" Lyse cried, racing toward them.

"It's okay," Daniela said, as she set the girl down in the grass, careful to keep the back of her head from hitting the ground. "I think it's all right now."

Lyse knelt down in the grass beside her. Hessika joined them, but at remove.

"Are you sure?" she asked, concern rife in her blue eyes.

"It was Niamh," Daniela said. "What she did when she healed me? The creature she put inside me . . . it protects me."

Lyse was thunderstruck by this revelation.

"No . . . that's amazing . . . and wonderfully *insane*."

Daniela didn't tell Lyse the worrying part. The creature

wanted something from her and she didn't know what. She was sure it would let her know its demands soon, but for now it was protecting her from empathic brain circuitry overload and she was thankful for that.

"It just means I don't need these anymore," Daniela said, and she removed the gloves from her hands and set them on the ground. "It's pretty damn freeing."

Niamh took that moment to open her eyes. She looked first at Hessika, who nodded, and then she turned her gaze to Daniela.

"So sorry," she murmured, and sat up. She was groggy and wiped out, shaky from all the emotional and physical exertion of getting them to the Red Chapel.

"Just sit there for a moment," Daniela said to her. "You've worn yourself out."

Niamh couldn't argue with that. Instead, she took Daniela's advice and pulled her knees to her chest, resting her head on her arms. She closed her eyes and rocked back and forth, disappearing into her own head.

"Let her be," Daniela said, smiling over at Lyse—and Daniela was happy to realize her little crush on Lyse had dissipated, replaced now by familial love.

"Okay," Lyse said, smiling back at Daniela. "And I'm going to hold on to these guys just in case."

She picked up the leather gloves, folded them, and stuck them in her back pocket.

"You don't have to do that," Daniela said, but Lyse wouldn't argue with her, just stood up and offered Daniela her hand.

"Take it," she said—and for the first time, the two women touched. It was a strange sensation, like when you touched your own face and were surprised by the softness of the skin covering your cheek. There was an immediate familiarity and the awareness that Lyse was a part of who she was . . . the same blood flowed in her veins that flowed in Daniela's own.

"I always wanted a sister."

"Me, too," Lyse said. "Funny how you sometimes get what

you wish for, but it comes at you in the strangest of packages and long after you'd forgotten you'd ever asked for it."

Daniela laughed. It was true. They weren't really sisters, not by birth, but they were sisters in all the ways that counted. Even if it had taken over two decades for them to connect.

"I'm better now," Niamh said, looking up at them. "Can we go inside?"

"Of course," Lyse said, helping Niamh climb to her feet.

The three of them headed to the front door of the wooden building, Hessika following behind them, but Daniela noticed that the Dream Walker was distracted. She kept glancing back, eyes narrowed, a thoughtful expression on her face.

"Don't worry," Hessika said to Daniela as the others crossed the threshold and disappeared inside. "It's coming, but not as quick as it could be. But don't let them dawdle too long. Only so much a lady can do to distract."

"You're not coming in?" Daniela asked.

Hessika shook her head.

"My time is near," she said, her Southern drawl more noticeable than before. "Eleanora will look after you all from here on in, *ma belle*. But I'll be thinking of you."

There was an ominous sound to Hessika's words that Daniela didn't like.

"You're speaking around your meaning," she said, frowning at Hessika as the larger woman began to meander away from the door.

"No riddles, dear heart. Only what is supposed to be. It's long past my time."

"I—" Daniela began, starting to become alarmed by their conversation. But Hessika waved her away.

"Now you go on in before the door closes on you," Hessika said, gesturing at the entrance to the Red Chapel. "It'll be too late then for even me to help you if that happens."

Daniela didn't like being told what to do, but something in Hessika's tone frightened her.

"Come in with me," she implored, but Hessika shook her head.

"Keep them safe inside," Hessika said, smiling sadly. "Keep the ones you love close to your heart, *ma belle*. What's written can be unwritten. Don't forget. Promise me that."

Daniela didn't understand, but she could see it was important for Hessika to hear her say it.

"I promise."

The sadness left the giantess then, and she giggled like a little girl.

"What a pleasure to know you. To know you all."

She blew Daniela a kiss, and then she began to slowly walk away from the Red Chapel, taking her time as she went, her long body swaying with every step. Daniela stood in the doorway for a few moments, watching her go. Then she turned around and went inside, the door gently closing behind her.

As soon as she was inside, she knew she'd made a grave mistake. She whirled back around, not wanting to leave Hessika alone outside—but what she found instead of a door . . . was a blank white wall.

Hessika

Hessika had known her time in the dreamlands would not last forever. Nor would she want it to—a lady got tired, wanted to ease her weary bones, take the weight of responsibility she'd been carrying and set it down for a while. It had been a long road, full of waiting . . . and her patience was just about done.

She knew the dreamlands well enough now that there were no worries. The young ones would not find their way out to see her go. The dreamlands would protect them from that sight. Only Eleanora . . . and Temistocles . . . would know what she was intending. The three of them, all Dream Walkers, drew their energy from this place, and thus they were in tune with everything that happened here. Eleanora and Temistocles would feel her go, and only *they* would understand her reasoning.

The darkness was coming. She still called it *The Flood* in her head because the phrase was so ingrained after all these years. It had stolen one of them and it wanted the rest. If

Hessika could slow it down by sacrificing herself . . . give the others a little time to get away . . . she would.

And so she stayed outside. Stood her ground and waited, the last time she would be able to give her help to the ones she loved.

They said your life flashed before your eyes when you died—but that hadn't happened to Hessika. She wondered if it was because she'd already passed out of the human realm once before. When her time to die had come the first time, she'd made the choice to stay a Dream Walker instead of ascending to the next plane. She just hadn't realized that this meant her time would be mostly spent in the dreamlands . . . and not on Earth.

And when she *did* go back to Echo Park, she could only affect small things, her changes so minimal that no one really seemed to notice them. The dreamlands were more malleable, but she found herself getting bored when she stayed there . . . and so she'd waited, counting the days until the last Dream Keeper was born. Only then would Hessika not be alone.

Decades had come and gone. There had been no one. Sometimes she'd see other Dream Walkers, but they were few and far between—and they were stuck in their own loop, barely even acknowledging her existence.

And then, one day, *she* came.

She was just a little thing, frightened and lonely. She'd lost her mother, the trauma so great it had caused her powers to manifest early, and so she'd come to Hessika long before she was ready. She'd already stopped talking by then and so they communicated in other ways. But Hessika remembered her small face with fondness—the large eyes full of wonder at the strange new world the little girl had stumbled upon in her dreams.

Hessika was Lizbeth's late-night companion, and, as such, she thought she'd done a decent job of balancing the cruelty of the mental facility where Lizbeth lived. She knew the girl suffered terribly during her waking hours, and so she tried to make their time together in the dreamlands light and fun.

And, finally, when the time was right and her brother, Weir, was old enough that he could help her, Hessika had entered his dreams and encouraged him to go and save his baby sister from her untenable prison. It hadn't been a hard sell. Even without her nudging, he'd already been thinking in that direction. But Hessika's visits had given him the confidence to take the leap and do it. After the first dream, he'd immediately gone and retained a lawyer.

Not that Weir had remembered their dream meetings. She'd made sure they stayed buried deep in his subconscious.

She'd done what she could for the girl. She'd loved her as best she could—Hessika had always been a good mother hen, keeping a warm nest ready for the damaged little chicks that invariably found their way to her—but the time had come to let Lizbeth go. To free her so she could accept her fate.

Lizbeth had no idea that she'd just begun to walk her path. That dreaming the last dream and bringing magic back to their world . . . well, it was just the beginning. She would find her way, Hessika was sure of it.

But so that Lizbeth and the others might continue their journey, Hessika knew she must end her time here. She must give up "the self," the identity known as *Hessika*, under which she'd labored for so long.

The *crack* of thunder that sounded in the distance made her realize the time for rumination was over. She lifted her hand to shade her eyes, saw the darkness building as it drew toward her. She knew she couldn't let it get her too easily. She had to put up a fight, had to make it work to claim her.

She wanted a change of venue—she'd never been a fan of Lizbeth's desert landscapes—and so she began to call up memories from her own childhood. The land of her people was rich with greenery, lush with waterways and tall grasses. As a small child, she'd wandered through the woods, the treetops closing in all around her, letting her pretend she was the only human being in the whole of the world.

She could hear the gurgle of the creek that ran behind her parents' property, smell the moldering woodland so full of decaying things that would be used to feed the next generation of plants and animals. She closed her eyes, letting the air heat up around her, sweat breaking out on her lip and under her arms.

When she opened her eyes again, the Red Chapel was still there, but now it was a large, rambling plantation that had gone to seed, reclaimed by the trailing fingers of the kudzu. Trees blocked out the powerful sun—in Hessika's memories, the land of her people was always bathed in warm afternoon light—but she could still feel the humidity in the air condensing on her skin. She looked down at her hands and was surprised to discover that the dreamlands had given her one final gift.

Her youth.

She'd always been tall, dwarfing her siblings and the other children she'd played with. Her parents didn't know why she'd been cursed with such height, but they'd tried to convince her that it was God's will. That it was a punishment for something she'd done, some crime she didn't remember committing. *Sin follows you wherever you go,* her mother would say.

Hessika hadn't believed it then and she didn't believe it now. Her parents were poor and uneducated. They didn't know better. Merely took as gospel what the preacher sang down at them from his pulpit. Hessika had been born with the gift of curiosity, and so she was saved from repeating the life her parents had lived. She'd left the woods, left Alabama, left the South . . . moved to California and found her calling. It had reached out to her through her dreams and because of that inborn curiosity, she'd listened when it had said: *Los Angeles.*

Funny, though, how when the end came, her instinct was to go back to where she'd come from in the first place . . . back to a time that was both idyllic and scary to her.

It was good to be back in her childhood body. The aches and pains of the world had left Hessika when she'd died, but the joy and freedom of childhood had not come back until now. She was full of energy, her heart beating loudly in her chest, life moving in and out of her as she breathed. She wished she could stay in the here and now forever, but she knew she was only getting a little taste. A memory to remind her of what had been, and a gift to thank her for all her sacrifices.

There was another *crack* of thunder and Hessika looked up to see the treetops swaying in the wind. That same breeze ruffled her long hair, pulled at the thick strands flowing over her shoulders and down to her butt. She was wearing her favorite smock dress, a dirty white thing her mother had made her when she'd outgrown all her older sisters' hand-me-downs, and her legs were bare, her feet dirty from running through the woods without her sandals.

She knew such great happiness in those few moments that tears broke free from her eyes and poured down her cheeks. She thanked the Goddess for giving her this last, sweet taste . . . and then she steeled herself for what was to come.

"I'm here!" she screamed, as the sky grew appreciably darker above her.

The *hiss* of rain hitting the warm soil filled the air, and she shivered despite the heat.

"I've been waiting a long time for you," she murmured.

The darkness was not a person. It was not a thing, or a place . . . *It was a feeling.* A state of mind, a way of being. When it owned you, it made you see things through the filter of a darker lens. It heightened the bad, the small, the petty. It made things look hopeless. It stole the joy and the light. Not because it hated them . . . but because to the darkness . . . they were food.

It left desolation and emptiness in its wake. It turned everything monochrome when it should've been Technicolor.

The darkness was a leech, a parasite, a destroyer . . . the opposite of what it meant to be alive.

And it was coming for her.

The rain began to fall in earnest, a heavy stream of water that drenched her, slicking the white cotton dress to her body like a second skin. She pushed wet hair from her face, wiped the water from her eyes.

"Is this the best you can do?!" she yelled into the rain—the darkness was most successful when it was inside a host, but it could do damage on its own, too. She just needed to rile it up a little.

A lightning strike blew up the ground in front of her, and if she hadn't smelled the electricity in the air, hadn't felt the thrumming energy heading toward her and jumped out of the way, she would've been burned to a crisp.

"Come on now, *ma petite salope*," she said under her breath as she pulled her skirts around her knees and began to run. She wanted to get as far away from the Red Chapel as she could and draw the darkness away with her.

The rain continued to pelt her as she ran, her legs pumping hard. She dodged prickle bushes, jumped over tree roots that seemed hell-bent on catching her foot and sending her sprawling. She wove her way through the trees, head down so the water wouldn't blind her. She could feel a stitch forming in her side, but she didn't let the pain slow her down.

Finally, she came to the edge of the creek—the rainwater had swelled the small tributary to three times its normal size—and stopped, chest heaving. She looked around, but there was only the silence of the woods and the steady drumbeat of rain beating that silence into submission. She leaned forward, resting her elbows on her thighs, pulling in shaky breaths that made her head spin.

She wasn't sure where to go from here. It felt like the creek—a place she'd come to when she was little and needed to be alone—was where this was supposed to end. Something about it seemed inevitable.

She sat down on the muddy bank, her bare feet inches from the furious flow of water. She could feel the rain sluicing down her skin, running off her body into the soil. She stuck her fingers into the dirt, felt it slide in under her nails and lodge there. She lay back, face skyward, letting the rain have at her. It felt like tiny pinpricks all over her skin—and as she closed her eyes, she imagined her body as it had been when she died. The soft child's skin sloughed away, replaced by old, paper-thin flesh . . . but then that began to rot away, too, peeling back to reveal bright red muscle. The rain ate away at the meat of her, the muscle dissolving away until there was only white bone.

She was a skeleton now. The calcified remains of a human being.

The water continued its assault, her bones beginning to break apart and melt, leaving only a sludgy puddle behind . . . and even that, after a while, was eventually washed away.

The darkness had claimed another witch.

Devandra

They flew into her open arms. She held them as tightly as she dared and never wanted to let them go.

"*Mama, Mama, Mama,*" Ginny said, repeating the word over and over again as her voice was muffled against Dev's chest.

Marji was silent, but Dev could feel her older daughter's speedy heartbeat. She was like a little bird, all fragile and delicate winged.

"Are you okay?" Dev murmured, relief pouring out of her like sweat.

"We're okay, Mama," Ginny said, looking up and smiling at her mother. "Tem played Bananagrams with us and Marji won twice."

Dev looked over at Tem, who stood by the kitchen island, watching them. Lizbeth stood beside him. She looked older, her long hair pinned at the back of her neck, the skin under her eyes dark and swollen.

"The door!" Daniela called from the entranceway. "What the hell happened to the goddamned door?"

Lyse, who'd looked so awkward standing in the middle of the Red Chapel (which still resembled the loft where Lizbeth had grown up), took the opportunity to join Daniela, so she didn't have to engage with Dev and the girls or Lizbeth.

"How do we get back out there?" Dev could hear Daniela saying to Lyse—but then Marji grabbed her attention and Dev tuned everyone else out.

"Mama, we knew you were coming. We waited for you."

She smiled down at her older daughter.

"Thank you for waiting, sweet pea."

She didn't know *what* she would've done if they'd left without her. The thought of showing up and not finding Marji and Ginny here made Dev's blood run cold.

"But we have to go back home now," Marji said. "Auntie E says."

Dev looked over at Eleanora. The older woman was watching them carefully, Niamh beside her.

"The Flood isn't coming, Devandra," Eleanora said. "It's *here*. We have to go back, but we have to find a safe place for the girls first."

"And where the hell would that be?" Dev asked, not sure a safe place could exist in these dark times. It felt like wherever they went, the darkness, The Flood . . . whatever you wanted to call the evil that had infected all the worlds . . . was already there.

"I know where," Niamh chimed in. For hours now—all through the arduous journey to the Red Chapel—she'd barely spoken, but now she looked happy to be able to contribute something to the conversation. "The other women. We need to go where there is the highest concentration of blood sisters. We forget that we have magic on our side now. *Real* magic."

Daniela burst into the room, Lyse on her heels.

"Hessika wouldn't come inside and now there's no goddamned door—"

"Daniela's worried. She thinks Hessika did something

rash," Lyse said, interrupting her friend. She directed her words at Eleanora.

"She's not wrong," Eleanora said. "We needed a little time to plan, and Hessika was ready to give us that."

"What?" Lizbeth cried. "What does that mean?"

Eleanora gave Lizbeth a sad smile.

"She sacrificed herself so that the rest of you could do what was necessary."

Tem put an arm around Lizbeth and pulled her close. She didn't notice, her eyes stricken.

"Then she's not coming back?" Lizbeth asked—her voice monotone.

"No, pet," Tem said, murmuring in Lizbeth's ear. "She's not coming back."

"What about Arrabelle and Evan?" Daniela asked, her hands balled into fists at her sides.

"Arrabelle is gone," Eleanora said.

"Why didn't you tell us this before?" Lyse said, glaring at Eleanora. "We would never have let Evan go after her . . ."

She trailed off, the magnitude of Arrabelle's loss apparent from the expression on her face. Dev felt it, too, and she clutched the girls tighter.

"You can't make someone do what you want them to, Lyse," Eleanora said. "You, of all people, know this."

"Weir's dead, too," Lizbeth said abruptly, looking pointedly at Lyse. "It's my fault . . . and Daniela almost dying . . . I got mad at her and touched her even when I knew I could kill her . . ."

She couldn't finish the thought, her body shaking as she broke down, wrapping her arms around herself.

"No!" Lyse cried, rushing to Lizbeth's side. "It was *my* fault. Never yours . . . always mine. All of it. I was in charge and I let you down."

Lyse reached out her arms as if she wanted to hug Lizbeth but didn't know if the attempt would be welcome.

"I'm sorry. I was so cruel to you and I didn't want to be. I couldn't help it . . ."

Lizbeth swallowed hard, eyes shining, and looked up at Lyse. Then she launched herself into Lyse's arms, and the two women clung to each other, both crying now.

"It wasn't your fault," Lyse whispered, touching Lizbeth's wet cheek. "And Weir, wherever he is, he knows it, too. Daniela . . . ?"

Daniela smiled at Lizbeth.

"You got me to the hospital. You may have kicked my ass, but you saved it, too."

"You were under a spell, Lizbeth," Eleanora said, trying to ease the girl's mind. "You were compelled to do someone else's bidding—and you were meant to push the others away, and see Lyse as your enemy. For reasons that have nothing to do with any of you."

"I should've been able to fight it." Lizbeth disagreed, shaking her head.

"Magic is stronger than us," Eleanora said, thoughtfully. "At least when we're alone. But none of us have to be alone now . . ."

Dev tried to process everything she'd just heard, but the thought of sweet, beautiful Weir gone . . . it broke her heart. She didn't think it could be broken any more than it already was—but she had discovered recently that there were always new depths of despair to be reached.

In her mind's eye, Dev saw Freddy being dragged out of Eleanora's kitchen, and she felt nauseated with fear. She forced the image from her head, knowing if she went there now, she might never come back—and the girls needed her.

"Weir is dead . . . I just can't believe it . . ." Daniela covered her mouth with her hand and shook her head. Dev could feel anger emanating from the empath. "How do we stop this? We've pissed around for too long, letting them take everything and everyone away from us. How do we end it?"

Dev wanted to know the answer, too. She wanted a plan, a way to protect her girls and get Freddy back.

"It's a twofold problem," Thomas said, finally speaking up—but his wary eyes were glued to Dev. She realized he thought she still blamed him for killing her family and burning down her house.

"Thomas, I know it wasn't you," she said. "I know you cared for my mother and that you would never have hurt any of us like that."

He stared back at her, his lips trembling in surprise.

"Truly . . . ? You mean that?" he asked; he looked incredulous.

Dev released the girls, but they stayed close to her, not wanting their mother out of their sight.

"Sweetie pies," Dev said. "I want you to go in the other room while we finish talking."

"I can help," Marji said, but Dev shook her head.

"Not with this . . . but later I know you will."

"I'll take them," Niamh said, holding out her hands to Marji and Ginny. "Hello, there. I'm Niamh."

Ginny went to her easily, but Marji took her time, obviously hoping Dev would change her mind. Finally, when she didn't, Marji took Niamh's hand and let her lead the two of them into another room.

When the girls and Niamh were gone, Dev turned back to Thomas, who sat curled up on the couch, looking uncertain.

"I do mean it, and I'm sorry for blaming you when you were only trying to help."

He nodded, jaw working with emotion.

"I would *never* hurt a Montrose woman. *Never.*"

He looked over at his brother, Tem, who nodded in agreement.

"We failed you, but not purposely," Thomas continued. "And I take responsibility for that. We didn't keep the darkness in check. Didn't stop it from slipping through to your world."

"It would've gotten in one way or another," Eleanora said.

"There's no one to blame. Without the darkness there is no light. We need the balance of the two."

"That's true, but Tem and I became too enmeshed with your world. We were alone, here, in the dreamlands, two of the last of our kind. We were tasked with keeping your world free of what destroyed ours, and we failed you."

Eleanora crossed the room toward him. She did not look pleased.

"Do you not hear me?" she asked. "You could never have stopped it. It was futile. No one can stop it."

Dev couldn't believe this was true, that there was no way to save their world from being consumed by the darkness via the hands of its emissaries, The Flood.

"So that's it?" she asked. "We just give up? We let The Flood destroy everything, wipe out humanity?"

Eleanora frowned.

"Did I say that?"

"No," Daniela spoke out. "But you haven't answered my question, either."

Eleanora sighed.

"It's loose in your world now and we can't stop it, but we can balance it," Tem said from his perch by the kitchen island. "Well, Eleanora and I can't, but the rest of you living souls can."

"How?" Lyse asked. She was still with Lizbeth, her arm around the younger woman's shoulder.

Tem looked at Thomas, who nodded.

"Lyse?" Thomas asked. "Do you know who you are?"

She looked confused.

"I'm just *me*, I guess." Thomas continued to look thoughtfully at her. "I don't know what it is you want me to say."

"The tarot spread. The World, The Magician, The Hierophant, The Devil, and The Fool . . . which are you?"

"I have no idea," Lyse said, shaking her head.

Thomas got up from his place on the long white couch and began to pace.

"Think about it," he said. "We know The World stands for your world, correct?"

Lyse nodded.

"Sure, yes."

"And The Devil represents what we call 'the darkness' and the blood sisters call 'The Flood.' But it more literally refers to a specific minion on Earth—"

"Desmond," Daniela said with a low growl in her throat. "That's the devil we know."

"Or your son, David," Lyse said, addressing her words to Eleanora. "Only he's gone now. I took care of him."

All eyes went to Lyse.

"What did you do?" Eleanora asked.

"I brought him here and threw him into a singularity. It was a crazy idea, but I think it worked."

She looked around the circle of assorted faces and her posture changed, shoulders hunching. Dev realized that Lyse thought she was being judged, and she'd clearly taken on a defensive stance to protect herself.

"He killed you, Eleanora," Lyse continued, before turning to the others. "And he would've killed any of the rest of you if we'd given him half a chance."

"No one's upset with you, Lyse," Dev said. "I think you did the right thing. We all do."

She shot the others an imploring look: *Let Lyse see that we don't judge her for her actions.*

Daniela understood Dev's meaning and took a few steps toward Lyse.

"If you hadn't done it, I would've. And I think I speak for everyone when I say that what you did was necessary."

Lyse's shoulders relaxed.

"Thanks, Daniela."

Daniela shrugged.

"It's just a truth."

Dev was pleased that Daniela had been able to reach Lyse.

They did not need their coven master disabled by guilt. Every one of them needed to be functioning if they were going to stop The Flood from doing what it wanted with their world.

"Tem and I have an idea about two more," Thomas continued—now that Lyse was calmer again. "Who they represent—"

"I'm The Fool," Daniela said. Her tone was even, but there was anger in her eyes. "I was duped by Desmond Delay, who is my father and Lyse's grandfather."

Eleanora sighed deeply, lips pursed tightly together.

"I always wondered who your father was, but Marie-Faith refused to tell me. She kept it a secret from all of us."

"Francesca knew, and she hated you and Lyse because of it," Daniela said to Eleanora, her fists unclenching as she spoke. Dev wondered if saying these thoughts out loud—it was clear they'd been tormenting Daniela—was like lancing a wound, the poisonous infection slowly seeping out with each word. "Desmond used Francesca to infect Lyse with the dreaming spell when we were in Rome."

"After your mother went to Italy, we spent far less time together. I hardly knew Francesca," Eleanora said.

"Well, I think she hated you," Daniela replied, "because my parentage was kept secret and Francesca blamed you for it, Eleanora."

"I never met the great and powerful Desmond Delay," Eleanora said. "But now we know why."

"Because you'd have known him for what he truly was," Lyse said. "And if you're a fool, Daniela, so are the rest of us."

"I gave him Lizbeth on a silver platter—"

"The Fool played an important part," Thomas said. "It all happened as it was supposed to. Without the full return of magic, The Flood would not gain its power . . . and without magic, you and your blood sisters could not drive it back."

"That good old 'balance' you were talking about," Daniela said to Eleanora.

"Well, Lyse," Dev said. "Then you're either The Magician, who brings about change, or The Hierophant, who stands at the crossroads of time and space."

"I'm The Magician then," Lyse said. "Is that what you wanted me to see? There, I see it. I say it. I'm The Magician."

Tem looked at Lizbeth—and Dev felt their connection. It was more than just palpable. It was *electric*. She wondered if anyone else knew that Lizbeth was in love with the handsome dead man from another dimension?

Maybe Eleanora, Dev thought, *and Thomas, of course. But I don't think the others realize.*

"You're not The Magician—though everyone thinks you are," Thomas said to Lyse. "Even Eleanora. She believed it, too."

"I'm The Hierophant?" Lyse asked, confused.

"But The Magician is supposed to bring about change—" Eleanora began, but Thomas held up a hand for her to stop speaking.

"And Lizbeth did bring change to the world . . . big-time change," Thomas said. "The Hierophant is the crossroads. The place in time and space where anything is possible."

"I don't get it," Lyse said, bouncing nervously on the balls of her feet. "What're you talking about?"

Dev understood immediately—and she felt stupid for not seeing it before. She was the diviner, the interpreter of the tarot, and it had never occurred to her. And she'd *been* with Lyse when her friend had manipulated time and space . . . she could've kicked herself.

"You can change it all, Lyse," Dev said. "You can travel in time and space. It's how we went back to the hospital and saw your past self—"

"No," Eleanora breathed. "It can't be."

"I didn't think it was possible," Tem said, "but Thomas says it's true."

"Would someone explain this to me, please?" Lyse asked.

"I said before that the answer to stopping all of this was

twofold. Lyse has to search out the one moment in space and time when all of this could've been averted. The rest of us must go and fight the darkness and its Flood. Lyse will only have as much time as we can give her—"

"—unless I can pick apart the threads of time and space and stop all of this before it begins?" Lyse said, covering her face with her hands. "I have a headache just thinking about what you said."

"Yes, it's not for the faint of heart or mind," Thomas said, "but if you can figure out where the darkness tipped the scales in its favor, you can fix this. At least, here in the dreamlands and in your world. And possibly it will spread further . . . we can only hope."

"It's a suicide mission, Lyse," Eleanora said. "You can say no."

Lyse shook her head.

"I'm going to do it. It's not a question."

"I'll go with you," Lizbeth said, but Lyse was having none of it.

"Not gonna happen," Lyse said, her voice steely. "I'm the only one going on a suicide mission. I want the rest of you protected as much as possible."

Lizbeth nodded, but she didn't look happy about it.

"Well, with Hessika and Arrabelle gone," Lizbeth said, "that leaves the rest of us here at The Red Chapel to fight."

"And Evan, wherever he is," Daniela said.

"And Evan," Lyse agreed.

"Ten of us," Dev said.

"No pressure there," Daniela replied, snorting.

No pressure at all, Dev thought blandly. *Just the fate of the world in your hands.*

Niamh

Niamh had been sequestered away in one of the back bedrooms—a child's bedroom by the look of it—with Dev's daughters, Marji and Ginny. She liked the girls immensely; their connection to each other reminded her of the one she'd once had with her twin, Laragh.

"I don't think we'll be here long," Niamh said, sitting down on the pink canopy bed that took up the majority of the tiny bedroom. "They just need to talk about a few things."

Ginny and Marji plopped down on the floor in front of her, both eyeing her curiously.

"They're saying bad stuff," Ginny said. She was sitting cross-legged, her elbows pressed into her knees, her chin resting in her clasped palms. "Mama always makes us go upstairs when she and Daddy talk about bad things."

Marji rolled her eyes.

"She means when they fight."

Niamh remembered her own parents screaming at each other while she and Laragh hid under the square claw-foot table in the dining room. When their parents fought, she and

Laragh would just wait it out. They spent a lot of time there, playing with their Fisher-Price Little People, building cities for the flat-bottomed plastic dolls to live in.

She'd asked Laragh about it years later—when they were both older and, supposedly, wiser—and her sister had just stared at her like she was crazy.

"I don't know what you're talking about."

Her sister's denial had frightened Niamh, and she'd put the memory aside, not wanting to argue with her about something Laragh had—obviously—blocked out.

"They don't fight much," Marji continued. "Not like the other kids at my school."

"Or mine!" Ginny chirped, not wanting to be outdone by her sister.

"That's because they love each other," Niamh said. She assumed this was true. The others had said Dev and her partner, Freddy, really did care for one another, and no one had a reason to lie.

"They hold hands and kiss each other sometimes," Ginny agreed. "That means they love each other."

"Maybe," Marji said, looking skeptically at her little sister. Then she turned her attention to Niamh. "Do you love someone?"

"Uh," Niamh began, not sure how to answer such a loaded question.

"I do."

Ginny shook her head, her long dark hair flopping behind her.

"She does. She likes Thom—"

"Ginny!" Marji screeched, covering her sister's mouth with the palm of her hand.

"Stop it—" Ginny said, pushing Marji's hand away, a deep frown distorting her face. "Mama says you're not supposed to touch me when you're mad!"

"That was a secret, Ginny!" Marji squawked, humiliated that Niamh knew the secret identity of her crush.

"Thomas seems very nice," Niamh said, trying to be diplomatic.

"He's old," Ginny said, matter-of-factly.

Niamh laughed because Thomas looked like he was about twenty-five years old. Ginny's perception of him being elderly was humorous. She tried to think like a kid, to imagine that anyone over eighteen looked "old"—but it was hard to do. Still, she remembered other things from her childhood. The good parts of being a kid *and* the awful things. But those memories were at a remove—like her parents yelling obscenities at each other while their twin daughters played under the claw-foot table, Fisher-Price Little People sprawled all over the floor, the last remnants of a plastic doll apocalypse.

"Having a crush on someone is nice." Niamh finally decided on a neutral response.

Marji remained stubbornly silent in her humiliation.

"He smells old, Marji," Ginny said, and Niamh had to bite her tongue. She appreciated Ginny's bluntness, but she doubted Marji liked it very much right now.

The girls' dynamic really reminded Niamh of the relationship she'd shared with Laragh. Spending time with Dev's daughters made her miss her sister so much. She fought back the lump in her throat, not wanting to cry in front of the kids—Goddess, she'd already cried so much recently, she just couldn't take another round of tears.

Marji noticed her distress, her dark eyes suddenly round with compassion.

"You miss your sister," the girl said.

Niamh wasn't sure how Marji knew about Laragh, but in that moment she didn't care.

"Yeah, I miss her a lot."

Ginny climbed to her knees, then scooted over closer to the bed. She put her smaller hand on Niamh's larger one.

"Marji talks to ghosts."

Niamh couldn't help herself. The little girl was so earnest that she had to laugh.

"I'm not joking," Ginny continued, but she didn't seem to be offended by Niamh's laughter.

"I don't think you are," Niamh said. She'd realized all the emotion she was feeling had to get out somehow—and it was either laugh *or* cry. She'd chosen laughter.

"She misses you, too. She says you always stole the green man from her and she forgives you."

Niamh hadn't doubted Marji before, but now she knew for a fact that Marji was somehow communicating with Laragh. The little green plastic man with the blond hair and loopy smile had been both of their favorites. They used to fight over him all the time when they were small—and the only way Marji could've known this was to get the information straight from Laragh's mouth.

"Where is she?" Niamh asked.

But Marji shook her head.

"I don't know. I just hear her voice. I don't see her."

"But Marji sees ghosts, too, sometimes," Ginny chimed in, not wanting to be left out of the conversation.

"Tell her I love her," Niamh said.

Marji nodded, listening.

"She knows you do."

The door opened and Dev came in, her shoulders hunched with worry.

"All right, little bits," Dev said, stepping into the middle of the room and gesturing for the girls to get up. "Time to go."

The girls hopped to, clinging to their mother now. Niamh climbed to her feet, leaving behind the pink canopy bed and the white wicker furniture of the child's bedroom and following Dev and the girls to the door.

"Where are we going, Mama?" Marji asked.

"A place where there are lots more of us," Dev said, taking Marji's hand.

"Me, too!" Ginny said, taking Dev's other hand.

Niamh followed Dev and the girls back into the main

room. Thomas, Tem, and Lizbeth were by the couch. Lyse and Daniela stood close to one another, shoulders touching. Only Eleanora waited alone, her hawkish gaze fixed on Lyse.

"We're going to find Jessika and the other Shrieking Eagles," Lyse told Niamh. "You were right when you said the girls would be safer there."

"Okay," Niamh said, pleased they'd listened to her.

"Lizbeth and Tem will stay here—they're going to see if they can find Evan."

"Lyse will leave us with the Eagles," Dev said. "And then she's going to go on . . ."

"Go where?" Niamh asked, not following.

"She's The Hierophant from your spread," Thomas said, though there was no joy in his words. "Lyse is going to find out where this all started and fix it for us if she can."

So Lyse was the mysterious Hierophant. The last card in the spread—and the only one Niamh hadn't really understood until now. But it made sense that Lyse would be the linchpin upon which they all turned.

"The keeper of the sacred mystery," Niamh said, softly, catching Lyse's eye. "Hello, Hierophant."

"If anyone had told me a few weeks ago that we'd all be here together in a totally alien world having this conversation, I'd have thought they were insane," Lyse said, by way of an answer.

"I wouldn't want to be here with anyone else," Niamh said, looking at each face as she spoke. They were all good people—alive and dead alike.

"Let's do this," Daniela said.

Niamh took a deep breath, readying herself for what was to come.

"My hand, please," Thomas said to Niamh, holding up his right one for her to take.

Lyse could've brought Niamh, too, but she was already

transporting Daniela, Dev, and the girls, so Thomas stepped up and offered his services. They'd watched the others go and now it was their turn.

Niamh would be sorry to see the end of the loft. She was certain this marked the last time things would be calm—it was only going to get crazier from here on out.

"I wish I knew how to do what you and Lyse do," Niamh said. Thomas was very good-looking, very charming . . . he made her nervous and she had trouble looking him in the eye as she spoke.

"You make things come alive in the dreamlands," Thomas replied. "Anything I create here is impermanent . . . but you, you make things real. I wish I could do what you do."

Niamh felt herself blushing, her palms getting sweaty under his gaze. She saw why Marji had developed such a crush on the man. Thomas was very crushworthy.

"I would teach you if I knew how," Niamh said, finally looking up at Thomas.

He had nice eyes. Welcoming eyes. They made her want to tell him secrets . . . not that she had any interesting secrets to impart, but there was just something about him that made her want to talk.

"Maybe one day we will all be lucky enough for you to try," he said, squeezing her (very sweaty now) hand. Then his face went serious. "I'm taking you now, Niamh, because I wanted a word alone."

"Sure," she said, without thinking. "I mean . . . of course. Um, yes . . ."

As she fumbled with her words, his serious expression lifted for a moment—but then it became serious once more.

"You must go with Lyse on her journey," he said. "She will need another with her. Someone who will not let her stay her hand when the time comes . . . I would go, but I don't believe any of you blood sisters truly trusts me. Not out of malice. There is just, shall we say, a lot of water under the bridge."

"You think she'll let me come with her?" Niamh asked, uncertain.

"No, I don't think she'll want to risk your safety. So you're just going to have to insert yourself into her plans."

"If you think that's the right thing," she said. "I mean, if you think she needs me?"

"I do. She's not going to want to do what will be asked of her. You are removed from it. You will help her."

It was amazing how easy it was for her to just accept what Thomas said at face value. She didn't question his motives or ask him why he felt so certain that she needed to go with Lyse.

"I should warn you," he added, "that you will feel slightly compelled to do as I ask. At least while you're looking into my eyes. It's a quirk of my power and it's not something I can control. But I find when I make a person aware of this, it lessens the pull."

He was right. Once he'd told her about his little trick, she didn't feel the need to blindly do as he asked anymore.

"That's crazy," she said, shaking her head. "You could do terrible things with that."

He grinned back at her.

"Luckily, the effects go away completely once you're away from me . . . I think it's an olfactory power. Something about my pheromones. Once you can't smell me, you stop wanting to please me."

She hoped it was true—because there was a part of her that still felt under his sway.

"I will look after Lyse, if I can."

"Good, I knew you would understand," he said, leaning forward and giving her a gentle kiss on the cheek. His lips were soft and there was a touch of stubble on his chin. "You're very compelling yourself. A truly lovely scent."

She blushed as he pulled away.

"Shall we?"

She nodded, her heart beating very quickly. She wished

that knowing his charm was of the magical variety would make her like him less, but it didn't. She was super nervous around him, and the kiss he'd placed on her cheek only made it worse.

She waited for him to do what Lyse did and call up a magical blue orb that would take them to another dimension.

"I do things a little differently," Thomas said, quirking an eyebrow at her. "You won't even know—"

She blinked and they were standing on the prow of a boat, the pull of the sea rocking them very, very gently.

"—it's happened," Thomas finished.

He released her and she took a step back, impressed.

"Wow, that was amazing," she said, in awe of the man.

He had the good grace to look abashed.

"Please, it's nothing."

It *wasn't* nothing, but he was embarrassed by her compliment, so she let it go.

"I wonder where the others have gotten to?" Thomas asked, changing the subject.

They were alone on the deck of what appeared to be a decommissioned destroyer. There were only clear blue skies and sea wherever Niamh looked, and she suspected that Jessika had chosen to be far away from land because it was safer for the women they'd rescued.

Niamh had never been on such a large ship before—and never one that had a giant gun stationed on top of it, the long steel-gray barrel pointed out ahead of them in warning. Thomas had brought them to a spot toward the front of the ship, at the edge of a long runway where they were a safe distance from the edge. But Niamh still felt vulnerable. The sides of the ship were very low and it looked easy for someone to fall overboard.

"Look," Thomas said, pointing at the ground underneath them where someone had painted a white circle with a line through it. The circle stood at the end of a long runway whose asphalt-gray surface and yellow demarcation lines made it resemble a road more than a ship.

"Helicopter landing spot," Thomas added, indicating the circle. "I think."

The sun broke through the line of clouds above them, and Niamh lifted her hand to shield her eyes from the bright sunlight.

"Oh no," she murmured as she caught sight of something terrifying out on the horizon.

"What?" Thomas asked, instantly on guard.

"They're coming," Niamh said, eyes pinned to the fleet of small ships heading toward them. "The Flood is here."

"Time to find out where everyone is," Thomas said.

And then he took Niamh's hand and they ran.

Desmond

Desmond knew a terrible fate had befallen his son. He should've been upset by this odd and unsettling turn of events, but, instead, he found himself merely resigned to the fact.

I never really liked him, Desmond realized. *He was rotten and I knew it. But, still, I used him to further The Flood's needs.*

Guilt was not an emotion Desmond wasted time on, but now it blossomed inside him like a parasitic flower, cutting into his heart and forcing him to acknowledge something he'd buried deep down inside himself.

He'd made a mistake. A serious one. A reprehensible one. And it had happened because of *her.*

God help him, he'd loved Eleanora Eames from the first moment he'd laid eyes on her. She'd opened the front door to her grandmother's house, pushing strands of damp brown hair out of her glorious face, her wide pink mouth smiling at him. She'd been working in the kitchen, her cheeks flushed from the heat.

She'd looked up at him, those gorgeous eyes locking onto his own, and his heart had swelled with such need that he'd almost been unable to speak. He remembered asking for her grandmother—the woman who'd contacted his superiors—and she'd led him inside the house. He'd had a job to do, and he'd done it. He was there to help save her soul . . . but what he hadn't realized was it was actually *his* soul that was going to need saving when it was all said and done.

He'd tried everything he could to keep away from Eleanora. But she was too incredible and he'd failed miserably, spending entirely too much time in her company. She'd been so intelligent and kind . . . and they'd really connected. He was supposed to be watching her, making sure she wasn't communing with the Devil—which was what witches like her did—but instead he'd fallen more in love with her.

He would've thought making love to her would be the most important experience they shared, but after all these years, there was another evening that stayed closer to his heart.

She was sitting on the cot, her back pressed into the corner, arms wrapped around her knees. She was wearing Desmond's white undershirt and a pair of his striped pajama pants that he had given her from his own stash of clothing.

She'd twisted her long brown hair into a knot at the back of her neck, and she wore no makeup. Her eyes were thoughtful as she played with the striped fabric, running her fingers along the curve of her knee.

"I like that you think about things," she said. "There are just so few people in this world who truly think."

He was on the floor, a cigarette in his hand, his back against the wall. He'd unbuttoned the top two buttons of his plaid shirt and she'd watched him, eyes fixed on the bit of curly brown chest hair poking up from beneath his undershirt.

"I don't know what any of the answers are," he said, putting the cigarette to his lips and inhaling deeply. He so badly wanted to look

"cool" for her. "But I think there's more in this world than we can see or hear or touch or taste with our senses."

"Like we have a sixth sense?" she asked.

He nodded and then leaned his head back against the wall.

"A sixth or a seventh—"

"—maybe an eighth sense," she said, laughing.

"Yeah," he agreed, and smiled at her.

Their eyes caught for a moment, held, and then, finally, she looked away. In his heart, he knew that part of her goodwill toward him was selfish. She wanted to escape and she hoped he'd help her.

This was not going to happen. She didn't understand that she was here for a reason. She needed their help. Only with The Flood's backing could she be cured of her condition. Witchcraft was evil and it corrupted women; corrupted absolutely. He and the others were going to save Eleanora and then the two of them could be together. Forever.

Because that was what he knew was going to happen. They would fix Eleanora Eames and then she would marry him. They would have children and be in love and everything would be perfect.

It was a naïve point of view to embrace, but he was young, barely a man, and his optimism knew no bounds.

"My grandmother used to burn me when I was younger," Eleanora said suddenly. He was unprepared for this revelation and out came the first thing his mind latched onto, without thinking:

"That's not right. She shouldn't do that."

Eleanora shrugged, the white undershirt showing off the curve of her breast. He tore his eyes away from the sight, but the image was burned into his brain, and he knew he'd think about what lay beneath that undershirt the next time he touched himself.

"She wanted to burn the magic out of me."

Desmond had never heard anyone be so blunt about magic before.

"Because it's evil," he said.

She shook her head.

"It's not evil. It just makes her remember my mom. She blames magic for her death."

"What happened to your mother?" he asked, pulling on the cigarette again.

"Can I tell you a secret?" she asked.

And all he wanted, more than anything in the whole world, was to hear that secret.

"Of course," he said, trying to sound nonchalant. "You can tell me anything."

She sat forward, eyes gleaming with excitement. He was pretty sure whatever she was about to tell him, she'd never told anyone else, ever.

"I can visit other places in time."

He wanted to clear his ears out, make sure he'd heard her correctly.

"You can do what?" he asked.

She grinned, pleased that she'd unsettled him.

"I can't change anything, or even really talk to anyone, but I can go back in time and see things how they happened."

He shook his head.

"That's not real."

She frowned, her shoulders slumping.

"It is, too."

He tried another tack: "I believe that you believe that you can do that, but I bet you're just having some kind of lucid dream."

She didn't disagree with him, but from the expression on her face, it was clear she thought he was wrong.

"Suit yourself," he said, stubbing out the butt of his cigarette.

"It happens," she said, a note of defiance in her voice. "Whether you believe me or not."

He hadn't believed her then . . . it was only later—much later—that he'd understood just how right she was.

"Have you ever been in love?" she asked, changing the subject.

He shook his head.

"Nope," he said. "You?"

"Never."

He caught her eye again and he felt an almost electric jolt shoot through him. He'd never made love to a woman before, but more than anything he wanted to do that with Eleanora.

"I could fall in love with you," she said, still holding his gaze. "If things were different. I think I could."

His heart skipped a beat, but he spoke calmly: "Why's that, Eleanora?"

She smiled—and it was the sweetest smile the world had ever seen.

"Because I can talk to you."

It had all gone to hell after that. He'd tried to fix it—after the fact—but she wanted nothing to do with him. He'd learned, too late, that she'd borne his children, twins, a boy and a girl, and then given them up for adoption. She hadn't consulted him about any of it, and he had been devastated.

He spent many long years searching for his children.

David he found first, but he'd known immediately there was something not right about the man. His daughter he'd never gotten to meet. She and her husband had died in a car accident before he could meet her. She'd left behind one child, but Eleanora had snatched Lyse from him before he'd realized what was happening.

Once again, Eleanora had ruined his ability to connect with his family.

By then, he'd infiltrated the Witches' Greater Council and become a trusted member of the blood sisters' world. Out of revenge, he'd seduced Eleanora's closest friend, Marie-Faith Altonelli, forbidding her from telling anyone about their affair. She'd begotten Daniela and he'd made sure he was a part of *that* child's life from the get-go.

Now here he sat, on the back of a speedboat, racing toward the attainment of everything he'd worked so hard for: The Flood would have its day and the world would be changed for the better.

Or would it?

It was hard to even *think* this, but much of Desmond was starting to believe he'd been misled. All these years of wanting something, of pushing an agenda to fruition . . . and only at the end did he see the truth. That he might be on the wrong side.

But there was nothing he could do about it now. The plan had been set into motion and they'd passed the fail-safe point. The Flood was going to take control of the Earth, a war would come, and then everything would be over . . . purification and the beginning of a new order. The witches would bring about their own end as it had been written in *The Book of The Flood*.

Up ahead Desmond could see the decommissioned battleship floating on the buoyant blue sea. It was larger than he'd imagined, but they'd brought a battalion of foot soldiers with them, all under his control. With or without David, the next twenty-four hours would mark the end of the blood sisters and any control they had over humanity.

"We're close, sir," the young man who was piloting their speedboat called out over the roar of the engine.

Good, he thought. *I want this done soon so I never have to think about it again.*

The one positive thing that had happened was that Daniela had come out of her coma. True, she was back with her coven sisters, but that wouldn't be for long. He would send someone to fetch her and then she'd be at his side before the bloodshed had even begun.

"Send Helen and her team around behind them. Let's hem them in and make sure they can't escape."

Another young man—Desmond was having trouble remembering so many different names . . . or maybe his brain was failing him faster than he realized—barked his orders into a walkie-talkie and then listened as someone squawked a reply.

"They're already on it, sir," the young man said, letting the walkie-talkie fall to his side.

"Thank you," Desmond replied.

The two women he'd loved were both dead. His son had disappeared. One daughter was dead, another injured, and his granddaughter hated his guts.

My family is in the crapper, he thought, *but my work is about to bear its long-gestating fruit.*

A part of him wished they were reversed. There was something very appealing about sitting on a wide wooden porch in a rocking chair, the two loves of his life, Eleanora and Marie-Faith, on either side. Their children and grandchildren coming by for family gatherings . . . meals shared around a giant table. It was a daydream he'd had before . . . but it was just that. A dream. None of it would ever come to pass, and if he hadn't been so exhausted, he would've secretly wept for what could have been.

What could've been but never would be.

There was no one on the deck, but this didn't bother Desmond. The destroyer was surrounded by his boats. It would not be going anywhere. The women were somewhere on the ship, and he knew, eventually, his people would find them.

With David missing, Helen was now his second-in-command. He trusted her to do what was necessary . . . and do it efficiently. She'd done an excellent job of rooting out Yesinia's coven, even finding one of the rare and coveted "evolved" witches to bring back with her to the research facility. She was good at what she did, and she had an aptitude for magic . . . a talent he'd augmented with his research into witches' powers.

"Do you want to stay on the deck, sir?" The young man with the walkie-talkie was back. "Or would you like to enter the hatch with us?"

Desmond was not well. His time on Earth was limited and he got exhausted easily by physical activity. As much as he wished he could go belowdecks with his people, he knew he'd be better served staying up above.

"I'll be fine up here," Desmond said.

"Shall I leave some men up here with you?" the young man asked.

Desmond shook his head. "Leave me that walkie-talkie. If

I have a problem, I'll radio down to Helen or someone on one of the boats."

The young man nodded, his light red hair and freckled skin reminding Desmond of Devandra Montrose. He'd felt bad destroying the whole line of Montrose women, but he consoled himself with the knowledge that it was better to die now than to be smitten by the hand of the creator when The Flood took control.

He took the radio from the young man, slipping the clip over his belt. He had trouble maintaining his balance, and the cane he used to prop himself up was all he could manage. The walkie-talkie would be safer on his belt.

There was a raised partition by the gunwale and Desmond perched atop it, watching as a phalanx of Flood converts, both male and female, streamed down into the lower regions of the battle destroyer. Their black combat gear reminded him of insects—ants with guns, actually, who were about to march into battle.

As the last of his followers disappeared into the hatch, Desmond was left alone on the prow of the ship. It was silent, the beat of combat boots on metal having ceased once the last of the men and women went belowdecks. Sunlight bore down on the top of Desmond's head and he wished he'd worn a hat. He could feel the sweat pouring down his neck, pooling at the small of his back. He closed his eyes, and the calls of seabirds and the gentle crash of waves against the hull of the ship began to lull him into complacency.

"Desmond."

He started awake, the timbre of Eleanora's voice reverberating in his ears. He turned his head, scanning the deck of the battle cruiser. There was no one there. He cleared his throat and then coughed up a plug of mucus. He spat it onto the ground, where it began to ooze and bubble. It was disgusting. He hated how foul his body had become as it rotted from the inside out.

He took a deep breath and let it out slowly, turning the lion-headed cane slowly in his hands.

He closed his eyes, once again letting the gentle rocking of the ship lull him.

"Desmond."

His eyes flew open. Eleanora was standing in front of him . . . but not the old woman he'd met again so recently in Elysian Park. No, this was the Eleanora of his dreams, the beautiful young woman he'd fallen in love with and lost his virginity to all those years ago.

"Eleanora?" he said, a hitch in his voice.

Her long brown hair hung loose and free around her shoulders, the soft curve of her throat visible through the wide lapels of her light blue blouse. He stared at her wide pink mouth, and even all these decades later he felt himself stirring at the sight of her.

"Why are you here?" he asked.

She floated toward him, her long blue skirt trailing along the asphalt-gray surface of the deck.

"To ask you to reconsider," she said. *"To beg you not to do this."*

Her words made him sad. He wanted to grant her wish, but it was impossible. There was nothing he could do. His hands were bound.

"It will all be over soon," he said instead.

She pursed her lips, her skin translucent beneath the heat of the sun.

"Yes, it will," she agreed. *"But not in the way you think. As we speak, my blood sisters are breaking the morale of your people. You think you can come at us with guns, but we have magic, Desmond. And magic trumps everything."*

He was confused. What was she talking about?

"And we have you to thank for that," she continued. *"Thank you, Desmond."*

He dragged himself to his feet, using the cane Daniela had given him to hold himself up. He felt dizzy, his head swimming. He reached for the walkie-talkie at his belt but couldn't find it. He looked down and saw that it had disappeared.

"What do you mean? What are you talking about?" he cried, taking a step toward Eleanora's apparition.

She didn't stay where she was but backed away from him.

He lifted his cane and pointed the tip of it at her.

"You're not going anywhere until you tell me what you mean!" he yelled, his face getting red with the exertion.

"Hello, Dad."

He wheeled around to find Daniela standing behind him, holding the walkie-talkie in her hands. She let it fall from her grasp and it clattered onto the deck. She lifted her foot and smashed the radio's plastic body with the heel of her shoe, so that it splintered apart, useless.

"Daniela . . . ?" he moaned, surprised to see her here on the deck of the boat.

"Where else would I be?" she asked him, her eyes narrowing into slits as she surveyed his ravaged body.

He knew he looked even worse than he had when she'd seen him last, could see her disgust and fear reflected back at him.

"I told you I was dying," he said.

"I don't think you can die soon enough for me, Desmond," she said.

Her words shouldn't have bothered him, but they did. She was the one child whom he thought he had a decent relationship with, but he'd been wrong. Daniela hated him as much as the others. Maybe even more.

"Why did you do it?" she asked.

"Do what?" he said, his mouth suddenly dry.

"Kill my mother and Francesca . . . use Francesca's spirit to cast the spell on Lizbeth that would destroy our world . . . ? I'm sure there's more, but looking at you makes me sick to my stomach, so I won't go on."

He laughed, which sounded more like a croak because his throat was so parched. He'd always enjoyed Daniela's plain-spoken bluntness. She was a woman unafraid of saying something that might offend, and he'd appreciated that about her.

She didn't like being laughed at. He could see the anger growing in her eyes. She stepped toward him, grasping for his upper arm with her bare hand.

Her bare hand, he thought. *But she can't . . . I'll kill her.*

He tried to sidestep her, but he wasn't fast enough. She latched onto him and—

—they were no longer on the prow of the destroyer.

"Where are we?" Desmond asked—everywhere he looked, there was only black, empty space as far as the eye could see.

He blinked and then Daniela was standing in front of him, her rainbow-hued hair a staticky mess as she stared at him with flashing eyes. She lifted her arms in the air and electricity shot out of her fingertips.

"You're in my head," she said. "Only I'm not alone in here. The monster you created in your lab is here with me. And this is its true form!"

She lowered her hands and as she did, light exploded all around him. He tried to cover his face, block out the pain in his eyes, but he found that he was unable to move.

"They're all here to say hello . . ." Daniela gestured around her and what Desmond saw chilled him to the bone.

He was surrounded by a sea of women . . . old women, young women, girls . . . he recognized some and others he did not. They were pale blue and shimmering, their bodies like floating crystals all around him.

"You created this monster," Daniela said. "You murdered my blood sisters and stole their powers . . . but you couldn't steal their souls."

"I didn't know," he said, weakly.

"Yes, you did," Daniela said. "And now you're going to pay."

The women descended on him . . . and Desmond began to scream.

Desmond was sitting alone on the deck of the destroyer, hands lying limply in his lap, the lion-headed cane resting against the inside of his thigh. A slight breeze blew in from the sea, carrying with it the heady scent of salt and decay . . . but Desmond, the bringer of The Flood, was no longer alive to smell it.

Daniela

They'd stayed inside Daniela just long enough to get their revenge on Desmond. But when Daniela had opened her eyes again . . . she was alone. The creature was gone.

"Laragh? Is she still there?" Niamh asked, but Daniela shook her head.

Niamh looked crestfallen, her eyes filled with a grief Daniela could taste. It made sense. Niamh and her twin, Laragh, had been like two halves of the same person. Now that Laragh was gone, a part of Niamh was dead.

They were sitting inside a maintenance closet. They'd been stashed away in there as soon as everyone had realized Desmond was not coming belowdecks.

"You'll take Desmond Delay out from here," Jessika had said, before she'd handed them a shortwave radio and locked Daniela and Niamh inside the closet. "We'll be out here kicking ass and taking names."

And now their job—hers and Niamh's—was done.

"Lyse?" Niamh said into the radio.

There was a crackle and then Lyse came online.

"Stay there. We're on our way."

The radio went dead and Daniela raised an eyebrow.

"Where the hell does she think we're going?"

Niamh smiled, her nervousness off the charts.

"What's wrong?" Daniela asked.

"Nothing—" Niamh started to say, but Daniela could tell that Niamh was going to lie to her, so she reached over and took the other woman's wrist.

A flash of a conversation . . . *Thomas telling Niamh to stay with Lyse* . . . and then Daniela was back in the closet with Niamh.

"What did you just do?" Niamh asked, shocked by Daniela's ability to invade her mind.

"You want to know if he's lying to you?"

Niamh stared back at Daniela, dazed.

"I . . ." She didn't finish the thought, just nodded.

"It's hard to tell unless I touch him for myself, but, honestly, I didn't get a bad vibe. If he wants you to go with Lyse, then you should probably do it."

Niamh visibly relaxed, the tension leaving her body.

"Really? Are you sure?"

"I think so," Daniela said. "And I agree. He's pretty hot. You could probably make out with him when this is all over."

Daniela had added this last bit because she had sensed how embarrassed Niamh was by her attraction to Thomas—and Niamh did not disappoint, blushing bright pink.

"Oh, no, is it that obvious?" Niamh asked.

Daniela laughed.

"No, I'm an empath and I just touched you. It's what I do."

"Oh, yeah," Niamh said, bouncing on the balls of her feet. "Okay, good."

There was a knock on the door and then the hatch opened to reveal Lyse and Jessika standing in the semidarkness of the passageway. Jessika was holding a gun, and she used it to indicate that they should follow her. It was very quiet on the ship, and the red emergency lights only added to the surreality of the situation.

Jessika put a finger to her lips, encouraging them to stay silent as they moved down the darkened passageway. A blast of gunfire rang through the air.

"Get down!" Jessika yelled before shoving Daniela to the ground.

A second later, Lyse and Niamh were on the floor beside her as Jessika returned fire. Someone at the end of the passageway screamed, and Daniela knew they'd been hit. There was more gunfire, which Jessika returned, and then she was grabbing Daniela by the shirt collar and lifting her to her feet.

"C'mon, there'll be more of those where that came from."

Daniela had never been manhandled so gracefully by another person before. Jessika was tough and gorgeous, and the woman knew her way around munitions. It was not the time to be getting all hot and bothered, but Daniela found herself completely turned on. She'd never had the best of luck with the ladies, but, dammit, she sure hoped when this was all over that she could spend a little time with Jessika.

"Stop drooling over our escort," Lyse whispered in her ear as they followed Jessika farther down the passageway.

"Can't help it," Daniela whispered back.

Their back-and-forth got a hiss to be silent from Jessika, and they stayed quiet after that. At the end of one passageway, they encountered two bodies, both in black combat fatigues . . . The Flood. Daniela was just glad they didn't have to step over any dead blood sisters.

After winding through passageway after passageway, they eventually arrived at their final destination: the mess hall. The interior was lit up like a shopping mall. Table after table filled with women . . . the blood sisters they'd rescued from the underground research facility.

"They're doing a lot better," Niamh said, her voice filled with surprise.

"They perked up as soon as you guys arrived," Jessika said, and they followed her as she threaded her way through the tables until she found Dev and the girls. Dev had given them stacks of napkins to play with and Marji was trying to show Ginny how to fold paper planes with them.

"It's working," Dev said as soon as they approached. "It was such a good idea."

She was smiling, but underneath the smile she was stressed.

"We took care of Desmond," Daniela said. "He's not gonna be messing with anyone ever again."

She knew her words sounded harsh, but she would cry over his death at a later date . . . and she wouldn't be mourning the man upstairs, she'd be mourning the death of the man she'd *thought* he was.

"I'm sorry for your loss. Both of you," Dev said to Lyse and Daniela, but she didn't look sorry at all.

"Don't be," Daniela said, and Lyse nodded.

"Tell us about the spell," Lyse said, changing the subject.

"Well, the girls and I got the women together and we worked it into being . . . I think it will hold as long as necessary."

It had been Thomas's idea. There was so much magic on this ship, why not use it to fashion a protection spell? So he and Dev had worked to weave a spell that would make the mess hall and everything in it invisible to anyone who meant the women on the ship harm.

"We gave them each a symbol to cast in their minds, and it's working," Thomas said as he came to stand behind Dev.

Daniela was glad to see that the two of them seemed to have put aside their differences and were working together. It was stupid to have any infighting when there were about a hundred armed Flood members roaming the halls.

"Well, you've made it easier for us to take them out without anyone else getting hurt in the crossfire," Jessika said; the gun that was in her hand was sheathed now. "With that said, time for me to go back out there."

"Thank you," Daniela said. "Thanks for looking out for us."

"Let's just say that when this is all over, you and I will figure out a better way to thank me," she said, giving Daniela a wink before she walked away.

Daniela watched until Jessika was gone, but her mind was already working out ways to show her gratitude to the sexy woman with the gun.

"I think she likes you," Niamh said.

Lyse laughed and shook her head at Daniela.

"There's way more than 'like' happening there, Niamh."

"Yes, I would have to agree with Lyse on that front," Thomas said.

I seriously hope Lyse is right about that, Daniela thought, but she didn't weigh in.

Daniela could feel the spell working all around them—it gave a sharp, metallic taste to the air.

"So what? We just hang out here until Jessika and the Eagles take everyone out?" Daniela asked.

"That's it exactly," Lyse said. "You guys stay here. I think you have it well in hand."

"Does that mean you're going now?" Dev asked, her eyes welling with tears.

"Yeah," Lyse said. "I think it does."

"Don't go!" Ginny said, clambering out of her seat and throwing herself at Lyse's waist. "Marji says you might die. Don't die, please."

Marji was still sitting at the table, but her head was down and she looked like she was crying. Dev went over to her older daughter and knelt beside her.

"What's wrong? What's happened, Marji?"

But Marji just shook her head, tears falling down her cheeks and onto the tabletop.

"Baby, tell me—"

Thomas came to stand on Marji's other side.

"Why don't you let me?" he said to Dev.

"Well, I—"

"Let him, Dev," Daniela said. She'd seen the way Marji looked at Thomas. Maybe her hero worship would get her talking.

Dev nodded and stood back up, letting Thomas have a moment with her daughter. She sat down in one of the chairs and pulled Ginny onto her lap.

Daniela watched as Thomas inclined his head toward Marji.

"It can't be that bad. Why don't you whisper it in my ear?"

Marji shook her head no.

"Please?" Thomas continued. "It's always better to say it out loud. Takes the power of it away."

Marji thought for a moment, and then she leaned over and whispered in his ear. He nodded, listening.

"I see," he said, nodding again.

When she was done, he stood back up and laid his hand on her shoulder.

"It's hard to know these things, my dear. But sometimes we are forced to bear things we think will break us."

He kissed Marji on the top of the head.

"You did beautifully," he added. "Now go give Lyse a hug and tell her that you love her."

Slowly, Marji climbed to her feet.

"I'm sorry, and don't die," she cried, and ran to Lyse, burying her face in Lyse's waist.

"It's okay," Lyse said, stroking the girl's hair. "You know that this isn't the end . . ." Lyse continued, but Marji pulled away, looking up at her.

"I know it's not," she said, in between hiccupping tears. "I love you, Lyse."

She wouldn't say any more after that, just held on for a moment longer and then went to join Ginny and Dev.

The moment passed, but it had made Daniela feel very, very sad.

Lyse hadn't asked Thomas to tell her what Marji had said to him. She didn't seem to want to know.

Well, the first thing I'm gonna do is harass the information right out of him, Daniela thought as she, Thomas, and Niamh waited in the galley to see Lyse off.

"So I just scroll through the past and try to figure out what went wrong?" Lyse asked.

"You'll know it when you see it," Thomas said.

Lyse nodded.

"Okay, I guess it's now or never."

"Be safe," Daniela said, hugging Lyse tight and then releasing her.

"I'll try," Lyse said, and gave Daniela a wink.

"Be careful," Thomas said, letting Lyse hug him, too.

"Like I said. I'll try."

Lyse took a step back and lifted her arms in the air. A glowing ball of blue neon light crackled in between her hands.

"Well, I guess I'll see you on the other side," Lyse said, giving them a halfhearted grin—and Daniela watched as the orb grew large enough to encapsulate Lyse's entire body.

"Go now!" Thomas said to Niamh.

Niamh didn't blink. She just hurled herself at the glowing orb, slipping inside just as it popped out of existence.

"Holy crap," Daniela said.

Niamh and Lyse were both gone.

And that was when shit on board the destroyer really hit the fan.

Lyse

"*Waaaait!*" The word was muffled and elongated, as if it were coming from the bottom of the sea.

Lyse turned her head, her view tinged in neon blue. The world beyond the confines of the orb was static, time slowing to a crawl. Niamh, who'd been running toward Lyse before the orb had popped, was still going, her arms and legs caught in an exaggerated pumping motion, one hand extended, the fingers touching the glowing edge of the neon-blue bubble.

Then she saw the tip of Niamh's finger pierce the side of the orb—and the sound it made was like someone breaking a plate-glass window with a ball-peen hammer. Her gut reaction was to end the spell—but she'd never tried to stop it before, not once she'd called it into being. She wasn't sure it was even possible.

This is nuts, Lyse thought. *She's gonna get herself killed.*

So she did something scary. She attempted to stop her passage into the dreamlands. But she quickly realized that things were already in motion, too far along to be stopped.

That breaking the spell might kill them both. Instead, Lyse turned her attention to helping Niamh climb inside the orb.

Grabbing Niamh's hand, she began to pull the other woman through the neon-blue membrane.

"C'mon," she muttered under her breath as she threw all her strength behind her efforts, determined to keep Niamh safe.

Lyse could still see the outside world, could tell Niamh's lower extremities were caught there, trapped between the two realities. She felt Niamh's arms wrap around her, crushing her throat with a terrified clutching that made it hard to breathe. She had to push Niamh away, had to or she would've passed out from the lack of oxygen.

"Let go, can't breathe!" Lyse gasped, tearing at Niamh's grasping fingers.

Niamh was frantic, obviously regretting her impetuous decision, but it was too late. Lyse had to find a way to get her in the orb, or God knew what would happen to her.

"Niamh, calm down," Lyse said. "Let me concentrate on making the circle bigger."

She felt stupid for not thinking of this before, but Niamh's surprise stowaway move had thrown her.

"Relax," Lyse murmured—and she felt Niamh go limp in her arms. "Good."

She needed to focus on making the orb larger.

You can do this, she thought, and closed her eyes, letting all other thoughts drift away. She directed all of her energy toward this one goal, pushing out with her mind, harnessing the psychic energy inside her to expand the orb so that it covered both of them.

A feeling of intense calm settled over Lyse, her breathing slowing down and her focus laser sharp. In her mind's eye, she saw the orb surrounding them, a massive glistening soap bubble in shades of electric blue growing larger to encompass the rest of Niamh.

With a *pop*, Niamh fell against her, knocking them both backward and onto the ground. Lyse opened her eyes and had to close them again, the bright blue sky above her so intense it was nearly blinding. After a few seconds, she opened them again, giving them a few stinging minutes to adjust, then turned her head to find Niamh a few feet away, also having trouble adjusting to the brightness of the day they'd fallen into.

"You all right?" Lyse asked, and Niamh nodded.

Lyse propped herself up on her elbows, exhaustion flooding her body, making her feel woozy.

"What were you thinking? That was crazy. You could've killed us both," Lyse said.

"Thomas thought you'd say no if I'd asked to come," Niamh began.

"Damn right, I would have," Lyse agreed.

"I'm sorry," Niamh said.

Lyse sighed and let her eyes drift across the landscape, taking it all in. They were on a flat, sandy expanse of beach. The crash of the waves a few hundred feet from where they lay was omnipresent and intoxicating. Lyse wanted to close her eyes and lie back down, let the echoing roll of the sea calm her down, wash away all the stress and tension in her body and brain.

Not gonna happen, she thought, and then she exhaled, trying not to let her anger surface.

Instead, she said: "You shouldn't have tried to come with me. This is something I needed to do on my own."

She pulled herself up into a kneeling position, the knees of her jeans turning dark blue from the moisture in the sand. "You had no right trying to stop me."

Niamh frowned, shielding her eyes with the heel of her palm.

"You think I was trying to stop you?"

"What *else* were you doing?" Lyse asked.

Niamh shook her head.

"No, I wanted to help you," she said, the bright sun making the freckles on her cheeks stand out against her pale skin. "I think Thomas wanted me to come with you because I can make stuff happen here in the dreamlands. He can, too, and he would've come instead of me, but he was afraid you wouldn't trust him."

"He wasn't wrong," Lyse said.

"It's a death sentence being here and not having the ability to make the world bend to your will," Niamh said—and Lyse realized she'd been mistaken. Niamh really *had* come to help. She felt foolish for not seeing Niamh's motives earlier.

"I wish I hadn't had to come here," Niamh added, grabbing a handful of pale white sand in her hand and letting it slowly trickle out through her fingers. "You think I want to tag along? Well, you're wrong. This place scares me. I hate it here in the dreamlands."

Lyse agreed. The dreamlands were out of control, unpredictable . . . *scary*. But she instinctively knew that they would lead her where she needed to go. She had to find the moment in time when The Flood—or the thing that appeared as The Flood in her world—came into its power. She had to stop that moment from happening before their universe was destroyed forever.

"I appreciate you coming with me," Lyse began, then stopped, realizing how lame that sounded. "Thank you."

Niamh seemed to accept this as if it were an apology.

"You're wel—"

Her words were drowned out by the crash of waves, appreciably louder now than they'd been not ten seconds earlier.

"What were you saying—" But the words were hardly out of her mouth before a cacophonous roaring overwhelmed her ears and she was enveloped in a wash of seawater. She sputtered, her lungs taking in the salty brine, and she dug her hands into the sand for purchase as the wave began to retreat, creating an undertow that tried to take Lyse with it as it returned to the sea.

She was able to remain on the shore as the wave dissipated, but just barely. She gulped down oxygen as she climbed to her feet, her legs shaking, her body drenched.

"Niamh?" She looked around for her friend, but she was gone. Only sand and surf as far as the eye could see.

She whirled around, eyes scanning for any sign of movement—and then she saw it. A small blue boat broke the surface of the water way out on the horizon, popping up from the depths like a bouncing buoy marker.

"Niamh!" Lyse screamed and began to run toward the tide line, the fingers of the sea reaching out to embrace her.

The small boat moved fast, slipping over the waves. As it got closer, she could make out Niamh's face, her hair plastered to her head with ocean water. She'd wrapped her arms around herself for warmth, her body shivering.

When the boat was close enough to approach, Lyse ran out into the water, the splash her shoes made swallowed whole by the crashing surf. As she clambered on board, she saw that Niamh's teeth were chattering.

"If I hadn't . . . I could be . . ." Niamh tried to say in between hiccups of tears. "I would be . . . dead."

Lyse didn't know how she'd escaped being dragged out to sea, but obviously Niamh hadn't been so lucky. The shock of it all had scared her badly.

"But you aren't and you didn't. You saved yourself."

Niamh nodded, the chattering of her teeth and the pale blue of her lips worrying Lyse.

"Can you wish yourself a blanket? You're freezing," Lyse added.

In less than a second, a heavy woolen blanket—that smelled like wet dog—appeared around Niamh's shoulders.

"Boy, does that thing stink," Lyse said, holding her nose.

"It's . . . the blanket our dog, Angelbetti, slept on when Laragh and I were kids."

"Well, it still stinks," Lyse teased. "But it's a good stink."

Niamh gave her a tentative smile in return.

"She was the stinkiest dog that ever existed. But the most loyal and kindest and sweetest dog ever," Niamh said. "I miss her even now."

The talk of her childhood pet seemed to cheer Niamh up, knocking away some of the fear that had been circling her.

"As much as I like this boat, I don't think we're where I need to be," Lyse said as the percussive crash of waves broke against the beach.

"I don't want to leave here," Niamh said. "It feels safe."

Lyse shook her head.

"Nothing's safe in the dreamlands."

"I know," Niamh said, softly, her eyes downcast.

As if to remind them of the truth of this, Lyse felt the water beneath them begin to churn.

"We need off this boat," Lyse cried. "Now!"

She grabbed Niamh's hand and dragged them both to the edge of the boat. She pushed Niamh off the side, then followed her overboard just as the boat was caught in a giant riptide that yanked it backward like it was a toy.

Niamh screamed as they watched a giant whirlpool open up under the boat, sucking it down into the icy depths of the sea. Lyse grabbed Niamh's hand and began to run for shore. She didn't stop to look back, she just held fast to Niamh's hand. The water was freezing as it lapped at their ankles, the cold water trying to stop them from reaching the beach. Lyse imagined her feet were engulfed in flame—and then they just *were*, the heat pushing back the tentacles of ice water and helping Lyse to pull them from the clutches of the sea.

The sensation of heat and flame dissipated as they reached the shore, but Lyse didn't stop running. She knew the water wasn't done with them yet, felt its need to consume them, and she had no intention of letting that happen.

"Don't stop! Keep running," Lyse screamed—and then she felt it. It was like the entire sea was being sucked back by a giant vacuum cleaner, and the powerful wave that Lyse knew was coming terrified the hell out of her.

"It's a tsunami!" Lyse cried. "We need a wall—something to block it!"

"If you imagine it, through me you can make it happen," Niamh yelled back at her.

Lyse did as Niamh said, imagined a wall so tall that nothing could ever breach it, and channeled the other woman's power through their physical connection. She felt the wave behind them, towering over their path like a twenty-story skyscraper about to crash onto them—but she knew that the wall she and Niamh had built would keep them safe.

"Keep going forward! Don't stop for anything," Lyse screamed into the wind, her words looping back to Niamh.

"Okay!" Niamh yelled back, but because she was behind Lyse, her response was barely a whisper in Lyse's ear.

She knew Niamh could be trusted to listen and act accordingly. Things were crazy, the world out of control—hell, they weren't even *in* the real world—and so long as Niamh trusted her, she knew she could get them out in one piece.

As she ran, she imagined that the sand beneath them was actually a set of steep stairs—and then a set of steps was forming beneath their feet as they climbed. They were buffeted by the wind, making it hard to keep their footing. So Lyse wished the wind would die down—and the thought was hardly in her head before the wind died away.

She could hear the crash of water against stone and knew the wave had come into contact with the stairs. She wondered if the onslaught of water had washed the path behind them away, or if the stairs she'd imagined into being were made of sturdier stuff.

"I can feel water on my back," she heard Niamh murmur behind her. "Like little tentacles trying to touch me."

"Ignore it," Lyse called back to her, still holding on tight to Niamh's hand.

They left behind the arid sandscape as they climbed, the bright sunlit sky turning thick and hazy with moisture as they climbed ever higher. They were being led up into the atmosphere, the blue sky becoming not just something to admire but something to be touched. The color began to melt away around them, morphing from a crisp, clean blue to a more foreboding shade of gray-green that reminded Lyse of a bruise.

A drop of water fell on Lyse's head and then another on her nose. The wave was getting smart—it was letting itself condense into the atmosphere and then it was going to rain all over them.

"Shit," Lyse said, coming to a stop in the middle of the stairs—which continued to grow higher and higher above them until they disappeared into the clouds. She didn't know what to do. She hadn't expected the wave to follow them.

She took a deep breath and closed her eyes, feeling Niamh shivering with fear behind her.

"Close your eyes, Niamh. If you're scared."

Niamh squeezed Lyse's hand, letting her know that she had.

"What do we do?" she asked Lyse. "It's all around us."

Lyse swallowed back her own fear. She had to be strong for Niamh, but it was hard to be the hero when you just wanted to curl up into a ball and hide. She returned Niamh's squeeze, her own palm slick with nervous sweat.

"We're gonna take a page from the Greek myths—we're gonna make ourselves some wings and fly," Lyse said.

She focused her mind like a scalpel, willing it to do the delicate work she needed. There was a slight pinch at the apex of each of her shoulder blades, and then a searing hot pain danced across the flesh of her back, rippling out from her shoulders.

"What's happening?" Niamh asked her. "Are you okay?"

Lyse hadn't realized she'd cried out—but then she heard herself give another whimper as she felt the wings begin to extend out of her skin. She bit back pain as muscle and flesh tore apart and rearranged inside her.

"Okay . . ." She gasped, the pain exquisitely intense. "Just . . . a few more . . . seconds."

She heard—then felt—something snap into place above her, and though she could hardly see them, she'd imagined the wings into being, knew exactly what they looked like.

"That tickles," Niamh said, and Lyse felt her friend push away the white feathers brushing her nose.

Lyse turned so the flat of her back was to Niamh.

"Hold tight to me," she said, then grunted as Niamh wrapped her arms around her neck.

Lyse wasn't sure what would happen if they lost their connection and her borrowed ability to manipulate the dreamlands disappeared. She tried not to think about it. Instead, she felt the wings unfurl around her, their weight pulling down on her back and shoulders. The feathers themselves were light, but strung all together in such a mass of fluff and keratin, they were heavy and unwieldy.

"You know Icarus flew too close to the sun and died," Niamh whispered in her ear. "Be careful. You can die here in the dreamlands, too."

Lyse knew she was right, but, at that moment, she didn't feel like there was another choice to be made.

Take us out of here, wings, she thought—and she felt them extend into the air.

In seconds, she was buoyant, her feet floating a few inches above the safety of the stairs. She hovered in place for a few moments, trying to adjust to the strangeness of the new experience. Then, satisfied she could control her wings, she took off, carrying Niamh with her up through the atmosphere and into the rain-heavy clouds.

They sailed through the air for what felt like an eternity. Lyse navigated them through the desertscape, soaring high enough that she was able to bypass the spindly spires of burnt red stone. She knew she couldn't hide up in the clouds forever, but it was the first time in weeks she'd felt even a little safe.

She loved the sensation of flying. Was quickly addicted to the utter freedom she felt as she glided over the outcroppings of rough-hewn rock, layers upon layers of faded gradations of orange and brown and red stone all stacked together like a complicated game of Jenga.

You can't stay up here forever.

It was Eleanora's voice in her head. More and more her subconscious had adopted her grandmother as the voice of reason, gently reminding her to get back on track whenever she ventured too far from the path of what needed to be done.

You're wasting time. Get the girl back to where she belongs. This is your fight and yours alone.

She knew the voice was right. She'd been dodging her fate. This was her battle to win or lose . . . and having one of her blood sisters there would only slow her down, make it impossible for her to act. She'd be too worried about Niamh getting hurt, and that would give The Flood the advantage.

They were far away from where the wave had almost caught them when Lyse felt safe enough to touch back down on land. She didn't say anything to Niamh, just slowly began her descent, aiming for one of the larger towers of rock.

"Is something wrong?" Niamh murmured, speaking close to Lyse's ear. "Why are we going down to the rocks?"

Lyse didn't answer until her feet had touched down on solid ground. She waited for Niamh to let go of her, severing their physical contact and causing the wings to vanish.

"Why did you do that?" Niamh asked, reaching for Lyse's arm.

"You can't come with me," Lyse said. "I know what Thomas said, but it's not your journey, Niamh."

Niamh's face fell, an expression of sadness similar to one she'd seen on her best friend Carole's little boy, Bemo, right before he began to cry.

"Niamh, don't cry—"

But as Lyse reached out to try to comfort her, Niamh shook her head.

"I keep losing the people I care about," Niamh said. "I don't want to lose you, too."

"We have to accept our fate," Lyse said. "Whatever it is. We like to think we're in control, but we're not and we never will be."

Niamh swiped at her wet face with the sleeve of her shirt.

"Are you sure about that?" Niamh said, as she drew in a shaky breath. "Isn't that what you're doing now? Changing all of our fates?"

She was right, of course. That was exactly what she was doing. What they were all doing.

"Thomas told me that I should come with you," Niamh continued, "because he said you might not want to do what needs doing. When the time came."

"What does that mean?" Lyse asked.

"I don't know," Niamh said. "I wish I did."

Lyse felt like she'd just stepped onto shaky ground. She didn't like that Thomas knew things that she didn't.

"Okay, we're going back. You'll be safer there . . . and then I can ask Thomas what the hell he meant by sending you with me. Fair?"

Lyse took Niamh's hands. They were thin and clammy.

"Fair," Niamh said, a little defeated.

"Think of Devandra. Think of the real world. Think about the girls. They're who we're doing all this for," Lyse whispered as her eyes unfocused and a pale blue orb grew around them.

Lyse opened her eyes just as the orb's neon-blue sheen died away. They had come back to the ship . . . but not the same one they'd left behind. What they found, instead, was the scene of a massacre. One with no survivors.

The Flood had been thorough.

The mess hall where they'd left Daniela and Dev and the girls . . . had been the scene of a bloodbath. Innocent women mowed down like animals. It was a party for the dead, decorated in spilled blood and viscera that blanketed the walls and tables and floor.

Lyse felt like she was being watched by a thousand dead glass eyeballs, all blank and unfocused, yet somehow still staring. Still calculating what was happening around them. Tracking every tiny movement, every flutter of eyelash, every tic of a cheek. The dead were fascinated by Lyse and Niamh. Curious about what the women were doing there, what they were thinking and feeling.

Niamh dropped Lyse's hands and took a step back, face white with dismay. She took another step, unconscious of where she was going, and the heel of her shoe slipped in a puddle of congealing red. Lyse caught her arm before she went down, but not before a terrified whimper escaped Niamh's lips.

"Oh God," Niamh cried.

"There is no God," Lyse said, her throat tight with anger.

It was so quiet you could hear a pin drop. The only sound—and it was a faint, repetitive one—was the steady *drip* of a water tap somewhere in the galley. Someone had probably been washing up back there when the attack started. Caught off guard, they hadn't managed to get the water turned off before they'd joined the fray . . . or maybe they'd just been shot right where they were standing.

Lyse covered her mouth with her hand, bile threatening to come up into her mouth. She was having trouble believing this was possible. How had it happened so quickly? They'd just left. Why hadn't someone realized The Flood was about to attack? Why hadn't they stopped it?

"It can't be," Niamh said, her lips trembling. "How?"

Lyse didn't have an answer for her. Whatever had gone down, it had occurred in a matter of moments . . . and none of the unarmed women had been ready for it.

"It looks like it was a blitz attack."

Niamh nodded, but she was already scanning the dead . . . looking for their friends.

"Why would someone do this?" Niamh asked, still trying to make sense of the carnage. "I don't see them. Do you?"

Lyse didn't want to look at the blank faces. Didn't want to see Dev or Marji or Ginny lying there in the blood-splattered mess hall, their bodies limp as marionettes . . . couldn't bear the thought of Daniela being among the victims. Her mouth grew taut with anger as she remembered how excited Daniela had been to meet Jessika. She wanted Daniela to fall in love and have a normal life. She wanted bright, happy futures for all the people she loved—not this. Not this death and suffering and fear.

". . . should check and make sure . . ." Niamh was saying, but Lyse had totally blanked.

"What?" Lyse asked. "I'm sorry. I wasn't listening."

"Let's find Dev and the girls and . . ."

Niamh broke off, eyes on Lyse.

"I can't," Lyse said, fighting back hysteria. "There are just too many of them. I can't bear it. I'll lose my mind . . ."

Niamh didn't reply. Just stood there, surveying the butchery that lay before them. They stayed that way for a long time, both of them lost in their own thoughts. Finally, Niamh knelt down and began to examine one of the bodies, her long brown hair hanging down like a curtain across her face.

Lyse saw that there were also dead Shrieking Eagles mixed in with the other women, and some of The Flood's combat troops had been taken down in the melee as well, recognizable by their black camouflage fatigues and guns. They may have been on different sides, but in death they were all united. It was clear that none of these deaths had been easy ones.

"What do you think happened?" Niamh asked. "*When* do you think it happened?"

"I don't know," Lyse said, because she had no idea where they were in the timeline. Had they been gone for hours? Minutes? Days?

"I can't . . . I just . . . I can't . . ." Lyse began, but her mouth was having trouble finishing the sentence.

"Easier to live in denial," Niamh said with no judgment in her voice. She was just stating a fact. "To just pretend that none of this happened. That everything was okay again."

"You're closer to the truth than you know," Lyse said, thoughtfully. "There's no need to pretend . . . not when it's so much easier to just go back in time and make sure it never happens in the first place."

Lyse smiled, knowing that this was only the first stop on her journey. It was a moment in time, meant to remind her of what would happen if she didn't succeed . . . *and Lyse did not plan to fail.*

Evan

The landscape was dark and oppressive and Evan had been walking for miles—at least, it felt like miles. It was hard to tell time or speed or space here because the emptiness of the desert was unwavering in its sameness. He'd stopped calling Arrabelle's name long ago because it had begun to seem like a moot point. It was becoming very clear that Arrabelle wasn't here, and that screaming his throat raw wasn't going to bring her back.

There was a part of his brain that said she'd been taken away because he hadn't wanted to be with her. He'd planned on telling her soon. That, though he cared for her, he didn't . . . no, *couldn't* . . . be in a relationship with her. He just couldn't be a partner to anyone. Couldn't give her what she needed emotionally. He was happy with his life . . . with who he was . . . he couldn't be put in a position again where he had to defend his right to be himself.

He knew she would protest, tell him that she loved him and wanted to be with him no matter what—and then he would have to tell her the truth. That he'd been in love with someone once, before he'd met Arrabelle, and that the person he'd thought he loved—and who he'd thought loved him back—had left him when they'd discovered more about Evan than they'd wanted to know.

He'd thought the pain he'd suffered would go away—but the rejection had opened a wound deep inside him. One that would not heal. He would tell Arrabelle the story. He would make her see that no matter how much he cared about her . . . he could *not* be vulnerable like that again.

"Arrabelle!" he called out, the gesture futile. "Arrabelle, please! Wherever you are, listen to me!"

He stopped walking, just stood there in the semidarkness, swaying on his feet, and then he sat down in the sand. But that wasn't good enough . . . he lay back and let the sand fill in around him, slipping inside his clothes so that the tiny granules scratched at his skin.

He stared up at the sky—there were three moons the size of cantaloupes circling each other. He reached up, wanting to touch them with his hands, but they were too far away . . . so far away that to claim them, he'd need a spaceship and the ability to travel at light speed.

"Arrabelle," he said, her name soft on his lips. "Where are you, Arrabelle?"

She didn't answer him, but it almost didn't matter anymore. He was content in the knowledge that no matter where she was, he was with her in spirit. This was how he'd expected to go . . . alone . . . and now it was happening. Just as he'd imagined.

"Arrabelle, if I'm being completely honest with myself here—and that's something I should be, honest with myself, because why lie to me, right?" He said all this out loud. "Besides, there's no one else here to lie to anyway."

He lifted his arms, making angels in the sand, and he wondered if the Goddess was watching him.

"Arrabelle, I'm terrified of you. I have been since the moment we met."

He was talking, words coming out of his mouth that he didn't even know he had inside him.

"You are everything I could ever want, but I'm too scared to let you love me. I'm a pusillanimous fool and I hate myself for it."

The first raindrop hit Evan on the forehead. It was so unexpected that he recoiled, sitting up and wiping at his face. But then he realized what was happening and started laughing.

"Your rain scared me!" he said, yelling up at the sky. "Who the hell is afraid of a little water?"

A lyric from a song danced through his head . . . something about *needing someone like a desert needed rain*, and he laughed even harder. He was sitting in the sand, laughing his head off, getting rained on . . . and he wasn't happy, per se, but he wasn't so miserable now, either.

"Arrabelle!" he screamed, his voice reaching up to the three moons. "I love you!"

The rain began to fall in sheets. He was getting drenched, but he didn't care. He lay back in the sand, his clothes and hair plastered to his body. He closed his eyes and let the rain wash everything away.

He woke up to the smell of growing things. It was a rich, loamy scent and it filled his nostrils and made him smile as he shook away the last fingers of sleep. He rubbed his eyes, the memory of the impromptu rain shower making him laugh.

The smell of damp soil was only getting stronger. He turned his head, surprised to find himself smack-dab in the middle of a field of mushrooms. He sat up, brushing his hair out of his eyes, and looked around.

"Whoa." The word slipped out of his mouth before he could stop it.

No matter where he turned, as far as the eye could see . . . *mushrooms.*

He got up and stretched, surprised at how one rainstorm had changed the whole tenor of the landscape. He was so busy marveling at the bizarreness of the dreamlands and not paying attention to where he was going that he almost missed it. The hillock in the middle of all the flat land. It was the only part of the landscape *not* covered in mushrooms and once Evan had seen it, he was obsessed. He walked over to it, crushing little mushroom bodies under his heels as he went, drawn irresistibly to whatever lay beneath it.

It was a large rectangle of dirt, a mound of soil that looked as though it had lain undisturbed for a long time. Without understanding why, Evan knelt down beside the mound and thrust his hands into it. He began to dig, slowly at first and then faster, shifting soil out of the way with a frenzy that made him light-headed.

Finally, he stopped, his fingers touching something soft. He brushed the dirt away . . . and discovered Arrabelle's sleeping face.

He tried everything to wake her up. He called her name. Gently slapped both cheeks. Shook her. Yelled her name. He tried everything until there was only one option left.

It feels like a test, he thought. *And I hate tests.*

But he wasn't the same man he'd been—something had happened to him during that rainstorm. He'd been purified by a supernatural event greater than himself. It almost felt like a religious experience, like he'd gone out into the desert and waited for the Goddess to find him and lay a kiss of absolution on his brow. With that accomplished, he had the confidence to do anything.

Like wake up a sleeping princess.

"Arrabelle," he said, as he knelt before her, a prince with dirt-covered knees.

He ran his finger down the side of her cheek, then lowered his face until his lips were inches from her left ear.

"Arrabelle, I love you. I know that if I do this and it works, I will be tied to you for life," he said, and cleared his throat, his mouth dry. "So I promise to always be honest with you and tell you what I'm thinking. I'm ready to be vulnerable again, to have a better life with you at my side."

He stopped and closed his eyes.

"Arrabelle, please wake up."

He placed his mouth gently against her lips, felt the dry crackle of his own parched skin as he kissed her. She tasted like dirt and growing things, her lips moister than he'd expected. He felt her stirring and then her arms were encircling the back of his neck and pulling him toward her.

"I thought you'd never get here," she breathed against his mouth.

"Me neither," he said—and then he kissed her again.

She held him close, her body warming under his. She was lithe, yet firm, and he could feel her taut muscles tensing as she ran her hands up and down his back. He enjoyed the feline grace with which she moved underneath him, wanted to get closer to her, fill his senses with her.

"You're so beautiful," he murmured as he kissed her throat. "So damned beautiful."

"Thank you for not letting me go," she said, her voice thick with emotion.

He stopped what he was doing and rolled onto his side so he could see her face. Her eyes were dry, but deep lines cut into the skin around her mouth and between her eyebrows.

"I couldn't do it," he said, tracing the curve of her jaw with his finger.

She shivered at his touch and closed her eyes.

"It was like being dead, but with dreams. It's not bad . . . not really."

"What're you talking about, Bell?" he asked.

She opened her eyes and shrugged.

"I don't know. It feels so far away now. Like with each breath I take, it gets further and further away."

She smiled at him, her dark brown eyes clearer than they'd been only a few moments earlier.

"You're feeling better?" he asked.

She nodded.

"I am."

"So what next?" he asked.

She sat up, pulling her knees into her chest. She yawned, but the exhaustion was beginning to fade from her eyes, the lines disappearing from her forehead and around her mouth.

"Well, I think we should try to find the Red Chapel. It's the only place I know of in all the dreamlands," she said, arching her back and stretching like a cat. "I don't know how we find it, but maybe if we just think about it, it will come to us."

"It's an awful place in real life," Evan said, wishing they would go anywhere but there.

"It's where you lost your coven," Arrabelle said, in understanding.

"Lost them . . . ? It was a massacre. The Flood stole Laragh, then burned Yesinia and Honey on a pyre in front of the Red Chapel. Niamh saw the whole thing." He didn't get into the fact that Niamh was the reason the chapel had been burned down to its foundations. Suffice it to say, it had been a horrific night. He and Niamh had both almost died and their coven had been destroyed . . . all because of The Flood.

"We don't have to go—" Arrabelle started to say, but Evan took her hand in his, brought it to his lips, and kissed it.

"I go where you go, Bell."

It was funny, but they didn't have to go far.

They'd set off as soon as Arrabelle had felt well enough to

walk, their hands intertwined. He found himself just happy
to be in her company, pleased he was the reason she was up
and moving, alive, not buried in a field of mushrooms.

"I ate it, like an idiot," she said, swinging her arm as she
walked—and by proximity and connection of their hands, his
arm went with hers as they matched their steps. "I'm an herbalist and I ate a poisonous mushroom."

She laughed, a clear throaty sound that made Evan's heart
beat faster.

"It happens," Evan said. "I'm just glad I found you."

"How'd you know where I'd be?" Arrabelle asked, swinging their arms faster.

"I didn't," he said—which was the truth. "I just started
walking. The others thought you were dead, but I didn't care.
I just felt like I had to go and find you."

"I'm not mad at them for leaving me," Arrabelle said. "I
get it."

"You were there one minute and the next you were gone,
Bell," Evan said. "It was surreal."

"I walked for so long," Arrabelle said. "And there was nothing. Do the dreamlands scare you as much as they do me?"

"They do," Evan said, nodding in agreement.

"And I haven't been hungry since we got here. Except when
I was being compelled to eat those mushrooms."

Evan realized he hadn't had a meal since they got to the
dreamlands, but when he did a mental check of his hunger
level, he found it at zero.

"Very strange."

"I wish Lizbeth or Lyse or someone would just swoop in
and find us," Arrabelle said—and before the words were even
out of her mouth . . . a shadow cut across the sand.

Eleanora

That horrible witch—the excommunicated blood sister, Helen Cordoza—had breached the carefully constructed spell that Devandra and Thomas had so elegantly crafted. It happened in a heartbeat. One moment the mess hall was full of women working magic under their breath in hisses and murmurs, the next, the evil bitch had crossed the threshold, snapping the delicate web of their spell.

A surge of black-camouflaged men and women streamed into the large room, semiautomatic guns at the ready. Thomas ran for the hatch, magic crackling between his fingers as he tried to stop Helen from destroying the invisibility spell completely. But it was too little, too late. A man with a black grease-painted face lifted his gun and blew Thomas's head off.

He was the first casualty—and then all hell had broken loose. The Shrieking Eagles attempted to stop The Flood's men, but there just weren't enough of them. Daniela had run into the room from the galley kitchen and that Helen bitch had slammed the empath with enough magic that she'd been thrown back ten feet in the air, her head hitting the wall at a funny angle. Eleanora had been sure her neck was broken.

Dev tried to hide Marji and Ginny under one of the tables and had gotten a gunshot to the back for her trouble . . . the girls hadn't lived much longer after that. It was a holocaust . . . innocents killed because of *what* they were: blood sisters.

Eleanora's ability to affect the real world was very limited, and so she'd only been able to offer her blood sisters a little help. When it was all over, there were dead from both sides, but to Eleanora it was clear that The Flood had won this battle. Eleanora had watched them check for survivors, shooting anything that moved, and then they'd gone, so callous they'd even left their own dead behind. She didn't think they knew Desmond was gone, but she thought they'd discover it soon enough.

She was alone in the mess hall for a long time . . . and then a flash of neon blue had shot through the room and hope had flared to life once more in Eleanora's breast. She sensed that now was the time for her to make her move. She floated toward her granddaughter, gently placing her hand on Lyse's shoulder. It was like being plugged into an electric socket and she immediately felt more real.

"Eleanora," Lyse said, as her grandmother came to life out of the magical ether.

"I think I know where your journey starts, my dearest," Eleanora said. "And it's not in the dreamlands—"

"Take me with you," Niamh said, not wanting to be left out. "I can help you."

"I can't, Niamh," Lyse began, but Niamh cut her off.

"Please," Niamh begged. "I know that it's important for me to go with you. Please, Lyse."

"I think she should go with you. It was important to Thomas," Eleanora said—but she waited for Lyse to decide.

Finally, Lyse spoke: "I appreciate all that you've done, Niamh. You're alive and well and I don't want that to change . . . especially if I fail. But I won't tell you no. Though I can't guarantee your safety."

Niamh nodded.

"Of course. I understand."

Lyse turned to Eleanora.

"You said you would set us on the right path . . . ?"

"Yes," Eleanora said. "Go back to the house on Curran Street. Open the remaining Dream Journal . . . and it will take you where you need to go."

"I love you," Lyse said. "Thank you."

Eleanora smiled.

"I love you, too. So much more than you will ever know."

And then Eleanora watched as her granddaughter, the person who had taught her what love was, enveloped herself and Niamh in a neon-blue orb and disappeared.

Lizbeth

Lizbeth had resigned herself to the fact that the dreamlands couldn't get enough of her. They were obsessed, mining her memories, and using them to clothe the landscape around them.

"They like you, pet," Tem said. "They're drawing spiritual blood from you."

She hadn't thought of it in those terms before, but it made sense. The dreamlands liked her magic, and they were siphoning off bits of it for themselves.

"Ew," Lisbeth said. "You make it sound like the dreamlands are a mosquito."

"And you must be tasty to them," Tem teased her. She smiled, liking when he flirted with her. It made her happy.

"Shall we?" she asked, pleased by the mode of transportation he'd rustled up for them.

She'd specified she wanted to fly, and he'd obliged her by calling up a giant hot-air balloon for them to travel inside. It was made of blue and green patchwork fabric, the basket a soft faun wicker that was smooth to the touch.

"Do you know how to operate one of these things?" she asked, and he grinned.

"Do I know how to operate one of these things?" he said, mimicking her. "Climb aboard and you will see."

He offered her a leg up and a moment later she was standing in the basket, her hands grasping the edge as Tem climbed in beside her.

"So how do you operate one of these things, again?" he asked, and she gave him a playful swat on the arm.

It was strange to feel so light and happy in these moments with Tem when all of this terrible dark stuff was swirling around them. Lyse and the others were back in the real world dealing with The Flood and she was here taking a hot-air balloon ride with a man she loved.

Yeah, she'd used the word *love* and she meant it. When this was all over, she'd already decided she was going to stay in the dreamlands with Tem. She didn't care if she never went home again . . . besides, what home was there to go back to? Weir was dead. Her mother was dead. Her father was a terrible person, and who knew what was going to happen to the covens? No, she would throw her lot in with Tem and let what would be . . . *be*.

"You do know what you're doing," she said, as they'd sailed up into the clouds.

"You're precious and I would never risk your safety like that," Tem said, settling his arm around her as they climbed higher and higher.

She leaned her head against his chest and they stood like that, eyes trained on the ground as it flew past them. The desert was the dreamlands' default, and the sloping dunes of pale yellow sand stretched on and on like pats of butter melting in the heat of the sun.

"Do you see him?" Lizbeth asked over the hiss of the fire.

Tem shook his head.

"Nothing, lovey."

This went on for a while, both of them scouring the ground for some signs of life.

"Maybe the darkness took him, too?" Lizbeth said.

"I suppose that's a possibility."

They didn't continue down that line of thinking.

"Wait, I think I see something!" Tem cried, pointing down to where two small specks were walking in the sand, hand and hand.

Lizbeth's heart swelled as she realized . . . that the second speck was Arrabelle.

Lyse

Lyse and Niamh stood on the red lacquer bridge that spanned Eleanora's koi pond, listening to the tinkling song of wind chimes (from somewhere in the neighborhood) as they danced on the wind. Lyse had chosen to return to a time before she'd come back to Echo Park. Before Eleanora had learned she was sick. Before The Flood had entered Lyse's consciousness.

She took a moment to look around, one final time, knowing she might never see this place again—the place where she'd grown up, where she'd known what it was to love and be loved by someone who was your family. The breeze blew through her dark hair, pushing her bangs in her face. With the breeze came the familiar scent of jasmine, a smell she loved more than any other.

She closed her eyes, bathing in the scent-filled air. When she opened her eyes again, all she wanted was for her time on Curran Street to last forever. She turned her head and smiled at Niamh, who was holding the Dream Journal in her hand.

"I'm almost ready," Lyse said.

"Time doesn't really matter right now, does it?" Niamh said—and Lyse shrugged.

"I suppose not."

She took one last look at Eleanora's small bungalow . . . so many memories, so much heartbreak and joy. It was where she'd fallen in love with Weir, where she'd discovered who and what she really was, where she'd said good-bye to the woman who'd raised her.

"Good-bye, house," she whispered.

"Mama! Someone's up there!" It was Ginny's voice and it cut through the sound of the wind and the dancing wind chimes . . . and that was when Lyse knew it really *was* time to go.

She could hear Dev and the girls climbing the hill and knew they were only seconds away. She felt Niamh's hand on her shoulder as she began to call up the blue orb.

"May I have the Dream Journal?" Lyse asked as the orb coalesced around them.

"Of course," Niamh said, and handed the book to her.

The air around them began to shimmer with magic as a golden light erupted from inside the book and, suddenly, the blue orb that enveloped them was a bright and shining gold.

"I'm sorry, Niamh," Lyse said—and then she shoved Niamh out of the orb just before it popped.

She felt bad leaving Niamh behind, but she knew that when she opened her eyes again, she would be facing something great and terrible: *The Past*. And she did not want to take anyone there with her.

Take me to the beginning, she thought—and when she opened her eyes again . . .

. . . she found herself in the potting shed of the nursery in Georgia that she had once owned with her best friend, Carole. There was a gap in between the door and the frame, and she was able to peek out through it and see what was happening inside the greenhouse.

She watched, the Dream Journal still clutched in her hands, as a past version of herself hunted through a small mini-fridge looking for a beer. Like a mini-earthquake, the cell phone in the back pocket of her past self's cutoff khakis began to buzz. The abruptness of the vibration in the still of the nursery startled the past Lyse enough that she dropped the beer, the foamy head pouring out over the concrete floor.

"Really?" her past self said, and sighed, looking down at the cracked phone screen and staring at the name on the caller ID. Her past self picked up the half-empty can of beer and set it on top of the mini-fridge.

For a moment the other her debated not answering it, but then guilt got the better of her.

Lyse remembered this moment clearly, knew from experience that the other her would close her eyes and press accept.

"Hello?" past-Lyse said, placing the phone against her ear so she could return to the mini-fridge, yanking another beer from the plastic ring of the six-pack.

Lyse knew that it was Eleanora on the other end of the call. Knew that she was saying Lyse's name through the phone line.

At that point, Lyse hadn't actually spoken to Eleanora in about three months—their conversations were always less fraught over email—and Lyse remembered hearing a resigned quality, a reticence she had never heard from Eleanora before.

"You got me," past-Lyse said as she walked over to the potting table and leaned her weight against it. "I'm at the nursery."

Lyse imagined Eleanora sitting at her round oak kitchen table, elbows pressed into the tabletop as she held the oversized beige handset to her ear, worrying the coiled telephone cord between her fingers as she decided the best approach to take with her niece.

She didn't remember what Eleanora said, but past-Lyse's response was curt.

"It's fine. I stay late here all the time." The tone was noncommittal.

Under normal circumstances, Lyse and Eleanora were never at a loss for words. She remembered the awkward pauses as she'd waited for Eleanora to get down to business. There had been something off about the phone call.

She remembered how the next few moments of the conversation had changed her world forever. Past-Lyse closed her eyes but wasn't fast enough to stymie the flood of salty tears as they slid over her bottom lids and cascaded down the curve of her cheeks.

"You're dying?" past-Lyse said into the phone, and her voice was taut as piano wire. "But it's not fair." Past-Lyse's voice stretched out into a plaintive whine.

Lyse remembered that on the other end of the line, Eleanora had laughed. Not a harsh sound, but one that was as soft as a sigh.

Then she'd spoken the truest words Lyse had ever heard: "What's fair about life?"

Lyse realized that this was not the place in time that she was looking for. She closed her eyes.

Take me to the moment, *she thought.* The one I'm looking for.

And when she opened her eyes again . . .

. . . she was standing on the red lacquer bridge that spanned Eleanora's koi pond. Niamh was beside her, holding the Dream Journal. Lyse looked down at her own hands, saw that the journal was indeed gone, and became very confused.

"What happened?" she asked Niamh.

"What do you mean?" Niamh asked, frowning.

Lyse knew better than to elaborate. She'd been pitched back in time because somehow she'd done something wrong.

"Nothing," Lyse said. "I was just thinking out loud."

"Well, so you think we should go soon?" Niamh asked—accepting Lyse at her word. "Not that time really matters now."

Niamh had said those very words the last time they were here.

"Yeah, I think we should go. Doesn't matter about time," Lyse said.

"Shall I open the book?" Niamh asked.

"Yes," Lyse said, and watched as Niamh flipped open the cover of the journal and a glowing gold light shimmered all around them.

Lyse knew she was going to have to take Niamh with her this time. She waited until Niamh placed a hand on her shoulder and then she called up the orb. Just as before, the blue light turned gold . . . but this time, Lyse allowed Niamh to come with her.

Take me to the moment when everything changed for me, Lyse thought—and when she opened her eyes . . .

. . . *she and Niamh were squatting together in a tangle of bushes near the edge of Echo Park Lake.*

"Where are we?" Niamh whispered.

"The lake the night I killed someone for the first time," Lyse replied.

Niamh gave her a funny look.

"You're kidding, right?"

Lyse truly wished she were.

"Wait, is that you?" Niamh asked, distracted by something ahead of them.

Past-Lyse was curled into a ball on the path in front of them. As she cried, her body shook from the shock of just having helped kill a man. The luminous shade that was Eleanora knelt beside Lyse's past self . . . reaching out as if she could cradle past-Lyse like a child.

"I miss you," her past self murmured, pushing pieces of dark bangs from her eyes.

"Don't."

Eleanora's tone brooked no argument, and past-Lyse nodded, beaten. Then she opened her mouth to speak but instead pressed her hands to her face, covering her eyes. Blinding herself to the reality of what was before her.

"The Flood is coming, Lyse. Prepare yourself," Eleanora whispered—and then the Dream Walker dissolved into the ether.

When past-Lyse removed her hands, her face was ugly with tears. She turned her head, looking for the ghost, but Eleanora was gone.

"Eleanora?" past-Lyse whispered, swiping at her eyes with the back of her hand, her hot tears finally spilling.

There was no reply. Only the gentle hum of the night. Past-Lyse sat beside the broken body of the Lady—only a few feet from where Lyse and Niamh sat hunched in the bushes—for what seemed like hours, her gaze far away. Then she climbed to her feet, and with an unsteady gait, she walked out of their view.

"That's so creepy," Niamh whispered.

"It's even creepier when it's your own body that you're watching," Lyse replied.

"So now what?" Niamh asked.

Lyse sighed—she wasn't sure about what came next, but she had an inkling.

"C'mon," Lyse said. "Let's go take a look."

She crawled out from the bushes, Niamh behind her. The two of them walked over to the broken body of the Lady of the Lake . . . and the dead man who lay pinned beneath her. But he didn't really count.

Lyse stared at the beautiful stone beauty that lay smashed to smithereens. The moon hung back, hidden behind a sheet of clouds, not willing to shine its light on the abomination. The abomination not being the Lady and her destruction, but the man trapped beneath her stone body.

Flesh and meat that once held human form—yet there was almost nothing human about him now . . . except for one pale arm peeking out from beneath the stone, its long fingers curled into the approximation of a claw. He was crushed like a cockroach under a shoe, and there was too much blood for him to be anything but dead. The Lady of the Lake was not a waif; her body was large and imposing, and when the man found himself under her as she toppled forward, his fate had been sealed.

Lyse didn't feel bad for the way the Lady had been used as a murder weapon by Eleanora and past-Lyse. Her uncle David deserved what happened to him.

The moon chose this moment to reveal itself again, illuminating the lake. The face of the water reflected back the moonlight, the surface sparkling like diamonds on black velvet. As if called down by the moon, the prickling fingers of a cold breeze tickled the Lady's broken body.

"Lyse?" Niamh whispered in her ear. "Why are we still here?"

"Because we have to undo what was done here."

Niamh stared at her.

"Bring someone back from the dead?" she said, indicating the corpse under the broken statue. "That's not possible."

Lyse smiled, but there was no warmth in her eyes.

"Oh, I think it's entirely possible," Lyse said. "Besides, I can't throw my uncle into a singularity if he's not there to be thrown. And if we do this . . . I think it will be the thing that returns the balance of power to our world and takes away The Flood's advantage."

Lyse was sure that returning her uncle to the living . . . was the moment she had come here to change.

The breeze was almost a warning that magic was fast approaching. There was a slowing down of time, a swirling of the ether around them, and then the air split apart like someone shucking the husk from an ear of corn as a bolt of lightning shot across the sky.

"Are you sure we can do it?" Niamh asked Lyse. She sounded tentative, unsure of herself.

"We are both capable of so much more than we even know," Lyse said, and then she began to hum.

The song was not something she knew consciously, but once she opened her mouth, it flowed out of her. The tune was rambling and old—no, not old . . . but timeless. It came from before, when the world was new and magic lived in every living thing that took its sustenance from the Earth and sun. The song called to the Lady, to the stone she was made of, which had been taken from the Earth and would one day go back to it. Lyse felt the great stone body begin to stir.

Niamh rested her palms against the Lady's shattered torso, the tune Lyse hummed encircling the splintered pieces of the statue's body. With the grinding of stone on concrete, the pieces began to move back toward one another as if they were magnetized. Lyse continued to hum, while Niamh moved the pads of her fingers along the Lady's back. When she finally took her hands away, a powerful magic linked both her and Lyse to the statue.

"I can move through space and time," Lyse murmured to Niamh. "And you are the maker."

Niamh left her kneeling position and rose to her feet. The magical link between them pulled the Lady into the air, where she floated weightlessly. Using the same magical tune, Lyse sung the Lady forward, swinging the heavy stone figure back onto the pedestal from which she'd watched over Echo Park Lake for almost a century—all without so much as lifting a physical finger.

Niamh came to stand beside Lyse and grinned at her.

"We did it," Niamh murmured, her voice soft with wonder.

But Lyse knew it was not over yet. She took Niamh's hand.

"Now we raise the dead."

Niamh shuddered.

"Are you sure?" she asked Lyse.

"We leave him there and past-me goes to jail," Lyse said. "I get up tomorrow morning and come running down here, all set to tell the police that I'm the murderer. Though I don't know how anyone could think I was capable of toppling over our lovely Lady here."

Lyse reached out and patted the Lady's stone pedestal.

"Still, we don't need past-me rotting away in jail right now," she continued. "Not when The Flood is just about to make its big move."

"No, I have to agree with you about that," Niamh said. "So how do we do it?"

"We cast a circle of life," Lyse said, "using the Dream Journal."

She didn't know how she knew this would work. It had just come to her as soon as Niamh had asked the question. She went back to the bushes where the two of them had been hiding and found the Dream Journal sitting in the dirt. She picked it up, brushing off the soil, and carried it over to her uncle's body.

She placed the tattered old journal on her uncle's crushed chest and then quickly stepped away. The less she had to look at the dead man, the better.

"Now take my hands," Lyse commanded, reaching for Niamh—and as soon as their fingers touched, the book burst into a golden flame that encircled them both.

The light was so bright that Niamh closed her eyes, but Lyse refused. She wanted to see every second of what was about to happen. As they raised their arms into the air, the golden light shot upward, sparkling like a Roman candle between their wrists, both sets as slender as the trunk of a birch sapling. Lyse opened her mouth—and she thought she was going to hum the same tune as before . . . only it wasn't her voice that poured from her lips. Instead, it was a chorale of men and women, a cacophony of different tones and timbres, each vying to be heard over the din of the others. As the voices wove together into one, the golden light became something alive and malleable. It coalesced into something solid . . . a glowing mail made of golden chain.

As the song grew in pitch, the voices became frenzied, and the mail expanded in response. It began to lengthen and stretch, blowing itself up like a hot-air balloon until it was a large sphere that encapsulated both the Lady of the Lake on her pedestal and the dead man on the ground. With a loud boom, the Earth began to rumble. Lyse closed her mouth, abruptly ending the song and invoking a silence that cut the air like a scythe. But the glowing globe of chain mail continued to shimmer and grow as if it had a mind of its own.

Then the silence was replaced by a low growl. One that started under the Earth and bubbled up like a geyser, splitting the concrete around the Lady's pedestal with its power.

"With enough pressure, even the blackest coal can be transformed," Lyse said—and lowered their hands, the action ratcheting up the pressure inside the sphere. "Now return as you were."

She dropped Niamh's hands and clapped twice. The sphere popped, sending a shock wave out into the universe, one that echoed like a shot through the dreams of anyone nearby who had the misfortune of being tucked up in bed. Many people would wake up the next morning and wonder if there'd been an earthquake in the night. One they'd managed to sleep through, though it had *managed to somehow infiltrate their dreams.*

"It's done."

Lyse spoke the words, breaking the spell they'd cast.

The Lady was whole again, returned to the state she'd been in when Eleanora and past-Lyse had called upon her to act. Below her, the dead man was whole again, as well. His handsome face had filled out once more with flesh, bone and skin uncrushed. He had a head of steely gray hair, buzzed short against the crown of his head.

Niamh reached out with a toe and prodded the dead man's shoulder. The dead man did not stir.

"Are you sure he's alive?" Niamh asked.

Lyse knelt beside the prostrate figure and picked up the Dream Journal, tucking it under her arm. Then she leaned forward so her face was within inches of the dead man's ear.

"You will remember nothing. You will know you have failed in your task, but not how or why. And you will leave me alone. For now, you will not act until you see me one final time at the hospital in Italy."

Lyse whispered these words into the dead man's ear, careful not to touch the dead flesh with her lips. The dead man continued to stay where he was, but Lyse stood up and pointed to the careful rise and fall of his chest.

"He's alive. I hate it and I hate him, but it's done," she said, turning back to look at Niamh.

Lyse and Niamh watched from their perch behind the bushes as the Lady of the Lake stood vigil over the dead man until the morning light crested the hill and split open the day. Luckily, the dead man started to stir just as the first jogger of the morning hit the playground and began her lonely circuit of the park. She passed him, already breathing hard from her exertions, as he sat up and groaned, grabbing his head in pain.

To the jogger, he was just another homeless drunk sleeping off a bender. Only Lyse knew who and what he was. She watched as the dead man climbed to his feet, his dark clothes stained with dirt and sweat. He coughed and spit a globule of phlegm into the grass before stumbling off in the direction of Sunset Boulevard.

Lyse watched him go—and she cursed him:

May your end be painful, Uncle David. Painful . . . and long . . . and in a dark place of my choosing.

Once her uncle David was gone, Niamh turned to Lyse.

"That wasn't the moment, was it?"

Lyse shook her head.

"No." She wished that it had been . . . had hoped that it would be. But it wasn't. She felt gutted. She didn't know what to do now.

As if reading her thoughts, Niamh asked, "Where do we go from here?"

Lyse sighed and said, "You don't go anywhere."

Niamh stood up and walked back over to the Lady of the Lake. There was a bench not far from where the Lady stood, and she sat down on it. A moment later, Lyse joined her there. They stared out past the water at the massive downtown skyscrapers that rose up in the distance like metal mountains.

"You have any clue where you're going?" Niamh asked, finally.

"I think so."

Lyse was a liar. She had zero idea of what the next step would be.

"And will I be stuck here when you go?" Niamh asked.

Lyse shook her head and held up the Dream Journal—it was brown and singed where the magic had burned a hole through its middle.

"I'm taking you back to when we left."

"No," Niamh said, shaking her head. "I can't let you go alone. What if you don't come back?"

All Lyse could think to do was to hand Niamh the Dream Journal.

"I have to come back. You have the Dream Journal."

It was a lame attempt to reassure Niamh—and she could see from the look on Niamh's face that it hadn't worked.

"C'mon, it isn't the end . . . just hold on to this and give it to me when you see me again," Lyse said, forcing a smile onto her face. "If I do this right, then the power will shift and we can stop The Flood from killing everyone on the ship . . . or maybe even stop The Flood from coming into power at all."

Niamh's eyes filled with tears, but she took the Dream Journal and held it to her chest.

"Until we meet again," she said—and then she leaned over and hugged Lyse tight.

As soon as they arrived on the ship, the others surrounded Niamh, surprised to see them back so soon. While Niamh kept them occupied—like they'd prearranged—Lyse took her leave, calling up the neon-blue orb as quickly as possible. She didn't have the heart to say good-bye . . . again.

Once more, Lyse stood on the red lacquer bridge over the koi pond at Eleanora's house in Echo Park. It was the place she felt safest, her refuge. She had come here because she didn't know where else to go. Everything she'd done had failed. She wasn't sure what else there was to try.

And then a thought popped into her head. If she was The Hierophant . . . then that meant she was, literally, the crossroads. *She was the place where everything started and everything began. As soon as she realized this, she knew how—though not where—to go.*

Take me to the beginning of me, *Lyse thought—and closed her eyes . . .*

. . . and when she opened them, she knew immediately that something was different. Lyse was not a watcher this time; she was a participant. She was inside the body of someone else.

The cot she was sitting on was hard, her back pressed into the corner between two concrete walls, arms wrapped around her knees. She looked down and saw that she was wearing a white men's undershirt and a pair of men's striped pajama pants. Both were too big for her.

She reached up and instinctively twisted her long brown hair into a knot at the back of her neck. Then she began to nervously play with the striped pajama fabric, running her fingers along the curve of her knee.

He was on the floor, a cigarette in his hand, his back against the wall. He'd unbuttoned the top two buttons of his plaid shirt and he was staring at her. She knew that face. Knew instantly who he was and who she was . . . Desmond and Eleanora.

"I don't know what any of the answers are," he was saying, as he put the cigarette to his lips and inhaled deeply. She could tell that he wanted to impress her. "But I think there's more to things than we can see or hear or touch or taste with our senses."

"I'll say," Lyse replied. "You have no idea."

He frowned, then nodded, leaning his head back against the wall. "A sixth or a seventh sense—"

"Maybe a millionth sense," Lyse said, rolling her eyes. She didn't like this guy one bit.

"A what?" he asked, not smiling at her.

Their eyes caught for a moment, held, and then, finally, feeling really uncomfortable, she looked away.

This was not going to happen. She was not *going to have "a moment" with Desmond. She didn't understand why she was here, but obviously there had to be some kind of a reason for it.*

"Eleanora Eames, I think we should get married. Have some children. You don't need to be in love with me. We can work on that."

Lyse stared at him, gobsmacked. And that was when she realized that The Flood had used Desmond's broken love for Eleanora to swing the balance of power in their direction . . . and she instantly knew what she had to do to change their fate . . . and in doing so, seal her own.

She had to make them fall in love.

"Do you believe in magic?" she asked.

"What you call magic is just the Devil getting inside you," Desmond said. *"It's evilness."*

Lyse shook her head.

"It's not evil. It's magic. And it's just what I am. A witch. I know you're scared of it and later on you might do some really stupid shit because you think I'm rejecting you . . . but I just hope that you think about it. Really, really *think about what kind of man . . . no,* human *. . . you want to be when you're old. Because you were not a happy man in the future when I knew you."*

"Uh?" Desmond squeaked, stubbing out the cigarette on the floor.

"Can I tell you a secret?" she asked.

He stared back at her, utterly confused.

"Uh, sure, of course," he said, trying to sound nonchalant. *"You can tell me anything."*

She sat forward, eyes gleaming.

"I'm not Eleanora. I'm your granddaughter, Lyse, and one day in the future you tried to destroy me. But I didn't let you."

He looked like he wanted to clear his ears out, make sure he'd heard her correctly.

"Beg pardon?" he asked.

She grinned, pleased that she'd freaked him out.

"I'm The Hierophant, the point of intersection where all magic meets. I can go back in time and I can change things. I'm the crossroads, and it starts and stops with me."

He shook his head.

"That's not real. You're not making any sense."

She frowned, her shoulders slumping. She thought she'd say her piece and everything would be fixed . . . but, no, she was still stuck here.

"It is, too, real," she said, after a long silence.

Desmond tried another tack: *"I believe that* you *believe that you were your granddaughter and you did all that, but I think you were just lucid dreaming."*

"Suit yourself," she said. "It will all happen just as I say . . . whether you believe me or not. Unless you do something about it."

He didn't believe her now . . . but maybe he would later. That was all she could hope for.

"Have you ever been in love?" he asked, changing the subject.

She didn't want to talk about Weir with the man who'd had him killed.

"Nope," she said. "You?"

"Never."

He caught her eye again—and she felt his love for her growing inside him.

"I really could fall in love with you," he said, still holding on to her gaze. "If things were different. I think I could."

"Why's that?" she asked, despite herself.

He smiled up at her—and it was the sweetest smile she'd ever seen.

"Because I can talk to you, Eleanora."

He took her hands and looked deeply into her eyes.

"If it makes you feel better about me, I promise here and now that I will never do anything to hurt you or your children or your grandchildren . . ."

And that was when Lyse felt herself dissolve into a million pinprick points of light.

Epilogue

*E*leanora Eames sat at the station waiting for her train. She'd bought the ticket that morning and now she was nervous as a cat, wanting to be in California already without having to sit up on the train for days on end to accomplish the feat. Her excitement soon wore through her worry, and then she found that she was giddy with unbridled energy. She couldn't believe she was actually doing it, she was actually leaving Massachusetts and starting her life.

It seemed like a dream.

"I bought us some coffee."

Eleanora looked up into her savior's eyes. She didn't know how or why it happened, but Desmond had changed his mind. He'd seen that the men he was aligned with weren't doing the Lord's work. Instead they were torturing and terrorizing young women, trying to get them to confess to witchcraft. He'd helped Eleanora escape and now he was joining her on her trip out West.

Nothing had occurred between them, but she knew he liked her. Liked her the way a man liked a woman . . . and strangely enough, she was starting to think that maybe she had similar feelings for him.

But she wasn't going to jump into anything. There was a whole world she wanted to see, and he was going to join her on the adventure.

Their first stop would be Echo Park, California. In her mother's Bible—the most cherished possession Eleanora owned—she'd found the address of a woman called Hessika. She didn't know how this woman knew her mother, but Eleanora aimed to pick this Hessika's brain, find out anything she could about her long-dead mother.

"I think it's time," Desmond said, interrupting her thoughts.

She grinned up at him and waved their tickets in the air.

"I'm glad you decided to come with me," she said—and, darn it if she didn't blush.

"Me, too," he agreed, looking embarrassed but happy.

He reached down, picked up their luggage, and then offered her his arm.

"Shall we?"

She slipped her arm through his and, together, they walked to the train that would take them away from Massachusetts and on to their destinies.

Amber Benson is the author of the Echo Park Coven novels, including *The Last Dream Keeper* and *The Witches of Echo Park*, and the Calliope Reaper-Jones novels, including *The Golden Age of Death* and *How to Be Death*. She cocreated, cowrote, and directed the animated supernatural Web series *Ghosts of Albion* with Christopher Golden, which they followed with a series of novels, including *Witchery* and *Accursed*, and the novella *Astray*. Benson and Golden also coauthored the novella *The Seven Whistlers*. As an actress, she has appeared in dozens of roles in feature films, TV movies, and television series, including the fan-favorite role of Tara Maclay on three seasons of *Buffy the Vampire Slayer*. Benson wrote, produced, and directed the feature films *Chance* and *Lovers, Liars and Lunatics*. Visit her online at thewitchesofechopark.tumblr.com, facebook.com /AmberBensonWroteThis, and twitter.com/Amber_Benson.